D0837523

The UNDESIRABLES

The
UNDESIRABLES

Chad Thumann

LAKE UNION
PUBLISHING

This is a work of fiction. Names, characters, organizations, places, events, and incidents are either products of the author's imagination or are used fictitiously.

Text copyright © 2016 Charles Thumann
All rights reserved.

No part of this book may be reproduced, or stored in a retrieval system, or transmitted in any form or by any means, electronic, mechanical, photocopying, recording, or otherwise, without express written permission of the publisher.

Published by Lake Union Publishing, Seattle

www.apub.com

Amazon, the Amazon logo, and Lake Union Publishing are trademarks of Amazon.com, Inc., or its affiliates.

ISBN-13: 9781503939967
ISBN-10: 1503939960

Printed in the United States of America

*On June 22, 1941, Nazi Germany launched a surprise
invasion of the Soviet Union. Within a few short
months, the Germans conquered Ukraine and Belarus.
Then they surrounded Leningrad. And they drove
onward to the gates of Moscow.
By December of that year, the Russians' Red Army was
in complete disarray, and the citizens of Leningrad
were paying for its failures. The Nazi Hunger Plan,
or Starvation Policy, called for the destruction of
Leningrad by firebombing the city's granaries and
preventing any food from reaching the starving
citizenry. As winter loomed, the men, women, and
children of Leningrad were so desperate for food that
some even turned to cannibalism.*

CHAPTER 1

THE CELLIST

The first thing Karen did when the Leningrad trader kissed her was hold her breath. The second thing she did was wonder where he got the fish. She hadn't eaten anything but stale bread since early November—no one in this starving city had—and that was more than a month ago. But somehow, the Leningrad trader's breath tasted like anchovies. He must have bartered for them, just as Karen had agreed to trade him this kiss.

The trader tried to separate her lips with his tongue, but that wasn't part of the deal, so she kept her mouth locked tight. She could feel him trying to grope her, but he couldn't unbutton her coat with his gloves on, and it was far too cold to take them off. Eventually he let go of her and removed his lips from hers. Karen was glad of that because she couldn't hold her breath much longer.

The Leningrad trader begrudgingly opened his duffel bag and handed over a shovel. Karen had brokered a four-way trade. She'd given her gold locket to Kaleena, who'd given a bale of chicken wire to Inna, who'd given a cup of flour to the Leningrad trader, who'd agreed to give

Karen the shovel. It had taken Karen more than a month to organize the deal, to figure out who wanted what and how to get it for them. The Leningrad trader turned out to be the most difficult link in that chain because he wanted more than a cup of flour. He also wanted a kiss.

Karen felt vaguely guilty, as if she were cheating him somehow. You couldn't eat a kiss. A kiss couldn't ease your hunger or start a fire. And yet this savvy and successful trader twenty years her senior had wanted little more. Karen felt bad for him but was relieved that he stayed true to his word.

She had big plans for that shovel. In the spring she intended to plant a garden. She had the seeds her aunt had sent with her across the ocean—tomato, cucumber, and squash. She'd never bothered to plant the seeds or even open the little envelopes they were packed in. She didn't like gardening, not like her aunt did, so she'd used the seed packets as bookmarks and had completely forgotten about them.

She caught her breath when she found them, tucked away in a book that was destined for the fire. She didn't dare tell her father about them. He would have bartered them away for something useless, like a pencil. She hid them in her pockets and began scheming a way to plant them. Tomatoes could be traded for potatoes or even bread. Cucumbers could be pickled if she could find the salt. And squash could be roasted or boiled into a soup. But first she had to survive until the thaw. Right now the ground was frozen solid.

Karen pressed the shovel to her chest and turned to leave, but she hesitated. The Leningrad trader looked so depressed, staring vacantly at the drawstring of his duffel bag. He twirled it around his finger, over and over, just as unwilling to remove his gloves and tie a proper knot as he had been to unbutton Karen's coat.

She leaned close to him and whispered, "You're a good man," and kissed him on the cheek. He smiled at that, which made Karen smile, too. "I'll save you a cucumber," she promised before turning to trudge through the snow back to her apartment. She glanced over her shoulder and was surprised to see the man still watching her, absentmindedly rubbing his cheek where she'd kissed him.

Karen focused on her journey. The route home wasn't long, only about twenty minutes on foot. She'd made that same walk hundreds of times before. But everything required concentration now. It wasn't just the frigid temperature; it was because she was hungry. Her hunger made her weak, and sometimes her mind played tricks on her. Just last week she'd become unfocused and gotten lost. That twenty-minute walk turned into a desperate hour-and-a-half hike as she tried to find her way back. She could have died. Others had. Corpses lay frozen in the street where men or women had fallen, too cold and fatigued to keep walking. That could have happened to her, and if she didn't focus, it could happen again.

She reached her first landmark—the State bakery where she collected her ration of bread—and turned right. She stopped three blocks later, as she always did, to stare at her second landmark—the old woman's dead body.

Karen had first noticed the old woman a week and a half ago, and at the time she hadn't even realized the woman was dead. The old woman lay at the base of an ornate fountain sculpture. Her face was as pale as the white granite of the statues she was crumpled against, and at first Karen thought she was part of the stone sculpture. Behind the old woman rose three strong laborers hoisting a steel girder. Karen's best friend, Inna, had described enough of these patriotic statues that Karen believed she understood the symbolism. The old woman at the laborers' feet represented Mother Russia, long suffering under the corrupt capitalistic system of the former ruling czars. She lay exhausted from her labors, but her struggle had not been in vain. For she had three strong sons who embraced the new Communist regime and helped build great monuments for the people—not just palaces and cathedrals for bishops and princes, but factories and apartment blocks to ease the suffering of the working poor. Only this time the symbolism was wrong. This

Mother Russia wasn't a statue; she was an actual human being, or at least she used to be. Her body lay on the iced-over water.

Karen saw the woman's cadaver every day on the way to the bakery. And she couldn't help but stop and stare. Even when it was snowing, even when the wind rubbed her cheeks like icy sandpaper, Karen would halt a moment, eyes narrowed, and wonder: How had the old woman died, and why? Had she been trying to chip away at the ice to fetch water? That made little sense. Like everything else, the fountain was frozen solid. If it was water she'd been after, she would have had an easier time gathering and melting snow.

A new theory had popped into Karen's mind. She once read a story about an old Eskimo who left his village and walked out into the snow. He knew his time had come, and he no longer wanted to burden his children and grandchildren with the task of keeping him alive. So one night he got up, trudged into a forest of white-dusted fir trees, and died. Karen couldn't remember where she'd read that story. It might have been Jack London. But she had burned her books weeks ago in an effort to stay warm, so she couldn't be sure.

Perhaps, Karen thought, the old woman had done the same thing. Perhaps she knew it was her time to die and had walked into the fountain so that others could eat her bread. But that didn't really make sense, either. If she were dying to ease the lives of the living, she would have found someplace private. She wouldn't have chosen so grand a fountain.

This left Karen with only one conclusion: the old woman had chosen the fountain for the very reason that it *was* grand. She knew people looked at the fountain, and she knew people would be forced to see her dead body. She wanted people to see.

But why did she want them to see her body? Karen couldn't figure it out. The woman had died to make a statement. Karen felt stupid that she couldn't understand what that statement was. Every time she looked at the corpse and failed to understand, she felt like she was letting the old woman down.

So for the tenth day in a row, Karen turned and walked on, all the more frustrated. After two more blocks, Karen should have reached her third landmark. This, too, was a dead body: an old man who must have stumbled and never gotten up. But today she saw no sign of him.

Panic crept into her mind. Had she taken a wrong turn? Should she have turned right instead of left at the fountain?

No, this was the correct corner. She was able to pick out other details that confirmed it: the metal pole for the missing street sign—stolen for firewood—was bent at nearly a forty-five-degree angle, just as Karen remembered. The storefront beyond it, once boarded up, now had broken windows bare to the elements. The glass shards still sprinkled the sidewalk in exactly the pattern she recalled. This was definitely the right place. Someone had finally cleared the old man away, that was all.

As Karen continued her journey back home, she discovered that other bodies had disappeared, too: the fat wine seller crushed under his storefront, the woman hit by a tram and left in the street, the child fallen from a rooftop while watching the sky for German bombers. Each of these dead bodies had served as a gruesome signpost for her, points on a map telling her how much farther she had to walk to get home.

And now they were gone.

Karen was so happy not to have to see them anymore that she turned around and walked back to the State bakery. Soldiers were there, standing uncomfortably on their skis, banging their forearms against their chests to keep warm. They weren't just male soldiers. In Stalin's Russia, women could fight, too. Inna's older sister was there, her machine gun slung over her shoulder. Karen smiled and waved as she approached.

"Thank you, comrades, for finally clearing the streets!"

Even though Karen had grown up in New York, her Russian was so good she could often pass for a native, especially since plenty of citizens didn't speak perfect Russian. Although she couldn't quite pass as a full-blooded Russian, her exotic accent, dark hair, pale skin, and haunting eyes left many Leningraders thinking when they first met her that she came from one of the Soviet Union's far-flung republics—from Azerbaijan or Kazakhstan or Turkmenistan. Karen had gotten her dark features from her father, but she'd learned Russian from her mother, who'd been a Russian ballerina. They'd spoken to each other exclusively in her mother's native tongue until Karen was ten. Then her mother had abandoned her. But Karen's knowledge of the language had not.

The soldiers stopped flapping their arms and eyed Karen. "What are you talking about?" asked Inna's sister.

"The bodies," Karen explained, still smiling. "You removed all the dead bodies."

Inna's sister shook her head. "Why would we do that? We're too busy guarding the food and the trenches to bother cleaning up bodies that stay frozen until spring anyway."

Karen's smile fell. "So you didn't remove them?"

Inna's sister shook her head. "It wasn't us, Comrade."

Karen nodded and turned to leave. She hurried back to her apartment, carefully counting the city blocks until she reached the fountain where the old woman's body had been. She jerked to a stop. The old woman was gone, too.

Now Karen felt even more confused. The corpse had been there only ten minutes ago. But if the soldiers hadn't moved her, who had?

Then she smelled something delicious. It was like a smell she remembered from New York, an aroma she associated with Thanksgiving or Christmas. Not quite the same—not roasted chestnuts—but similar. It made her mouth water.

Someone, somewhere, was cooking, and not just one person, lots of people. Karen desperately wanted to find out where, find out who. She followed the aroma through the snow. She was no longer careful to follow the route she knew. The scent of cooking proved too strong a lure to resist. She wasn't just hungry; she was starving. Her bread rations should have provided enough calories for her to survive, but the government had been replacing some of the flour with sawdust. As a result, the population was slowly dying.

Karen followed her nose through bombed-out buildings, across streets pitted with shell holes into frozen courtyards and through snowy alleyways. In one of those alleys she finally found what she was looking for. Men and women were crowded around a trash can. A fire burned inside it, and over the fire was meat.

But it didn't look like Christmas. The men and women didn't look like Santa Claus. Their cheeks were drawn, their eyes sunken, their teeth gapped and sharp. They carried pieces of metal pried from concrete rubble or busted street signs. And when they saw Karen, when they turned toward her, they gripped those clubs in both hands as if threatening to use them.

Karen ran. She shouldn't have had the energy to run, but somehow she found it. She was younger than they were, and they couldn't catch up, at least not at first.

She bounded across a street and rounded a corner, her breath puffing steam. She glanced over her shoulder and saw two men still chasing her. She reached the bank of the Neva River, and still the men chased her. She was losing energy fast. Even if she kept running, they would catch her. And no one else was out in the freezing cold, just her and her two pursuers. So she swallowed her fear and raced straight out onto the river's ice.

The Neva was spotted with dark holes where people had broken the ice to draw water. As a result, the river's surface was precarious despite the cold. Every time Karen stepped near one of the holes, the ice began to splinter.

But, as it turned out, starving had one advantage. Karen was seventeen but weighed only as much as she had when she was twelve.

The ice didn't break under her. The men pursuing her weren't so lucky. Barely had Karen reached the far shore when she heard a loud crack. She glanced over her shoulder to see the two swallowed by the icy current.

Karen closed her eyes in relief. She knew what would have happened if they'd caught her. They would have eaten her. Where else could they have gotten the meat? Anyone who had meat would've eaten it months ago. And no fresh meat was coming into the besieged city, only sawdust-filled bread. There was a reason the bodies had disappeared from the street. And Karen was no longer happy they were gone.

She wished she had a gun. But at least now she had a shovel. Now she could start a summer garden. Now she wouldn't starve to death.

CHAPTER 2

THE ORGAN-GRINDER

That same day, December 9, 150 miles away, the Red Army was preparing for battle.

"Ready to fire!" yelled Petr. He was nineteen years old and tall for his age, with a boyish face and a military haircut that made him look even younger. Petr had been thin before he was drafted, but constant marching and digging had filled out his muscles, so he had a boy's face on a man's body.

Petr had been drafted from a little village east of Moscow. Now he was in the woods, outside the industrial town of Tikhvin, an important railroad hub for the historic city of Leningrad. The Germans had captured Tikhvin a month ago. Petr's unit had been sent to take it back.

"Ready to fire!" he repeated, glancing expectantly at his commander, Lieutenant Gromoslavsky.

The lieutenant didn't look Petr's way. He only gazed up at the cold sky and squinted at the clouds. "A bear," he said.

"What?" asked Petr.

"Look, a bear." Lieutenant Gromoslavsky pointed at one of the clouds, roughly in the shape of a bear. "It's a sign." The lieutenant punctuated the remark by taking a long draw from his canteen.

This was when Petr realized that the lieutenant was drunk. He always seemed to be drunk before a battle. Petr didn't know how or where he got the vodka. But he always had enough liquid courage hidden away to numb his senses and dull his brain.

Petr didn't really mind. The lieutenant didn't know how to work the Katyusha rockets anyway. None of them did, at least not when they had first been assigned to the battery. But Petr could read the instruction pamphlet. So eventually he figured out how to launch the rockets, which had made him the battery's de facto leader. The arrangement worked out fine so long as the lieutenant didn't try to interfere. And so long as the lieutenant was drunk, there was little danger of that.

Petr ignored the lieutenant and ignited the rockets. They rode in plumes of smoke off the bed of the three-axle truck, moaning and screaming as they rose into the bleached winter sky. It was strange music, the reason the Germans had nicknamed the Katyusha launchers Stalin's Organ.

The instructions showed Petr how to launch the Katyushas, but aiming them was far more complicated. They had a range of over three miles, which meant Petr seldom saw where they landed. He couldn't just aim and fire. Instead, he had to solve a complicated equation involving the rockets' angles of ascent, their fuel, their acceleration, and the force of gravity. The charts and tools that came with the rocket launchers should have helped Petr with those calculations, but no one ever taught him to use them, and he couldn't figure them out on his own. So he just pointed the rockets high enough so they wouldn't hit his own troops, and let them fly.

Back in Petr's rural village, his father, a former university professor and a theoretical mathematician, was teaching arithmetic at the local schoolhouse. When the Red Army conscription commission discovered that the new recruit was the son of a former math professor, they assigned Petr to the Katyusha rockets in the 285th Rifle Division. Who better to make the highly precise calculations required to aim the Katyushas properly?

Unfortunately for the Red Army, Petr hated math. He respected his father's command of numbers, the more so because he himself couldn't understand anything more complicated than algebra. Petr preferred the real world to the theoretical world of numbers. Especially nature. He loved trees heavy with snow, streams crusted with ice, and the absolute silence of a winter day, a day like this one.

Petr's uncle had taught him to hunt, and the young man loved it. He loved the traces animals left in the snow. He loved outwitting them, tracking them back to their lairs. He loved shooting because he'd discovered he was a natural shot. He even enjoyed the cold.

To Petr, his father's move from Moscow to a rural village had been invigorating. It was freedom. The army, of course, was the opposite. The army was tedium. It was taking orders and digging ditches. It was pushing trucks stuck in the mud. It was carrying heavy ammunition and supply boxes. And it was marching, endless marching. Petr's unit had a truck, but it was for the Katyusha missile racks, not the men. Petr already felt as if he had marched all the way across Russia, and now that they were constantly in retreat, it seemed like the Germans were forcing him to march right back.

Dull explosions in the distance told Petr that the Katyusha rockets had struck some barren patch of snow, and he hurried to reload the missile racks on the back of the truck. He'd quickly learned that he was not judged by where the rockets fell but by how often they fell. The political officers who kept an eye on the army for the all-powerful Politburo couldn't see where the rockets landed any better than Petr could. But they could know how quickly Petr and his team reloaded the battery, how long it took before they ignited the next salvo. Petr and his team had become quite good at loading rockets. So theirs was judged one of the finest Katyusha batteries on the front, even though they had absolutely no idea how to aim.

As Petr's team finished reloading the Katyusha for him, he checked the angle of the launch rack and adjusted it slightly downward so the rockets would travel more straight ahead than upward. This way the rockets would land farther away. If Petr's comrades managed to break through the German lines, he wanted to be sure his rockets didn't land on them, the advancing Red Army.

He needn't have worried. He'd barely ignited the new salvo before the Russian infantry appeared in the trees on the other side of the river before him. Like Petr they wore warm *ushanka*—fur hats—under their steel helmets; *valenki*—felt boots; and *telogreika*—quilted jackets and trousers. The whole uniform was dyed green and offered no concealment against the white snow and bare birch trees. But these men didn't even bother trying to hide. They were far more concerned with running away.

They ran right for Petr.

His heart sank. Once again the Red Army was retreating. Already Petr could hear the political officer screaming at the rush of fleeing infantry, pleading with them to hold their ground, ordering them to stand fast for their country, and, pistol drawn, threatening to shoot the first Russian soldier who tried to cross the bridge to the other side of the river—Petr's side.

It was to no avail. Russian soldiers had no fear of pistols. They feared German machine guns.

Peter heard the staccato report of those machine guns and ignited a Katyusha salvo that briefly drowned them out. The rockets exploded harmlessly in the distance. And the machine gunfire returned, closer.

Then came another sound: the rumble and clank of metal plates slapping against steel wheels. It was tank treads: German panzers. A shot boomed, louder than the machine guns, and a tree blew apart, showering burning splinters in all directions. The Russian soldiers who crossed the stone bridge were passing Petr now, dropping their rifles and grenades so they could run faster. A rout was under way.

Petr and his crew had never been in a battle that hadn't turned into a rout, so they knew exactly what to do. They packed up the ammunition trailer while Lieutenant Gromoslavsky wheeled the truck around. Then they attached the trailer to the truck's hitch, jumped on the running boards, and hung on tight, waiting for Lieutenant Gromoslavsky to hit the gas. Drunk or not, the lieutenant was wise enough to keep the truck's fuel tank topped off. Their truck burned less gas than a German tank, so they all knew that the panzers would be forced to stop and refuel eventually, allowing them to outrun the surging German attack.

But the lieutenant hadn't hit the gas, not yet. He was waiting for Petr, the only crew member who hadn't jumped aboard. Petr looked around. One of the other trucks had failed to start. It was still facing the advancing panzers, rockets loaded and pointed up into the sky. That truck would make a valuable prize. The Germans loved capturing abandoned equipment and using it to kill Russians. And the truck stood, abandoned. The Katyusha rocketeers manning it had joined the mad dash to flee.

Lieutenant Gromoslavsky leaned out his window, shouting at Petr to jump on the running boards, warning that they would leave him behind. Petr knew it was no idle threat. He wouldn't be the first man the lieutenant had sacrificed to save his skin. But Petr was tired of marching, and this battle was supposed to have been different. It wasn't supposed to end in a Russian rout. It was part of a new winter offensive. Winter was to be Russia's greatest weapon. Had it not destroyed Napoleon? Now it should be destroying Hitler. Russians were used to winter. They were prepared for winter. Their quilted *telogreikas* were warmer and far less cumbersome than the long coats the Germans wore.

Or at least Petr had heard that that was what the Germans wore. He'd never seen a German. He'd always been too far removed, firing his rockets from well behind the Russian lines. He'd looked forward to

seeing a German, finally. The great winter offensive was supposed to end
with captured German prisoners, after all. But here instead was another
Russian retreat. Once again, he'd only been close enough to hear the
enemy's guns and tanks, and once again, he'd been too far away to see
a single actual German soldier.

Petr didn't jump on Lieutenant Gromoslavsky's truck. Instead,
he calmly wandered over to the abandoned truck that wouldn't start.
Gromoslavsky shouted at him again, but Petr raised his hand and gestured at the lieutenant to go on without him. The lieutenant didn't have
to be told twice. His truck disappeared down the rutted road, leaving
a wake of icy mud.

Petr had the vague intuition as he walked toward the stalled truck
that he was being foolish. He wasn't a stupid or dim-witted boy. He
couldn't really have said what made him do what he did that day. He
was certain that his refusal to retreat would result in his death. A sensible voice in his head urged him to turn around and run, trying to
convince him that it still wasn't too late. But it wasn't a loud voice,
because in that moment Petr didn't care whether he lived or died. His
life no longer mattered to him. He just wanted to see a German, finally,
and to stop the endless marching.

CHAPTER 3

THE CHOIRBOY

More than four thousand miles away, it was still December 8 in New York City. There, at roughly 11:30 p.m., Bobby picked up a pen—and hesitated.

He was in an Army Air Forces recruitment center, and he wasn't alone. He'd had to wait in line just to get inside the door. Japan had just bombed Pearl Harbor, and in retaliation, America had declared war on both Japan and Germany. The outrage of that sneak attack was fresh in everyone's minds. Army recruitment hit an all-time high in December of 1941. Everyone wanted to enlist; everyone wanted to fight back against the Japanese. But that was not why Bobby was there. Bobby was there because of Karen Hamilton.

The papers before him demanded his signature, but still he hesitated. He knew that if he scribbled his name on the dotted line, his parents would be furious. They'd always been so proud of him, and he had never done anything to make them waver in that pride. He'd been a model son, which is why they so looked forward to seeing him during

Christmas vacation. But his train home left the next morning from Grand Central Station, and if he signed his name now, he would miss it.

Bobby didn't like going back to Minneapolis. It felt provincial, isolated, and small. The desire to get out of that city had driven him to graduate high school early, when he was only sixteen. Two years before, he had chosen to attend Columbia University, solely because it was in New York City. There was no bigger stage in America.

Bobby hadn't been disappointed. Columbia was a challenging intellectual environment; his high school lessons seemed remedial by comparison. At first he'd fallen back on old habits, coasting along in his studies, completing his assignments right before they were due. Then he'd realized he was falling behind, and for the first time in his life, Bobby started working hard. He paid attention to the study habits of his most successful classmates and mimicked them until he developed his own, even more efficient, methods. He didn't find the hard work difficult; he found it invigorating.

Basketball was more exciting, too, especially because he was now competing with boys two or three years his senior. No longer could he count on driving to the basket for an easy layup; long arms and strong bodies inevitably barred his path and threatened to strip the ball. So he perfected his outside shot and moved from the post to the back court. He studied game strategy and the abilities of his teammates, so he knew whom to feed the ball to and when. By the end of his freshman season, he wasn't a scoring champion like he had been in high school, but he was leading his team in assists. And he was having more fun on the court than he could ever remember.

The only place Bobby continued to be bored was on dates. The high school girls he dated back home had all been Catholic. They were tall and pretty, but they were reluctant to embrace him, timid at his touch, and frightened by his kiss.

The Catholic nuns who ran their private schools ruled with velvet tongues and iron fists. Boys and girls alike were treated to terrifying sermons describing the spiritual agony that assailed the bodily curious. Only in the sanctity of marriage could men and women finally explore their carnal desires, content in the knowledge that pregnancy, supposedly the inevitable consequence of even light petting, was no longer to be feared. Those who were suspected of ignoring these sermons were assailed first with words and then with rulers and belt straps if necessary.

The girls attending Barnard, Columbia's sister college, weren't Catholic. But the Protestant girls who seemed to rule the Ivy League's sister schools were even worse. They were cold fish. When one finally allowed Bobby to kiss her after he had tried for weeks, she closed her eyes and grimaced as if it were some torture to endure rather than an exquisite pleasure to share.

As Bobby became more familiar with upper-class Protestant culture, he began to realize that they had a lot in common with the Catholic families he'd known in Minnesota. They were repressed in the extreme. Married couples never seemed to touch each other. In public, husband and wife addressed each other as "Mr." and "Mrs.," like perfect strangers. Bobby often wondered how these people managed to have children at all.

This attitude was unique to the upper social stratum, Bobby knew. He wasn't naive. Other communities within the city reveled in their passions and suffered the consequences. He'd seen men and women huddled outside taverns and nightclubs, ignoring falling snow, lost in the feel of each other's embraces and the taste of each other's lips. On more than one occasion, he'd passed a parked car, noticed the steamed windows, and knew exactly what was happening inside.

He would have felt more envy if the consequences of those tawdry affections weren't equally apparent. Orphaned children and single mothers were everywhere, as were fathers laboring long hours or even begging to feed too many children. Even if these consequences weren't so abundantly clear, Bobby knew he was a prisoner of his social class.

His family would never condone his fraternizing with what they saw as the working poor. So he never considered it.

Bobby met Karen Hamilton in the winter of 1939.

He was attending a concert—Stravinsky's *The Rite of Spring*. He had a music history class at the time and chose the event because that week's subject was Russian composers. He brought his girlfriend at the time, Elizabeth—a pretty, blonde nineteen-year-old who'd allowed Bobby to kiss her good night on their previous date. In the cab on the way to the concert, she even allowed Bobby to hold her hand. But as soon as they arrived, as soon as they found themselves in public view, she let go of him and returned to her reserved Protestant self.

The music was like nothing either of them had ever heard. Elizabeth hated it. The fast tempos and percussive beats gave her a headache. She described the music as "savage." She even went so far as to complain that all the concert was missing were bare-breasted islanders dancing in grass skirts. She meant it as an insult, but Bobby was quite taken by the image.

Bobby disagreed. He not only loved the music but admired one of the cellists in particular. She played with both skill and passion. And she was beautiful. Her brown eyes were almost black, and her raven hair formed a striking frame around her pale face and red lips. The strenuous score made her and the other performers sweat, making her cream-colored gown stick to her skin. The silky material outlined the curve of her chest, the roundness of her hips, and the long, sensuous lines of her legs. That fine silk let Bobby see her muscles tense and relax with each forceful thrust of her bow. He was mesmerized.

When Bobby took his girlfriend back to her dormitory, he didn't even try for a kiss. He waited on the snow-swept stoop until her proctor opened the door, then tipped his hat and went back to the cab. But he didn't go home. He paid the cabbie double to take him back to the concert hall as fast as possible. There he waited with a crowd of admirers at the backstage door. For forty-five minutes the fans huddled together, inadvertently keeping one another warm. Then the doors opened and the musicians poured out.

The waiting fans clapped politely while Bobby studied each face, looking for the cellist.

Then the conductor emerged with his daughter beside him, and the polite applause magnified. Music critics and orchestra patrons crowded around to congratulate him on the performance and to ask him to sign their programs.

At first Bobby was disappointed, thinking his cellist must have slipped out through a different exit. But then he caught the gaze of the conductor's daughter and recognized her almost-black eyes.

He flinched, shocked. On stage, with her cello, she had seemed to be in the full flower of womanhood, more experienced in love and passion than Bobby could ever hope to be. Now, clad in a bulky wool coat, dark hair tucked into a felt beret, standing demurely beside the tall man, who was surely her father, she looked like a child.

Bobby pushed forward and waited his turn for a word with the conductor. When the moment came, he ignored the man and faced his daughter. "My name's Bobby Campbell," he said, "and I'm a prodigy, too."

Karen's father frowned with disapproval.

At first Bobby assumed the conductor was jealous that someone was congratulating his daughter instead of himself. Later, after Bobby got to know Karen's father, he came to realize that wasn't it at all. Even though he was a composer, a conductor, a pianist, an artist—even though his livelihood was entirely dependent on the approval of others—he was embarrassed by praise.

This was a quality common among socialists, Bobby would learn later. They preferred to share credit, so it was a perverse act of love when the conductor interjected to correct Bobby that Karen was no prodigy—talented, yes, but she still had a lot to learn—and in any case, she was fifteen, and in the world of music one could hardly call a fifteen-year-old a prodigy.

Karen ignored her father. She looked up at Bobby with those deep, black eyes and allowed a smile to cross her red lips. "I'm Karen Hamilton. So what sort of prodigy are you?"

Bobby explained that he was only seventeen but already a sophomore at Columbia. That led to a longer discussion about New York and how it compared to Minneapolis, which led to a lengthy report on his family and its history. How his grandfather had emigrated from Ireland, developed a hardy strain of strawberry resistant to frost, and made a fortune in manufacturing jam.

Bobby had always been an easy conversationalist, but he wasn't generally a braggart. Pride was the deadliest of the seven sins, and he'd studied enough history to know that even the pagan Greeks counted hubris as dangerous. But he also had an overwhelming feeling that this might be his only chance to impress this girl and that he needed to impress her. She stirred something in him that made him want to be his best.

He found himself walking beside Karen and her father, still talking, describing how proud he'd made his parents and teachers, when Karen interrupted.

"Do you think your grandfather made his own parents proud?" she asked him.

Bobby hesitated, confused. "My grandfather?"

Karen nodded. "Wasn't he the one who made your family's fortune? Wasn't he the one who emigrated from Ireland? What must his parents have thought when he abandoned them?"

Bobby was befuddled. He admitted that he had never considered this, but Karen didn't let it go. "So now that you are considering it, what do you think about it?"

Bobby didn't even understand the question. All he could do was stare. They'd arrived at the conductor's apartment, a modest building on the Lower East Side. Bobby looked up at the building's dirty facade, hoping to find some direction, some answer, in the lines of its brickwork.

The conductor came to his rescue. "What I think my daughter is saying," he suggested, "is that sometimes it is more important to follow your heart than to do what others expect of you."

Karen nodded. "What is it you want to do? What is it that your heart desires?"

Bobby stared at her a moment longer. Then he told her the truth. "I don't know."

Karen smiled again. It wasn't a joyous smile, and it wasn't mirthful or even polite. It was the worst kind of smile—a pitying one. "When you do find out," she said, "you tell me."

Bobby's heart was sinking fast. He had failed to impress this girl. His bragging hadn't elicited interest; it had brought out only charity. He'd been given his one chance, and he'd fallen flat on his face.

But then Karen did something unexpected. She stepped forward, took his hand in both of hers, stood on tiptoe, and brushed his cheek with her lips. "Good night," she said before ascending the steps to her building with her father.

"Good night," Bobby responded, in a daze. And as he watched her disappear into the dark foyer and watched the door shut behind her, he suddenly knew the answer to her question. He knew what his heart desired.

It desired her.

CHAPTER 4
THE CELLIST

While Karen bartered for a shovel, while she trudged back and forth to the bakery, her father stayed home at his piano, gnawing down the point of his last pencil and continuing to compose music.

Karen hated her father. He was the reason they'd left New York in the first place. He was the reason they'd traveled across the Atlantic and then up through the Baltic Sea to this beautiful but isolated port city of ice towers and blue skies. Leningrad was where Dmitri Shostakovich lived and worked, and Karen's father lionized the Russian composer, who was perhaps the most famous composer of the twentieth century. Shostakovich was only thirty-one years old when his Fifth Symphony had become a worldwide success.

Karen's father had conducted that symphony in America, and Shostakovich was so impressed by the performance that he invited him to join the orchestra in Leningrad. He even offered Karen, a budding cellist, the opportunity to study with him at the Leningrad Conservatory.

Karen's father jumped at the chance. Despite Karen's wishes, he dragged her with him across two oceans and an entire continent, leaving her boyfriend, Bobby, behind. When she left New York in 1939, Karen was fifteen. She'd been gone for only a year and a half, but it seemed like a lifetime now.

Mr. Shostakovich wasn't only the reason they came to Leningrad. He was also the reason they didn't flee in June when the Germans invaded. Their work here was too important, Mr. Shostakovich claimed. The defenders needed music, and the world needed music, because Shostakovich was working on a new composition, a Seventh Symphony written *in* Leningrad, *for* Leningrad. He told Karen's father that the symphony would be performed all over the world, a firm declaration that Leningrad was besieged but not broken, that one European nation at least was able to stand up to the German war machine, take the worst that it could offer, and remain unconquered.

It was a beautiful sentiment, one that Karen's father, with all his impractical romanticism, fully believed in. He joined the civilian corps that helped build the trenches and antiaircraft pits surrounding the city. He volunteered for the conservatory's fire brigade so that he could stand and serve beside his hero, Dmitri Shostakovich.

Every single day, as the ground froze and food grew scarcer, Karen's father walked to the conservatory and helped Mr. Shostakovich work on his new masterpiece. And every single night, after returning to the apartment, Karen's father transcribed the day's progress, tried out experimental elements on his piano, and wrote down the ones he liked.

Shostakovich had abandoned them in September of 1941, hypocritically escaping Leningrad on a plane to Moscow. Even after that, Karen's father still worked on the symphony. He never stood in the ration lines with Karen. He never helped her scrounge for wood or food. He just worked all day and all night on the symphony and criticized her for not practicing the cello.

Karen hated Mr. Shostakovich. She hated him almost as much as she hated her father.

Her father even refused to wear gloves because he could not play the piano with gloves on. Karen begged him to give it up. Nobody cared about the stupid symphony. Her father wasn't even Russian. But he didn't give up. He just kept on working, finally having agreed to wear gloves a few days earlier. But they were thin women's gloves, not warm at all. Yet he had absolutely refused to wear anything thicker—until today.

When Karen arrived home with her shovel, she was overjoyed to see her father wearing his mittens. He had finally taken her advice. She was so happy that she didn't even mind picking up the paper and pencil and writing down the last few notes as he dictated them to her. She didn't question why he didn't write them himself. Together they ate the last of their bread ration and went to sleep, huddling together for warmth.

Karen woke up cold. She was confused. She expected to feel cold, of course, but not so frigid. Why was there no warmth under the blanket? And then, with horror, she realized why. Her father's body was not producing any heat. She shook him. He wasn't asleep. He was dead.

And Karen feared that she suddenly knew why. Filled with dread but needing to know the truth, Karen pulled off her father's mittens. His fingers were black and rotting from the inside out. One after the other they came off in her hand, rotten from frostbite. That's why he'd worn his mittens—not to keep warm, but so that Karen wouldn't see his fingers.

In that moment, Karen hated her father more than she ever had before. He had nothing to worry about anymore, nothing to accomplish, no responsibilities. He'd abdicated it all, leaving all those burdens to Karen. He'd gotten her into this mess, and now she was the only one left who could get herself out.

She dragged her father's body into the courtyard, where Mrs. Kudaschova used to tend her summer flowers. The flowers were long dead, and, as Karen expected, the soil was frozen solid. She knew she couldn't break that soil, but she had to try. She knew what would happen to her father's body if she didn't bury it—it would meet the same fate that had befallen the old woman at the fountain and the dead child and the wine seller. She smashed at the frozen soil, trying desperately to chip away a hole. Her shovel broke. She tried not to weep, but the tears came hot and thick, and despite her best efforts, uncontrollable sobs followed. Now there would be no garden. Not without a shovel. One more reason to hate her father. It was his fault.

She was no idiot. She knew better than to try digging in the courtyard in the middle of winter. She knew the frozen soil was as hard as rock. But what choice did she have? She couldn't just wait until summer. Her father's body lay beside her, already frozen stiff, his face calm, his eyes open, serene in death. She glared at the broken shovel on the icy soil. And she gave up. She just covered her father's body with snow.

Karen dragged herself back to the apartment. She smashed her father's piano to pieces. She smashed her cello next. Then she fed both to the fire, using photographs of her boyfriend, Bobby, as kindling. In her fit of rage, she almost threw her father's compositional notes into the fire as well, but she stopped herself. She folded the papers inside her coat. She cried, then, and she didn't stop crying until she fell asleep.

Meanwhile that fire blazed. And for the first night in weeks, she felt truly warm.

The next morning, Karen went out to the courtyard. The snow mound had been dug up. Her father's body was gone. She knew she couldn't wait any longer. Even if she could find another shovel to start a garden, it would be pointless, because she wouldn't survive until summer.

She no longer needed a shovel. She needed information. She needed to know where the Germans were, the location of the nearest unoccupied town, and how to reach it. She needed food so that she could travel. She needed identification papers that would allow her to pass Red Army checkpoints. And most of all, she needed a weapon and the courage to use it.

Karen didn't know how she would get any of those things. Even finding a simple shovel had been difficult. But she promised herself to find a way, because without them she would never escape Leningrad.

CHAPTER 5
THE ORGAN-GRINDER

A sort of madness had come over Petr. His heartbeat had slowed. It seemed to him that the woods had grown quieter. They had grown much louder, in fact, as the German panzer tanks neared and their guns fired more often. It only seemed quieter because Petr's mind was focusing on the stalled truck, on the missile rack in its bed, on the Katyusha launcher, and the hump-backed stone bridge that rose like a steep hill almost directly before the truck. The sound of the guns and the tank treads meant nothing in Petr's mind, pushed back to his subconscious.

Petr began to manhandle the launch rack, lowering it farther than he'd ever done so that the rocket tips practically rested on the top of the truck's cab. Then he crawled up underneath the rockets to peer through the cab's rear window, over the driver's seat and steering wheel, and through the windshield.

The German tanks were coming into view. These were the twenty-five-ton Panzer IVs, pride of the Wehrmacht—the German Army. Their wide, boxy frames were slung low to the ground, and they squeezed between the bare birch trees, knocking down trunks where the passage was too narrow. A short howitzer protruded from each tank's turret like the chunky nose of a prizefighter. Their three-inch-wide shells could reduce concrete fortifications to rubble, Petr knew, and the machine guns extending from their lower hulls added deadly firepower. Petr had to admit that a panzer had a terrifying beauty, like a Siberian tiger.

Here he was, finally seeing his first Germans. The infantry ran beside the tanks, keeping pace, and carrying rifles, machine guns, and boxes of ammunition. The German soldiers' uniforms seemed designed to intimidate. Their steel helmets angled slightly backward, framing each man's head in a way that suggested the sharp beak of an eagle. Long, gray coats were draped over each soldier's smart gray-green uniform and knee-high black leather boots. They looked like stern school headmasters, industrial foremen, or even politicians. They gave Petr the uneasy feeling that they were men born to command—to expect and demand obedience from all they faced.

Petr noted with satisfaction, however, that the Russian winter had already begun to degrade the psychological impact of that carefully designed German uniform. The soldiers' heavy gray coats tangled their legs, slowed their pace, and sopped up the wet snow. Their boots looked soaked through and caked with ice. Their eaglelike faces were pale with cold, and the misty breaths that puffed from their mouths showed their mounting fatigue.

The lead panzer rumbled up to the other side of the bridge, its black exhaust climbing behind it into the still air. Then it paused, Petr heard ice cracking, and a hatch swung open on top of the tank's turret.

A soldier pulled himself up and half-out of the hatch. He wore a black leather jacket and a peaked cap, and he looked both warm and calm. He lifted a pair of binoculars to his eyes and began to scan the area across the river.

Petr knew the man wouldn't see much to give him concern. The Red Army had already fled, leaving nothing behind but empty rocket cases and abandoned rifles or machine guns. The truck in which Petr hid was the only vehicle left. And a single shot from the tank's three-inch howitzer would make short work of that.

The tank commander's binoculars halted on Petr's stalled truck, trained directly at the windshield, directly at Petr. Petr froze. He was staring right at the tank commander, and the commander was staring right back. But he couldn't see Petr. The sun was bright in the white sky, brighter still as it glistened off the blinding snow blanketing the river's ice; and the area in which Petr was hiding, under the missile launch rack, was shadowed by the Katyusha rockets.

The truck's bright exterior and dark interior turned the windshield into a one-way mirror. The tank commander surely couldn't see through it, couldn't see anything but his own reflection looking back at him. And yet the commander held his gaze, as if reassuring himself there was nothing on that side of the river to fear, that the Katyusha truck really was abandoned, really was the fat prize it seemed to be.

Petr held his breath. And then, finally, the tank commander lowered his binoculars and yelled something in German. A young soldier, probably an infantry sergeant, trudged up to the tank commander. The tank commander yelled again, sweeping the riverbank with a pointing finger. The infantry sergeant turned to bark at the troops, relaying the tank commander's orders.

Three machine gunners and their assistants hustled up to the riverbank and plopped down into the snow. The machine gunners slung their weapons off their shoulders and propped the barrels onto folding bipods while their assistants cracked open metal boxes and slapped belts of ammunition into the guns' chambers. When they were ready, the infantry sergeant barked again.

The bullets tore into the snow, gravel, and mud on Petr's side of the river. But they didn't hit the stalled truck. The machine gunners carefully traced their fire around the vehicle—clearly, the orders were not to damage the prized Katyushas.

Once the ammunition belts were spent, riflemen ran forward with more ammo boxes, and the assistants loaded new bullets into the guns. But this time the machine gunners didn't fire. They just stared across the river, fingers likely resting gently on their triggers.

The tank commander yelled something and banged on the turret. A gearbox ground as the unseen driver shifted the panzer into low gear. And the heavy tank disappeared from Petr's view, hidden by the tall, humped bridge as it inched onto the stone and began to climb across.

Petr couldn't see the panzer, but he made out its black exhaust puffing into the sky. Soon the tank would be on his side of the river. Then the infantry would follow, and they'd capture the Katyusha launcher, and they'd capture or kill Petr.

The tank commander's head appeared over the crest of the bridge, then his chest and arms. He looked back and forth, squinting at the bright light reflecting off the snow, wary of any potential ambush. Then Petr saw the turret and the snub-nosed howitzer, then the hull and machine gun, so close that he could see the whites of the driver's eyes behind the view slit.

Petr saw the tracks, and finally the bottom of the tank—the under hull. It rose up over the hump of the bridge. This was the tank's weakest point—the unarmored underbelly between its tracks. An instant later the tank would clear the hump and descend to the other side, showing only its steel-plated armored front of more than two inches, impervious to all but the biggest Russian guns.

Nobody fired at a tank from nearly beneath it. But Petr could. In a single motion he squeezed the trigger and dove from the truck. Before he hit the ground, he felt a searing pain in his legs as the rocket exhaust burned through his *telogreika* trousers.

He was only dimly aware of explosions. The snow enveloped him. For a moment he could think of nothing but the excruciating pain in his legs. He heard a supersonic zip—bullets passing right over his head. The machine gunners had seen him jump from the truck and were zeroing in. He rolled to his right. This drenched his smoking legs in more wet snow, a moment's relief from the pain, but more important, it sent him directly under the truck, its three axles shielding him from the German machine guns for now.

Their slugs ripped into Soviet steel, into the truck's bed, cab, and tires, deafening Petr with their impact and rocking the truck back and forth above him. He pulled himself forward on his elbows and peered out between the truck's front wheels.

Petr had hit that panzer with over a dozen Katyusha rockets, each packed with eleven pounds of high explosives. At least two rockets must have struck the tank's soft underbelly. The explosions multiplied as the panzer's ammo ignited, leaving a charred and smoking twist of steel. The vehicle was no longer a tank, it was a roadblock. Until its wreckage could be cleared, no German panzers would be crossing the bridge.

Another tank tried to cross the river directly. It rumbled out onto the snow-covered ice, rolling fifteen feet across before the ice broke with a terrific crack. The tank plunged like a boulder into the shallow depth, the icy water surging through gun slits and view ports. Hatches popped open everywhere at once, and the five-man crew struggled to wade through the frigid current to the safety of the German-held shore. Petr suspected they would die of hypothermia.

The Panzer IV unit had three more tanks, and these began taking control of the chaos. Two had driven up to the bridge, where they slowly tried to push the destroyed hulk of their comrade panzer off the bridge and into the river.

The third maneuvered to the river's edge, dug itself in with a twist of its treads, and directed its turret at Petr's truck.

As Petr watched the gun turret swivel around, the pain in his legs returned with a vengeance. But he knew he wouldn't have to endure that pain for long. The machine guns might not have been able to reach him, but the panzer's howitzer could launch the truck into the air like a toy with its highly explosive shell, pulverizing Petr with the force of its shock wave.

When the turret stopped, Petr was left staring right down the howitzer's barrel into the black breech of the gun. He gritted his teeth, but he didn't close his eyes. He didn't care what he would see. He just wanted to die with his eyes open.

Then the Panzer IV burst apart.

An instant later Petr heard the shrieking impact and crunching metal of the tank's destruction. A moment after that came the sharp report of the gun that fired the armor-piercing round, as the shell had moved much faster than the speed of sound.

Petr pivoted to the right and could hardly believe what he saw: T-34s charging the German flank, threatening to seize the opposite shore of the river. Round of body, almost organic in their contours, Russia's T-34 tanks were all angles and curves. Whitewashed to blend in with the snow, their diesel exhaust colorless and therefore invisible, the T-34s had taken the Germans completely by surprise.

And although their forward-slung turrets gave them the appearance of dim-witted slack jaws, Petr thought the Russian tanks even more beautiful than the German ones. To him they looked like white stallions, drawing long chariots of avenging angels into battle, for ropes were strung behind the tanks, pulling soldiers on skis.

Petr watched as the soldiers began to let go of the ropes, pushing hard with their ski poles and picking up speed as they descended through the forest toward the German flank.

In only moments they were skiing past the churning tanks that had pulled them there, but they didn't wait for the T-34s to catch up. They kept pushing with their poles and skis, like ice-skaters, picking up downhill speed until they stopped poling and crouched to reduce wind resistance.

These angels looked nothing like the conscripts Petr had just seen fleeing for their lives. Instead of the green quilted uniforms, they wore white camouflage snowsuits complete with hoods pulled tight over their steel helmets. They were moving so swiftly that they blurred against the white trunks of the bare birch trees.

German rifle fire barked in the cold air, and here and there a Russian fell, tumbling over his skis. But the German rifles were bolt action and had to be cocked after every shot. Without their machine guns, the German soldiers couldn't sustain a high enough rate of fire.

Meanwhile, the tanks dueled. There were fewer T-34s in a Russian tank platoon than Panzer IVs in a German one. At full strength the Germans would outnumber the Russian armor five to three. But Petr had already helped destroy two of the German panzers, and the lead T-34 had just disabled a third with a shot that struck the panzer's side between turret ring and hull. Now it was three to two.

But these Wehrmacht tank crews were disciplined, hardened veterans of the German conquests of Poland and France. Already the remaining panzers were reversing off the bridge and turning to show the Russians their thicker frontal armor.

One Panzer IV landed a direct hit on a T-34, ringing the Russian tank like the loudest bell Petr ever heard. The crew inside had to have been deafened. But the explosion only blackened the T-34's whitewash. The Russian crew returned fire, their shell striking a glancing blow on the apron of steel around the howitzer but not penetrating.

All five opposing tanks stopped now, engines idling, their drivers giving their gunners a stable platform. They fired back and forth, pausing between loud booms to reload. The Russian infantry kept advancing. They carried submachine guns—the lead soldiers knelt on their skis while still moving and let loose long bursts at the German machine gunners. Their comrades continued surging forward, firing from the hip, the submachine guns' recoil slowing their descent while the guns' inaccurate but rapid fire pinned down the German riflemen.

Petr forgot the pain in his legs as he watched, fascinated. Petr had loved American movies, especially cowboy films, when he was a young boy. His favorite was *The Big Trail*, starring John Wayne, which he saw when he was eight, the last cowboy movie he ever saw. Stalin had banned foreign films in 1932. Petr remembered that the hero and the villain always seemed to end up shooting at each other in the middle of a dusty street. The two enemies would stand straight and still, firing relentlessly with their six-shooters until one was shot dead. This tank duel was a lot like those movies. The huge, armored machines stood their ground and blasted away at each other, pausing only to reload.

Despite the Russian advantage in numbers, the battle seemed to be at a stalemate, with neither side able to penetrate the armor of the other.

"Come on, come on," Petr heard himself growl, urging the T-34s to rush forward, surround the panzers, and fire away at their weaker side and rear armor. But the Russian tank crews seemed content to sit back on the top of the hill and shoot from there.

This was looking more like the battles he was used to, he thought bitterly. Russian cowardice was going to result in yet another Russian defeat.

Then Petr noticed that the infantry combat was over—the Russians had completely overwhelmed the elite German troops protecting the panzers. The Russian soldiers lay on their bellies now, half buried in snow, their skis abandoned as they crawled toward the German tanks.

The panzer crews couldn't see the Russians because they were "buttoned up," their hatches closed tight to protect them from incoming T-34 rounds. They were relying on periscopes to target the enemy tanks, and the periscopes had a very narrow field of vision.

Now Petr realized it wasn't cowardice that kept the Russian tankers back; it was experience. The T-34's armor was vulnerable up close, so they'd let their superior infantry destroy the German tanks for them.

Several Russian soldiers lit petrol bombs—so-called Molotov cocktails. Petr had been taught about them but doubted their efficacy. How could a glass bottle filled with gasoline hurt a German tank? Now he watched them toss the bottles onto a panzer's engine deck. That made Petr a believer. The Molotov cocktail's burning fuel coated the tank's armor plating, but it also dripped through the cooling vents.

The erupting engine blaze sent the Germans popping up from their hatches with arms raised in surrender. The Russians gunned them down.

The last panzer backed away from the bridge, retreating into the woods. It reversed slowly, not daring to turn around and present its vulnerable rear to the guns of the T-34s.

The Russian infantry easily kept pace, jogging beside the tank and tossing RPG-40 antitank grenades onto its deck and turret. The image reminded Petr of dogs baiting a bear. The heavy grenades detonated on contact, pitting the panzer's thick armor but not penetrating it. The bombs popped and banged all over the German tank, first a dozen, then two dozen.

With each explosion the tank seemed to jerk. Finally, it stopped. A tall Russian hoisted himself onto the deck, climbed up onto the turret, and began to pry open the hatch.

The hood of his snowsuit had blown back, revealing a deeply tanned face and a blond beard. Three of his comrades helped with the hatch while a forth stood with one leg propped on the howitzer priming an antipersonnel grenade, a short stick attached to a metal cylinder packed with explosives called a potato masher.

The men finally pulled open the hatch, and the soldier tossed in the potato masher. There was a flash, a boom, a puff of smoke.

The battle was over.

———◆———

The soldier with the tan face and blond beard leaped with great agility off the panzer's turret and crunched through the snow toward the bridge. He vaulted atop the crumpled heap of metal that had been a German tank before Petr destroyed it.

The blond soldier peered inside blackened hulk. Then Blondie turned his head toward Petr, tracing a line through the air from the destroyed vehicle to Petr's hiding place. He smiled, slid down the tank to the bridge, and strode toward the stalled truck. His companions followed, exchanging brief words Petr couldn't hear.

Blondie examined the three-axle truck. Its windshield was broken, its cab punctured with countless bullet holes, its tires flat. But there was no corpse. He bent down, his white smile flashing, and held out his hand. Petr took it and was yanked out into the open by the blond soldier's strong grip.

Petr screamed in pain.

When Blondie saw Petr's legs, his smile dropped. He reached into an ammunition pouch, pulled out a flask, unscrewed it, and took a quick pull himself before holding it under Petr's nose. "Drink," he said. "Drink."

Petr drank. It wasn't his first vodka. He and his uncle often celebrated a successful hunt with a round of stiff drinks. But this was finer than the spirits Petr knew, not the liquid fire that made his stomach churn. This was ice-cold and smooth. It coated his throat as he swallowed, and he was surprised by how quickly he emptied the flask.

He heard cloth tear and recognized that someone was doing something to his legs. He tried to lift his head, but Blondie shoved him back down. "Don't worry," he assured Petr, "you'll be fine."

"Where did you come from?" Petr asked.

"We came from Siberia."

Petr's head swam. He had the odd sensation of flying and realized he'd been lifted between two of Blondie's comrades.

And Petr noticed that the sky had turned a perfect shade of blue, and he saw a cloud that he mistook for the same one Lieutenant Gromoslavsky had pointed out earlier. "A bear," he muttered.

"What?" asked Blondie.

"It really does look like a bear."

Blondie followed Petr's gaze and nodded. "Yes, I guess it does at that."

CHAPTER 6
THE CHOIRBOY

Winter, 1939

The day after Bobby met Karen at the concert, he skipped class and left a card in her mail slot asking for a date. She accepted, so they spent that Saturday strolling in the park, her father acting as chaperone but respectfully keeping his distance.

They watched skaters on the lake and kites in the sky.

"So. Did you figure out the answer to my question?" Karen asked him.

"Yes," he replied, "I did."

Her face lit up. "What is it, then? What is it you want to do?"

He held her gaze for a moment and said, "I can't tell you yet."

Her smile continued to play across her lips as she read the mischief in his eyes. "Is it a mystery, then?"

"For the moment, yes."

Still smiling, she bit her lip before turning and continuing to stroll along the path with him. As they walked, she slipped her hand into his.

Bobby asked her out every weekend. They went to the park, to the zoo, and to the movies. He even invited her to come watch him play basketball. This time it was her turn to marvel at him, at all the bare skin revealed by his athletic shorts and jersey, sweat glistening off toned shoulders, arms, and legs. She loved it, all of it—except the cheerleaders, who she thought were silly.

Winter turned to spring, and still they went out, but only during the day. Karen and her father worked nights, rehearsing or performing. Bobby attended all the performances he could and waited with the admirers by the stage door. He got to know her father better, along with the other musicians. He was even invited to their postconcert soirees, where he was introduced to their intoxicating avant-garde lifestyles. They talked of art and politics and love and sex all in the same breath. They didn't consider themselves Americans but rather world citizens, since the music they loved came from all over Europe.

And as he got to know them better, Bobby began to realize why, despite their obvious talent, the more traditional theaters and critics shunned them. They didn't believe in the ownership of music. They believed in the complete freedom of all intellectual ideas. They refused to be bound by traditional compositions. Like jazz musicians, they would add their own improvisations whenever inspiration struck them. They openly criticized one another, deeming the performance as a whole, rather than the feelings of a single individual, to be of paramount importance. They were musical as well as political socialists, and Bobby's family would have been scandalized to know that he was making their acquaintance.

On each and every date, Karen asked him if he was ready to tell her the answer to that first night's question. And on every date Bobby disappointed her.

She told him she didn't believe him, said she thought he was stalling for time, and even threatened to break up with him. But she never did.

Bobby was afraid to tell her. It was a strange feeling. He'd been so confident in the rest of his life; he still was. But he dreaded telling Karen the truth. What if she rejected him? He'd be devastated. So he held his tongue until May 30. It was at a particularly lively soiree after a particularly successful concert. And it was an unseasonably warm night with a full moon.

The shades were open, the lights off, and the burning glow of cigarettes lit smiling faces and flashing eyes. Ice clinked in glasses, and conversation spilled through the open windows out into the street. Karen and Bobby sat close on the sofa, their knees touching.

"Tell me," Karen said.

"I want you to marry me," Bobby blurted out.

Karen looked shocked. No one else had heard it amid the dozen conversations twittering in the background. But it felt to Bobby as if the room had fallen suddenly, dreadfully, silent.

Karen stood up unsteadily. She smoothed the front skirt of her dress. She looked down at Bobby. He suddenly felt very small in his corner of the sofa. Then she nodded as if making up her mind, cuddled up in his lap, and kissed him on the lips.

From that point forward, Bobby and Karen couldn't keep their hands off each other. At any opportune moment, Bobby would pull her onto his lap and kiss her, or Karen would pull Bobby under the shade of a tree and kiss him. No embarrassment came when they embraced; no shame followed their kisses. And their constant touch only made them yearn for each other even more.

They couldn't get married, of course. They were both too young. Karen was fifteen and Bobby only seventeen. He knew his parents would never approve, but he also knew that once he was legally an adult, he wouldn't require their approval. So he promised Karen he would wait, and she returned that promise.

Something else happened while they dated. Bobby began to pay more attention to the world beyond America's borders. Because the musicians all considered themselves world citizens, they were personally affected by the continued Nazi takeover of Germany and the regime's subsequent invasion of Czechoslovakia. They lost contact with Jewish musicians living in Prague and were shocked by the reports of artists who'd managed to flee the country.

Then, in the summer of 1940, Karen left for Leningrad. Before her departure, they spent an entire day together. Bobby rented a horse-drawn carriage, and they toured Central Park. Then he took her to a Yankees game, where they watched Joe DiMaggio hit a home run. They had dinner outdoors at the Café Brevoort, where they made up stories about the New Yorkers hurrying past them while they ate. Bobby had organized the entire day to combine both his and her favorite activities; he didn't want her to remember only him, but also the city and the country she loved.

The next morning Bobby saw her off at the dock, where they repeated their promise to wait for each other. He gave her a golden locket with his photograph inside so she wouldn't forget him. And they said good-bye.

"I'm so glad you told me," she said.

"Not as glad as I am," he replied truthfully.

They wrote to each other constantly over the next year and a half. One didn't wait for the other to reply before firing off a new letter, so the effect was like having four separate conversations all at once.

Karen confessed her melancholy to him. She described how much she missed America.

Bobby tried to keep her spirits up by describing New York in its tiniest details. He began to carry a journal with him wherever he went so he could jot down observations that he would later send to Karen via letter. She seemed to love these observations and always asked for more.

Although they were apart, Bobby convinced himself that they were experiencing a bodiless love, a purer love of the mind and the soul. Then Karen stopped writing. Bobby wrote, begging her to tell him what had happened, what had gone wrong. But she simply wouldn't respond.

Bobby fell into a deep depression. He didn't just feel rejected; he felt lost. He had dedicated his entire future to Karen, and now that she didn't want him anymore, he didn't know what to do with himself.

He threw himself into basketball and his schoolwork. He tried to work so hard that he wouldn't have time to think about Karen or his future. But that just brought his future closer. He finished his course work at nineteen. He was about to graduate, but he had no idea what to do with his life. His teammates tried to cheer him up. They took him to a movie.

There, in December of 1941, he saw a newsreel about Leningrad. He'd known that Germany had invaded the Soviet Union, but he hadn't known that the Germans had already advanced to Karen's city, let alone that they'd surrounded it. If he'd understood the mortal danger Karen faced every day, if he'd had any idea how many people had already frozen to death and how many more would eventually starve, he would have been terrified.

But newsreels weren't news. They were propaganda. And this newsreel was Soviet propaganda. In his commanding baritone voice, the narrator described Russia's heroic efforts to defy the German siege and feed the soldiers and citizens defending Leningrad. Russian truck drivers waved as they ran supplies through the snow. Army engineers laying railroad track to the edge of Lake Ladoga paused in their work long enough to smile at the camera.

Then the background music assumed a more ominous tone. Red Army soldiers manned their trenches—grim, resolved, and alert. One pointed to the sky, shouting, "Over there!"

German dive-bombers roared in formation through the sky. They were trying to cut the supply lines! But the Russian antiaircraft gunners put a stop to that. Blasts of flak burst like dark clouds in the sky. A German plane swooped with a roar, but it wasn't diving, it was dying. Smoke plumed from its rear. The Soviet gunners cheered. And the newsreel was over.

Bobby felt something like relief. This was why Karen had stopped answering his letters. It wasn't that she'd stopped loving him. Leningrad was surrounded, and no mail was getting in or out.

Bobby paid no attention to the feature film. His mind raced.

Japan had attacked Pearl Harbor only the day before. Everyone was rushing to enlist. He had originally planned to join up right after graduation. But now he worried that that would be too late. Russia was struggling for its life against the Nazi menace. Karen and her father were heroically defending themselves against German aggression. Bobby had to do something, anything—*now*.

Bobby left his teammates right after the movie. He didn't return to his college dormitory. Instead, he went straight to the Army Air Forces recruitment center.

The papers they put before him demanded his signature. And yet he hesitated, keeping the pen in his fist. His parents would want him to come home first. They would want him to graduate from Columbia. If he signed on the dotted line now, he would miss going back to Minneapolis, miss his graduation ceremony—all of it. His parents would be furious, and so disappointed. He squeezed the pen with indecision.

"Do you think your grandfather made his own parents proud?" Bobby suddenly remembered Karen asking him.

He uncapped the pen and scrawled his name.

CHAPTER 7
THE CELLIST

One month later, in January of 1942, Karen found herself facedown in a frozen potato field a dozen miles outside of Leningrad in the pitch-darkness. The icy ground sucked the heat from Karen's legs, arms, and chest. Her thick coat and layered wool sweaters had protected her for a few minutes, but now the cold penetrated her clothing and was slowly spreading through her body. In her mind's eye she saw her skin turn black, like her dead father's fingers, but she knew that was only her imagination. A voice in the back of her head screamed at her to get up off the icy ground, but she closed her eyes and ignored that voice. She knew that as bad as the cold was, the German soldiers only a few yards away were even worse. Her gloved fingers closed more tightly around the shovel in her right hand and the sack of frozen potatoes in her left.

The farmers had abandoned this potato field the previous summer when they were forced to evacuate their collective farm. The German advance had been so fast, the resistance of the Red Army so futile, that the agricultural workers barely had enough time to collect a few meager belongings, let alone harvest their fields. So the collective farm had fallen under the snow of an early winter, and the potato field had fallen under the tread of German marching boots. The unharvested potatoes were left to rot.

But the early frost saved the potatoes. Hidden beneath the snow, they were forgotten by the Germans. And the subterranean spuds could still be a source of carbohydrates and calories for the man or woman brave enough to dig them up.

Inna and her friends were plenty brave, Karen had discovered. She had been sticking closer to Inna since the death of her father. It was how she survived, though it wasn't getting her much closer to what she needed to do to escape Leningrad. Just staying alive used up all her time, energy, and ingenuity. Karen liked Inna—she always had—even though their first meeting a year and a half ago hadn't been particularly pleasant.

It was late-summer 1940, and the weather was brilliant. White puffy clouds had spotted a bright-blue sky, and yellow sunlight glinted off the white granite facades and open windows of city buildings. Karen was fresh off the boat from New York, and she was walking to her first class at the Leningrad Conservatory. She had worn a fine silk dress for the occasion, the most expensive garment she owned, which she had carefully packed in her father's trunk. She loved that outfit, all the more because she had worn it the previous winter when she'd first attracted Bobby's attention. She wanted to make an impression at the Conservatory, too.

She noticed people staring at her as she walked, and she became conscious of the fact that her dress was finer than the clothes worn by anyone she passed. Their garments were simple blouses, shirts, skirts, or tunics, dyed in practical, earthy colors that helped hide stains and dirt. Karen's dress, on the other hand, was a shiny cream color, the hem of which she had to lift to prevent it from getting soiled as she walked. The fabric clung to her porcelain skin and outlined the shape of her legs with every summer breeze. The women stared at her, envious, and the men seemed to undress her with hungry eyes, which worried her. Her self-consciousness grew until she stopped glancing around her and only looked down, watching her feet step one in front of the other.

But she couldn't ignore the girl who brazenly crossed the street to block her path on the sidewalk. The girl looked like a street urchin. Unlike most Russians' simple but clean and dignified garments, this girl's clothes were filthy. Her hair was cropped short like a boy's, yet red tufts stuck out in every direction. The girl stood sideways like a traffic officer and held up one hand, signaling Karen to stop. She sneered at Karen over her raised shoulder, then yelled a series of angry Russian words. Karen didn't know what to make of the girl, who appeared to be her own age. Karen tried to move past her, but the girl adjusted her stance to block Karen, never pausing in her angry diatribe of insults.

The girl was shorter than Karen, but stockier, and despite her filthy appearance she held herself with a confident, almost military bearing. Nonetheless, Karen refused to be intimidated. Late for class, she forced her way passed the girl, almost knocking her down. The girl threw a handful of mud square at Karen's back.

This filthy girl had ruined her best dress! Karen was the furious one now. Momentarily forgetting her Russian, Karen let loose a stream of unladylike English obscenities. The girl's eyes widened at the sound of them. But for Karen that wasn't enough. Along the street, a horse pulling a grocer's cart had left a pile of steaming dung. Karen picked up the dung and pitched it at the girl, scoring a hit right in the girl's chest. A moment passed. Karen was prepared to fight. She was certain the angry girl would leap at her at any moment.

Instead, the girl laughed. She wiped the dung off her chest and apologized to Karen. "I didn't realize you're an American tourist," she explained. "Tourists usually have Communist Party guides with them." She offered to shake Karen's hand. "My name is Inna."

Karen learned that Inna had mistaken her for a bourgeois hooligan. Bolsheviks hated the bourgeoisie, who adorned themselves in expensive fashion and jewelry for the sole purpose, Inna believed, of stealing husbands or boyfriends. This time it was Karen's turn to laugh. She explained that Inna had nothing to fear from her. She already had a boyfriend, she said, and she didn't need another.

That fascinated Inna, who demanded to know everything about Karen's boyfriend. Karen then learned that the root of Inna's Bolshevik fanaticism wasn't her love for the Communist Party; it was her obsession with a boy named Sasha.

Sasha Portnov was a member of the Komsomol, a Communist Party–sanctioned youth group. He was also an aspiring novelist. Inna and Sasha had known each other from childhood, and she had fallen in love with him when she was six. He'd joined the Young Pioneers, which was the Soviet version of the Boy Scouts, so Inna had joined, too, just to be close to him. When he graduated from that organization and moved on to the Komsomol, so did Inna. Sasha was always happy for Inna's company, and he respected Inna's dedication to radical Communist ideals. But Inna feared he thought of her more like a sister than a girlfriend.

Karen helped Inna make Sasha change his mind about that. She convinced Inna to drop the affected filth and intentional ugliness of a Bolshevik radical. Inna absolutely refused to drape herself in the "shameful" bourgeois fashions of the West, but she did allow Karen to lend her individual items from her wardrobe to create a more flattering image. A neat, tailored jacket pulled tight against Inna's bosom revealed the feminine rise of her chest. A thick leather belt buckled around her waist looked like part of a paramilitary uniform, as did tight sand-colored breeches and calf-high riding boots. But they also successfully showed off Inna's developing figure. Karen washed, combed, and clipped Inna's hair, transforming the boyish cowlicks into the shaped bangs of a bob cut that framed Inna's piercing blue eyes. The net effect was to transform Inna from a dirty street urchin into a cute but dangerous young militant. And the true miracle of the transformation was that nothing about Inna's new appearance suggested anything less than complete dedication to the Communist cause. The uniform worked. Within weeks, Sasha and Inna were dating.

Despite Karen's affection for Inna, she felt uncomfortable around Sasha. He didn't seem to trust Karen, and even before the German invasion, he was always criticizing America. That criticism grew louder as the Germans marched toward Leningrad. He resented the fact that America remained neutral, and Sasha once told Karen to her face that, since she was American, she might as well be a German collaborator. After that, Karen stopped visiting Inna at the Komsomol clubhouse. She knew what happened to German collaborators—they were hung. She didn't think Sasha meant it that way, but she also knew better than to take any chances.

Then America did enter the war, and Sasha finally began treating Karen with respect. After Karen's father died, she began to realize that she needed the Komsomol. Karen ingratiated herself further with Inna's friends by parroting back to them their Communist propaganda. To hear her at the clubhouse, one would have thought she was as radical as Inna. But Karen hadn't really changed her political views. She was just being practical. The Bolshevik fanatics in the Komsomol might have information Karen could use to escape Leningrad. She had already noticed that although the Red Army soldiers manning the trenches and bakeries never talked to her, no matter how hard she tried to talk to them, they often chatted and traded gossip with Inna.

This was how Inna found out about the potato field where Karen found herself now, facedown on her stomach and freezing. It was also how Inna had gotten hold of the shovels.

They were military shovels, so-called entrenching tools distributed to the soldiers along with their uniforms and rifles. And the soldiers didn't willingly part with them. Inna's sister, a machine gunner, explained the importance of the shovel before she relinquished it to them. She described how she had been admonished about the lifesaving qualities of her humble shovel during her time with the training battalion. "When given the order to halt," her instructor had howled at her, "you must lie down and immediately start digging!" In three minutes she was expected to dig deep enough so that she was lying flat, and enemy bullets would whiz harmlessly over her head. But that wasn't good enough. Unless given the order to advance, she was expected to keep digging, so that eventually she could kneel in her trench and then stand. Even then, if not given the order to advance, she had to keep digging, always to her left, never to her right. Every member of her squad was taught to dig left so that they wouldn't interfere with each other's labor. Eventually all that digging would result in communications trenches connecting her comrades' foxholes to her own. It was in that manner that the trenches protecting Leningrad had been dug. And Inna's sister knew that if her superior officers ever caught her without her shovel, she could be beaten or worse.

But the promise of potatoes was too great a temptation even for soldiers. When Inna promised her sister's fellow soldiers a share of the harvest, they agreed to lend her their precious shovels. They had to be returned, of course; nothing as valuable as a shovel could simply be given away in Leningrad. Inna distributed the shovels to Sasha and Karen, keeping one for herself. Then they began to plan the raid, referring to one another as the First Potato Army.

It was a dangerous raid. The potatoes were behind German lines. Karen, Inna, and Sasha didn't only have to cross under the German guns covering no-man's-land; they also needed to sneak past German patrols. They had waited for a moonless, overcast night.

The darkness was their only advantage. They'd spent so much time without electricity in Leningrad that they were used to seeing in the dark. The Germans, however, seemed entirely dependent on machines and electric light. Karen, Inna, and Sasha had seen the headlights of their Opel trucks long before they heard the engines. That had given them plenty of time to jump off the road and roll into a frozen ditch, where they hid until the trucks passed.

Then, finally, they reached the potato field unseen. It was time to get digging, and they worked with all they had. Until they heard something and crouched in the dark.

German soldiers were coming their way. They nearly walked right into Karen, Inna, and Sasha—almost catching them by surprise, but the crunch of their boots on the icy topsoil gave them away. Karen and her friends immediately stopped digging and dived onto their bellies, onto that frozen ground, where Karen wondered and worried how long they could hold out, facedown, the heat draining from her.

CHAPTER 8

THE ORGAN-GRINDER

"What do you intend to do after the war?" The question came from Jillian Croogar, a young American newspaper reporter working for the *Los Angeles Times*. Miss Croogar had been allowed access to Petr while the Soviet Union's newest hero was recovering in a field hospital.

It was now January of 1942. Native Russian reporters had already visited him. Desperate for good news, they interviewed him for Pravda, Russia's mouthpiece for Soviet propaganda. The story they wrote had made Petr out to be a supersoldier, a warrior so dedicated to his great leader, Stalin, that he fearlessly held back an entire German tank battalion and destroyed two of the Wehrmacht's most expensive war machines.

The Pravda story made Petr famous. Even this American reporter had heard of him, so Soviet propaganda ministers directed her to his bedside. "Get married, perhaps?" the reporter suggested. "Start a family?"

Petr stared at Jillian. The answer was so obvious that he didn't quite understand the question. "After the war?" he repeated, making sure he understood just what the reporter was asking.

"Yes, after the war." Miss Croogar nodded, her pencil hovering over a steno pad. "You got a sweetheart back home waiting for you?"

Petr shook his head. "Nothing."

"Nothing? You mean no one," Miss Croogar corrected him, scribbling in her pad. "No matter. You're a hero now. I'll bet the girls will be lining up for a kiss—"

"No. I mean nothing. I won't do anything after the war."

Now Miss Croogar looked confused. "You gotta do something—"

"I think he means that he will continue to serve his country," interrupted Miss Croogar's Russian advisor. Stalin and his Politburo didn't trust foreign journalists, so they assigned "advisors" to watch over them. The advisor's truest purpose was to prevent Miss Croogar from writing anything that might embarrass the Communist Party.

"I'll never survive the war," Petr declared with complete confidence.

It was not the answer Miss Croogar was expecting, but she only hesitated a moment before writing down his response. "What makes you think so?"

"You said I'm a hero, yes?"

Jillian nodded. "That's why I'm here."

"Russian heroes always die."

Miss Croogar paused and stared at Petr. This interview was becoming far more interesting than the propaganda puff piece she had expected. "Why's that?"

"Because they're always given the most dangerous jobs."

The advisor nodded at that. "They're fearless. It is part of the Russian character."

No, not because they're fearless, Petr wanted to say. *Because they're expendable.* He didn't dare say it out loud, though. He knew better than to criticize the army or the government, especially with an official right there at his bedside. Petr was slightly surprised that he had even consciously summoned the thought. He had grown adept at burying his thoughts, especially potentially subversive ones, deep in the back of his mind.

Miss Croogar continued to stare at him in the silence. He had the odd sense that she could read his mind. But it wasn't disturbing. It actually felt comforting somehow.

"Is John Wayne joining the army?" Petr asked.

Miss Croogar looked confused. "Who?"

"John Wayne," Petr said earnestly. "Your paper, it is from Hollywood, right?"

"Los Angeles, not Hollywood."

"That's not the same thing?"

"Not exactly. And John Wayne's an actor, not a soldier."

Petr was disappointed. "I'll bet he'd kill a lot of Germans."

Miss Croogar smiled. "But not a lot of tanks," she replied, referring to Petr's heroics. "You just gave me an idea . . ." She scribbled something down on the pad of paper. "I'm gonna call you the Russian John Wayne."

Petr turned red with embarrassment. "Don't do that."

Miss Croogar smiled and winked. "Already done." She folded up her steno pad, shoved it in her breast pocket, and patted it before standing up. "You Russians are always so pessimistic. You'll survive this war, you'll see. You're the Russian John Wayne now. John Wayne never dies."

Petr didn't respond. He only watched as the reporter and her government escort exited the hospital.

Despite Miss Croogar's claims to the contrary, Petr's suspicions about his impending doom were confirmed by his subsequent transfer. The political officers now believed that his talents were being wasted in the

Katyusha battery. He was a tank killer, they thought, and should be trained as such. So that same January, with his legs fully recovered, Petr remained in a rear training battalion. They would teach him to fire the new PTRD antitank rifle.

The PTRD was a simple weapon. It was basically a giant rifle that fired a huge bullet. Fyodor, Petr's new teammate, told him not to shoot it at a tank's turret or engine but at something more vulnerable.

Fyodor Malenkov was a short, stocky man who used to work on a collective farm east of Moscow. Judging from his round face and almond eyes, his ancestors had likely come from somewhere in the Asian steppes. Fyodor had taught himself to drive and maintain his farm's single tractor, and this was the skill that convinced Red Army recruiters to make him a tank driver. He was trained in the operation of the T-28 infantry support tank, an obsolete vehicle quickly being replaced by the new T-34s. Such experience gave Fyodor unique insight into what tankers feared.

Armored vehicles were claustrophobic, loud, uncomfortable, and confusing. Their thick steel plating was supposed to protect their crews, but, psychologically at least, the opposite was true. "I always felt vulnerable," Fyodor once confessed to Petr, "as if I were driving a gigantic bullet magnet straight at the enemy lines. Once I saw the tank right next to me simply disappear, blown from the inside out by hidden artillery. Another time we were assigned to recover a vehicle that had been hit by a flamethrower. It was still hot, and the corpses inside smelled like roast pork." Life as a tank crewman meant constant uncertainty and terror, Fyodor explained. "One moment you'd be leading an assault, seemingly invulnerable in your steel coffin, and the next moment you'd be a puddle of burned flesh."

Even worse, tank crewmen were often running blind. They could open hatches to see, but that was suicide during combat. As a driver, Fyodor was entirely dependent on the eyes of his commander. Unlike the rest of the crew, the tank commander dared stick his head out of a turret hatch and had much greater awareness of the battlefield around him. "Kill the tank commander," Fyodor advised, "and the crew will be helpless." Fyodor lost his own tank that way. When his commander was killed in his open hatch, Fyodor and the rest of the crew panicked. They bailed out of the vehicle and ran for the Russian lines. After having lost so many expensive weapons in the opening months of the German invasion, the Red Army now had more tankers than tanks. So, like Petr, Fyodor had been reassigned and retrained.

Petr doubted he could follow Fyodor's advice. But he was committed to try, because the only alternative was to rely on his mine dog. Mine dogs—brand-new secret weapons—were the second weapons for which Petr was trained. Petr wasn't exactly the one being trained, of course—the dog was. Petr and Fyodor were simply assigned a dog and instructed on how to command him.

Petr's dog was named Duck. He was an eighty-four-pound Alsatian wolf dog, the breed later called a German shepherd. Duck was larger than most mine dogs, no doubt because he'd been well fed as a Moscow family's pet. Duck was named by the family's two-year-old son, who'd only known three words at the time: *Momma*, *Poppa*, and *duck*. The name seemed to fit, since his favorite pastime was chasing ducks and geese in Moscow's parks.

The military requisitioned Duck after he'd lived with the family for three years. By that time the young boy had learned quite a few more words, such as *patriotic*, *defender*, and *fascist invaders*. It wasn't difficult for the Red Army agent to convince the boy that his pet should be trained as a soldier and that Duck would become a true hero of the Soviet Union.

The Red Army agent didn't tell the boy that Duck would be strapped to a bomb and trained how to blow himself up. Thus the designation of mine dogs: they were living, breathing antitank mines. They were attached to several pounds of TNT and trained to run under panzers, where the tank's armor was weakest. The action would knock down a wooden stake mounted so it stuck straight up on the dog like an antenna. The trigger would detonate the explosives, killing the dog and destroying the panzer, or so the theory went.

The problem was that Petr liked Duck. He was a smart and affectionate dog. He'd often push his snout up under Petr's hand, forcing Petr to pet him. And it took Duck less than a day to recognize Petr as his new handler. He responded to Petr's voice commands immediately but absolutely refused to obey anyone else. Petr thought he was a brilliant dog, as well as a fine physical specimen. Petr believed he would've made a good hunting companion and often thought what a waste it was to make Duck commit suicide under some German tank. But Petr was not in charge of the Red Army, and neither was Duck. Their job was simply to do as they were told.

After a month of retraining and recovery, Petr was reassigned to his old division. But now he was in a rifle battalion instead of a rocket-artillery battery. The Red Army was finally seeing some success against the seemingly invulnerable German war machine. The winter offensive outside of Moscow was pushing the Germans back, and it saved the capital. That, and the successful liberation of the Tikhvin railhead, convinced Stavka, the Russian high command, that the Germans simply didn't know how to fight in the bitter cold. So they decided to extend the winter offensive and break the German siege of Leningrad. They reorganized the Leningrad front and called the new force the Second Shock Army. It was a name designed to give the soldiers confidence: they weren't just an army; they were an elite Shock Army!

Already the first assaults had stalled. Petr's unit was tasked with relieving them by opening a second front. But apart from the newly arrived veterans from Siberia, the Second Shock Army was still made up of the same terrified conscripts who had, to this point, retreated from combat. As Petr led Duck forward through the masses of marching infantry, he saw nothing in their frightened, downturned faces that gave him any hope. This February attack seemed likely to result in the same defeats he'd always experienced. At least the ground was frozen hard. That would make retreat much more manageable.

Negative-thirty-degree nights had frozen the ground so hard that digging trenches and foxholes was impossible. Petr and his comrades were barely kept warm by an ample supply of heating oil. But the Germans didn't have even that. Already German supply lines were stretched long, and the winter made them seem longer. Petrol was in short supply, and it was required for the vehicles. So without the insulation of trenches and without proper heating, the Germans were forced to encamp in villages using homes abandoned by fleeing refugees as makeshift barracks. The fields in between them, and the forests, were a no-man's-land. The winter front lines had none of the contiguous lines of bunkers and trenches that many had experienced in World War I.

The new winter offensive sought to take advantage of this. The Russian infantry was ordered to approach the German-held villages using gorges and "dead ground"—undulations in the landscape—to avoid detection. Then, with an order from their political officers and a shout from their commanders, the riflemen were to rush forward from the German rear and flanks, clearing each village house by house. That was the first wave. As antitank gunners and mine-dog handlers, Petr and Fyodor were part of the second wave. Once the riflemen had secured the village, Petr, Fyodor, and Duck were expected to rush in and defend the newly liberated town from the expected panzer counterattack.

<hr/>

Shortly before another frigid dawn in late February 1942, Petr, Fyodor, and Duck crawled to their start positions on the edge of a frozen, rolling wheat field. Once again Petr was impressed by Duck's training and intelligence: the big wolf dog could crawl on his belly as well as any frontline rifleman. From their new position, Petr and Fyodor could peer over a crest in the field and witness the assault on the village firsthand.

Like everything in this war, it didn't go according to plan.

At first the attack seemed like a success. The screaming infantry appeared as if from nowhere, rising up from the folds in the ground only fifty yards from the village cottages. But the Germans weren't surprised. Rifle and machine-gun fire spat death at the Red Army. The muzzle flashes weren't coming from the cottage windows and doors, as expected; they came from the bottom of the buildings' walls where the Germans had cut out firing slits. They were standing in the cottage potato cellars, firing as if from a trench, as well protected as if they were in concrete bunkers.

Petr watched it all. The most courageous Russians were the first ones cut down, dancing with the impact of each German bullet before crashing headlong onto the hard ground. Now the first wave hesitated. But commanders and political officers urged the soldiers onward, and once again they lurched forward, trampling fallen comrades under foot. Already the wounded made a horrific clamor, their moans and screams for help rising above the sounds of gunfire. In this weather they would freeze to death before help could arrive.

The Germans continued to fire, taking a terrible toll on the Russians. But there were simply too many infantries. The Germans couldn't kill them all. Soon the surviving Russians reached the buildings, kicked open the doors, and threw grenade after grenade into the perimeter cottages. A series of dull booms shook the buildings. And the Russian soldiers rushed inside.

Petr could not see the brutal hand-to-hand fighting occurring within. He only saw the results. Some Russian soldiers were repulsed, killed by German bayonets and dumped back outside to form barriers against further attacks. Other soldiers were victorious, liberally spraying their submachine guns into rooms and basements before firing off flares to indicate that their objectives were secure. Still others faced no fighting at all, as the German veterans escaped out the back of their cottages to take up prepared positions deeper in the village.

Petr couldn't take his eyes off the spectacle of blood. He'd never been so close to the front line, apart from his own duel with the panzers. And he noticed he was shivering. It wasn't from the cold. And it wasn't from fear. It was from anticipation. His muscles tensed. He had to force himself to sit still; it took every ounce of willpower not to scramble to his feet and join the riflemen in their orgy of killing.

Petr noticed Duck reacting the exact same way. The dog straightened, half standing in a crouch, ears upright and alert and nose pointing forward, anxious for the slightest command to pounce into battle. Looking at the dog, Petr realized he was looking at himself. They were both warriors, he and Duck. They hadn't really lived until now. Civilian life had been a waking dream. They were born to fight, and it had taken a German invasion for them to discover the truth about themselves.

An officer was blowing his whistle. It was the signal for the second wave.

"Come, Duck!" Petr yelled, and he and the dog were racing across the tundra. Duck was like a tan-and-black version of a Katyusha rocket, tearing across the field with incredible speed, his frozen breath trailing behind him like exhaust. Somehow Petr managed to keep up. Fyodor lagged somewhere behind them, but Petr didn't look back. He only focused on his objective—a small cottage where he'd seen the all-clear flare fired by their infantry sergeant only moments ago.

Duck reached the cottage door first, leaping up and scratching at the wood planks. Petr hit the door an instant later, splintering it and crashing inside.

The cottage wasn't cleared. Moments after their infantry sergeant fired his flare, German soldiers must have rushed him from the basement. They had him pinned to the wall with a bayonet, clubbing him with rifle butts.

Duck didn't hesitate. With a flash of white teeth, he lunged at the first German, knocking him to the ground, snapping and ripping his clothes to get at the soft flesh beneath. Petr attacked the second German with his shovel. He didn't remember yanking it from his belt, but it was in his hands. His first blow split the German's helmet. His second split the German's skull.

When Fyodor entered, he found Petr and Duck standing over the dead Germans. He stared wide-eyed as Duck sat on his haunches and calmly licked his bloody snout with his long tongue. Petr was leaning against the wall now, catching his breath from the long sprint and the adrenaline rush of the fight.

Fyodor leaned over where Petr had ditched his PTRD rifle for the brutal efficiency of his shovel. "You're still gonna need this," Fyodor said, picking up the rifle and handing it to Petr.

CHAPTER 9
THE CELLIST

Karen could just make out the German soldiers' steel helmets in the darkness as she lay facedown on the frozen potato field. There only appeared to be four of them, and for once they weren't using lanterns or flashlights. Sasha lay about ten feet to Karen's right, and Inna was snuggled up next to him. For a moment Karen envied them. They, at least, were keeping each other warm.

There was no cover between Karen and the German patrol, nothing to hide behind. Karen felt naked and exposed on the flat ground. But so far the Germans hadn't seemed to detect Karen and her friends. The soldiers just chatted in their foreign language and stood around like lazy workers. As Karen lay there, her fingers, along with her toes and her legs and her chest, continued to grow numb with cold. She shivered and clenched her teeth so they wouldn't chatter.

One of the German soldiers popped a cigarette into his mouth and lit a match. Karen immediately looked away from the flame, knowing that exposure to the sudden light could ruin her night vision. But she was grateful for the German's nicotine addiction, because he passed out matches to each of his companions, and soon the glowing end of a cigarette was dancing like a firefly in front of each soldier's face, and Karen knew that even those dull embers made it more difficult for the Germans to peer through the protective darkness.

Sasha came to the exact same conclusion. He reached into his bag and pulled out a frozen potato. Karen immediately recognized what he was planning to do and shook her head silently, trying to tell him—beg him—to just lie still. But Sasha wasn't looking at her. He was looking past the soldiers at the darkness beyond. He lifted himself onto one elbow, pulled back his arm, and launched the potato in a high arc over the Germans' heads.

The potato landed with a thud. The Germans turned away from Sasha, suddenly quiet, searching the darkness. One threw down his cigarette and picked up his rifle.

Sasha charged.

Karen wanted to scream for Sasha to stop but instead rolled farther to her left, putting more distance between herself and Sasha and Inna. She felt like a coward, but she didn't want to die just because Sasha had more courage than sense.

But Sasha's gambit worked. By distracting the Germans with the potato, he reached them before they could turn around. He threw his arms around the soldier with the raised rifle, and the gun went off with a bang. Sasha and the soldier struggled, Sasha pinning the German's arms to his side. In a fair fight, Sasha might actually have won.

But it wasn't a fair fight. Not even close. At first the three other soldiers were paralyzed with indecision. They raised their rifles but didn't shoot, realizing that if they missed Sasha, they might kill their friend. But the confusion only lasted a moment. The smallest German flipped his rifle in the air like a baton twirler, caught its barrel, and swung the butt at Sasha's head. The wooden butt smashed Sasha full in the face. Broken teeth spilled from his mouth, reflecting the glow of the cigarettes.

Sasha let go of the German and lay on the ground, hands over his bloody face, twisting in agony. His legs moved back and forth against the frozen soil of the potato field as if he were trying to create a snow angel. The German he assaulted stared down at Sasha a moment. He spoke to his fellow soldiers while he reached down and picked up his rifle. Karen noticed the other Germans pulling long blades from scabbards on their belts and realized with horror that they were bayonets. She wanted to warn Sasha, but she couldn't do so without giving away her own position. And Sasha couldn't see them, his hands still over his face, still writhing on the ground. One of the Germans chuckled as he fixed the bayonet to the end of his rifle. Then he raised the spearlike weapon over Sasha's body, got his back behind it, and drove it down.

Karen caught her breath at the sound of the blade puncturing Sasha's chest. Sasha mewed like a cat. Then he went still, and silent. That silence seemed to last a full minute. Then Inna screamed.

Karen knew she could do nothing now to save her friend. Instead of helping Inna, she used the scream to cover the sound of her own movement. She crawled to the edge of the potato field and didn't stop until she reached the short stone wall that enclosed it. Flipping herself over it, she crawled back to her knees and risked a glance back.

Inna was still screaming. She hadn't attacked the Germans. She'd rushed up to Sasha and knelt beside him, holding his bloody face against her heaving chest.

The Germans didn't bayonet Inna. They simply raised their rifles and shot her.

Karen had never let go of her sack and shovel the whole time. She hadn't thought about it; she just held on to them out of pure instinct. But that instinct saved her life, because the Germans spent the next hour searching the field. They established a methodical pattern, moving in slowly expanding concentric circles from the center of the field to the perimeter wall. They found the holes from which Karen and her friends had dug out the potatoes, having been lucky enough to pry the frozen soil loose. They found Sasha's and Inna's sacks as well as their shovels. But they never found Karen crouching low behind the stone wall. Two shovels, two sacks, and two dead Russians led the Germans to conclude that Sasha and Inna were alone. Besides, it was cold. The soldiers wanted to get back to their warm quarters, so eventually they left. They took the potatoes and the shovels. They didn't bother with Sasha or Inna. They left their bodies to freeze in the field as a warning to other partisans who might risk stealing potatoes from the Wehrmacht.

After the soldiers left, Karen climbed the wall and crept back into the field. She first knelt beside Sasha and stared at his bloody face. A well of hatred rose up in her chest. She had grown to hate so many things in Russia, and now this boy had made her hate him, too. She almost hated him more than the German soldiers who'd killed him. They were the enemy. Of course they would kill him. But Sasha hadn't needed to let them. He hadn't need to attack them. If they'd waited, if they'd been patient, the soldiers would eventually have finished their cigarettes and returned to their camp. Karen was sure of it. Sasha's attack had been suicide. No, it had been more than suicide; it had been murder. He had murdered Inna. Karen pulled open Sasha's coat. It was soaked with blood from his punctured chest. She tried to keep her hands as clean as possible while she rifled through his coat pockets, only to find them empty. She found his belongings in his trouser pockets instead, and it was a good thing, too, because there his identification papers and ration card were still dry, not stained with blood.

Karen wiped Sasha's blood off in the snow. Then she fell onto her knees beside Inna. Inna's blue eyes were open, and frozen tears glistened on her cheeks like tiny icicles. Karen wondered whether she could ever sacrifice herself for Bobby the way Inna had sacrificed herself for Sasha, and she couldn't help but feel cowardly and inadequate. She hoped Bobby would never force her to find out. Bobby wasn't stupid like

Sasha, was he? Bobby would never charge a squad of German soldiers armed only with his fists. It was Sasha's fault that Inna was dead.

Karen opened Inna's coat and searched through her pockets. She found her identification papers and ration card, an apartment door key, and a bundle of folded letters. The bundle was tied with a lock of hair. Inna had never mentioned that Sasha wrote her love poems. She'd kept them private and secret. Karen stared at the bundle before returning them to Inna's coat, unread. She would respect her friend's privacy. But she stuffed the identification papers, the key, and the ration card into her pockets along with Sasha's. Then she turned and began the long twelve-mile walk back to Leningrad.

—◆—

By the time she reached the trenches surrounding the dying city, Karen faced a new problem. She couldn't just walk up to the Red Army sentries and announce herself; she'd be mistaken for a German infiltrator and shot on sight. She, Inna, and Sasha had worked out a signal with Inna's sister, who would be waiting there for the "potato army." They would whistle, wait until the machine-gun team returned the whistle, and approach the trench. But Inna's sister expected three people: Inna, Sasha, and Karen. She might even have heard the Germans' gunfire. How could Karen tell Inna's sister that Inna and Sasha were both dead? She wished she didn't have to talk to Inna's sister at all. But it was that or risk getting shot.

Karen got down on her belly, crawled out from the edge of the woods, and whistled. Someone in the trench whistled back. Karen stood up and crept forward in a crouch. She reached the edge of the trench and jumped down beside a Maxim machine gun, its small, scalloped barrel protruding from a little trolley with spoked wheels. It looked like a toy. No wonder the Germans were winning, Karen thought—their weapons were so much more intimidating than the Russian ones.

Inna's sister grabbed Karen's hand. "Where are Inna and Sasha?" she asked.

"Just inside the woods," Karen lied. The lie came easily to her—more easily than she expected. "They decided to cut some firewood. They'll be here soon." The lie made sense, Karen realized, because she herself should have cut firewood when she had the chance. Her military shovel was sharp enough to hack through dead tree branches.

Inna's sister peered at Karen. "Why didn't you stay with them?"

"It's too cold," Karen explained, reaching into her potato sack and pulling out the machine-gun team's share. Once again, she knew Inna's sister would accept the lie. Karen was American, so the Russians considered her weak. Of course they would believe that an American girl couldn't endure a Russian winter. Besides, the machine-gun team was already eyeing the potatoes, their mouths watering. Karen twisted shut the sack and lay the shovel down next to the potatoes. She regretted giving up the shovel even more than giving up a share of the food. But she had no choice.

"Tell Inna I'll meet her at the usual place tomorrow," she added.

Inna's sister nodded, but she wasn't really listening. She took off her steel helmet and piled snow into it while a companion sparked up a fire. She placed the helmet on the growing flames and gazed at the concoction hungrily. Soon enough she would have boiled potatoes.

Karen grabbed what remained of her sack and climbed out the other side of the trench. Now on the outskirts of Leningrad, she knew better than to return to her apartment. Too many people knew her there. And for what she had planned, no one could know her.

She went to Inna's apartment instead. Inna lived in a housing block down the street from the Kirov Tractor Factory, where her father used to work. It was in southwest Leningrad, much closer to the German lines and the German guns, and the tractor factory had been an important target for those guns, since it produced Russia's impressive new T-34 tanks. The Germans had bombarded the neighborhood in an attempt to shut down the Kirov's production. The bombardment had failed to destroy the factory, but it left Inna's neighborhood a landscape of crumbling walls, broken pavement, and black craters. Vehicles could no longer pass through the rubble. Residents emerged from their homes only long enough to scurry to the bakeries or into work at the factory, afraid of getting caught in the open during the next German shelling. The broken streets were usually abandoned, which made Karen's trek easier.

Despite the bombardment, Inna's housing block was remarkably unscathed. The modest apartment was luxurious by Soviet standards, since it had two bedrooms. Inna's father earned such luxury by being an *udarnik*, a "shock worker," at the tractor factory in faraway Chelyabinsk. Shock workers set an example for other laborers with their enthusiasm, endurance, and superproductivity. His absence would help Karen.

It was a surprise to Karen that Inna's apartment was a jumble of color and clutter. Inna's mother had died when Inna was a baby, but her influence lived on in the apartment. Clearly, she had knitted the hundreds of colorful throw blankets, as well as the doilies under lamps and picture frames. Before living in Russia, Karen thought there was no such thing as property in the Soviet Union—that all items were shared. After all, her father told her that the Soviets had abolished all private property. What she didn't understand at the time, and what she had soon come to learn, was that Russians distinguished between "private" property and "personal" property. Private property was defined as "capital," which was anything that could be used to build or create something else. Factories were capital because they were used to build industrial goods. Farms were capital because their land was a productive source of food. Even a loom or a bicycle-repair shop could be considered capital. But personal items, like clothing and watches and radios and books, were commonly recognized as possessions.

Inna's apartment was loaded with intensely personal items. Her mother's smiling face was everywhere in those picture frames, standing beside sentimental souvenirs representing where each photograph was taken: the dried leaf from a birch tree in Moscow, a broken paving stone from outside the Winter Palace, ticket stubs from the State Academic Theater of Opera and Ballet. There were countless other tchotchkes that Karen didn't recognize. She briefly wondered whether Inna would be given the same treatment, the same places of honor within her father's apartment. But then she pushed the morbid thought out of her mind. She couldn't think of Inna as dead. Inna had been her best friend—her only friend, really. But Karen couldn't afford to mourn for her. Not yet. She had to trick herself into believing that Inna was still alive. And she had to study everything in this apartment. She had to learn as much about Inna, her father, her sister, and her dead mother as possible, because Karen had a plan.

She would become Inna.

CHAPTER 10

THE ORGAN·GRINDER

Petr took a good look at his new surroundings once he'd recovered from his savage fight to take the cottage. At the center of the open room was the hearth: a huge fireplace and chimney. Around it were cluttered benches and tables where the Germans had apparently slept in an effort to avoid the rats. Every crack in the doors, windows, and walls was stuffed with old newspapers in an attempt to insulate the building from the cold. That, combined with decades-old goop smearing the windows, left the cottage in perpetual twilight. The Germans had tried to fight off the darkness with improvised lanterns. Old mess tins, schnapps bottles, and even helmets hung from the ceiling were filled with grease, the twine wicks sputtering with weak flames. How could proud German soldiers live in such deprived squalor? At that moment Petr realized how precariously the Wehrmacht was holding on. Perhaps the Red Army could win this war, after all.

More gunfire and a series of explosions ripped Petr from his thoughts. He crept to a window on the opposite side of the cottage, smashed it with his shovel, and peered outside.

The village was in chaos. Bodies littered the frozen dirt roads, the Russian dead outnumbering the German corpses by more than two to one. Several buildings were on fire, including the Russian Orthodox church, its onion dome blazing like a huge Olympic torch.

Each cottage was its own unique battlefield, Germans fighting in isolation to defend themselves against a band of Red Army soldiers closing in.

"Over there!" Fyodor had moved up beside Petr and was pointing at a two-story building on the edge of town. It was a big log cabin, built from piled tree trunks, and had probably served as a workers' barracks before the German occupation. The windows on both stories made it an excellent choice for an antitank position.

Petr nodded and moved along the wall to the cottage's back door. Fyodor took up position on the other side and motioned with his fingers. "One, two, three . . ." On "three," he threw open the door, and Petr bolted for the two-story log house.

The cold hit him like a slap. His lungs constricted in pain, but he forced them and his legs to keep pumping. He heard bullets zip near his head and felt Duck beside him, matching his pace like a shadow. He passed a group of Soviet riflemen crouching behind a stone wall, trading fire with Germans trapped in a cottage. He was dimly aware that the helmet of one of the riflemen flew off the man's head in a spray of red, but then he was beyond them, still running, still alive. The two-story log house loomed ahead, its big wooden door seeming to promise safety inside. But just as he reached it, Petr noticed something strange out of the corner of his eye: Duck had stopped short and fallen to his belly, whimpering.

The dog hadn't been hit; he wasn't wounded, but something was wrong. Perhaps the cold had numbed Petr's brain as well as his arms and legs because it took him another two full strides before he realized that Duck's actions were a warning. Then he let himself crash to the ground. He landed on top of the PTRD rifle he'd been clutching to his chest, and the force of the fall against the gun's hard steel knocked the wind out of him. He gasped for breath as Fyodor stomped passed him. Petr tried to yell a warning, but his lungs still weren't working. His shouted "Stop!" came out as an incomprehensible moan.

Fyodor didn't stop; he didn't even hesitate. Bullets still zipped past them both, the lightning flashes of tracer rounds cutting through the air all around them. The door and the log house promised protection from those deadly projectiles, and Fyodor was desperate for that safety. Petr could only watch as Fyodor lifted the wooden latch and threw his shoulder into the planks, breaking the ice that caked the frame and knocking the door wide-open.

A piece of twine was tied to that door—and to six potato-masher grenades bundled together. The violent force with which Fyodor smashed the door ripped the twine from the grenade bundle's fuse, priming the explosives. Petr's breath came back to him, along with his voice. "Get down!" he yelled, and Fyodor heard it.

Fyodor and the grenade bundle hit the plank floor at the same time, Fyodor with a soft thump of quilted tunic, the grenades with a metallic clank. The bundle bounced, half turned in the air, and exploded. Fyodor died instantly.

Petr closed his eyes, not in terror but in grief. He couldn't bear to look at the bloody corpse that had been his friend and his teammate. Duck was grieving, too. The dog was on his feet again, slouching up to Fyodor and trying to lick his bloody face.

Petr saw the danger to the dog. The air still bristled with the zip of bullets and the flash of tracers. Petr struggled back to his feet and ran to the door. He leaped over Fyodor's body, grabbed Duck's collar, and dragged the big dog after him into the log house. He stumbled, landed on his side, and kicked what remained of the door shut behind him.

The inside of the log house was oddly peaceful. The crackle of gunfire, the boom of grenades, and the screams of the terrified, the battle mad, and the wounded were muffled by the heavy log walls. Petr rolled onto his back and stared at the gabled ceiling, catching his breath, enduring the pain of the blood returning to his numb extremities.

He'd been right about the log house: it was a communal barracks. He could see discolored patches on the sawdust-covered floor where cots had once stood. The hardwood floor was unevenly laid across the frozen dirt; the absence of a cellar was probably why the Germans had chosen to booby-trap it instead of occupying it. But Petr had been wrong about one thing—it didn't have two stories. Instead, the tall walls were ringed by a wooden loft accessible by a pair of rustic ladders.

For Petr's purposes, a loft would do just fine. He lurched to his feet, slung his big PTRD rifle over his back, and climbed one of the ladders. Then he hunkered down next to a window, smashed the glass pane with the barrel of his PTRD, and peered out at the frozen ground, where he saw an untended vegetable garden surrounded by a short wooden fence. Beyond it stretched the ridged surface of a plowed beet field. And beyond that was a rutted dirt road that cut into a boreal forest. Petr knew he was staring west, toward the German lines. Somewhere beyond those spruce, fir, and pine trees was the German artillery and motor pool; beyond that, German field hospitals, supply depots, and ammo dumps. And still farther would be the supply lines, columns of German trucks and horse-drawn wagons stretching to rail heads, and then thousands of miles reaching all the way to Berlin. This was the way the German panzers would come charging like cavalry in an American Western, rescuing the settlers from Indian attacks. Petr and his Red Army comrades were the Indians this time. And this time the Indians would have to win.

Petr heard scratching and whimpering behind him. He turned to see Duck precariously trying to mount one of the ladders. Petr let go of his rifle, reached down, grabbed hold of the harness that held Duck's mine-dog explosives, and hoisted the big dog into the loft.

Duck, as exhausted from the ordeal as Petr, curled up beside him. Petr welcomed the furry warmth, and he stared at Duck's chest rising and falling with each breath. How had Duck known about the booby trap? Had he smelled the explosives in the grenades or the latent scent of the German engineers who had rigged them? It was a mystery Petr would never solve. But as he gazed at the dog, he realized he owed Duck his life.

CHAPTER 11
THE CHOIRBOY

Hank Harris was the first casualty of war Bobby knew personally. Hank was a twenty-three-year-old Kansas City native who loved jazz. Hank was the one who convinced Bobby and his fellow flight cadets to spend their valuable evening pass at the Alibi, a Palm Beach bar that was hosting one of Hank's favorite bands.

"Cool," Hank had assured them all. "The joint will be jumping, and the whole night will be cool." That sounded good to Bobby and the other cadets, who were miserable in the stifling heat of their Florida training facility. It was February 1942. Bobby had been in Palm Beach for over a week, and he still hadn't gotten used to the weather.

The Alibi turned out to be even hotter than their base. It was packed with people who were standing shoulder to shoulder. But that didn't stop the lindy-hop dancers from swinging in place, kicking up a ruckus with flailing elbows and flying feet. The packed bodies, the swinging musicians, the jumping dancers, and the tropical humidity all thickened the air to make the Alibi feel like a smokehouse. Eventually

Bobby and his fellow cadets dragged Hank out of the joint and onto the street. Their uniforms dripping in sweat, they stumbled into Mel's All You Can Eat for a predawn breakfast.

Mel's was a railroad car transformed into a diner, but it was not like the polished silver-and-chrome establishments Bobby knew from New York. Mel's railroad car looked like little more than a heap of junk left on an abandoned side track. Mel wasn't cashing in on a trend, it seemed. He'd probably only moved into the railroad car because it was empty.

Not that Bobby or the other cadets met Mel. The woman who greeted them was a fifty-year-old waitress named Daisy. She took their orders and seemed disappointed that most of them wanted only ice water. It was too darned hot. Bobby couldn't even think of eating in the stifling heat. Hank didn't have that problem. He ordered a stack of pancakes, a side of bacon, and three eggs over easy.

Daisy hesitated before informing the cadets that everyone had to order "all you can eat," or none of them could. It was restaurant policy, she explained apologetically. After all, how could she be sure Hank wouldn't just feed the rest of them from his order?

Hank convinced the other cadets to eat with him. They weren't likely to find a better deal, and it had to be tastier than the slop served at the base's mess hall, he told them. It wasn't a very convincing argument, but once Jack Wright said he would do it, Bobby and his fellow cadets agreed to pitch in. They all liked Jack Wright. Jack was always smiling. It wasn't a goofy smile, and it wasn't even a smile just on his lips. Jack had smiling eyes and a mischievous grin.

Bobby, Hank, Jack, and the other boys were more than ready for a taste of freedom and adventure. Besides, they weren't boys anymore. All except Bobby were in their early to midtwenties. They had to be college graduates to be flight cadets, which meant they were among the oldest new recruits in the army. Only Bobby was still in his teens, having graduated early from Columbia. He'd missed his graduation ceremony by signing up early, but he had already completed his college credits, and that was good enough for the US Army Air Force.

They cadets didn't care who called them "boys" anymore. In any other walk of life, in peacetime, calling a grown man "boy" was a sign of disrespect, but not in the military. Referring to soldiers as "the boys" or "our boys in uniform" was an expression of proud endearment. Even their thirty-five-year-old flight instructor was one.

Jack smiled as he ate his pancakes and gave Hank a good-natured ribbing about the Alibi. The bar's patrons had been 80 percent men, Jack complained. How was he expected to charm a girl in a place like that? The others agreed with Jack and began to plan an alternative outing for their next pass. Their imaginations soared as they explored wildly impractical ideas like hosting a clambake, or expensive ones like renting a yacht. Soon they'd all forgotten about the heat. As they brainstormed about the future, they ordered more and more platters of food.

When Bobby pointed out how much they were eating, the other cadets took it as a challenge. "We gotta get our money's worth," declared Hank as he waved down Daisy for another order of steak and eggs.

Jack grinned with mischief in his eyes. "Let's see if we can put this place out of business."

They'd each had three full meals when Mel finally came out of the kitchen. He was a big man, well over six feet tall, and not an ounce under three hundred pounds. He wasn't alone. Two Dominican dishwashers stood at his side, and it was hard to say which of the three was the largest.

"Boys," Mel announced in a threatening growl, "you just had all you can eat."

Hank was spoiling for a fight, but he was smiling, too. Trying not to laugh, Bobby and Jack pretended to drag him out by the shoulders.

It was almost morning, anyway, and their base passes had expired hours ago. Their plan was to sneak back into their barracks, but the base sentries didn't let them off the hook. As a result, they spent all day

Sunday digging latrines. Still, it seemed cooler digging latrines than it had been in the Alibi.

Hank kept trying to convince them to go back to the Alibi the very next chance they got. But he died three days later. His plane was overtaken by an unexpected squall during a training exercise. The storm had blown in from the Atlantic, its dark clouds completely enveloping the two-seater, wrapping the plane in a blanket of static electricity that cut off all radio communication. By the time the squall passed, Hank, his flight instructor, and his plane were all gone. They had vanished into thin air.

It wasn't until two days later that search crews found the wreckage hundreds of miles away, in an Everglades swamp. Bobby hoped Hank and his instructor had been killed on impact, because alligators had devoured their bodies.

Hank's death shocked Bobby into reality. He had volunteered for a dangerous if not deadly duty, sure, but he'd always assumed that his own intelligence and competence would keep him alive. Hank's fate demonstrated how random and sudden death could be.

Bobby knew Hank wouldn't be the last. During the course of the war, thousands of cadets would be killed in training. A few weeks of training simply couldn't prepare would-be pilots for the actual dangers of flight. And even the best, most naturally gifted, pilot could be brought down by bad luck and faulty equipment.

That happened to Parker. By then they were all flying solo and had grown confident in their piloting skills. Parker's plane developed a leak in its hydraulic system. When his flight returned to base, Parker circled overhead, waiting patiently for his turn to land, never suspecting that every moment was costing him more hydraulic fluid. By the time his turn came, his flaps and wheels locked in place. Parker didn't even have a chance to eject—the ground was coming up way too fast. Without flaps to act as brakes and without wheels to cushion its fall, the plane disintegrated out from under him.

Bobby himself had a scare when he came out of a cloud and flew head-on into a flock of migrating geese. Three of the big birds slammed into his plane, cracking the windshield of the cockpit and smearing it with blood. One of the two engines went out, its propeller tangled with guts and feathers. Bobby's plane was crippled, and he had to land completely blind.

He would've ended up like Parker if Jack hadn't saved him. Jack flew right beside Bobby, holding perfect formation, instructing him over the radio in a comforting, reassuring voice. He told Bobby exactly where to go, how far to turn the yoke, how much to pull the throttle, and how best to compensate for the dead engine. Bobby managed a rough but safe landing.

Jack was most likely the reason Bobby's training group didn't have even more casualties. Jack was a natural pilot. He flew as though he'd been born with wings, and he seemed to know more about flight than even their instructors. No one knew where or how Jack had learned so much, and the cadet remained tight-lipped about his past. When prodded, Jack simply shrugged his shoulders and said, "Just lucky, I guess."

Bobby finally wrote about all of this to Karen, despite never hearing from her. He told her about his new friends, the instant camaraderie they shared, and the sudden sense of loss caused by Hank's and Parker's deaths. He expressed his love for her, wrote heartfelt admissions about how much he missed her, and apologized for the months when he had given in to despair and stopped writing. He'd thought she'd stopped loving him, he explained, but now he knew better. He knew no mail was getting in or out of Leningrad, and he knew that even these letters might never arrive in her hands. But he had faith that she still loved him and that somehow, some way, they would find each other again.

Bobby wrote to Karen every single night, but he never received a single letter in return.

CHAPTER 12
THE CELLIST

The day after Karen returned to Leningrad, the sole survivor of the First Potato Army, she visited the Moscovsky Rail Terminal.

East of Leningrad, a critical ice road stretched across vast Lake Ladoga. This was the so-called Road of Life, the only access to the besieged city that was not controlled by the Germans. The Germans tried to dive-bomb and strafe the supply trucks running the road, but the trucks kept coming, kept going. Once safely across the lake, the trucks were unloaded at the town of Osinovets on the lake's shore, and their cargo was hauled by train to the terminal in Leningrad.

Judging from the amount of traffic in the Moscovsky Terminal, a significant amount of supplies was getting in and out. Karen saw it with her own eyes. She also watched important refugees board outgoing trains to safety. Refugees like Dmitri Shostakovich.

She no longer resented the composer. She no longer blamed him for abandoning her and her father. If she had been offered the chance to evacuate, she would have taken it in a heartbeat. Wouldn't anyone?

It was why she had come to the rail terminal herself. It was why she watched the trains load and unload. She needed to see the operation. She needed to learn how it worked, because she was certain that soon she, too, would be motoring across the ice to safety.

Two days later, Leningrad's mayor addressed the citizens over the public-announcement speakers that had been strung throughout the streets. Mayor Popkov reassured his people that the worst was behind them. The mayor announced the creation of the Second Shock Army and the beginning of a major winter offensive that would break the German siege and rescue Leningrad from starvation. In the meantime, they merely had to survive. He admitted that food had become scarce, but he blamed the black market. He warned Leningraders that profiteers would be harshly punished.

The mayor's words rang hollow. Everyone participated in the black market now. They had to if they wanted to survive. Two hundred grams of bread, the current ration, were clearly not enough to survive on, especially since the bread was cut with sawdust. Those who did somehow manage to survive had to drag the bodies of their loved ones on sledges to mass burial pits. They braved the cold and exhausted themselves in the journey because they knew what would happen to the corpses if they didn't make the trip—cannibals would eat them. The very thing that had happened to Karen's father.

Despite the mayor's words of encouragement, an attitude of rebellion surged through the city. In the weeks that followed, Karen constantly overheard criticism of the government. The Communist Party was accused of hoarding food. Mayor Popkov himself was suspected of purposefully causing the shortage so he could profit. Karen even found anonymous pamphlets brazenly tacked to bulletins that encouraged open revolt. "We need not fear the NKVD," the pamphlets insisted. "Nor the army. They are our fathers, brothers, and sons. They cannot be compelled to fire on us!"

Karen was less convinced by the revolutionary sentiment of the pamphlet than she was by the mayor's speech. Meanwhile, the State police, the NKVD, *was* feared, and with good reason, because it had done far worse than fire on women and children during its brief history. NKVD agents were everywhere in Russia, spying on citizens, noting and recording subversive sentiment or activity. They might not massacre demonstrators in the street, but you could be sure they would round up the organizers afterward and make them disappear, never to be seen or heard from again.

Despite the NKVD, people grumbled in despair and openly criticized their leaders, which was rare in Russia. It indicated a new level of desperation. But that didn't mean people were willing to march on the Smolny, the seat of the city's government. For one, they were far too weak to march. Starving citizens make poor revolutionaries.

Things only got worse when the State-run bakeries began to shut down. City officials claimed that it wasn't a lack of food but a lack of water that caused the closures. Leningrad's last pumping stations had failed, and without water, the bakeries couldn't make bread. In an act of remarkable solidarity, cold, starving, and exhausted civilians once again emerged from their homes. They stood in long lines that stretched from the city's various bakeries to the Neva River. The lines became bucket brigades, passing water hand over hand, delivering it to the bakeries to keep the ovens working. Winter still gripped the city. The temperature was well below zero, and each hand that passed the bucket also had to break the ice forming on its lip to prevent the water from freezing solid before it arrived at the bakery ovens. It was exhausting work. But the purpose it gave to the citizens of Leningrad was also invigorating.

Until she joined those lines, Karen wouldn't have believed that so many ordinary men and women still survived in Leningrad. And although the work was hard, it kept her warm, as did the body heat of the men and women standing on either side of her. Karen no longer felt alone. For once she felt a part of a greater community, part of a family working together for a greater good.

Everyone else felt the same. Spirits had risen. Somewhere in line a man began to sing. He had a deep, booming voice well suited to patriotic songs. But he wasn't singing a patriotic song. He was singing a love song. It was a popular show tune intended for a line of chorus girls, so the man's baritone rendition sounded almost comical. Others immediately joined in, men and women alike. Soon the whole line was singing together. Karen added her own voice, trying to learn the words as she went. But the words weren't important. The song wasn't important. The singing was.

Everyone sang louder and louder, and other voices began to echo the song, from other lines, and from Russian soldiers in their trenches. The Germans could hear them now; Karen was sure of it. The Germans could hear and, upon hearing, would know that Russians still breathed in Leningrad, that their strategy of starvation had failed.

It was one of the happiest moments of Karen's life. Perhaps she wouldn't have to flee, after all. Perhaps she could survive in Leningrad, if everyone could work together, if everyone could just keep the bakeries open. And as public sentiment swung from despair to optimism, Mayor Popkov made another announcement: the Second Shock Army was enjoying remarkable success. Soon they would link up with the Leningrad defenders at the Nevsky Bridgehead. The ice road across Lake Ladoga was still secure. So tomorrow the bread ration would be increased from two hundred to four hundred grams daily.

The city was ecstatic. Karen was ecstatic. Their nightmare seemed to be over. Soon their heroes in the Red Army would liberate them.

But despite the bucket brigades, despite the individual sacrifice of Red Army soldiers, despite the promises of the mayor, the next morning, on January 24, the State-run bakeries closed. It wasn't about the water, after all. City officials had lied. There was no more flour. The rationing was over because there was nothing left to ration.

There was no public outcry, no riot in the streets. Starving people are too weak for that. All that was left now was to lie down and conserve their strength—to try to preserve what little energy they had left, to try to simply survive until the trucks brought more flour over the Road of Life.

The end of rationing in early 1942 was a great tragedy for Leningrad. But it was, from a selfish point of view, fortuitous for Karen. With the closure of the bakeries, her potatoes became that much more valuable. In addition to the potatoes, she had two extra ration cards. They weren't as valuable now that the bakeries were closed, but so long as people still believed the bakeries would eventually reopen, they were still worth something. And, of course, she still had her aunt's seeds. She no longer needed a garden—not where she was going—so everything she had, all the possessions that might mean the difference between survival and starvation in this city, were on the auction block.

She didn't want anything physical in return. There was nothing physical, other than food or the means to produce food, that was worth anything in Leningrad, anyway. But the two things Karen needed most weren't objects. She needed access, and she needed information.

The soldiers were her best hope. Even the soldiers were beginning to starve. They had always been hungrier than their German enemies, but now they were growing as desperate as the civilians. And so they were more willing to provide information than ever before. The citizens of Leningrad weren't told much, of course, and the information was often contradictory. For the cost of three potatoes, sliced into quarters, Karen got twelve different versions of where the Germans were, what villages they still occupied, where and how they patrolled, and how far they had advanced past Leningrad. It was by comparing and contrasting these stories that, newly equipped with a map for which she traded the seeds, Karen was able to piece together what was really happening beyond Leningrad's borders.

The 65th Rifle Division had come from Manchuria, traveling thousands of miles on the Trans-Siberian Railway, and had arrived just in time to save Moscow from German capture. Then they had taken the train north as far as the German lines. There they had attacked the Germans and won, thanks to one heroic soldier who refused to abandon his Katyusha battery. They drove the Germans out of Tikhvin, a village southeast of Leningrad and an important railroad hub. When the Germans had occupied Tikhvin, they cut off the Leningrad–Moscow railroad. By recapturing Tikhvin, the Red Army reopened the rail lines all the way to Lake Ladoga. Tikhvin was a shattered town 135 miles southeast of Leningrad. The sole purpose of its existence was to serve the Leningrad–Moscow railway. This also made it a supply hub for the entire northern front and a valuable prize for both the Germans and the Russians.

Karen could now confirm that the Tikhvin railway station was in Russian hands. If she was just able to get there, the rails were open all the way to Moscow and beyond. Getting on that railroad would be difficult, however. It required a ticket. Karen's inquiries eventually led her to a nurse at Leningrad Hospital. Some of the wounded soldiers evacuated from heavy fighting around the Nevsky Bridgehead had tickets. From Leningrad Hospital they were to be transported across the Road of Life and then by rail to the retraining and recovery battalions. But a lack of medicine and food meant most never survived their stay in the hospital. So the nurses stole their train tickets. After all, they weren't doing the dead soldiers any good.

Karen traded her two extra ration cards—her real ration card, and Sasha's—for three of the train tickets. Not Inna's, however. Karen was still pretending to be Inna, and keeping her card made her false identity seem more legitimate.

To get to Tikhvin meant crossing Lake Ladoga. She first needed to get to Osinovets and then onto the evacuation trucks. No path across that ice was safe, not with Luftwaffe raiders flying overhead.

Leningraders had begun to refer to it as the Road of Death. But the road was safer than trying to cross alone, without antiaircraft gun protection, on foot. Without access to a truck, Karen knew she would get lost and freeze to death long before she reached Tikhvin.

———

Karen had all her plans in place before she visited the Moscovsky Rail Terminal again. She knew that, once she got there, the supply sergeant could get her on a truck. All he had to do was write her name in the book. But he wouldn't do it for free. And he didn't want food. Why should he? He was in charge of unloading the supplies and inventorying everything that came across the lake. He stole all the food he needed. He didn't ask, not directly, but Karen could tell exactly what he wanted from her. He looked at her the way the Leningrad trader had, but with even more directness. The supply sergeant clearly wanted far more from her than a kiss.

Fortunately, Karen had something he wanted more: an extra train ticket. The supply sergeant might have been better off than any ordinary citizen of Leningrad—he might not be starving—but that didn't mean he liked it there. His life was still in danger. He was still cold. And he could still freeze to death. And Leningrad was beyond depressing. Even the grand faux-Renaissance Moskovsky Rail Station was gloomy. Dark clouds hovered beyond its Venetian windows, and silence echoed against its Corinthian columns. The clocks had all stopped at different times. And, without electricity, its station platforms were dark and grim. Only during the departure or arrival of trains or trucks to or from Osinovets did the station come alive. At all other times it was empty.

The supply sergeant hated it there. He had an aunt in Moscow—Karen had heard him talking about it. There, at least, he could finally laugh again. But although he could easily write his own name down in the book, secure his own place on a truck across the ice, what would he do then? Once he was across the lake, he'd have nowhere to go.

Karen's offer of a train ticket changed all that. With a ticket, he could escape just like her. So he accepted her offer, took her extra ticket, and Karen watched as he wrote her name—Inna's name—in the book.

It was now the last day of February. It had taken more than a month of planning, of wheeling and dealing, but Karen had finally made it. She still had a long road ahead. She still had to figure out how to escape Russia. But she was confident she could tackle that problem later. After all, America and Russia weren't that far apart, were they? Perhaps she could get to the Bering Strait. That was how the Eskimos had made it, across the Bering Strait to Alaska and then to America. The hardest part was getting out of Leningrad. If she could do that, she could do anything. And she *had* done that. Her truck across the lake was leaving in the morning. Just one more night of hunger, a short trip from the Moskovsky Terminal to Osinovets, and the nightmare would be behind her.

As she left Inna's apartment building for her early train from Moskovsky Rail Terminal, Karen saw a glow in the sky. At first she hoped it was the aurora borealis. But it wasn't. It was the reflection of flames. People were now too weak with hunger to watch their stoves. Those untended stoves, stoked with garbage instead of heating oil, were catching fire. And since the city's pumping stations weren't operational, there was no way to fight the flames. The fires spread from apartment block to office tower. The city would burn for days. At the front door, Karen stopped on the top step and watched the flames. She was fascinated, not frightened. She thought she was no longer a part of Leningrad, her fate no longer tied to the dying city.

But she was wrong.

A man was sitting on the bottom step of Inna's building. Despair washed over Karen, for she knew he was State police. He had to be.

She didn't know how he'd found her, but she did know that her plans were ruined. She'd participated in the black market. She'd bribed public officials. She'd forged a name on important documents. She would be arrested and imprisoned, maybe even shot. But she had to keep a straight face, had to remain calm. She couldn't let this man see fear or panic, because if there was any way out, any way at all, it would be by pretending. Pretending to be what, she was not sure. But she'd figure out something. She'd have to.

The man stood. "Inna Kerensky?"

Karen nodded. "Yes, that's me." She took one step down to him.

The man stared up at her, suspiciously. Karen knew he was trying to place her imperfect Russian accent. "You live alone?" he said.

Again, Karen nodded, relieved for the opportunity to lie about her accent. "My mother is dead, my father works in Chelyabinsk, and my grandparents still live in Azerbaijan."

The man seemed to accept the explanation. "I am with the NKVD. I would like to ask you some questions. Would you come with me?"

"Certainly."

Karen didn't speak as the man walked her along. She did not like pretending. It went against her very nature. Her father had driven that lesson home: be true to yourself. That was not conventional wisdom in the 1930s. It was, instead, quite an avant-garde notion. But Karen had taken to it like a fish to water. Her father had been proud of her independent spirit, especially when she refused to conform in school. He celebrated the fact that she craved neither approval nor praise from her peers. But that same lesson had often turned against him. Karen didn't share her father's dream that she would become a cellist, and she never hesitated to let him know it. And when she was talking back to him, not her peers or her teachers, her independent spirit didn't seem quite so endearing. This was one of the reasons she loved Bobby so deeply. She and Bobby were more alike than she and her own father had been.

Up until this point, pretending to be Inna had been easy. It was simply lying. All she'd had to do was use Inna's name. Inna's sister was stuck on the siege lines, so Karen had lived alone in Inna's apartment. She hadn't even had to pretend to be a young Communist ideologue. But with this man, it would be different. He was an NKVD security officer, surely trained in interrogation psychology. Karen wondered whether she'd be tortured. Whatever happened, she could admit nothing. Her only salvation, however remote, lay in somehow convincing this man that she was innocent.

She had to consider running. Fight or flight was the natural reaction of a cornered animal. But Karen was a fighter. And she knew that to run away would be to give in to panic. Fleeing into the cold, empty streets of Leningrad would make her guilty. And this man would easily run her down. He knew the streets of Leningrad far better than she did.

After a few minutes, the NKVD man stopped in the middle of the sidewalk. By the direction she knew he was taking her to the Smolny, the city headquarters, for interrogation. She had seen the Smolny before the war but hadn't noticed it since. It surprised her now—it had been so effectively camouflaged that it took her a long moment to recognize the building across the street. Not only had it been covered with special nets and tarpaulins; it had also been painted by theatrical scenic artists to disguise its shape. It looked like an entirely different building. Of course the Russians would disguise it, Karen realized. They would have to. The city headquarters would be a top priority for German bombing. And yet here it stood, unscathed. It wasn't the act of camouflage that was so impressive, but the degree of skill with which it was accomplished.

Working this out in her head had helped keep Karen calm, but now her heart sank. Russians were so good at hiding, at pretending. They could make a whole building disappear. What chance did she, a mere American girl, have of fooling Soviet State security?

CHAPTER 13
THE ORGAN-GRINDER

Petr woke from the stomach-turning sensation of falling. What had happened? Had he rolled off his bed? No, it was worse than that. He had almost rolled off the second-story loft. For a moment he was confused. Where was he? Then he felt an abrasive, wet tongue on his face, and it all came back to him. Duck, the dog's name was Duck. He was in the middle of a battle. That was the sound of crackling and booming outside the door. The Germans must still hold the center of the village, must still be resisting. How had he fallen asleep in the middle of a battle?

Petr suddenly recognized that he was a combat veteran. Veterans slept whenever they could, whenever they weren't needed. He, only twenty years old, was already a hardened warhorse and hero of the Soviet Union. The thought was more absurd than it was comforting. There was nothing special about being a veteran, Petr realized. All it meant was that somehow you had survived. You had been lucky.

A machine gun purred. It wasn't the tinny rattle of a Russian gun but the threatening growl of a German MG-34. The sound made Petr realize that perhaps one thing was special about being a veteran, after all. Veterans were hard to kill. Blondie and his Siberian unit had been veterans of the war in Mongolia. And the Germans still holding the center of this village were undoubtedly veterans of Poland and France. Look how hard they were to kill. How long had they been holding out?

Petr wasn't sure. He'd lost track of time while he slept . . . hours, at least.

The raspy tongue swept across Petr's face a second time, prompting him to sit up and push away the Alsatian wolf dog's snout. Petr noted with satisfaction that he had already set up his big PTRD rifle before he'd fallen asleep. It was pointing west on its bipod, a big bullet already cocked in its chamber. But it wasn't pointing out of one of the log house's windows. Petr had taken a tip from the Germans. He'd carved a hole in the plaster where the logs joined, and the barrel of his rifle was sticking through it. It wasn't invisible—not exactly. Someone in the frozen field outside could spot it if they knew exactly where to look. But they'd be looking at the windows first. This way Petr could surprise the Germans the way the Germans had surprised the Russians during their assault on the village. That was another sign of being a veteran, Petr realized with even more satisfaction—learning from your enemy.

Petr rolled over and lifted the PTRD stock to his shoulder, wrapped his finger around its trigger, and peered out through his peephole at a beautiful winter scene. Snow had fallen. It coated the fallow beet field and the straight road beyond, a pleasant landscape with white rolling hills. The distant forest had been dusted as well, the glistening flakes and icicles making the spruce look like Christmas trees. But climbing up above the trees was another color: black. It was the inky smoke of gasoline engines, the dark exhaust of German tanks.

The panzers were still too distant to hear over the sound of rifle and machine-gun fire, but the smoke was approaching fast. The German cavalry was on its way.

Petr was not the only one to notice the tanks. A series of shrill whistles blew over the gunfire. This was the tank killer's signal—time to ready their weapons. Petr's gun was ready. So was his other weapon. It sat on its haunches and panted, a smile stretched across its snout, its red tongue lolling out and wagging with every breath.

Petr stared into the dog's brown eyes. It was his duty to arm the explosives. Duck was trained for this, to blow himself up against German tanks, a canine suicide bomber. Petr knew that all over the village, other dogs were being prepared, their packs unbuttoned, electronic batteries charged, wires connecting primers to the wooden antennas. But Petr couldn't do it. Duck had saved his life. Now it was Petr's chance to return the favor.

The German panzers began to emerge from the woods, and Petr's heart sank. The tanks were buttoned up, the hatches locked tight. The commanders and crew were leaving nothing to chance, relying on viewports and periscopes instead of the naked eye. "Shoot the commanders," Fyodor had advised, but now Fyodor was dead, and there were no commanders to shoot.

As the lead tanks churned through the virgin snow of the beet field, more emerged from the woods behind, dozens of them. It must have been an entire company, at least.

Another series of whistles blew. This time it wasn't a signal to the soldiers, but to the dogs. Duck recognized the cadence immediately and leaped from the loft. Petr tried to call him back, but the dog's training was too ingrained. He raced like a shot out of the log-house door so he could circle back around to the tanks crossing the field.

Petr returned his finger to the trigger and his eye to the peephole. He heard the bang of first one and then another antitank rifle. The bullets sparked on a panzer's armor but had no other obvious effect.

Suddenly the lead panzers halted. Their turrets swiveled, and their howitzers roared. A cottage disintegrated under the impact of high-explosive shells.

The Russian antitank rifle team there would have already evacuated out the back door; they knew better than to stay in one place. But the howitzers were again swiveling on their turrets. The guns roared, and timber flew from the next cottage in line. Soon the riflemen would have nowhere left to hide. Those howitzers would flush them out of their holes and right into the fangs of German machine guns.

The rear tanks now overtook the ones that had halted to fire their howitzers. They churned forward fifty yards in the snow before they, too, stopped and fired. Petr ducked his head just before a window beside him exploded into deadly shrapnel. He hadn't yet fired to give away his position. But the seasoned panzer crews weren't taking any chances. They preemptively destroyed any building that might hide an antitank gun or rifle.

They were veterans. But so was Petr. Another window exploded far from Petr. The enemy's own trick of burrowing through the wall had worked. Nonetheless Petr didn't feel safe. Every instinct in his body screamed for him to run. It was only a matter of time before the panzers would fire into the walls, too. But Petr didn't run. His body shivered uncontrollably from fear. He clenched his teeth, but that only made him shake even harder.

Another shell exploded, and suddenly Petr fought the urge to piss. He had to run out back, where it was safer, and find some ditch to piss in. But that would mean running, would mean giving up his position. This was the only two-story building in the village, other than the church, and the church was on fire. The log house's height was his only advantage. If the tanks got close enough, if he could angle a shot down through the weak armor of a turret hatch, he could kill a commander.

Petr pissed himself instead. He'd heard stories of soldiers pissing themselves out of fear. But in this moment Petr knew those stories were false. You didn't piss yourself from fear; you pissed yourself from courage.

The rear tanks had started moving again. They passed the front tanks, drove for another fifty yards, and halted to fire. This is how it would be, Petr realized, until they were right on top of him. Only half the tanks would move at any one time, the other half covering their advance with howitzers and machine guns. It was like watching a giant mechanical game of leapfrog.

Smoke was everywhere—smoke from the guns, smoke from the explosions, smoke from the panzers' exhaust. Then Petr noticed movement in the smoke and heard barking. It was the dogs, leaping through the snow toward the panzers. Petr held his breath, anticipating the carnage when the tank crews opened up with their front machine guns. There was absolutely no cover in the open field, and the charging dogs would be cut down in seconds. Yet those machine guns remained silent.

The dogs on all fours were barely half as tall as a running man. The viewports and periscopes had trouble spotting them. Between that and all the smoke, the dogs were effectively invisible. Petr felt proud and ashamed all at once. He'd been wrong to question Red Army tactics and even more wrong to refuse to arm Duck's explosives. The mine dogs would work. They outnumbered the panzers two to one. They'd destroy the tanks, the village would be secured, and Petr would live after all.

Then the dogs reached the lead panzers, and everything went wrong.

The dogs had been trained on Russian tanks, not German ones. Russian tanks ran on diesel fuel, not gasoline like the panzers. That fact confused the dogs. The German panzers looked like the tanks the dogs were used to. They were big and metal. But they didn't smell like tanks because they didn't smell of diesel fuel. And there was another odor, the smell of gunpowder. The dogs recognized that smell. Their handlers smelled like that. Maybe their handlers were somewhere inside these panzers? The dogs didn't attack the tanks the way they were expected to;

they didn't run under the tanks. Instead, they hesitated and ran around and around them, like sheepdogs herding giant robots.

One dog slipped on a patch of ice next to the panzer it was stalking. As it rolled onto its back, the wooden stake tied to it triggered its explosives. The dog died instantly, and although the resulting explosion didn't destroy the panzer, it did split the tank's treads, immobilizing it.

That got the Germans' attention.

Suddenly the tank crews noticed the dogs and realized the threat. They opened up with their machine guns.

But the dogs were inside the German ranks now. They wove in and out between the panzers, hard to track and even harder to hit. Some of the dogs ran for cover under the panzers, finally fulfilling their destinies by blowing themselves up. Two tanks exploded.

Now the panzer hatches popped open. Commanders showed their heads, then their torsos, from their top hatches, yelling at the machine gunners and leaning over to point out the canine targets.

Petr pulled the trigger of his PTRD.

A commander's head exploded. A gruesome sight. Petr hadn't considered what a slug from his big PTRD rifle would do to human flesh and bone. He wanted to vomit. He squeezed his eyes shut to flush the image from his memory, but he couldn't, so he reimagined it—that was no human head; it was a melon. They were all melons, put on a fence for target practice. He was shooting the melons with his uncle's shotgun.

Petr slid the bolt, rechambered a round, and fired, again and again. More melons exploded.

Petr wasn't shivering anymore. He was calm, going about his business, doing his job. He was still afraid, but what he was doing felt more important than fear. He was defending the dogs, defending Duck, defending a friend.

He should be moving, though. He had been trained to move after every shot so he wouldn't be killed by return fire, but there was no return fire, at least not yet. There was too much confusion among the panzer crews. And Petr knew in his gut this was a unique opportunity, one he had to take advantage of. Not every one of his bullets hit; he wasn't that good. But if he could destroy enough melons, perhaps the panzers would be forced to turn around.

The panzers never turned around. The dogs had stopped exploding, the survivors having faulty demolitions or, perhaps like Duck, overly sympathetic handlers. Now the panzer crews were realizing the dogs were no longer a threat. The real danger was that marksman in the log house.

Machine-gun fire raked the log-house wall. Petr couldn't see the howitzer barrels swinging in his direction, but he sensed it. He abandoned the heavy PTRD rifle and leaped from the loft to the sawdust-covered plank floor.

He landed on his side, flattening his arm under his ribs and the cold, hard surface hammering his ear, which felt like getting smashed with a red-hot skillet. He'd lost his wind and lay gasping, unmoving, on the floor.

The wall behind him exploded. The thick logs transformed into thousands of flying splinters, some as long and thick as his arms. But the angle of the burst sent them flying over the top of him, missing his curled body altogether.

Petr unfolded himself, scrambled to his feet, and stumbled out of the log house as the entire structure collapsed behind him.

The center of the village was largely still intact. Red Army soldiers surrounded the interior cottages, finding shelter from German small-arms fire behind fences or the dead bodies of their fallen comrades. A few managed to cut through the frozen ground and dig shallow fox-holes. But they were at a stalemate, unable to advance farther. Petr knew the stalemate was about to be broken. It was only a matter of minutes before the tanks would resume their advance, roll through the village, and cut down the Russian infantry from behind.

Petr started calling for Duck. If the big wolf dog were still alive, Petr didn't want to leave him to the mercy of the Germans. But he didn't stop moving, either, running, half crouched, through cottages and leaping over the bodies of dead Russians and Germans. He couldn't go back the way he'd come; the German attack would take that route in an effort to cut off the Russian retreat. He couldn't escape through the field; that ran straight into the guns of the panzers. But there was another way. The village was built beside a river that it used to channel water for irrigation. If the river was frozen hard enough, it just might provide an escape.

Duck appeared just as Petr reached the riverbank. The big dog leaped on Petr in his excitement and knocked them both tumbling down the bank and onto the ice. If the ice had been thin, the fall would have been disastrous; neither Petr nor Duck could have survived getting wet in this cold. But the river was frozen solid, despite its swift current. Petr ruffled Duck's fur and ran, half crouching, straight down the middle of the river, using it like a road, slipping and sliding and losing his balance on the ice but somehow keeping his feet. The river's steep banks rising on either side hid him from the Germans' view.

Petr and Duck reached a stone bridge that arched over them. That gave Petr pause because he didn't remember passing a stone bridge on the way to the village. He must be running in the wrong direction, away from the Russian lines and into the German ones. Then he heard the roar of automobile engines and saw a column of German troop-transport trucks driving toward the bridge, rushing soldiers to reinforce the attack on the village. Petr grabbed Duck, pulled him under the bridge, and plastered himself against the stonework in the shadow of the bridge's arch. The vibration of the heavy trucks rumbling overhead ran through him. He held Duck tight and quiet, waiting for the trucks to pass. There must have been a dozen of them. But he realized he had a better chance of surviving here than trying to pass back through the village, even if he was heading straight to Berlin. When the rumble of the last truck faded into the distance, Petr let go of Duck, and they continued on their way.

The thunder of the tanks and the crackle of the machine guns gradually grew more distant. Poplar and birch trees lined the riverbank. Petr hoisted himself up out of the river by grabbing the trees' bare branches and roots.

He ran away from the river now, deeper into the taiga. At any sign of civilization, he automatically turned in the opposite direction. If he was behind German lines, villages would be held by the Wehrmacht and the roads patrolled. He grew exhausted, but he didn't feel its full effect until the sun sank low against the horizon. He collapsed against a thick tree trunk, welcoming the darkness. It would hide him, protect him from German patrols. He didn't know where he was, but for the moment at least he was safe. He closed his eyes and felt the warmth of Duck's body curled up against his own.

Petr didn't sleep. He wasn't that kind of tired. He was fatigued. His muscles ached from the tension of the battle and the duration of his run. He lay there waiting for the lactic acid to seep slowly out of his muscles, for the pain of the fatigue to give way to stiffness. He had to get up before he lost feeling in his extremities. He'd escaped the Germans, but the cold could still kill him.

His back cracked as he pulled himself into a sitting position. He twisted his spine to loosen his muscles, but it did little good. He glanced down at Duck and noticed that the dog was chewing his paws, digging ice out from where it had lodged between his toes. Petr ruffled the fur on the dog's head, muttered "Good boy," and stood.

They plunged deeper into the woods. He couldn't tell which direction he was moving in, but the night sky was slightly brighter in one direction. That might be a sign of the aurora borealis, or it might be the glow of Leningrad's lights. Either way, that was north, and north offered Petr the best chance of escape.

As Petr would later learn, he was partially correct. The sky was reflecting the glow of Leningrad, but the light came from Leningrad's burning fires. Petr knew the Germans had surrounded Leningrad and held the city in a tight blockade. He wasn't aware of the true desperation, starvation, and privation of every citizen caught within the city. He didn't know that the electricity had been cut. He didn't know that the gas lines didn't work. He didn't know that the water-pumping stations had broken down. And he didn't know that thousands of people were starving to death every day. The Soviet government didn't want people to know what was happening in Leningrad, because it didn't want anyone, especially not soldiers, to know how close they were to losing the war with Germany. So the officials and bureaucrats and commissars carefully controlled all information coming out of the city. The NKVD opened and read all mail. Refugees who managed to escape and began to describe what was really happening were arrested and warned to keep quiet.

No one outside of Leningrad knew how bad it truly was in the city. Everyone believed the citizens were courageously and patriotically holding out against the Germans, waiting for the glorious moment when they would finally be liberated by the Second Shock Army. That, the Soviet leaders believed, was best for morale.

No one outside the city knew it was a death trap.

So Petr headed toward Leningrad, believing that, since he was behind enemy lines, the besieged city offered him the best chance of safety. If he could only reach the guns and trenches of Leningrad, he would be safe.

CHAPTER 14
THE CELLIST

The NKVD man looked well fed. Everyone here did. That was all Karen could think of while she stared at the man across the big wooden table. She could even smell the food. It was somewhere in here, a commissary perhaps, feeding important Communist officials, high-ranking military officers, and their families. She could smell boiled cabbage. When was the last time she'd eaten vegetables? She could only vaguely remember. She briefly considered stealing some on her way out. But that was her stomach thinking, and she knew such thoughts were unwise. She reminded herself to concentrate. She was playing a dangerous game—a game at which men like the NKVD officer were masters. If Karen lost, she knew she would never leave this building alive.

The NKVD man read from his notes. "You met Sasha Portnov in the Young Pioneers?"

Karen blinked. Sasha Portnov? What did he have to do with her crimes? Sasha had been a true believer, a Communist, a patriot. He had nothing to do with the black market. "Why are you asking about Sasha?"

The NKVD man's expression didn't change. "I will ask the questions here. Did you or did you not meet Sasha Portnov in the Young Pioneers?"

"I did not."

The NKVD man looked up from his notes and peered at Karen across the table with the expression of a strict schoolmaster. "It is important that you understand. I know when you are lying. I will let this first lie go unpunished. But next time there will be consequences."

"I am not lying."

"Do you enjoy pain?"

"Of course not."

"Then tell me the truth."

"I am."

The NKVD man sighed, then pushed back his chair and stood. "Don't you think we have records from the Young Pioneers?" he asked as he walked around the table toward her. "Don't you think we have official documents proving that you and Sasha Portnov served together in the same group?" He took her wrist in both hands. "Why are you pretending not to have met him?"

"I'm not pretending—" Karen's words caught in her throat as the NKVD man twisted her wrist. The pain was excruciating. She couldn't think, couldn't hear, couldn't even see. She could only feel the pain and wonder what he was doing to her, wonder if it would ever stop. And then it did.

"I know everything about you," the man warned her. "I have investigated your father and your sister. I have even searched your apartment."

Karen's head swam. For a moment she couldn't speak. She wanted desperately never to feel that pain again. But some part of her mind told her there was something worse than pain. You could recover from pain. The only thing you couldn't recover from was death. "My apologies,

Comrade," she forced herself to say. "But you misunderstood. I don't
claim never to have met Sasha Portnov. But I did not meet him in the
Young Pioneers. I met him before that. I joined the Young Pioneers
so that I could be with him. I will try to be more clear in the future."

The NKVD man flinched, shocked. He quickly regained his composure, circled back around the table, and sat down. "You see, then?
That was not so difficult. The truth is much easier."

"Absolutely, Comrade."

The NKVD man picked up a pen and twisted off its cap. "You say
you joined the Young Pioneers to be with him. Why? Did someone
force you? A foreigner?"

"I was in love with him."

Again, for the briefest moment, Karen saw shock wash across the
face of the NKVD man. Karen realized with some satisfaction that this
interrogation was not going as he had planned. Perhaps the old saying
was right; perhaps the truth really would set you free. But this time it
was not Karen's truth. It was Inna's.

"You joined when you were eight."

"Sasha was nine."

"And you claim to have already fallen in love with him?"

"Desperately."

"You were not yet mature enough for romance."

"You do not need to be mature to love someone."

"And am I to believe the two of you . . . an eight-year-old and a
nine-year-old . . . were, what, sweethearts?"

"No, comrade. Sasha Portnov barely knew I existed."

Inna had told Karen the story at least half a dozen times. It was a
quaint story, and cute, one that Karen loved. Inna, as a little girl, had
taken off her gloves to admire a necklace. It was a cheap piece of jewelry,
with a tiny beaded doll serving as its pendant, but to young Inna it was
magical. She had wanted to feel it, to run her fingers over the beads, so
she had removed her gloves. She so coveted the pretty jewelry that she

completely lost track of the world around her. She was distracted, and someone used that distraction to steal her gloves.

Inna knew that when she got home her father would ask about the gloves, and Inna would be punished for letting someone steal them. So Inna didn't go home. Instead she just sat on the stoop and cried until a boy came and asked her what was wrong. That boy was Sasha. He said he was in the Young Pioneers, and that part of his code was to help someone once a day. He gave Inna his gloves.

As Karen told the story to the NKVD man, she remembered Inna telling the story to her. It had been such a small thing, a common thing, a moment motivated by a child afraid of a spanking. But the good deed and the handsome boy had turned it into something special for Inna. Without realizing it, Sasha had also turned it into an act of romance, because from that point forward Inna was obsessed with him. Her love for Sasha went unrequited for eight long years. Inna couldn't help but smile when she told the story to Karen and now, when Karen retold it, she couldn't help but cry.

The NKVD man looked puzzled. "Why are you crying?"

What could Karen say? That she missed Inna and Sasha? She couldn't tell the NKVD man *that*. Or could she? The truth will set you free.

"Because he is gone," she said.

The NKVD man put down his pen, sat back in his chair, and stared at her. "Gone where?"

"I don't know. But I think he's dead." Karen sobbed then. She couldn't help herself. They were real, these tears. Until now she had never had a chance to mourn for Inna, to grieve. It had been such a senseless death, but also a beautiful one—beautiful in its selflessness. So she grieved now, and her sorrow came out in convulsive sobs that shook her body and turned her empty stomach.

The NKVD man stared at her in silence. Then he stood up again and circled the table. He was going to hurt her again. Karen knew she had to get hold of her emotions, stop crying, say something to prevent the NKVD man from torturing her. But she couldn't. Try as she might, she couldn't stop crying.

The man stood above her and reached into his pocket. He was going to cut her, Karen realized, or stab her or worse. She'd read that in stories: torturers forcing blades under their victims' fingernails.

But the NKVD man didn't draw a knife from his pocket. He took out a handkerchief. He handed it to Karen, who didn't hesitate to use it to wipe her runny nose and blot the streaming tears from under her eyes. The cloth was oddly comforting, as was the closeness of the strange man. He leaned against the table next to her, stoically watching her as she regained her composure. She drew one last sniffle before handing back the handkerchief. "Thank you. I think I ruined it."

The NKVD man tossed the dirty linen on the table but ignored the comment. "Do you know what happened to him?" he asked.

Karen did know what happened to him. But she'd already told a lie to Inna's sister, claiming that Sasha had stayed behind to collect wood. She couldn't be sure the NKVD hadn't already spoken to Inna's sister, so she didn't dare contradict herself. "No," she lied.

"I spanked him."

Now Karen was confused. What was going on? What was this interrogation all about? Why was this strange man talking about spanking? Spanking whom?

"He never told me he'd given his gloves away," the NKVD man continued. "He said he'd lost them. So I spanked him."

If Karen had any tears left, she would have cried again. She'd misjudged everything and everyone. This wasn't about the black market; it wasn't about profiteering. It was about Sasha, a boy she'd resented for wasting eight years of her best friend's life. A young man she'd thought she had to trick into becoming Inna's boyfriend. A hothead who'd gotten himself and his girlfriend killed for no reason.

But now Karen realized that none of those things had been true. The nine-year-old Sasha hadn't given away his gloves because it was his duty as a Young Pioneer. He did it to impress a pretty little girl. Those eight years of love hadn't been unrequited, after all. Inna had never needed Karen's makeover. Sasha had always been attracted to Inna but had been as afraid to approach Inna as she had been afraid to approach him. It meant that Sasha hadn't attacked that German out of blind, stupid patriotism. That, too, had been a misguided attempt to protect the girl he loved.

And the man sitting across from her? He was not just some impersonal State security officer.

"You're Sasha's father," Karen said.

The NKVD man nodded, and Karen's heart went out to him.

"Is he dead?" the man asked. He had to know the truth already, but he dreaded its confirmation.

"I hope not," Karen reassured him. And then she told the story, about how she and Sasha had gone hunting for potatoes, about how they called themselves the First Potato Army, about how they'd almost been caught by a German sentry. This, however, was when Karen began to bend the truth. In her new version of the story, Sasha had been successful in the attack. He'd killed the German, and they'd escaped together back to Leningrad's trenches. But there Sasha decided to stay behind. He told her he wanted to gather some wood. He gave Inna his potatoes and instructed her to go on ahead without him.

Karen could tell that the NKVD man was proud of his son, of his courage and of his patriotism. But he seemed to be ashamed of letting his son take such big risks, of failing to protect him. "There is nothing you could have done," Karen reassured him. "Sasha purposefully kept it all secret because he was afraid you wouldn't let him go."

The NKVD man nodded, stoically. "Can you show me where? Show me where you left him, where he stopped to gather wood?"

"Of course," Karen lied.

It was well after midnight when Karen and the NKVD man left the Smolny together. But with the city still burning, it was bright enough to see. It was a long walk; the trams hadn't run for months, and even if the NKVD could have procured a vehicle and petrol, the streets were too clogged with rubble to allow a car's passage. Eventually they reached the edge of the city, and the Red Army's defensive trenches.

Thank goodness Inna's sister wasn't on duty. Sasha's father showed the sentry his NKVD identification, and they crossed into the no-man's-land beyond Leningrad's defensive perimeter.

Karen held her breath as they crossed the open ground. She knew that German artillery was already aimed on this position and that German spotters on the surrounding hills would call to the guns if they suspected someone was trying to escape the doomed city. But once again the darkness was her friend, or perhaps the smoke from the city fires protected her, because they weren't detected, and soon she was leading the NKVD man through the frozen boreal forest.

Karen didn't know where she was going, and she didn't really care. Her plans had already been spoiled. The truck with her name on it had long since departed, and the train tickets in her pocket were worthless.

They came to a clearing. It seemed as good a place as any. Karen stopped and looked around before pointing at a tree. "There," she said.

Sasha's father walked to the tree and looked at its branches. It was a young spruce, green and sappy, and it didn't look good for firewood. "How?" he asked.

Karen detected the suspicion in his voice. "Not that one, the oak," she corrected herself. She walked up to the trunk of a big barren oak tree and pointed up at its gnarled branches. "He said he would climb up and hack off a limb."

"Did you see him?"

Karen looked up through the dark branches. "I helped hoist him up, and then he told me to leave."

"None of the branches are broken."

The NKVD man was right. If her story were true, some of the branches would have been cut short. "Perhaps he didn't succeed."

"There are no tracks."

Karen looked down. Inside she was beginning to panic. She'd almost convinced him, but now she was making fatal mistakes. Her story was beginning to unravel. Then she remembered: "It snowed three days ago. It must have covered up the tracks."

"I see. So, who is Karen Hamilton?"

Karen's blood froze. She slowly turned around and saw that the NKVD man had a pistol in his hand. He was pointing it right at her.

"I found another ration card on the same woman who had Sasha's. She said you had given it to her."

Karen stared at the gun, and her mind raced. Maybe she could make a run for it. Maybe in the forest and the darkness she could get away. But it wasn't dark anymore. The sun had begun to come up, and already there was enough light for him to shoot her easily. And they were only a few feet apart. The NKVD man wouldn't miss at that range. Karen knew she was dead.

She was about to say something, a desperate lie about how this Karen was a neighbor who had died and had left her an extra ration card. But a new voice interrupted them.

"Hello, comrades!" the voice called out. "Are you from Leningrad?"

A boy dressed in the uniform of a Russian soldier had appeared in the woods behind the NKVD man.

The NKVD man spun, pointing his pistol at the smiling boy.

Karen jumped at the NKVD man, trying to tackle him to the ground.

CHAPTER 15
THE ORGAN-GRINDER

Petr's journey to Leningrad lasted several days. He had nothing to eat but the meager rations in his mess kit, bread frozen solid that he had to cut using his sharp shovel like an ax. He shared every meal with Duck. He didn't dare build a fire for fear that its smoke would give his position away to the Germans. The water in his canteen was soon frozen, leaving him nothing to drink but snow. He traveled only at night, because it was easier to see the glow in the sky, and he felt safer surrounded by darkness. It was colder at night, too, and the ceaseless march helped keep him warm. Compared to the days, Petr's nights were almost pleasant.

On the second night, Petr crossed another river. It was frozen solid, and the troughs of tire tracks were dug right down its middle. Apparently the Germans were using it as a road, so Petr called Duck deeper into the woods and they avoided the river.

On his third day, he saw smoke where the glow had been in the sky the night before. Now he knew he was heading toward Leningrad, but he incorrectly assumed the smoke was the result of artillery duels between the Germans and the Leningrad defenders. That night the glow was brighter, too, and it motivated him to keep marching even after the rising sun slowly turned the darkness gray. Petr knew he was close, maybe only a few miles from the city's trenches, and he knew that meant the Germans must be nearby, too. He decided to keep marching.

Petr came to a road. It led in the exact direction he was marching, so he had to follow it somehow. He moved parallel to the road, deep enough within the coniferous forest to stay hidden from the view of any trucks passing by.

He heard voices up ahead.

He and Duck crouched. Petr was unarmed. He'd lost his big PTRD rifle in the log house and hadn't found a secondary weapon. So he held his breath and stayed hidden. But then he heard the voices a little more clearly. And his heart leaped. They weren't speaking German—they were speaking Russian.

Petr rose from his crouch and bounded forward with a smile. Duck trotted beside him. They passed through a wall of spruce and into a narrow clearing.

A man and a girl stood there, on the opposite side—the girl's back to a tree and the man's back to Petr. Petr waved and called out to his comrades in greeting, asking about Leningrad.

The man turned to him. Petr froze. The man had a pistol in his hand. It had been pointed at the girl and now was pointed at him. The girl lunged at the man, trying to knock him down.

CHAPTER 16

THE CELLIST AND THE ORGAN-GRINDER

The moment Karen clamped her arms around the NKVD man, she knew she'd made a mistake. She should have run while she had the chance. The NKVD man was half a head taller than she and physically fit, much better fed. Grabbing him felt like grasping at the trunk of a tree. All she could do was deflect his arm, spoil his aim. The gun went off, and a bullet plunged into the ground. Maybe that saved the young soldier who'd appeared, but not her. The NKVD man grabbed her, threw her down. Karen felt herself falling onto the cold ground and saw the pistol moving toward her, the barrel pointed at her forehead. She tried to squirm away, but the NKVD man only tracked her with the aim.

Then the NKVD man was thrown to the ground. An animal was on him, a wolf, ripping at his coat. No, it wasn't a wolf. It was a dog. Snarling, it ripped out bundles of wool and flesh with every bite. Karen kept scurrying backward, as terrified of the dog as she was of the NKVD man. But the dog didn't seem interested in her. It kept biting and tearing at the NKVD man.

The NKVD man put up a good fight despite the torment of being eaten alive. He managed to climb to his knees, protecting his face and neck from lunging fangs with his bleeding left forearm. The dog's silent attack had knocked the gun from his hand, but now the NKVD man patted the ground, searching for it. As the dog kept lunging, his fingertips groped for the steel barrel.

Karen heard a voice: "Duck! No! No, Duck!" The voice was getting closer—it was the soldier, running toward them.

Karen swallowed her fear and lunged for the gun. Her hand wrapped around it at the same time as the NKVD man's did. But he was so much stronger, she knew she could only hold on a few moments before he yanked it from her grasp. So she tugged at the trigger. The pistol boomed, and she felt it kick, but she kept pulling the trigger, over and over. The bullets zipped harmlessly into the forest. She wasn't trying to aim; she was only trying to empty the gun before the NKVD man could turn it on her. The gun clicked empty just as the NKVD man wrestled it from her grasp.

Still fighting off the dog with one arm, the NKVD man dropped the gun and reached into his coat. The soldier grabbed the dog's collar, pulling the animal backward even as he lunged and lurched in the man's grasp. "Off, Duck! Down! Down!"

Freed now, the NKVD man drew an ammo clip from his pocket, picked up the gun, and ejected the empty clip.

Karen saw a spade hanging from the soldier's belt loop. As he struggled with the dog, she scrambled to her feet and grabbed the military shovel—just like the one she'd used to dig potatoes and just as sharp.

The NKVD man slammed the new clip into the gun and pulled back the bolt, chambering a round. Before he could raise the gun, Karen hammered the shovel into the back of his skull. Blood splattered, and the NKVD man pitched forward into the snow. He twitched, so Karen speared him with the point of the shovel.

The dog stopped struggling. The soldier stepped back, horrified. Karen reached for the NKVD man's gun. She held the gun out to the soldier, but she was shaking, almost uncontrollably, and she couldn't hold it steady. "Don't . . . don't let that dog come anywhere near me," she warned.

The soldier raised his hands. "Stay, Duck," he said. But there was no need for the command. The wolf dog, so vicious mere seconds ago, now sat on his haunches, looking up at Karen, licking his bloody lips. The death of the NKVD man had made him perfectly calm.

Karen noticed red out of the corner of her eye. The NKVD man's blood was spreading through the snow. She glanced down at his body; she couldn't help it. What she saw made her vomit. Then she passed out.

Karen woke to the pleasant smell of burning wood and the crackling of a fire. The soldier crouched beside a small blaze, coaxing it with kindling. Karen was relieved to see that he'd placed a latticework of evergreen boughs over the fire to hide the smoke. She also noticed that the soldier had the NKVD man's gun within arm's reach on the ground. The soldier wasn't looking at her, but his big wolf dog was. He lay beside the fire, resting his chin on his paw, seemingly relaxed. But his brown eyes never left her face.

Karen looked at the gun and then at the soldier. The first thing she noticed was that he didn't look starved. He couldn't have come from Leningrad, then.

She refocused on the soldier's face. The beginnings of an unkempt blond beard had begun to grow over his pale cheeks, but the nearly invisible whiskers couldn't hide his sharp, angular, almost patrician nose and jawline. His hair had begun to grow out from what was not long ago a crew cut, now sticking up at odd angles. It all made the soldier look like a boy with a drawn-on play beard, which he was, really. He couldn't have been much older than Bobby. His uniform was filthy. He probably hadn't washed in days. Well, neither had Karen. She could hardly fault him for that. Especially considering that she had dried, caked blood on her hands and vomit on her coat.

Karen sat up but froze when the big dog growled, alerting the soldier.

The soldier stopped feeding the fire and grabbed the NKVD man's pistol beside him. He pointed it at Karen, warily. "Who are you?" he asked.

Karen eyed the gun and considered her response. She had no way of knowing where this soldier came from or what his mission was. With no safe response, she decided it was better to continue the lie that had served her so far. "My name is Inna. I'm from Leningrad."

The boy soldier eyed her, then pointed his chin to the left. "And who was he?"

Karen followed his gesture to a pile of snow. Obviously the soldier had tried to dig a grave and failed. Not even the military shovel could cut through the frozen ground. So he'd contented himself with burying the body in snow instead. Karen wondered how long she'd been passed out. "I don't know his name. He was with the NKVD."

The boy soldier turned ashen. "You killed an NKVD man?"

"He would have shot you."

"I'm a soldier."

"So? If I hadn't grabbed him, you would be dead. He had good aim."

The soldier stared at Karen a moment, still aiming the gun steady. He conceded her point. "Yes. He shot at me. But why?"

"Because he didn't want you to see."

"See what?"

"See him kill me."

The soldier looked skeptical. "You are an enemy of the state. Why would he be ashamed to kill an enemy of the state?"

"Because I'm not an enemy of the state."

The soldier didn't move, but Karen could see his eyes glitter with understanding. He wasn't stupid. But would that make convincing him not to shoot her easier or harder?

"Then why else would he want you dead? You must be a subversive."

Karen sighed. She took a chance and dropped her carefully affected accent. "I'm not a subversive. I'm not even Russian. I'm American."

The soldier's eyes widened. "American? How did you learn Russian?"

"I've lived in Leningrad for a year and a half."

"Your accent is nearly flawless."

"My father says it is because I am a musician. I have a good ear."

"Your father is in Leningrad, too?"

"My father is dead."

"Because he was a spy?"

"Of course not."

"An American spy."

"Why would we spy? We're on the same side now."

"I am simply trying to figure out why the NKVD wants you dead," the soldier said.

"Not the NKVD. Just that man. He hated me."

"Why did he hate you?"

"Because he thought I murdered his son."

The soldier paused in thought. "Did you?"

"Look at me. I haven't eaten in days. Could I murder someone?"

The soldier's eyes narrowed. "You murdered an armed NKVD man."

"Only with the help of your dog."

"Soldiers kill. I've seen killers. I know what they look like. And I'm looking at one right now."

Karen peered across the fire at the soldier. "I didn't kill that man's son."

"Then who did?"

"The Germans." Karen told the story of the First Potato Army, and this time she told it in full. She felt ashamed. "I shouldn't have abandoned them. I should have fought for them."

The soldier shook his head. "Then you would be dead, too."

Karen nodded. It was the truth. But it didn't help to assuage her guilt. So what that she had survived? Was that so important? Death was everywhere.

The soldier reached into the fire, pulled out a slice of newly defrosted bread, and threw it to Karen.

Karen grabbed it, passed it back and forth between her hands to let it cool, then neatly broke it in half. She stuffed one part in her coat pocket and the other in her mouth.

"I thought you haven't eaten in days?"

"I haven't."

"Then why don't you eat the whole slice?"

"Because then there will be no food for tomorrow."

"Tomorrow we will be safe. Tomorrow we will be in Leningrad."

Karen laughed. "Leningrad isn't safe."

"But it hasn't been conquered . . ."

Karen felt her face tighten up, deadly serious. "Leningrad is a death trap. There is no more dangerous place in the world."

"I think I just came from somewhere more dangerous."

"I doubt that."

"What do you know? An American."

"I know that if you go to Leningrad, they will eat your dog."

The soldier straightened. "What? Who will eat him?"

"The soldiers manning the trenches. They will shoot your dog and eat him before they even let you into the city."

"Why would they do something so barbaric?"

"Because dogs taste better than rats. And the rats have already been eaten."

The soldier stared at Karen. He didn't want to believe her, but Karen could tell that he did. "I don't have a choice. There is nowhere else to go."

"You're from the army, aren't you?"

"Yes."

"So go back to your unit."

"I don't think my unit exists anymore."

"Why? What happened to it?"

"It was overrun."

"Where? When?"

"Out there, somewhere. Three days ago."

"Then find another unit. The Second Shock Army is mounting an offensive soon."

"I am the Second Shock Army."

The feeling of despair that washed over Karen surprised her. She had grown so cynical about Soviet propaganda, so skeptical of everything the mayor ever said, that she was sure the Second Shock Army's supposed offensive was only a myth. But what the soldier was telling her was much worse. The Second Shock Army wasn't a myth; it was real, or at least it had been real up until three days ago. It was real, and it had failed. It had been decimated—an entire army overrun by the Germans. How could the Russians afford to take such losses and continue to fight? They couldn't. No military could. They were going to lose this war. The Germans were invincible. Leningrad would never be saved. The ice road over Lake Ladoga would eventually be severed. Every man, woman, and child left inside that city would eventually starve.

"So you see," the soldier added, "there is nowhere else to go."

Karen shook her head in growing panic. "No, no, you can't go back to Leningrad." She had to stop him. She was finally free of that city, and she couldn't allow him to drag her back there. "There is no food, no electricity."

"But the army—"

"Even the soldiers are starving!"

"I have nowhere else to go."

Karen stared at him, her mind turning, desperately grasping for any idea, any thought that might stop the soldier from forcing her back to Leningrad. "I have train tickets. Two. I'll give you one."

"Train tickets? What good are train tickets?"

"From Tikhvin to Moscow. On a troop train. If we can get to Tikhvin, we can get to Moscow."

"How do you know this?"

"I paid for the information."

"Money?"

"Food."

The soldier looked across the fire at Karen. He clearly didn't trust her. "Show me the ticket."

Karen hesitated. If she showed him the ticket, he might shoot her and take it. But what choice did she have? She couldn't escape, not with that dog watching her. She had to trust him. She took off her glove, reached into her coat, and pulled out one of the tickets. She held it before her. "See?"

The soldier peered and reached across the fire to take it, but Karen jerked her hand away. "No. I paid for it. I keep it."

"It has a name on it."

"It belonged to a wounded soldier. We will have to pretend."

"You will pretend to be a soldier?"

"There are woman soldiers." She was right. But that didn't mean the plan would work.

"We will be caught," the soldier said.

"How?"

"Your identity will be discovered."

"No, it won't."

"How can you be sure?"

"I'm a good liar."

The soldier paused, considering this. "Are you lying now?"

Karen nodded. "My name is Karen."

"You said it was Inna."

"I lied."

"You lie about a lot of things, don't you?"

"Yes," Karen nodded. "Yes, I do."

"But you're not lying about Leningrad, are you?"

"No."

"Then who is Inna?"

"My friend. The one killed in the potato field that I told you about."

"You have her identification papers?"

"Yes."

The boy pointed to her pocket where the train tickets were hidden. "And what about those soldiers? Do you have their identification?"

"No."

"Then how do you intend to pass yourself off?"

"We were defenders of the Nevsky Bridgehead. Heroes of the Soviet Union. We were wounded, unconscious, lucky to be evacuated. We lost our identification tags, and our papers were burned during an artillery attack."

The boy soldier blinked, impressed. The story was believable. He had seen bodies without ID tags often enough and had wondered what would happen to him if he were wounded without any identifying information.

Karen interrupted his thoughts. "I told you my real name. What is yours?"

"My name is Petr. He is Duck." He motioned toward the big wolf dog.

"Duck?"

"I didn't name him."

"Where did he come from?"

"I'm not sure. A family in Moscow, I think. He was drafted. Just like me."

Karen sat up. "If we reach Tikhvin, we can take a train to Moscow. Duck can be reunited with his family."

Petr shook his head. "Even if we could bluff our way onto the train, we would never make it all the way to Tikhvin. It is more than a hundred miles away. We'll freeze to death."

"There is wood. We can find food in villages, in fields. Like the potatoes I told you about."

"The Germans occupy the villages." Petr shook his head again. "We will be intercepted long before we reach Tikhvin. Leningrad is our only hope." He stood up and kicked snow on the fire to put it out.

"Then we have no hope at all."

The soldier reached down, lifted his pack, and slid it over his shoulder. The wolf dog seemed to recognize the gesture and leaped up to stand at the soldier's hip.

Karen remained sitting, her arms around her knees, looking up at the boy in despair.

"We have to leave," he said.

"I can't go back."

"Eventually a German patrol will happen by."

"I'll take my chances."

Petr lifted the gun and pointed it at Karen. "Perhaps you will, but I can't."

"You're going to shoot me?"

"If you don't come with me, yes."

"Why?"

"Because you will tell the Germans where I am."

"I told you, I am not a subversive."

"And I don't believe you. So get up."

Karen looked into Petr's eyes. She couldn't tell whether he would really shoot her. She couldn't take the risk. So reluctantly, she stood.

"You go first," he commanded, waving with the gun.

Karen trudged forward, into the tree line. The boy soldier, the dog at his side, followed close behind, continuing to aim the gun at her back.

———

The woods were silent and beautiful. It was already March, but winter still held Russia in its freezing grip. Thick snow twinkled on the forest floor, and icicles glistened in the tree branches. Karen had been in the woods before, but always at night, and now she was practically blinded by the sun's white glare. But then, suddenly, the forest changed. The picturesque winter scene drastically transformed into black, scorched earth, splintered wood, and deep craters. Beyond the scarred ground were Leningrad's defensive trenches, bristling with machine guns, and beyond those loomed the still-burning spires of the city. Karen halted, not daring to take another step forward out of the cover of the trees and into the black despair of no-man's-land.

Petr moved beside her in an instant. "What happened here?"

"The Germans shelled it."

"Why?"

"To prevent anyone from leaving the city." Karen pointed out the surrounding hills. "They have spotters there, there, and there. If you cross during the day, they call in artillery. It's a death trap."

"Why doesn't the Leningrad Army shell those hills and kill the forward observers?"

Karen shrugged. "I am not in command of the Leningrad Army."

Petr took a deep breath and looked out on no-man's-land. "We will have to wait until dark."

"If they hear anything, if they suspect anything, they will fire flares. And then they will shell you."

"Then how did you get out?"

"I had the cooperation of the Leningrad Army. The first time, Inna's sister let us through. The second time, the NKVD man's badge let us through. We didn't make any noise, so the Germans didn't hear us and didn't shell us."

"Then we won't make any noise, either."

"Yes, we will. We don't have the cooperation of the Leningrad Army."

"So?"

"So, when we get close to the defensive trenches, they will challenge us. The Germans will hear, and they will fire their artillery."

"How did you intend to get back into the city, then?"

"I told you, I never had any intention of returning to Leningrad."

"But the NKVD man must have. How did he intend to get back?"

"I don't know. You could ask him, but he's dead."

"Get down!" Petr dove to his stomach, and the dog followed. Karen looked around, confused for a moment, until she saw a group of people climbing out of the trenches into no-man's-land. She dropped down. "What are they doing?" Petr asked.

"Trying to escape." Karen watched as the distant crowd, probably a dozen or so individuals, picked their way over the broken ground of craters and splintered trees that formed no-man's-land.

"They're not soldiers."

Karen shook her head. "They're refugees."

"Why did the army let them pass?"

"They must have given them money or food."

Karen watched with dread as the refugees moved farther across no-man's-land. They appeared to be coming right toward them, hoping to reach the shelter of the trees. They hadn't quite made it halfway.

The soldier shaded his eyes from the sun and looked to the hills Karen had pointed out. "Nothing's happening. There must be no one there."

"They're there."

"Then why haven't they called in the artillery?"

"They're waiting. They want to make sure the refugees can't escape.

"We should cross now, while we have the chance." Petr tried to climb to his knees, but Karen grabbed him and pulled him back down. Surprisingly, the dog let her. He didn't even growl. An instant later, the sky began to whistle. Karen and Petr buried their heads in their arms. The explosions deafened them, and shock waves blew over them like a hurricane.

Karen's ears were still ringing when she looked up. The landscape had changed, but the new craters, fresh splinters, and scorched earth only looked like the old craters, dead splinters, and scorched earth. Smoke curled upward into the sunlight. The rotten smell of gunpowder choked the air. The refugees had vanished. Their body parts were somewhere, perhaps buried in newly turned earth. But there was no obvious sign of them. The heavy artillery had erased them from the face of the earth.

"Perhaps we should try Tikhvin, after all," Petr remarked.

Tears of relief welled in Karen's eyes. "Yes. Thank God."

CHAPTER 17

THE CHOIRBOY

Bobby stared at the blank page. Writing love letters was so difficult. Everything was a cliché. What hadn't been said before, by countless authors, all far greater writers than he? Nothing. "Dear Karen" was as far as he'd gotten. The rest of the page remained blank.

Suddenly his unfinished letter was snatched away, and Bobby looked up to see Jack Wright with the piece of paper in his hand.

"What are you wasting your time on this for?" Jack asked, holding the paper out of reach. "We got business tonight."

In Palm Beach, Jack and Bobby had just survived flight school together. They'd both just made lieutenant and graduated at the top of their cadet class. Bobby had always been a quick study, and the flight lessons came as easily as anything else he put his mind to. As for Jack, at first Bobby thought he was just naturally gifted. He was also a few years older than Bobby. But Bobby began to realize that Jack's ability was more than raw talent. It was skill. Somehow, somewhere, Jack had already learned to fly. The first time Jack climbed into his training aircraft's cockpit, he'd already known far more about airplanes than the other cadets and was even able to give his instructor a few tips.

Bobby eyed Jack warily. The older boy was taller, so it was no use trying to grab back the letter. "What are you talking about? What business?"

Jack didn't answer. Instead, he walked to the Quonset hut door and propped it open with his foot. A warm, humid breeze carried into the barracks, bringing with it the sweet scent of the ocean. "See that?" Jack asked, pointing at the huge and bright full moon. "You know what that is?"

"It's the moon."

"No, it's not. It's an opportunity."

"What do you mean—"

Jack put his finger to his lips, shushing Bobby. "Listen."

Another warm breeze rustled through the Quonset hut, and Bobby detected another sound. Music.

Jack saw Bobby strain to hear the notes, and he broke into a smile. "A big band's playing at the Everglades Club."

The Everglades Club was the most exclusive seaside resort in Palm Beach, a winter playground for the New York and Philadelphia social set. "We're not allowed at the Everglades Club," Bobby said.

"Yes, we are. We're officers now."

Jack was right. Technically, the Everglades Club was members only. But after Pearl Harbor, a patriotic fervor gripped the nation to which not even the wealthy were immune. Overnight they'd become fascinated with their boys in uniform, and especially the local boys at Morrison Army Air Field. Common soldiers were still deemed unfit for polite conversation, but officers weren't common soldiers. Officers were mostly college educated, after all, and were gentlemen. So every Saturday night the Everglades Club opened its doors to these dashing defenders of freedom, hosting so-called at-homes for the flight commanders and newly promoted aviators. And every Saturday night young men met young women and danced to big-band rhythms until the Everglades Club closed its Spanish revival doors and everyone was forced to go home, nurse hangovers, and dream of the following Saturday.

Neither Bobby nor Jack had ever been, of course, because until now they had been mere cadets. But as of the previous day, they were full-blown lieutenants.

Bobby should have known that Jack would immediately want to take advantage of their new status. "Why do you like rich girls so much, anyway?" he asked.

Jack's smile broadened. "What's not to like? They're girls. And they're rich."

Bobby decided not to tell Jack about his own disappointing experiences with the rich girls of Barnard College. Instead, he just said, "You should just go along without me."

Jack wasn't having it. "I wish it was that easy. But I need you."

"How come?"

"If you wanna catch babes, you need candy. And believe me, nothing's sweeter to a babe than a guy like you. Look at yourself. You're a kid Jimmy Stewart."

Bobby blushed. He knew he was being swindled. But he also knew that no one, not even him, was immune to flattery like Jack's. Better just to give in now than drag this out. "Fine. I'll get dressed."

"Don't forget to wear your wings. The girls love a pilot."

The five-mile journey to the Everglades Club was a beautiful drive through West Palm Beach. As they crossed the channel bridge, Bobby stared out the open-topped jeep at the big, round reflection of the moon in the water below. "What's the moon got to do with it, anyway?" he asked.

"You'll see," Jack responded.

The at-home event of the Everglades Club was like nothing even Bobby had ever seen. It was a bigger, louder, classier high school prom, for starters. The clean white walls of the Grand Ballroom glistened with silver-framed photographs of members having fun on the beach, on tennis courts, and on golf courses. Crystal chandeliers cast warm, sparkling light over hundreds of champagne bottles; scores of exotic flower arrangements; and a dozen brass trumpets, trombones, and saxophones. Cigar and cigarette smoke twisted in a sultry dance toward the high arched ceiling. Below, couples young and old bounced back and forth in energetic fox-trots. Everyone was smiling, everyone was happy, and even Bobby had to admit that the women looked delicious.

Their chiffon, silk, and rayon evening gowns were folded into pleated petals that swept the ballroom floor. The girls' bodies were like the stems of inverted flowers. And what bodies they were! Halter tops formed plunging necklines and revealed bare backs that left little to the imagination. Ribbons, sashes, and belts cinched narrow waists, emphasizing the curve of hip and thigh. Cream, rose, and white cloth contrasted with Palm Beach tans. Blonde, auburn, brunette, and raven hair, carefully rolled back in curling waves, revealed even more sensuous skin on necks and shoulders, the visual feast of flesh broken only by the glitter of choker necklaces and flashing diamond earrings.

Jack had already cornered two of the prettiest specimens, confidently leaning forward with his arm propped against the wall behind them, effectively pinning the girls like beautiful butterflies in a framed display. Their names were Mollie and Ellen—the former, a perky auburn beauty, and the latter, a sultry brunette who reminded Bobby of Karen. The two girls were cousins, twenty and nineteen, respectively, and were down for the weekend from college, chaperoned by what they described as their "wild aunt." By their own admission, they were having the time of their lives.

Jack was right about the wings. Neither Mollie nor Ellen could keep her eyes off the chrome pins that marked the boys as pilots. Ellen even reached out to run her fingers over Bobby's silver wings, and he felt a thrill when she withdrew her hand and accidentally brushed her fingers against his neck.

"Why'd you join up?" she asked innocently.

Bobby was tongue-tied. What was happening? Had he had too much champagne? No, that wasn't it, he suddenly realized with shame. It was because he couldn't tell her the truth. Telling the truth would mean telling her about Karen. "Just, you know, felt it was my duty and all that."

"My brother joined the naval reserve," Mollie bragged.

"He'll be good, too," Ellen added. "He was the club sailing champion last summer."

Jack laughed. "I don't think the navy uses sailboats anymore."

Ellen reddened with embarrassment. "I know. I just mean he's a natural on the water, that's all."

"I'm sure he is," Bobby reassured her.

"He just hopes there'll still be fighting left for him when he graduates from college," asserted Mollie. "He figures we'll whip the Japs inside of six months."

"Sure," Jack agreed. "The Japs can't beat us in a stand-up fight. But the Huns, they're a different story. We'll lick 'em eventually, but it'll take a little longer."

Bobby picked up on Jack's braggadocio. "But we'll be sure to leave a few for your brother."

"How about you?" Mollie asked Jack with a flirtatious smile. "You joined up to fight the Germans?"

Jack suddenly looked serious, almost brooding. "No. I joined up to fly. Fighting's just a bonus."

"What's so great about flying?" Mollie asked.

"Everything," Jack insisted. And he left it at that.

A few hours later, Bobby found himself in the back of the jeep, his arms wrapped around Ellen's lithe body, feeling her stomach spasm as she laughed deliriously. Jack was behind the wheel, Mollie in his lap, and the ocean flowed beneath them all. The jeep cut into the surf like a speedboat, parting the water into two rooster tails of spray that glowed in the moonlight. Jack spun the wheel left, then right, and as the warm water splashed over him, Bobby realized that his friend was intentionally trying to soak the girls.

Jack finally pulled out of the surf onto the sand and put the jeep in neutral. "Maybe we ought to get you out of those wet clothes," he boldly suggested to the girls.

Mollie slapped him and climbed out of his lap into the passenger seat. Bobby inwardly groaned. Maybe he should have warned Jack about rich girls, after all.

Mollie straightened her wet evening gown indignantly. "I think you should take us home."

But Bobby had underestimated his new friend. This was all part of Jack's plan.

"I only thought, you'd want to learn to fly," Jack said with mock innocence.

Mollie looked at him, uncertain and wary. "What do you mean 'fly'? I'll have you know I'm not the kind of girl—"

"I mean really fly, in an airplane. Bobby and I could teach you." He glanced over the seat at Ellen. "We could teach you both."

Now it was Bobby's turn to stare, mouth wide in wonder. How far was Jack planning on taking this farce?

Mollie looked intrigued, but still she was cautious. "Isn't it hard?"

"No," Jack assured her, "it's not hard. I could teach you easy. Heck, I taught myself."

"I thought the army taught you," interjected a skeptical Ellen.

"Naw, the Army Air Forces didn't teach me anything. I knew how to fly before I joined up. Isn't that right, Bobby?"

"It's true." So it was true. Jack had never admitted it until now, and Bobby was fascinated. What was Jack up to?

"Oh yeah?" quizzed Mollie, arms crossing her chest for protection. "Then who taught you?"

"Like I said, I taught myself."

What followed was a story that Bobby could never verify but Jack insisted was the gospel truth. Jack claimed that he learned to fly when he was fourteen. That was when his father died, leaving him with a biplane, a crop-dusting business, and two younger brothers to feed.

Jack's mother decided to sell the plane and use the money to move to Chicago. She spent the last of their savings to put a "For Sale" ad in the paper and locked the biplane in the barn. Jack didn't want to move to the city. He just wanted to fly. He'd loved the wind in his face and the goggles over his eyes and the stomach-wrenching acceleration when his father dived low to the earth before releasing the pesticide. Jack knew what that felt like because he'd always begged his father to take him, and his father seldom refused. Jack had been in the plane so often, and he'd watched his father so closely, that he was absolutely certain he could take the controls himself.

Which was why, on an evening he'd specially chosen for its full moon, Jack crept out of bed, snuck out of the house, and cut the barn's padlock with a pair of his father's shears. The World War I–surplus Curtiss Jenny inside weighed thirteen hundred pounds. If Jack taxied it out to the field, the sound of the engine might wake his mother. So he hitched the plane to Bess, the family dairy cow, and forced the unhappy creature to help him move the airplane out.

The improvisation worked until Jack started the engine. The racket of the eight cylinders spooked Bess, and she disappeared into the neighboring woods. Jack decided to ignore her for the moment, turned the biplane into the slight breeze, and gunned the throttle. As he took off, he cleared the woods on the edge of the fallow field and caught sight of black-and-white Bess trotting away from him in terror. Jack banked and rolled and dived, buzzing Bess and sending the cow into a panic. She leaped and turned like a prize bull at a rodeo before bolting back in the direction from which she'd come, back onto the family's land. With his impromptu herding done, Jack decided to climb into the sky and enjoy the moonlit view.

He ran the plane almost to empty on that inaugural flight. He watched the Curtiss Jenny's moon shadow race across the fields and forests far below. When he finally reached the last of his fuel, he turned back and prepared to land.

Landing was a lot trickier than it looked. His first couple of attempts almost resulted in disaster. He pointed the airplane down toward the fallow field and dived. But that only increased his speed, and as the earth rushed up to meet him, he realized that his propeller, not the landing gear, would be the first to hit ground. Both times he pulled out of the dive in the nick of time.

Only his lack of fuel saved him. On his third landing attempt, he found himself once again in an unintentional dive. Once again he yanked up on the yoke, and again the Jenny jerked up to pull out of the dive. But at that moment it ran out of gas. The engine died, and Jack felt himself falling. The nose of the aircraft was pitching upward at over ten degrees, so Jack could no longer see the ground. All he could see were the twinkling stars on the horizon. But to his surprise and relief, the biplane began to slow as it fell. It fluttered like a kite without a string until Jack felt the force of the tail hitting the ground. He was thrown forward against his harness when, an instant later, the landing gear also slammed down. And then he was bouncing along uncomfortably as the Curtiss Jenny taxied uncontrollably across the plowed surface of the fallow field—and right into the communal watering pond.

The next day Jack and his mother hired a few transient laborers to help pull the Curtiss Jenny out of the mud and the muck. Remarkably, the plane hadn't suffered serious damage. A few days later it was dried out and ready to fly again.

His mother wasn't angry, just glad he'd survived. It also convinced his mother to let him try to take up his father's business. She secured the contracts, bought the leading arsenate for crop dusting and superphos-phate for top dressing, and even secured occasional postal-service sub-contracts for mail hauling. They hired a Canadian Great War vet turned American hobo, Jimmy Hunt, as a maintenance mechanic. Jack did the actual flying. And together they managed to save the family business.

But the more Jack flew, the more he yearned for greater challenges. Jimmy Hunt often told Jack stories about the "Knights of the Sky" who fought in the Great War. Jimmy hadn't been a pilot. But as a mechanic, he'd had a front-row seat for the acrobatic dogfights between aces like Kenneth Conn, Heinrich Kroll, Joseph Fall, and Paul Billik. Hearing those stories, Jack realized that air combat would be the ultimate flight test. He had to join the army. But he also knew he couldn't make the mistake Jimmy Hunt had made. Only officers could be pilots. So Jack needed a college education. He set aside enough money for correspon-dence courses, and as soon as he received his diploma, he enlisted.

"And so here I am," Jack concluded with a cockeyed smile. "Wearing my army wings and offering you girls a chance to fly."

Mollie bit her lip and glanced nervously over the car seat at Ellen. "What do you think?"

Ellen looked up at Bobby's face, his features soft in the warm moon-light. Whom did she see there? Bobby or a young Jimmy Stewart? She pulled his arms tighter around her waist. "I feel safe," she said. And that settled it.

Fifteen minutes later, the girls waited in the jeep while Jack and Bobby snuck into the hangar and prepared the planes. They were P-39 Airacobras, the most powerful aircraft either Jack or Bobby had ever flown. And Bobby was nervous. Not because he feared flying the high-performance airplanes, but because he was afraid they'd be caught.

Jack tried to reassure him. "You know how many girls I took up in the Jenny?"

"These aren't old biplanes."

"So what?"

"So we're stealing military property."

"Borrowing it."

"We could be arrested."

"You asked about the full moon earlier. They call it a hunter's moon because it's bright enough to hunt by. It's also bright enough to fly by, which means we won't need lights, which means we won't get caught. Trust me."

"But the Airacobra's a single-seater."

"All the better. That just means Ellen's gonna have to sit in your lap. She'll love it. I told you, I've done this before."

"These aren't farm girls, they're socialites."

"What's the difference?"

"It's a world of difference."

"That's where you're wrong. These girls, they've been sheltered their whole lives, chaperoned by crazy aunts everywhere they go, warned not to take risks. You take one of these girls up in a plane, you give her that thrill, and you bring her back down again safe and sound, you know what happens?"

"What happens?"

"She realizes Mommy and Daddy were wrong about taking risks. Risks can be fun. And they start to wonder what else Mommy and Daddy were wrong about."

Bobby gave in.

Jack was right about taking off. The Army's Third Air Force was still in an expansion phase, desperately trying to recruit and train as many pilots and ground personnel as possible, and quickly expanding beyond Morrison Army Air Field into the hotels and boardinghouses of West Palm Beach. The result was temporary chaos that wasn't helped by the tropical surroundings and friendly local females. Jack taxied quietly through the airfield, leading Bobby, with Ellen in his lap, through a maze of tarmacs until they bounced onto a little-used emergency gravel runway. Then he gunned the engine and roared into the night sky.

Bobby followed close behind. Ellen's breath caught in her throat at the g-forces of the sudden climb. But then she pressed her forehead against the cockpit canopy and gasped in awe at the lights of Palm Beach receding behind her. "They're beautiful!" she exclaimed.

"Have a closer look." Bobby twisted the yoke, and the plane yawed into a barrel roll. Ellen grabbed Bobby hard around the neck in terror as he leveled out upside down. "It's OK," he reassured her.

Ellen looked down through the Airacobra's bubble glass canopy at the city that lay before her, a twinkling map. She smiled in amazement at the cars, small as toys, leaving the Everglades Club. Bobby couldn't help notice that gravity had pulled the hem of her dress all the way up to her waist. He admired her garters for a moment before twisting back into a barrel roll and straightening the plane.

He'd adjusted the Airacobra just in time, for Jack suddenly dived and banked across the Florida peninsula, picking up speed and leaving Palm Beach far behind. Bobby barely kept up. It was only twenty-five miles to the massive Everglades swamp that dominated this part of Florida, and the fast Airacobras covered that distance in less than six minutes. Bobby followed Jack as he buzzed the pine forest that separated east Florida from the swampy wilderness; he matched Jack's every move. The two planes performed a high-speed aerial dance as Jack led them into a tall upside-down loop, a twisting corkscrew descent, and then buzzed so close to the flat waters of the tepid swamp that the downdraft created a rooster-tail wake as tall as the one caused by the jeep earlier in the evening. The bucking g-forces of each maneuver caused Ellen to clutch Bobby wherever she could, holding on for dear life. She completely forgot about Bobby's hands. Bobby found himself grabbing and holding taboo regions of flesh, her inner upper thighs, upper ribs, and even straight across her bosom. Before things got out of control, he straightened the plane and climbed higher into the night sky. As Ellen settled back into a modest position on his lap, they both had to catch their breath. Ellen looked over her shoulder at Bobby, staring at him, then sweetly asked, "Can I try?"

Bobby nodded, took his left arm out from around her waist, held her right hand in his own, and placed it on top of the yoke. "Just be gentle with the stick," he warned.

Ellen giggled. And then she was all concentration, biting her lip, staring through the canopy at the field of stars that spread out before them. "Like this?" she asked. She moved the stick to the right, and the plane responded instantly, banking into a wide turn.

"Perfect," Bobby said. "Now straighten her out and keep this heading. You'll fly us right home."

Ellen beamed.

As soon as the Airacobras landed, slowed, and the army's newest air force pilots had popped the glass canopies, Ellen and Mollie leaped to the gravel runway and ran off hugging each other with peals of excited laughter. Bobby and Jack leaped out after them and pulled them apart in a panic, cautioning them to stay quiet at least until they could get the planes back to their hangars undetected.

When they drove into the Everglades Club, Mollie directed Jack to a rear entrance because it was already well past curfew. Ellen pulled Bobby close and gave him a good-night hug. But as she held him, she lifted her lips to his ear and asked whether he'd like to come inside. Bobby was surprised. What about her crazy aunt chaperone? Mollie overheard and reassured both Bobby and Jack that their aunt would be asleep by now. They could sneak right past her into their bedrooms for a nightcap. Jack smiled at Bobby and winked. "What'd I tell ya?"

Bobby nodded at Jack and then looked down at the pretty girl he still held in his arms. Her rolled-back hair had been blown free, leaving her dark curls in a tangled, passionate mess. Her halter top, still damp and heavy from the wild jeep ride, hung even lower than designed, exposing the lacy top of her bra. The chiffon pleats of her dress had been made sheer by the water, and he could see the outline of her long legs. And when he looked into her eyes, he was once again reminded of Karen.

But she was not Karen. He slowly extracted himself from Ellen's embrace. "I can't. I've gotta get back."

Jack stared at him in disbelief. "Are you kidding me?"

"No, I'm not kidding. I gotta go."

Jack chuckled and shook his head with disappointment. "Then you can park the jeep back in the motor pool." He tossed the keys, and Bobby snatched them out of the air.

He turned his attention back to Ellen. "I'm sorry."

"Don't be sorry," she said gently. "I had the best night of my life."

That made Bobby smile. He climbed into the jeep and started the ignition. Then he put it in drive and turned away from the club. When he looked back over his shoulder, Jack, Mollie, and Ellen were long gone.

He spent the rest of the drive home thinking of Karen.

CHAPTER 18

THE CELLIST AND THE ORGAN-GRINDER

Neither Karen nor Petr knew how to get to Tikhvin. They had to travel during the day now, since their only point of direction was the sun. If they traveled at night, they could very easily walk in circles without even knowing it. Karen had a map, but it offered little help without landmarks. Every patch of woods looked like every other patch of woods. So, when after a day and a half of tromping through the thick snow they stumbled upon the icy ruts of a frozen road, Petr decided that their best option was just to follow it. This was dangerous, possibly exposing them to German patrols, but it was either that or remain lost in the woods forever. And, as Karen had predicted, Petr wasn't yet acclimated to the constant pain of hunger as she was. In a few days, he'd finished the last of his military rations, and the forest offered few nutrients. He grew desperate for food.

The road didn't exactly head in the direction of Tikhvin, but eventually, Petr reasoned, it would lead them to a crossroads or, at the very least, a village or farm where they might be able to find provisions. Karen was less convinced. But she wasn't in charge of this expedition, Petr was. He was the leader by virtue of having a gun. Karen didn't trust Petr, so she tried not to speak to him. When he asked her questions, she tried to limit her answers to short one-word responses. And she, in turn, asked nothing of him. He was a member of the Red Army, a Communist, and a patriot. He first met her when she was under arrest by an NKVD agent. Karen was certain that as soon as they reached Tikhvin, Petr would turn her over to the local authorities and report that she'd killed an NKVD man, thus satisfying his distorted sense of patriotic justice. For that reason alone, Karen had to try to get away somehow. But so long as Petr had that gun, she was at his mercy.

One night Karen tried to steal his gun. She waited until the sound of his breathing told her he was asleep. She crept onto her hand and knees. Then she moved silently toward him. But that wolf dog of his began to growl, waking Petr. Karen pretended that she'd woken up to relieve herself. Fortunately, Petr seemed to believe her.

The dog was growing hungry, too. Karen could tell. He'd always eyed her, but now he eyed her as though he wanted to eat her. The feeling was mutual. She even suggested to Petr that dog meat was quite tender. The implication horrified him. The truth was that Karen had never eaten dog. But she knew that so long as this dog Duck lived, she was trapped. She couldn't possibly steal the gun and escape with the dog eyeing her every move. She had to kill the hound. Yet if Petr got hungry enough, perhaps he could be convinced to do the job for her. It was the only way. He probably didn't realize that, having been much better fed recently, he'd have plenty of reserve energy to burn before he became truly desperate. Meanwhile, she had to bide her time. She didn't have much of it. She would starve before Petr, since she was half-starved already. She was growing weak, so weak. And the ceaseless marching wasn't helping.

They followed the road but always kept a line of trees between themselves and the frozen ruts. When Karen did try to walk the road, she slipped on the ice and tumbled painfully to her knees. The road was like an uneven and chunky ice-skating rink.

Though their purpose was stealth, the forest floor was simply easier to negotiate. Petr's boots and Karen's shoes were too small, and with every step they sank in the snow to their knees. But then Petr chopped four long walking sticks from the birch trees. They still sank with every step, but by using the sticks like ski poles, they were able to pull their legs from the grasping snow without even breaking stride.

At night they moved farther from the road, built a fire, and used it to warm their snow-encrusted shoes and socks. They hoped they were deep enough into the trees that German patrols would be unable to see the light of the flames or detect the fire's smoke. They made good progress in this manner, and, despite the winter conditions, Karen felt warmer than she had in Leningrad.

They ran into German convoys twice. The first time the sound of shouting and roaring machinery warned them well ahead of time. They sneaked deep into the woods and waited for the Germans to pass. But the Germans didn't pass. They kept yelling and revving their engines in the same spot. Eventually curiosity overcame Petr, and they crept up through the woods toward the sound. Three German trucks were stuck. Drivers, covered head to toe in hoods and overcoats, were trying to push the trucks. But every time they gunned the throttle, the wheels would spin against the ice, and the trucks would settle deeper in the hard ruts. Petr and Karen retreated into the trees undiscovered, giving the Germans a wide berth, and rejoined the road a mile farther on.

Clearly, the Germans were having trouble moving their supplies. The second time Karen and Petr didn't hear engines or yelling. They heard the clip-clop of hooves and the sound of heavy breathing. They dropped to the ground and hid moments before another German convoy neared. The trucks had been hitched to teams of heavy farm horses, and the trucks' windshields were folded down so the drivers could hold the reins. The big horses' hooves clattered against the icy road, and the beasts panted with every step, working hard to keep their balance on the slick surface and simultaneously drag the burdens hitched behind them. The trucks were like big sledges, sliding rather than rolling over the road. But the ad hoc arrangement worked. The trucks moved onward, passing Petr, Karen, and Duck. Then a soldier riding in the back noticed something. He banged on the truck's cab, and the driver pulled the reins, halting the big horses. The soldier jumped down from the truck bed and crouched, absorbing the force of gravity in his knees. He unslung his MP40 submachine gun, a dangerous weapon at close range. The German released the safety and started marching toward them, leaving the ruts.

All Karen and Petr had between them was the NKVD man's pistol. But any noise would only alert the rest of the Germans. Karen glanced nervously at Petr. Would he reach the same conclusion as Sasha? Would he sacrifice both their lives in a stupid act of pointless courage? She saw Petr reaching into his uniform jacket and had her answer—he was going for his gun. Why did men always do things that were so stupid?

But then Petr surprised her. When he pulled his hand out of his coat, he was holding a chrome whistle. What was he doing? A whistle would give them away immediately. Karen held her breath as she watched Petr blow. The whistle didn't make a sound. But Duck reacted instantly. He broke from his cover and ran straight for the trucks, passing right between the legs of the shocked German soldier.

The whistle had emitted a high-frequency sound that only dogs could hear. They were distributed to the handlers as a fail-safe mechanism—in case the antitank commander was killed before he could blow his lead signal, individual handlers could command their dogs to attack without giving away their hidden positions.

The Alsatian wolf dog didn't bark or growl; he just ran straight from the woods into the icy road. The Germans had no idea what Duck was. Nothing made him look like a Russian weapon. He wasn't wearing his mine jacket; Petr had long since stowed it in his pack. And since he was a German shepherd, the soldiers might even believe that he came from a German unit somewhere.

Instead of trying to shoot the dog, they jumped out of their trucks and tried to grab him. Duck jumped and sprang and sprinted under and between the vehicles. The Germans bounded after him, slipping on the ice and laughing. It must have felt like a wonderful game and a welcome distraction from the drudgery of soldiering. But they didn't know that Duck wasn't playing. He was working. He was running under the trucks because that's what he was trained to do. If he'd been wearing his bomb vest, he would have exploded. They couldn't catch him. The German with the MP40 managed to grab him around the neck, but the slick ice that coated both of them allowed Duck to wiggle away easily.

As Duck and the soldiers gallivanted in the snow, Petr and Karen fled. After blowing the whistle, Petr climbed back to his feet and waved silently for Karen to follow him. She hesitated. This was, after all, a chance to escape. But where else could she go? The road was swarming with Germans.

They moved through the woods at a careful trot, trying to avoid making more noise than Duck. But once they gained more distance, they broke into a full run, stomping through the snow and crashing through the tree branches. Then they slowed to a fast march, having exhausted themselves, and tried to catch their breath.

Petr blew on his silent whistle.

Unbeknownst to the German soldiers, Duck heard the ultrasonic shriek. He turned a full circle, leaped through a lunging soldier's arms, bounced like a rabbit through the snow, and disappeared back into the tree line. The laughing Germans pulled themselves up off the ice and gave chase. But Duck, with his four swift legs, easily outran his pursuers, and the Germans quickly gave up, leaning on their wet knees, panting.

Duck dodged under a fallen tree and leaped over underbrush to pass into a clearing dominated by a small hunting shack. It was a simple A-frame cabin constructed from hewn wood and corrugated tin. The dog knew where he was going—he just had to follow his nose. He trotted up to the hunting shack's plank door, jumped up against it, and scratched with his forepaws. A moment later, the door opened, and Duck tumbled inside. He immediately shook, spraying snow melted by his body heat all over the interior of the shack.

Neither Karen nor Petr cared one bit. They were busy piling tinder in the cabin's wood-burning stove. Finding the shack had been a miracle—one for which they had the German soldiers to thank. If the Germans hadn't sent them away from the road and into the forest, they never would've found this cozy little refuge. And if they hadn't had found the cabin, they never would have rifled through its crates. And if they hadn't rifled through its crates, they never would have found the paper bags of dried macaroni, untouched and unspoiled, just waiting to fill a hunter's stomach.

Karen began to eat the macaroni raw, savoring its crunch. But Petr ran outside to gather wood and snow. The snow he piled into his steel helmet, which he placed on top of the stove. Karen grasped what he was doing and lent a hand. But they had to wait until nightfall. The Germans were still out there, still close. They needed darkness to mask the smoke from the wood-burning stove. There wasn't much daylight in the far Russian north, so they didn't have long to wait, though it felt like an eternity. As soon as the sun sank beneath the horizon, they jumped into action, together coaxing the fire to heat up the helmet, boil the slush, and cook the noodles.

That night they ate like kings. It was just plain macaroni, overcooked to a soupy consistency in the boiled snow. There was no sauce, no butter, no cheese, and no meat. But to Karen it was ambrosia. Her palate had come to expect stale, sawdust-filled bread dipped in a broth made from wallpaper glue. Axle-grease and pine-needle tea had helped her survive through the darkest days of the Leningrad winter. Even her hard-won potatoes, which had cost the lives of two loyal friends, had been freeze-dried and unappetizingly chewy by the time Karen could eat them. These noodles, on the other hand, were warm and soft. She slurped them down her throat and filled the empty space in her stomach that she had never believed would be filled again. Predictably, her eyes were larger than her stomach, as her insides had shrunk with her emaciation. She and Petr cooked three bags of the macaroni at once, but Karen couldn't even finish a single meager bowl. She didn't care. She fed what was left in her bowl to Duck. The big dog grinned as he sucked up noodles with his long tongue.

Karen lay on the floor of the cabin next to the warm wood stove, closed her eyes, and savored the feeling in her gut. For the first time in months, it hurt not because she was hungry, but because she was full.

The next morning, Karen was alarmed to find Duck curled up beside her. She could feel his chest and stomach expanding with every breath. She opened her eyes and saw that Petr was asleep, too, his back propped up against the wall on the other side of the cabin, where, she realized, he was positioned to intercept anyone coming through the single door. Petr was no Sasha, Karen decided. He was smart. He was a survivor. He'd proven that over the past few days, which only meant it would be that much harder to escape from him.

She returned her attention to the sleeping dog. She wondered whether she could get up without waking him. She knew she couldn't. And, perhaps more important, she didn't want to. She could feel the warmth of his body radiating from his fur and through her coat. The warmth invited her to forget her fear of the wolf dog. She dared to take off her gloves and run her fingers through his soft winter coat. Duck didn't growl or snap or bite. Instead, he murmured some sound from under his breath and rolled over onto his back. Karen smiled and rubbed the coarse fur that covered the dog's belly.

"He likes you." It was Petr, who had woken and was watching her from across the cabin.

Karen didn't stop scratching the dog. "Only because I fed him."

"I thought you wanted to eat him."

"I did," Karen replied. But it wasn't the truth, and for some reason she felt compelled to admit it. "No, I didn't. Not really. I was scared of him. I wanted to get rid of him."

"Are you still scared of him?"

"I should be." But she wasn't. Not with him lying on his back like that, his neck curling around and his tongue lolling out of his mouth in ecstasy.

"Yes. Perhaps you should be. We're all three of us killers."

Karen laughed. She couldn't help it. It was so absurd. She, a seventeen-year-old girl, a musician—a cellist, of all things—ninety pounds in wet clothes, described as a killer. And this dog, so soft, so furry, making that strange noise—what was that noise? Was he purring? It sounded like purring. How could this creature be a killer? And the boy soldier, not much older than she—filthy, soft-spoken, so trusting of the NKVD man and, she suddenly realized, so trusting of her. How could he be a killer? If she'd met either one of them under normal circumstances, she would never have been afraid; she would never have felt threatened. They seemed like such gentle souls. But these weren't normal circumstances. They were dangerous circumstances. And, Karen knew, in dangerous times gentle souls died. Looks could be deceiving. This boy and this dog were no gentle souls. Like her, they were killers. They had to be because, like her, they had survived. And they were patriots. So they were dangerous.

"Why are you laughing?" Petr asked.

"You wouldn't understand."

Petr nodded. "Probably not." He looked at her in silence. "You know what I'm thinking?"

"What?"

"I'm thinking there's a reason there was so much macaroni."

"And what reason is that?"

"I wouldn't be surprised if there were wild mushrooms, too, during the summer."

"It isn't the summer."

"But there are deer."

"You think?" Karen said.

"There would have to be, wouldn't there? Why else would someone build this shack? It's a hunting shack—a shack built for hunting."

Karen peered at Petr, suspicious. "What are you planning?"

"How many bags of noodles are left?"

"About a half dozen."

"If I could find a deer, we could cook it with meat."

"How could you find a deer?"

"By hunting it."

"You know how to hunt?"

"Yes."

"In the winter?"

"Yes."

"Then what are you waiting for?"

Petr smiled and climbed to his feet. "Come on, Duck." The Alsatian wolf dog somersaulted to his feet and bounded for the door. Petr held it open, and the dog leaped outside. "Don't start a fire. The Germans might see the smoke."

"I'm not an idiot."

"I'll see you soon."

"Good luck."

Petr slammed the door behind him, and Karen continued to lie where she was, imagining the meat. It would be so good if Petr really did find a deer, if he really did manage to kill it. Karen wondered how much meat one deer could provide. A few days' worth? A week's worth? She had no idea. Even if it were only a few days, that would be a few days of heaven . . . a few days of not having to march, of not having to survive . . . a few days of just relaxing and eating and regaining her strength. It was so tempting. But she couldn't afford to give in to that temptation. She had to stay strong.

Karen could hear Petr outside, trudging farther away from the shack. She sat still and silent until she couldn't hear him anymore. And then she sat still and silent for ten more minutes. Finally, when she was sure that he was gone, she got up, carefully crossed the squeaking floor, and opened the door just a crack. No one was there. She opened it wider and stuck her head out so that she could look in every direction. The clearing was empty. She shut the door and moved back to the crates. She rifled through them and found the one with the macaroni. She grabbed two full bags and stuffed them in her pockets. She stuffed another bag in the hem of her skirt, and a fourth under her hat. She couldn't carry any more, and four bags of dried noodles ought to last her long enough to reach Tikhvin, anyway. Besides, she still wanted to leave some for Petr. She didn't dislike the boy soldier, and she didn't wish him any ill will. She certainly didn't want him to starve to death. She just wanted to leave him, to escape. So she took out her train tickets, unfolded the one she had extra, and left it in the crate for him secured between the two remaining bags of noodles. See? She wasn't a killer, after all.

Karen then opened the door and stepped outside. She looked up at the sun to get her bearings, turned southwest, and plunged into the woods, alone.

CHAPTER 19
THE GOATHERD

Unteroffizier Oster kicked the trunk of a birch tree in an effort to knock the crusted ice from his jackboot. He resented having to leave the village to patrol the woods, even if the tiny cottages that his platoon used as their winter quarters were awful. They were cramped, filthy, and infested with vermin. Never would Oster have believed he could live in such squalor. He thought of his own home in Bavaria, and his wife. She was not a beautiful woman—not by any objective aesthetic standards. She was plump and ruddy and even a bit hairy. But she was his, and he was hers. That was the worst part of the army, being separated from the woman he loved. He'd been serving on the Eastern Front since before the invasion in June, and he was due some time off. He wasn't just any *Unteroffizier*; he was a full sergeant and squad leader, after all. When spring came, he was sure, his unit would be rotated out of the line, and he would return home for two weeks' leave—two blissful weeks of peace.

He was not a rich man. His home, a shepherd's cottage, was not much bigger than the Russian building he lived in now. But it was much cleaner. He took pride in keeping his home whitewashed, replacing the shingles, and maintaining the grounds. His wife took pride in her cleaning. Not like these filthy Russian Bolsheviks. Thanks to them, he had lice. Thanks to them, he'd contracted parasites so that he could no longer have a meal without immediately having to defecate. Thanks to them, his uniform and beard and hair were filthy. No wonder the German leadership had declared them "undesirables." They had no pride, not in themselves or in one another. They deserved to starve to death. Such was official German policy: Don't feed the undesirables. Let them die out. This land would be better off under the stewardship of German, not Slavic, families.

But despite the squalor, the discomfort, and the humiliating filth, Oster had grown to love his Russian village. Because as dirty as the cottages were, they were warm. The woods, to the contrary, were freezing cold.

As Oster's reconnaissance squad patrolled the woods, many of his men gathered too close around him, raising the *Unteroffizier*'s ire. "Don't just laze about," he commanded. "Spread out. Watch out for the enemy."

"There is no enemy, *Herr Unteroffizier*," replied *Gefreiter* Krause, slapping his arms across his chest in an effort to stay warm. Oster swallowed his disgust. He knew soldiers like Corporal Krause, soldiers who Oster believed would never amount to anything. They shirked every duty, including combat. They'd joined the army before the war because they liked the prestige a uniform afforded them. That prestige grew after the battle of France, no thanks to them, and until the winter of '41, they'd thought soldiering was eating three square meals, marching in parades, and kissing a pretty Fräulein. In short, soldiers like Krause were a thorn in Oster's side, but the *Unteroffizier* didn't believe he'd ever be rid of the slacker.

Of course, Krause wasn't the only slacker in the *Unteroffizier's* squad; he was just the worst and most obvious culprit. It was an unpublicized fact that only half of any rifle squad did any actual fighting. When things got nasty and bullets began to fly, much of the squad simply shot their rifles into the air instead of actually aiming at the enemy. For some, like Krause, it was an act of cowardice: aiming required lifting one's head and exposing it to enemy fire. For others, it was an act of misguided compassion. They simply couldn't bring themselves to kill another human being purposefully, so they intentionally missed.

In France, *Unteroffizier* Oster had learned that most of his job as squad leader was identifying the cowards, the compassionate, and the killers. He armed and deployed each accordingly. The cowards were worthless, so, much to their dismay, he deployed them in the most forward positions. There they could act as decoys, drawing fire away from the more combat-ready members of the squad. And if they ran, they would have to run right past Oster, who would threaten to shoot them himself if they didn't hold their line. The compassionate were somewhat less worthless. They were unreliable in an assault, but they could hold their positions and defend themselves. In fact, if they survived an enemy attack, they overcame their natural inhibitions against killing. Once they faced the prospect of "kill or be killed," practicality prevailed over their Christian upbringings, and they began to aim for the enemy's heart.

The most important members of Oster's squad were the killers, and Oster's most ruthless killer was a man named Pfeiffer. He was small and scrawny, but he enjoyed fighting and sought out conflict, be it in a beer garden or a field of battle. Pfeiffer was the type of thug Oster would have avoided in civilian life. But in a combat squad he was invaluable. This was why Oster had assigned Pfeiffer his squad's most important weapon: the heavy machine gun. The MG-34 was, perhaps, too large a weapon for the diminutive Pfeiffer. Many leaders assigned the heavy gun to their largest and strongest squad member. Pfeiffer looked comical dragging around the big weapon. He preferred not to sling it over his shoulder like a rifle, since the strap dug into his flesh. So he carried it behind his neck, both arms propping it in place, and as he marched he looked like he was affixed to a cross. It was an ungainly posture, and in a firefight, valuable seconds were often lost while Pfeiffer untangled himself from the gun before setting it up. But Oster didn't care. He felt it was more important to have a killer like Pfeiffer manning the gun than someone stronger but less dangerous.

The MG-34 was the weapon around which every German infantry squad was organized. The only purpose of the rest of the soldiers was to support the machine gun. Their bolt-action rifles only served to keep the enemy pinned down until the deadly fire of the machine gun could kill them. For that reason, the other killers in Oster's squad were given extra machine-gun ammunition. So long as the machine gun was operational and was constantly fed linked belts of ammunition, it didn't much matter what the rest of the riflemen did. Pfeiffer was the one causing casualties among the enemy.

"If there's no enemy, why do you think we're patrolling the woods?" Oster asked Krause.

"To find the dog," Krause replied.

It was true. Their reconnaissance patrol had been hastily organized and sent into the wilderness after a supply convoy arrived in their village and described an odd encounter with an Alsatian wolf dog. Oster's platoon leader, *Leutnant* Schaefer, had ordered Oster and his squad to locate the dog and capture it. He was worried the canine would fall into the hands of Russian partisans. A fine dog like that was a piece of military equipment valuable to the Wehrmacht.

Oster hated the Russian partisans, many of whom were refugees from the very village Oster's platoon had captured. Unlike the more useful Russian peasants, who stayed behind to cook, clean, and labor for the German soldiers, the partisans ran away and hid in the woods. There they lurked like dangerous animals, waiting to prey upon solitary motorcycle couriers or poorly armed supply trucks, sniping with hunting rifles from the trees. Oster had never actually seen a partisan, but he'd spent more than one winter evening hungry and shivering because partisans had attacked a supply truck and stolen his platoon's heating oil and food. If Oster had believed this dog-finding patrol would somehow help strike a blow against these troublesome partisans, who were really nothing more than glorified bandits, he would have been much more enthusiastic about the mission. But he knew all Schaefer's talk about protecting military equipment from the Bolshevik bandits was nonsense. In truth, Schaefer just happened to love dogs.

Oster liked dogs, too, but not in the same way as his Prussian commander. Oster's family had relied on dogs for generations. Oster's business was cheese, a particular kind of goat cheese that was prized by Germans and had therefore kept his family financially secure for hundreds of years. Dogs were essential to the business of raising and herding goats, but they were simply a tool, like a hammer or a hoe. And they were a tool with extra, associated costs. You had to feed dogs. And so to maximize profit, you had to make sure that you fed the dogs who worked hard and got rid of the ones who didn't. That task was made more difficult by the fact that dogs didn't have just one or two pups; they had full litters. So whenever it was time to breed the dogs, Oster was faced with the task of identifying the hardworking puppies among the general rabble. That usually took a few months, at least. Oster then hiked the undesirable puppies out into the mountains, where he left them to starve in the wilderness.

It wasn't much different from organizing a combat squad. Perhaps that was why he'd been promoted to squad leader. After all, Oster realized with satisfaction, it was how the German government was treating the Russians. Humans were just like animals, weren't they? Those who could work and could contribute to the greater good should receive food and provisions so they could survive—such people, Oster believed, were the Germans. Those people who could not work efficiently—the slackers or naturally slovenly—should be eliminated. As Oster saw it, these people were the Russians, Bolsheviks, partisans, bohemians, and anyone else who didn't agree with official German policy. These were the so-called undesirables. And it was good and proper that Oster and his companions were ridding the world of them. The world would become a more efficient, and more pleasant, place to live.

"The dog is merely a means to an end," Oster explained to Krause after a long silence. "It is our manifest destiny to improve this land, to make it more productive. In order to achieve that goal, we must protect our army. In order to protect our army, we must reduce the capabilities of the Slavic partisans who seek to hinder our advance. In order to reduce those capabilities, we must find that dog."

"Then maybe we should just whistle." Krause halted, pursed his lips, and whistled a melodic call to the dog. The rest of the platoon broke into laughter.

Oster's face burned with embarrassment. His speech had been ridiculous. These men didn't care about manifest destiny. All they cared about was their own safety. "Keep that up and you'll make an easy target for a partisan sniper," Oster warned.

Krause stopped whistling at once, his face pale.

Oster turned to the rest of his squad. "Make no mistake. We may be behind our own lines, but this is still enemy territory." Oster noted that his words were finally having the desired effect. The men were gripping their weapons now, nervously eyeing the trees. Oster smiled inwardly, knowing it was the perfect time to instill some discipline. "Krause, take point."

Krause hesitated but didn't dare question the *Unteroffizier*. He cocked the bolt on his rifle, grasped it in both hands, and stepped forward through the slush, trying to make as little noise as possible.

The rest of the squad followed behind, Pfeiffer and his heavy machine gun dead center where he would be less vulnerable to ambush. Oster took up the rear. Despite their attempt at stealth, the soldiers' boots crunched loudly through the crusty snow with every step.

A startled flock of birds chittered overhead, their beating wings drowning out the soldiers' steps. Oster realized that those birds hadn't come from the neighboring trees—they hadn't been surprised by his squad patrolling. Something else had startled them. Oster mentally traced the trajectory of their flight back to its origin and pointed.

"There! Quickly!" He broke into a run, and his squad followed close behind.

CHAPTER 20
THE CELLIST

Karen had heard the whistling and was trying to move away from who-
ever had made the sound. She suspected it was the German soldiers
from the trucks, trying to find Duck. But when she startled a flock of
birds, she froze in terror. The birds would give her away, and if she was
right about the German soldiers, they would soon find her.

So she ran.

But that only made her an easier target. The sound of her coat
flapping and her feet crunching thundered in the quiet forest. And
she heard other feet crunching, the sounds coming up on her fast. She
changed direction to throw off her pursuers, only to come around a
bush only yards from a German soldier. She turned again into the forest,
but the weakness resulting from months of hunger was beginning to
affect her. She was tiring. She willed her legs to keep pumping, but there
was no strength left in them. They collapsed under her, and she tumbled
forward into the snow. Her arms still worked, so she began to crawl,
dragging herself forward on her elbows. It was pointless. Moments after

she collapsed, rough hands grabbed her coat and lifted her. Her spine jarred as they slammed her against a tree trunk. Her head swam. A German soldier pressed his forearm against her throat, preventing her from breathing, and said something to her in German she couldn't understand. She shook her head.

"Who are you?" he asked in Russian.

She tried to answer, but she could only wheeze through the pressure on her throat.

He released his forearm and repeated, "Who are you?"

"Inna . . . my name is Inna."

The soldier pulled her to him, spun her around, and quickly tied her wrists behind her back. Then he pushed her forward. Another soldier grumbled something in German, but her captor barked back, and the talking stopped. He pushed her onward, but again her legs collapsed. So the soldier lifted her and simply heaved her onto his shoulder.

As her mind raced, Karen realized this was the first time she'd seen a real German. Her muscles tensed in terror at that, and she could barely breathe as she bounced along, hanging off the German's shoulder.

CHAPTER 21

THE CHOIRBOY

As Bobby flew, he kept expecting an ocean of sand below him. That was what he'd seen as a kid in those old Rudolph Valentino movies: giant dunes rising like waves over an endless sea of bleached white sand. But those films had been made on Southern California beaches, not here in North Africa. The real McCoy was more rock than beach, jutting up in toothy lines to create a broken landscape that looked like a nightmare to traverse. Steep hills shot up haphazardly, spreading in all directions, spotted with ugly brown bushes. No wonder the Valentino movies hadn't been filmed here; it was hardly a landscape for making Hollywood dreams.

Bobby had been stationed at a secret US airbase in Eritrea for a little over a week. It was now April 1942. When they arrived, the pilots in Bobby's squadron had been disappointed. The airbase was a dump. Tents and shacks guarded a gravel runway surrounded by hand-painted signs that warned of unexploded mines. Bomb craters were being used as pre-dug latrines that were simply bulldozed over when they got too disgusting.

The air base had once belonged to the Italians, which was the reason for the bomb damage and the mines. Once the British Royal Air Force drove the Italians out, they handed the base over to the Americans. At the time, the United States had not yet entered the war, and the British wanted a top-secret yet neutral ally who could repair British aircraft without the fear of being attacked by the Germans. Now America was in the war, and it wasn't just repairing aircraft; it was supplying them—to England and the Soviet Union as well.

This was why Bobby had volunteered for the assignment. If he could help Russia, maybe in some way he'd also be helping Karen. So he and his new squadron had been shipped out on an oil tanker, their disassembled P-39 Airacobras packed in crates and disguised as tractor parts, bound for the oil fields of North Africa and the Middle East. In Eritrea a civilian crew assembled the fighter planes while Bobby and his squadron mates acclimated to the heat and the dust. Their job was flying the reassembled P-39s from Eritrea to Tehran, where the American pilots were to hand them over to Russia for use against the German invaders.

They had lifted off four hours earlier. North Africa was behind them. They passed over the Red Sea and dropped their disposable fuel tanks. Now they flew a straight shot through Saudi Arabia and into Iran. It was all a secret provision of the Lend-Lease Act, the first voyage through what officials in Washington hoped would be a safe and successful supply corridor.

Other, less expensive, equipment was traveling over a slightly different route. Hundreds of Studebaker trucks had been unloaded at Abadan in the Persian Gulf, and from there they drove in long convoys to Tehran, where they would be handed over to the Soviets, who would drive the trucks another fifteen hundred miles through Azerbaijan and Georgia all the way to Russia.

The line of trucks was coming into Bobby's view now, just over the distant horizon. That meant they were about to cross the border into Iran.

"They don't look too happy." It was Jack's voice on the radio. He'd decided to volunteer, too, hoping the mission might lead to combat.

Bobby glanced down. The squadron was flying over the road to Tehran, and Studebakers congested the route as far as the eye could see. A Bedouin caravan waited on the side of the road, black-robed nomads holding on to their camels and shaking their fists at the stalled trucks.

"Don't they know there's a war going on?" Bobby joked.

"Sure they do," responded Jack. "And I'll bet half of them are hoping the Germans will win." It would have been more funny if it hadn't been true. The British had taken control of Iran by force, exiling their leader—whom the locals called their Shah—replacing him with his unpopular son. Understandably, many of the natives were upset.

"You think the girls wear turbans, too?" It was Wally, the Texan. Wally had recently confessed his true reason for joining the army. He'd gotten kicked off the Texas A&M football team for getting caught in a dormitory at Texas State College for Women. He'd joined the army before he could be kicked out of college, too.

"Even worse," Bobby replied, "they wear veils."

"Even better," Wally countered. "You ever heard of the Dance of the Seven Veils? I saw it once in Mexico. Sure wouldn't mind a repeat performance."

"Not that kind of veil," Bobby said drily. "And these girls don't belly dance, either."

"I thought this was the land of harems?"

"Land of hairy legs, more likely," interjected Jack. "Not that you'll ever see a leg under those long black robes."

"Can't kiss 'em, can't dance with 'em . . . heck, the Germans can have 'em. I hear they like hairy legs."

"That's why they invaded France," Bobby quipped.

Laughter rumbled over the radio in response.

"Cut the chatter." It was their flight leader Major Bovington breaking in. "And keep your eyes on the sky."

The pilots grumbled inwardly. They were hundreds of miles from the nearest German air base. Chances were slim to none they'd see an enemy fighter. The fledgling American air force hadn't seen combat yet—not in the European theater of operations, anyway—and the pilots were dying to test their mettle.

The P-39s' powerful engines put miles of vast desert behind them. Then the sky started to turn dark. Bobby checked his watch. It was only half past noon.

And then he saw it, rising up over the horizon: a black curtain stretching from the desert up into the sky.

"What the heck is that?" asked Wally as the curtain drew closer.

"I don't know, looks like rain. Stand by, I'll find out." That meant the major was trying to make contact with the base at Tehran.

Bobby let his eye follow the traffic jam of trucks all the way forward to the black curtain. That was why the trucks had halted—the black curtain. He saw drivers getting out of their cabs, hastily removing the canvas tarps from their truck beds, and using the canvas to cover themselves in the roadside ditch. "What the heck are they doing?" Bobby wondered out loud. Then he understood.

"Pull up!" he yelled as he yanked back his control stick. "Pull up!"

"Why? What do you see?" the major demanded, scanning the sky for any sign of German attack.

"It's a sandstorm!" Bobby replied, continuing to climb as rapidly as he dared.

But the black curtain was approaching fast.

The P-39 was a low-altitude fighter, and its maximum fuel efficiency was at a mere ten thousand feet. For that reason, the squadron had been maintaining a low-level formation. But now, as the danger of the sandstorm loomed, they all pushed their engines to maximum capacity in an effort to climb over the inclement weather.

Bobby could feel the wind rattling his P-39's fuselage and buffeting the fighter in a roller-coaster ride of air turbulence. Just as he neared the highest point of the storm, the bottom dropped out from under him. His stomach caught in his throat. A downdraft forced his plane to plummet. Bobby adjusted his course, and the plane recovered, but now he flew inside the thick of the storm. He could hear the sand blasting his cockpit, could see the dust swirling through his propeller and entering the intake valves. But he kept climbing, clutching the control stick in a death grip.

The darkness cleared, and the bright sun practically blinded Bobby for a moment. He had climbed up and over the storm. His engine whined as if protesting the high altitude. But it didn't stall.

Bobby was safe, and the black curtain now stretched out like a pall below him.

He looked around and over his shoulders. He was shocked at the damage caused to the other planes by even such a limited exposure to the storm. Paint had been sandblasted off, and he had trouble reading identification numbers. So did Major Bovington, who asked each pilot to sound off. Bobby voiced his identification and counted the planes around him.

One was missing.

It was Jack.

"I'm going back for him," Bobby announced, twisting his control stick and corkscrewing back into the storm. Darkness and radio silence enveloped him before the major could command him to stop.

The wind kicked the P-39 around, and the sand tore at its cockpit. Bobby leveled out over the uneven desert, trying to penetrate the dust cloud for any sign of a signal flare from Jack. Sand was sucked into the P-39's intake valves. The engine sputtered and stalled. Bobby didn't bother lowering the landing gear—it would do more harm than good on the desert's craggy surface. He pulled up the aircraft's nose and braced for impact.

He was thrown forward against his safety harness as the bottom of the Airacobra ripped out from underneath him. Then his back pounded against his seat as the plane ground and jerked to a halt.

The whiplash knocked Bobby out. He slowly came to. The cockpit and even its glass canopy were still intact, but he could see sand pouring in through its seams. He unlatched his safety harness and tore open his ejection pack. He pulled the silk parachute out in billowing bunches and pressed it to his chest while heaving open the cockpit canopy.

The wind roared in his ears, and he felt searing pain as sand flayed his skin. He covered his face with the parachute and rolled out onto the P-39's wing. He fought against the wind and wrapped the silk parachute into a cocoon, as he'd seen the truck drivers do with their canvas tarps. The whipping sand still hurt, but at least now it was bearable.

There was nothing left to do but wait like this. Eventually he fell asleep.

When Bobby woke, he was disoriented. He could tell he was buried in sand, and he was having trouble breathing. And he was wrapped in something, something silky and white. He pushed and pulled and kicked, desperately trying to break free of the sand, desperate for a breath of fresh air.

Bobby's head thrust up out of the sand, and he gasped for air. As he caught his breath, he squinted into the sun-bleached desert. Now it did look just like one of those Rudolph Valentino movies, after all. Sand covered everything—the rocks, the bushes, everything. If Bobby hadn't bailed out onto the P-39's wing, he never would have been able to dig his way to the surface.

Bobby plowed through the sand back to the P-39's cockpit. It was all that was left of the Airacobra, protruding from the huge dune that had enveloped the plane. He sifted through the compartment for emergency supplies: a canteen of water, a flare, a pair of binoculars, and a map. He dug the sand away from the instrument panel and tried the radio, but dust had gotten inside and ruined its components. He climbed up on top of the cockpit and raised the binoculars. He saw a glint of metal in the far distance. Was it Jack?

Bobby stumbled down the steep dune, an avalanche of sand tumbling down with him. But he kept his feet and set out in the direction of the glinting metal. The sand was hot; he could even feel it through the soles of his boots. His eyes burned in the bright light, so he put on his goggles. It was only a few miles, but it felt like a marathon. Sweat poured off him under his flight suit, only to evaporate almost immediately into the dry air. His lips begged for moisture, but he knew licking them would only make it worse. He forced himself to take a drink of water, knowing he might pass out from dehydration even before he realized he was thirsty.

Bobby was right about the glint of metal. It was another P-39—Jack's plane. It, too, was buried in a sand dune, only the tail and the cockpit sticking out. Jack sat on the side of the dune, sheltered from the wind, watching with a smile as Bobby approached.

"Well, I guess I won't die alone," Jack announced.

"You won't die at all," Bobby responded.

Jack climbed to his feet and peered in a slow circle. "I don't see anything but desert." Then he lifted his canteen. "And we've only got a few days before we're dead from dehydration."

"There's a road out there somewhere." Bobby slapped Jack on the back and took his spot, sitting against the dune. He pulled the map out of his pocket and began to study it.

"Whole lot of good that will do you," Jack remarked. "Completely lost our bearings in that storm."

Bobby didn't respond. He was concentrating. He had an almost photographic memory. It was part of the reason school had been so easy for him. He envisioned the Bedouin caravan they'd flown over, remembering the curve of the highway where it had been stuck. He placed his finger on the map and began counting . . . to fifty, no, sixty . . . "That's how long it took before we saw the black curtain," he explained. "Cruising at 196 miles per hour, we would have covered three and a quarter miles in that time." He moved his finger that distance along the map. "Then it was another twenty seconds before we recognized the black curtain for what it was."

"Twenty seconds means another mile," Jack added, catching on.

Bobby moved his finger. "But then I gunned the throttle and began to climb. I'd lost track of time, then, concentrating entirely on controlling the plane. But I remember looking at the altimeter: it wasn't until we reached twenty thousand feet that we cleared the storm. That's a ten-thousand-foot climb from our cruising altitude, which would have required another two and a half minutes." Bobby moved his finger again. "It was only another twenty seconds before I realized you'd been swallowed up by the storm. I pulled the plane into an Immelmann"— half a loop combined with a roll—"which would have placed me there." Again he moved his finger. "Which means when I crashed, it would have been somewhere around here." He used a pencil to draw a circle around his finger.

Jack narrowed his eyes. "If you say so."

Bobby drew a line from the circle directly east. "And there's the road."

"You sure about this?"

"Anything beats sitting here waiting to die of thirst." Bobby checked his compass and turned to face east.

"Fair enough. Let's just hope we don't run into a bunch of Nazi sympathizers on the way."

Bobby patted the butt of the automatic pistol hanging from his hip. "You still have one of these, don't you?"

"Sure. But it's jammed with sand like everything else."

"The Bedouin don't know that." Bobby checked his compass again and started to walk away from the plane.

Jack jogged up beside him. "Sure is hot, isn't it? I can feel it through my boots."

"Yeah, but at least it's a dry heat."

Jack laughed. The humidity had been a common complaint during their basic training in Florida. Only a few minutes into a run or a hike, and they were all dripping with sweat. At the time, Bobby and Jack couldn't have imagined any heat worse. Their legs chafed against wet pants with every stride. It was like they'd just been thrown into a pool with their clothes on. Eventually, though, they'd all gotten used to the discomfort.

But this *was* something worse. The dry desert heat was dangerous. Bobby and Jack knew they were sweating just as much, maybe even more, than they did back in Florida, but they could barely feel it.

As they plodded on, the moisture evaporated faster than Bobby's body could replace it. He felt light-headed and weak. It wasn't uncomfortable, though. In a strange way, it was even a euphoric feeling. He could see the waves of heat rising off the white-hot sand. It didn't look like heat—it looked like water. He watched Jack move his hand up and down through the waves as if expecting his arm to get wet. No such luck. Thank goodness Jack was with him. Marching with a buddy improved a man's chances of survival by 200 percent.

They'd been briefed on desert survival. The British had already been fighting for months in Libya against General Rommel's Afrika Korps. American Army Air Forces commanders knew it was likely their pilots would see action in the Middle East, so they made it a point to give them basic survival training in case they were shot down. This was how Bobby knew they should force themselves to swallow gulps of water regularly before dehydration overtook them. Dehydration was the most likely cause of death. The buddy system was crucial for fighting it. If one of them began to pass out, the other could administer water.

It turned out to be a three-hour hike. They didn't seem to cover a long distance, but traversing hot, shifting sand proved even more difficult than they feared. Their canteens were empty after two hours.

By the time they saw the trucks, they weren't sure they were real. It wasn't until the drivers ran out to meet them, holding out bottles of water, that they knew they'd made it.

This time, they'd been lucky.

⎯⎯◆⎯⎯

The truck drivers were from the US Army Quartermaster Corps. As soon as Jack and Bobby explained who they were and what had happened, the drivers offered them rides in the back of their trucks and radioed ahead to report finding the pilots alive. Bobby and Jack sat on crates of canned SPAM as the convoy bounced over the bumpy road to Tehran.

Four hours later, they finally rejoined the rest of their squadron. Major Bovington and the other pilots met them in the Tehran officers' club, greeting the desert survivors with slaps on their backs and a round of stiff drinks.

Bobby felt guilty for going after Jack. If he'd been able to keep radio contact inside the storm, he suspected he would've heard the major ordering him to leave Jack behind. And he'd been responsible for the loss of a valuable plane.

To his surprise, Major Bovington was proud rather than angry. "You're in the army now, son," he explained. "We leave no man behind." He wasn't even angry about losing the planes. "We can build a plane in a couple of months. Know how long it takes to build a pilot? Twenty-one years."

"I'm only nineteen," Bobby responded with a cocky smile.

"And I try not to hold that against you."

Suddenly the room went silent. The Russian pilots had arrived. And they were women.

No one quite knew how to react. They hadn't expected women, and certainly not pretty women. They didn't wear makeup, but their pale, freckled faces and sparkling eyes gave them a girl-next-door appeal. Their hair was pulled back severely, like a schoolteacher's or librarian's, and their uniforms, cinched tight at their waists with wide belts, were oddly appealing, especially the glimpse they provided of cute little knees peeking out from between the hems of skirts and calf-high leather boots. It all served to create a divide of silent discomfort between the Russians and the Americans.

Then Jack spoke, welcoming the women to the officers' club and telling the Russian pilots that they were celebrating. His friend had just saved his life, rescuing him from the desert. Jack patted Bobby on the back.

Leave it to Jack to break the silence, Bobby thought.

The Russian pilots didn't understand. Apparently, they couldn't speak English.

Jack tried to speak more slowly. "Don't you know how to celebrate?"

The Russian women glanced shyly at one another and spoke quietly in Russian.

"Celebrate. You know, a drink, a cigarette." Jack pantomimed drinking and smoking.

The Russian women just nodded politely.

Jack narrowed his eyes, crossed the bar to the jukebox, and dropped a coin in its slot. He waited a moment for the record to flip. "Do you like Glenn Miller?"

Again, the women didn't respond. But then the music began to bellow out of the jukebox's tinny speakers. The girls broke into smiles; they couldn't help it—the music was jumping. Jack started tapping his feet and snapping his fingers. One of the girl pilots followed his lead and did the same. Jack grabbed the girl and dragged her onto the dance floor. She laughed as he spun her and taught her to jitterbug.

That was the first dance of the night, but it wasn't the last. The Russian pilots seemed to love American Big Band music and chattered among themselves, passing the American aviators from one to another, judging each as worthy of a kiss—or two or three. America may have been the land of the free, but Russia, it seemed, was the land of free kisses, for Jack had never had such an easy time coaxing a girl's lips to his own. It almost made that crash in the desert worth it.

At midnight, Bovington broke up the party. The squadron was scheduled to ship out by truck back to Eritrea at 6:00 a.m. The major decided it was time to turn in, and the female Russian flight leader seemed to agree. She called out to her pilots, clapped her hands, and hurried the women away, like a mother hen, to their chicken coops. But before she disappeared into the night, she left a tiny envelope with the major.

"What's that?" Bobby asked him.

"Microfilm."

"What, like spies use?"

"Yup." Major Bovington pulled out the film and held it up to the light, trying to read the tiny print.

"So what's on it? German military secrets? Japanese intelligence?"

Major Bovington scowled and placed the microfilm back in the envelope. "A symphony. Apparently the Russians want us to smuggle out music written by some fellow named Shostakovich."

CHAPTER 22

THE ORGAN-GRINDER
AND THE CELLIST

Petr wished he still had his PTRD rifle. It was too big a gun for deer hunting, but the little Tokarev pistol was too small.

He and Duck had been stalking a deer for hours. The young buck was running them in circles. Before they could get close enough for a pistol shot, the deer would hear them and bound off into the forest, well out of sight. They'd caught back up with it twice, largely thanks to Duck's keen sense of smell, but once again they'd spooked it before they got close. If he'd had the big PTRD, or better still, a simple Mosin-Nagant bolt-action rifle, Petr was sure he'd have bagged the buck an hour ago. Instead, he was considering giving up.

Normally, Petr would have thrown in the towel. He'd never been particularly resolute. When something proved too difficult, he would move on to some new, less onerous, task. But for some reason he dreaded returning to the hunting cabin empty-handed. Why? It wasn't as if he needed the food. They had plenty of macaroni; they wouldn't starve, not anymore. Meat was purely a luxury. Most of it would go bad, anyway, before he, Karen, and Duck ate it. So why did it matter so much to kill this deer? He wasn't doing it for the food, he realized. He was doing it to show off.

When Petr realized this, he gave up the hunt immediately. Why should he care about impressing some strange American girl? She wasn't even particularly pretty. No, that was a lie. She was skinny and filthy, and you couldn't even see much of her under her thick sweaters and fraying coat. But her eyes were beautiful. He'd never seen such intense eyes. To look into them was to be captivated by them. He couldn't look away. The dark-brown irises and deep-black pupils were mesmerizing. There was a saying that eyes were the window to the soul. If that were the case, Karen's had to be the purist soul in existence.

But the saying was a lie, too, because Karen's soul was dark. Petr had seen what she'd done to the NKVD man. Not that Petr had much love for NKVD men. They were the ones who'd taken away his father, and Petr knew his father had been extraordinarily lucky to escape that arrest with his life. Very few people returned from an NKVD interrogation alive.

Petr's father had never talked about what he'd been forced to endure during that interrogation. Petr had been afraid to ask. But he could imagine that, if given a chance, his own father, a normally peaceful mathematics professor, would have smashed in the brains of an NKVD man with just as much ferocity as Karen.

Maybe she didn't have that dark a soul, but neither was she pure. She was certainly no angel. That was part of what he liked about her, Petr had to admit. He couldn't trust her, not completely, and yet he felt some overwhelming desire to make her trust him. Hunting the deer was more than just showing off to a pretty girl. He wanted to demonstrate to her that he could find food. He wanted to prove to this girl, who he knew had almost starved to death, that he could provide for her, that she could trust him.

Well, he thought to himself, he would just have to find some other way, because the hunt had been a failure.

Petr marched through the snow, too lost in his thoughts to pay much attention to Duck. But when they neared the hunting shack, Duck suddenly halted and dropped to his stomach. Petr instinctively did the same, falling prone beside the big dog and drawing the pistol from his coat pocket.

They both lay there a moment, trying to control their breathing, Petr grasping the pistol with two hands and aiming it in front of him. He tried to ignore the discomfort of the cold seeping from the snow through the front of his uniform. He peered past the pistol's steel gun sight and focused on the shack. The front door was open.

The front of Petr's uniform was getting wet, his body heat melting the snow beneath him, but he resisted the urge to climb into a crouch and instead wormed his way forward—an awkward, uncomfortable, and excruciatingly slow way to maneuver. But it made him a small and very difficult target. The ground is the infantryman's best friend, Petr's drill instructor had often insisted, and Petr had learned that lesson well.

Eventually, now shivering with snow down his pants, Petr reached the shack. He had angled his approach to veer right of the doorway. Anyone inside peering out wouldn't have a direct line of sight to him. But neither could Petr see inside. So he wrapped his fingers around the bottom of the doorjamb, tightened his knuckles, and pulled himself forward silently until he could peer inside.

The shack was empty.

Petr immediately saw that he'd been the victim of one clever girl, and he felt the hot shame of gullibility. Karen hadn't cared about the venison. She'd just acted impressed as a way to encourage him and Duck to leave. She'd wanted to be rid of them so she could steal all the macaroni for herself. Maybe he shouldn't have given up on that hunt, after all, because Karen had just stolen his food and left him to die.

Despondent, he climbed to his feet and tromped into the shack. Snow fell from his clothes onto the wood-plank floor. He began to disrobe, throwing his uniform in a heap in the corner. Duck trotted into the shack behind him. Petr was down to his underwear when Duck decided to shake, spraying Petr with wet snow. Petr yelled and leaped away in shock. Duck pulled his ears back in apology and nuzzled his snout up to Petr's hand. Petr scratched the big dog behind his ears. He was cold, but not angry—at least not angry at Duck. It wasn't Duck's fault the girl had left them. Petr remembered how Duck had rolled over this morning, letting Karen scratch his belly. "She tricked you, too, didn't she?" he muttered to the dog.

Then, almost absentmindedly, Petr walked over to the cabinets and pulled them open, hoping Karen had missed some morsel of food. What he saw shocked him: two bags of macaroni, neatly stacked for him, maybe enough to survive the journey to Tikhvin. But that wasn't all. Slid between the bags was a train ticket. Karen had left him her most valuable possession. She hadn't left him to die, after all.

Petr wanted to go after Karen immediately. He felt irrationally compelled to get dressed, pocket his gun, and head back out into the woods. They were behind enemy lines, at the mercy of German patrols, and Karen was unarmed. He felt an overwhelming desire to protect her. But his clothes were still wet, and he couldn't risk building a fire, not until after dark, or the Germans would see the smoke and send a patrol.

Petr decided he would have to wait until morning. He tried to reassure himself that this was not unreasonable. Karen was far from helpless. She could take care of herself. She'd proven that again and again. She'd survived starvation, she'd escaped Leningrad, and she'd even escaped from him. But when night finally came and he lay down beside the warm stove, he couldn't sleep. All he could think about was that moment he'd first met Karen. He remembered the NKVD man and his Tokarev pistol. He'd had it pointed at Karen. If Petr hadn't arrived, and Duck hadn't attacked, Karen would be dead. She'd needed him then and, he worried, she might need him now.

CHAPTER 23
THE CELLIST

Almost a week later, Karen didn't sleep, either. She didn't want to. If this was going to be her last night alive, she wanted to experience it. She was locked in a storage closet, in the dark, so there wasn't much around her to experience. She was cramped and uncomfortable.

But so long as she lived, she still had her memories. Memories of her father, of New York, of Leningrad during the previous summer, of Inna, and, most of all, of Bobby. Those were the memories she wanted to cherish above all. But something strange kept happening. Whenever she tried to envision Bobby, she saw the face of the boy soldier instead. Her mind kept drifting to him, and even to his dog. She wondered if he hated her. She'd have hated her if she were him. She'd betrayed him. And she wondered if he really had managed to kill a deer.

The storage closet had no windows. But it was getting brighter. The shapes of the empty shelves were turning gray. She wondered what time it was. It must be well after dawn; the sun would have to be high and bright if its light was managing to penetrate this dark place.

Karen wondered how much longer she had left alive. She'd been told she would be executed at noon. That couldn't be very far off.

Karen knew there was no point in resisting. These men weren't with the NKVD. They were Germans. They were the enemy. If she told the truth, they would execute her. If she lied, they would execute her. There was no story, no matter how preposterous, imaginative, or believable, that could save her life. All she could hope for was to minimize the torture and die with her dignity intact. That, at least, she had achieved.

They had beaten her, of course. That went without saying. The Germans never would have believed her story if she hadn't made them beat her. As a result, her fat lip and black eye throbbed, and her ribs ached. But there was a big difference between being beaten and being tortured. She'd discovered that difference in the company of the NKVD man. He hadn't beaten her; he hadn't even left scratches or bruises on her body. But what he had done to her, even just for a moment, was ten times worse than what the Germans had done.

Karen had denied being a Russian partisan. So the Germans started beating her. After receiving a few licks, Karen let her Russian falter, revealing a foreign accent. This aroused their interest. They started paying attention to what she had to say. Karen had confessed that she was American and asked to be taken to the embassy. That was a ridiculous request, of course, because America had declared war on Germany. So, after a few more punches in the stomach, she asked to be taken to a prisoner-of-war camp and held until the end of hostilities. The Germans didn't take that demand seriously, either. Only soldiers were granted the right to be captured as prisoners of war, and Karen wasn't a soldier. If she was, she'd be wearing a uniform. So, when they started punching her in the face, Karen "confessed" that she was a spy.

The Germans had suspected this all along, and Karen played into those suspicions. She told them she had been sent there to determine

German troop strength and location. The Americans didn't trust their Russian allies, she explained, and they considered all Soviet military reports propaganda. So they'd sent a number of American spies into Russia to see with their own eyes.

That sounded believable to the Germans, for they didn't trust Communists, either. But they wanted to know where her equipment was—her radio and her codebook. Karen claimed to have lost both while trying to cross a river. But she offered to write down what little she remembered of the cipher she and the other spies were using.

This was a major intelligence coup for the Germans. With even bits and pieces of the code, cryptanalysts in Berlin could crack it and use it to entrap other American spies. They could also eavesdrop on American transmissions and intercept military orders and dispatches.

The cipher Karen wrote down was nonsense, of course. She made it up on the spot—a simple system of substituting numbers for letters. By the time her notes were sent to Berlin, the Germans would know she'd invented it. But by then it would be too late. Karen would be dead. That was what happened to spies: they were shot. But the Germans didn't want to waste bullets on a firing squad. They'd decided to hang her instead.

Karen was proud of her deception. She hadn't saved her own life, but she might have saved Petr's. The Germans never suspected she was traveling in the company of a Russian soldier, and she'd been able to avoid divulging the existence of the abandoned hunting shack. She was pleased with herself, she told herself, and she should be at peace—ready to die. And yet she couldn't help what she really felt. What she experienced inside that storage closet was terror.

Suddenly Karen heard a dog howling. It confused her for a moment. Then a new fear kicked in. She knew the Germans were looking for Duck. She'd overheard them, and they'd even asked her about the dog during her interrogation. The howling dog had to be Duck; the

Germans had found him. And if they'd found Duck, that meant they'd probably found Petr.

Karen knew she should be overcome with despair. If Petr were captured, that meant her carefully constructed story had failed to protect him. To make matters worse, the Germans would soon discover from him that everything she'd told them was a lie. She'd be interrogated again, and this time she wouldn't just be beaten, she'd be tortured. That made her all the more terrified now, but she wasn't sad. Illogically, unreasonably, she actually felt happy. Because for some reason even she couldn't quite understand, she couldn't wait to see Petr again.

CHAPTER 24

THE GOATHERD

Unteroffizier Oster suspected it was a trap. The safest thing to do would be to put a bullet in the dog's head. But *Leutnant* Schaefer wanted the creature alive, so the *Unteroffizier* had to obey.

A report had come in that someone had tied the Alsatian wolf dog to a tree near the village, causing the hound great despair. By the time they found it, the dumb beast's attempts to break free had only succeeded in tangling it more. The canine didn't stop howling when the German soldiers neared, but it did gaze at them with its big brown eyes and a mournful expression that begged them to set it free.

Oster had his men keep their distance. Unfortunately for the hound, Oster first had to make sure there wasn't a partisan sniper waiting in ambush. So he ordered Krause to go forward alone and see whether the dog was injured.

Oster was using Krause as bait. Fortunately, Krause didn't realize that. If he had, he might have figured out some way to refuse the order and shirk the dangerous duty. Instead, he moved carefully toward the dog, holding his hand out in greeting. The big dog stopped howling, pawed at the ground, wagged his tail, and even licked the palm of Krause's hand.

Oster was impressed. Maybe he'd finally found something Krause was good at.

Krause glanced back over his shoulder at the squad leader. "Shall I cut him loose, *Herr Unteroffizier?*"

"Not yet," Oster replied. If there had been a sniper, he would have killed Krause. And there probably was no booby trap, or the dog would have set if off by jerking on the line. But it still had to be an ambush. Why else was the dog left here like that, helplessly tied to a tree?

Oster had argued against investigating the barking dog when *Leutnant* Schaefer ordered it, trying to appeal to Schaefer's own sense of self-preservation. Their bivouac in the village was too poorly defended. Two of the platoon's squads were away—one on escort duty with a supply caravan, and another sent forward on a combat patrol toward Tikhvin. Only Oster's squad had been held back to guard the village's strategic bridge across the Neva River. And now *Leutnant* Schaefer was risking that important landmark by deploying his last riflemen? With Oster's squad gone, only the *Leutnant's* tiny support staff would be available to defend the village and the bridge from a partisan raid. But *Leutnant* Schaefer had brushed off Oster's concern, again citing his belief that there were no partisans. The attacks on their supply caravans had been the work of a young American spy who'd been captured.

"But if there are no partisans," Oster now muttered to himself as he stared at Krause and the animal, "then who tied up this dog?"

"What was that, *Herr Unteroffizier?*" Krause said. He already had his knife ready, despite Oster's order not to free the hound.

"I was wondering who tied up this dog," Oster admitted loudly, effectively posing the question to the entire rifle squad.

"Perhaps no one tied him up," proposed Pfeiffer, struggling as always under the weight of his machine gun. "It appears as if the dog tangled itself."

Oster had to admit that that was possible. "But then how did it get a rope around its neck in the first place?" The convoy that had first encountered the dog had reported neither leash nor collar.

Krause squatted and squinted at where the rope wrapped around a tree branch. "You are correct, *Herr Unteroffizier*. Someone definitely tied a knot."

Once again Oster was impressed, this time by Krause's initiative. Perhaps the troublemaker was finally taking soldiering seriously. He even felt a pang of guilt about having used the man as sniper bait. "Very well, cut him free," Oster announced. "But hold on to him tightly," he added. "Don't let him go!"

Krause's sharp combat knife made quick work of the rope. The dog didn't resist as the soldier carefully untangled the line from its legs. Soon the animal was back on all four paws, tugging at the rope like a hunting hound anxious for release. "He's a handsome creature, isn't he?" Krause said with admiration.

Oster nodded. "He resembles the Führer's dogs." Oster had never met the Führer, let alone his dogs, but he'd seen photographs of Hitler with his pets. Perhaps *Leutnant* Schaefer had been correct to send them on this mission, after all. Maybe it wasn't such a fool's errand.

Right then an explosion went off. It was near, but it wasn't a particularly loud blast—certainly no louder than a howitzer shell. But the unexpected sound startled Krause, who inadvertently let go of the dog's rope.

Oster cursed as he watched the dog bound away, disappearing once more into the forest. He was angry with Krause, of course, but he was mostly angry with himself for trusting a worthless soldier. That dog was their mission objective. He should have made Pfeiffer secure it, not

Krause. Oster had been right all along. Krause was good for one thing and one thing only: sniper bait.

He was about to order the squad to chase the dog, but then he heard a gunshot. And a moment later he heard a second. Now his brain connected the dots. All three sounds—the explosion and the two gunshots—had come from the village.

The bridge was under attack!

CHAPTER 25

THE CELLIST

The explosion knocked Karen off her feet. She hit her head against a shelf and blacked out. It was only for an instant, though, because the smoke in her lungs made her cough and immediately brought her back to consciousness.

She opened her eyes and was almost blinded by bright sunlight. A hole had been blown open in the side of the house the Germans had been using for their command post. The same blast had ripped her prison door—that of the storage closet—straight from its hinges.

The slumped body of a German officer lay on the rug outside Karen's makeshift cell. A big wooden splinter from the wall stuck out of the officer's neck. It was *Leutnant* Schaefer, the man in charge of her interrogations. She tried not to focus on the blood gushing from the wound onto the rug.

She heard the stomp of boots, and the front door swung open. Standing there was *Feldwebel* Krieger, Schaeffer's right-hand man—the very man who'd beaten her. He held an MP40 submachine gun and pointed it angrily at her, assuming she was somehow responsible for the *Leutnant*'s death. As he released the weapon's safety, a flash and a bang pierced the billowing smoke.

Krieger fell, a red splotch spreading on his tunic. Karen watched in wide-eyed shock as a silhouette, backlit by sunlight, emerged from the smoke. It was Petr. The boy soldier reached out and helped Karen back to her feet. "We should go," he said.

"Look out!" she screamed.

Petr spun at Karen's warning and fired again. Another German, the medical orderly, jerked back from the impact of the bullet. Karen scrambled across to the wounded platoon sergeant. Krieger was still alive, groaning and looking at her, unable to speak, his eyes begging for help.

She grabbed his submachine gun. As she yanked its shoulder strap free of Krieger's body, the big sergeant shuddered in pain. Petr kneeled next to the dead officer. He rolled the *Leutnant* over onto his stomach, revealing a holster on his right hip. Petr freed the German pistol from the bloody leather and stuck it in his waistband.

By then, Karen was beside him, grabbing his hand and pulling him through the hole blown in the wall. They didn't bother to loot the medical orderly—as a Red Cross medic, he was forbidden to carry weapons.

"We have to get across the bridge!" Petr told Karen, and they both broke into a run.

There were no other Germans in the village, just Russian refugees captured and forced to work for their conquerors. Most hid in their homes, only a few peering out from behind newsprint window shades at the fleeing soldier and the girl. But one old man emerged from a cottage right beside the wooden bridge and stood in Karen and Petr's way, forcing them to stop.

Petr raised his pistol at the old man, but the geezer wasn't trying to stop them. He was holding out a book and a hard loaf of bread.

Karen grabbed the bread.

Petr eyed the book. It was a well-worn copy of *War and Peace*. "Thank you," he said, "but we don't need it."

The old man refused to take no for an answer. He didn't speak but kept forcing it into Petr's hands. Finally, he gave up and took the book. "We'll read it later," he assured the man before retaking Karen's hand and breaking into a sprint.

The old man smiled as he watched the boy and the girl run across the wooden planks hand in hand.

Karen and Petr ran until they were exhausted. That didn't take long. For all her strength of will, Karen was weak of body. When they paused, she knew better than to sit, concerned she might never stand up again. So she stood with her hands on her knees, gasping for breath, feeling like she might vomit. When the nausea passed, she looked up and discovered Petr staring at her.

"What's wrong?" she asked.

Petr raised his index finger toward her face. "Your eyes."

Karen nodded. Both her eye sockets were purple and swollen from the beating. "My lips, too. It's OK. They'll heal."

"No, I meant they're still beautiful."

Karen blushed and looked down in embarrassment. Then she remembered something. She looked around. "Where's Duck?"

Now Petr flushed red—not in embarrassment, but in shame. "I had to leave him behind."

Karen was astounded. She'd seen how much Petr loved that dog. "How could you?"

Petr slumped, misinterpreting the question as an accusation. "It was either you or him. I had no choice."

"Yes, you did, and you chose me," Karen responded with a smile. She wanted to kiss Petr then. She wanted to leap into his arms and pull his face toward her and kiss him.

But she didn't.

Petr only looked baffled. "We . . . we should keep going."

"Yes," Karen said, nodding. "We should." But she didn't move. Not yet. "First, how do I use this?" She slid the loaf of bread into a pocket and unslung the German submachine gun from her shoulder.

Petr grabbed the stamped steel MP40 and examined it. "I don't know," he said. "If it's anything like ours . . . first you release the safety." He examined the bolt. "Which has already been done. That's dangerous."

Karen watched and nodded. "Then what?"

Petr shrugged. "Then just point and shoot." He handed the weapon back to her. "But don't hold down the trigger when you shoot. My drill instructor told me that. You only have one magazine, and the barrel will rise, making you miss. Try to fire in short bursts, like a pistol."

"I've never fired a pistol."

"Neither had I, until today."

Karen secured the MP40 as he'd shown her. "How did you blow through that wall?"

"I used Duck's mine."

"His what?"

"He was . . . a mine dog." Petr struggled as he referred to Duck in the past tense. Karen could see that his eyes were welling up. "Do you know what that is?" he added.

"No."

"He was trained to run under tanks. He wore a jacket stuffed with explosives. A mine. The idea is that once a mine dog is under a panzer, boom, the explosives go off and destroy the tank."

Karen was horrified. "Doesn't that kill the dog?"

Petr nodded. "This is war. Everyone dies."

"Not everyone."

"Not yet, anyway."

Karen desperately wanted to give in to her urge to wrap her arms around Petr's neck and kiss him on the lips. She was afraid of what he might say, how he might react. "Thank you," she said instead.

"You're welcome," Petr stammered before turning from her. "Are you ready now?"

Karen nodded. "I'm ready."

Petr looked at her hand, as if about to take hold of it. Instead, he turned and began to march. Smiling for the first time in months, Karen followed closely behind him.

CHAPTER 26
THE GOATHERD

Unteroffizier Oster huffed and puffed as he ran, leading his men back to the village. He was sure he would somehow be blamed for this fiasco, and he was preoccupied with how he could avoid getting demoted.

When he caught sight of the bridge, Oster was relieved to find it wasn't the target of the explosion, after all. But he could smell smoke. He stopped running and raised a fist, signaling his squad to proceed carefully as he led them in a crouch through the village, following his nose to the platoon's command post.

Outside the house, charred, splintered wood marked where a hole had been blown through the wall, apparently with dynamite. The platoon's medical orderly lay dead in the blast's scorch mark. Oster drew his pistol, inched quietly toward the edge of the hole, and peered inside. Schaefer lay in a pool of his own blood, bled out like a stuck pig. Not far from him lay Krieger. The big man apparently went down fighting, judging from his wound and his missing MP40. The storage closet door hung open. The partisans hadn't wanted to destroy the bridge. They'd attacked to rescue the spy.

Suddenly Oster realized he wouldn't be demoted. On the contrary—whether he liked it or not, he'd just received a field promotion. He then led his squad through the village to examine the bridge. He was satisfied to find it didn't appear booby-trapped or mined. But he noticed an old man staring at him.

"What happened?" Oster barked.

"Crime and punishment," the old man explained, and he pointed toward the command post.

That infuriated Oster, and he drew his pistol and shot the old man in the head.

CHAPTER 27

THE CHOIRBOY

After the loss of two valuable warplanes to a freak sandstorm, Army brass had decided that the route from Eritrea was an impractical and dangerous way to supply the Russians. So Bobby and his squadron were recalled to Palm Beach. Bobby's squadron mates were growing restless and bored.

But more than anything, Bobby was relieved. He hadn't heard from Karen since June of 1941, almost a year ago. And now, suddenly, he received hundreds of her letters all at once. They had obviously been held up by the Soviet postal service, trapped in Leningrad until they could be delivered across the ice road, and then delayed even longer while they were examined by the State censors. But they had finally gotten through.

And that meant Karen was still alive.

So Bobby spent his spare time trying to decipher what the Soviet censors had deleted in Karen's notes. Now he held a page up to a window, hoping the sunlight would illuminate the writing under the censor's thick, black ink.

It was no use. The censor had been too good at his job. Whatever was written beneath the ink was lost forever. So he picked up a different letter and reread from the beginning.

Dearest Bobby,

It's only been a few months, but it feels like a lifetime. My life in New York, my time with you, even my first year in Russia, they all seem like a dream I have trouble remembering. In that dream people laugh. They smile and they talk and they joke. In that dream no one hides food or steals wood. But now I've woken up and the dream is fading. All that's left is the real world, the world of cold and hunger. That's the world I live in, and try as I might I can't return to the dream.

Yesterday my neighbor's cat died. In the dream world my neighbor, Mrs. Kudaschova, loved that cat. She seldom let it out of her arms, let alone her sight. She carried it everywhere, stroking it, feeling it purr. But in the new world, the real world, she doesn't have time to take care of a cat. She needs to take care of herself.

She has been doing that by luring pigeons to her balcony, where she can snare them. She plucks the pigeons, roasts them, and adds their meat to her bread ration. Perhaps that sounds disgusting to you, in the dream world. But just writing about it is making my mouth water. That's the way it is here. Yesterday morning Mrs. Kudaschova put out her bait and set her snares like she always does. But the air-raid sirens interrupted her. When those sirens go off, we have to drop everything and race down into the basement. I don't know why—if a bomb were to strike, the whole apartment would just fall on top of us, wouldn't it? But everyone seems to think the basement is safe, so that is where we go. Mrs. Kudaschova always brings her cat down with her. But this time she couldn't find the cat. And when a bomb exploded across the street, she finally lost her nerve, stopped searching, and joined us in the dark.

That air raid lasted for almost an hour. Fortunately, our building was spared. But when she returned to her apartment Mrs. Kudaschova finally found her cat. It had escaped onto her balcony, where it had killed one pigeon and frightened away the others. It had eaten its victim, leaving nothing left over for Mrs. Kudaschova but blood and feathers. At that moment Mrs. Kudaschova stopped loving her cat. It stopped being a companion and started being a nuisance. By that evening, it had become a meal. She added its meat to her bread rations in order to make up for her loss of the pigeons.

That's the real world, the world that I live in every day. I spent seventeen years living in peace and only a few months living with war. But it's the war that feels real, not the peace.

You're the only part of the dream that I know was real. You're the one who makes me realize that it's the war that's temporary, not the peace. One day the hunger will be over, the war will be over, and I will see you again. It's that knowledge that helps me get up every morning, that helps me get dressed and walk through the bombed streets and stand in the bread lines. If it weren't for you, I'd probably be as dead as Mrs. Krudashova's cat.

Among the letters, this one was remarkably untouched by the censors. Perhaps someone had been lazy that day. In any case, comparing the letters helped Bobby piece together a history of what Karen was going through.

He put that letter down and picked up one she had written just a couple of months ago.

I don't know how I'll get through another winter without you. Whenever the clouds gather, I try to remember that first snowfall, when we walked together in the park, and we took off our gloves to hold hands. But soon we won't be able to take our gloves off here. It will be too cold. And our neighbor, Mrs. Kudaschova, says this winter is going to be even colder than last year. I asked her how she knows and she said she can feel it, feel it in her bones. I'm not sure whether to believe her or not, but the others seem to trust her. They say she's never been wrong before. And they think it's a good thing, a cold winter. A cold winter will defeat the Germans, they say. Russians thrive in the cold. It's how they stopped Napoleon. But I think—

The rest of the paragraph was covered in black ink, redacted by the Soviet State censor. So Bobby moved to the next part.

Classes have been cancelled at the Conservatory, but father still spends all day with Mr. Shostakovich. They aren't writing a symphony together, not anymore.

Instead they're digging trenches and learning how to put out fires. I think it's silly. If the Germans are coming, we should leave Leningrad, go home. We're not Russian. This isn't our war. But father says I'm just looking for an excuse to go back home and see you again. Maybe he's right. I miss you.

I love you, Karen.

Bobby put down the letter and picked up the next.

Dearest Bobby,
A little girl stands on the roof of our apartment every single day, watching the sky. I told her to come inside, but she insists. She says she is watching for German airplanes—

A large portion of the letter was blacked out with the black ink. It began again on the next page:

The air raid sirens go off day and night. We take every precaution, keeping the entire street dark so that the German pilots can't see where to aim their bombs. I have learned to walk in complete darkness, all the way down three flights of stairs into the basement. That's where we huddle, listening to the bombs drop, until we hear the all-clear signal.

The rest of the letter was almost all redacted. Only three words remained, isolated on the next page:

. . . the city granary . . .

What had she been trying to say about the city granary? Bobby could not know. But this one was the first letter, written in September.

The third letter had even more black ink, and the fourth, more still. Each letter got blacker and blacker, until eventually he couldn't read anything but "Dearest Bobby" and "I love you, Karen."

Bobby desperately wanted to try to find out what Karen had written under the black ink, and it unsettled him knowing that Russian censors had been reading her love letters. But it didn't matter, really, that he couldn't read much of what she'd written. He could read the dates of each letter, so he could organize them chronologically. Doing so proved to him that she was still alive, or at least she had been until Christmas Eve.

That was the date of the last letter. "All I want for Christmas," she had written, "is to escape from Leningrad. If I could just do that, maybe I could find my way home. Alaska is not really so far, is it?"

"Hey, the major wants to see you," Jack said.

Bobby looked up to see Jack ambling through the door of their Quonset hut in Palm Beach. Jack leaned against his bunk bed and glanced down at the blacked-out letters strewn across Bobby's bed. "Makes you proud to be an American, don't it?"

"What does?"

"Getting your girlfriend's letters like that. At least our postal service doesn't read other people's mail."

"It's what we're fighting for," Bobby responded with a wink.

"I could do with a little fighting."

"We'll be fighting soon enough."

"I hope so. I'm sick of the navy hogging all the glory."

In truth, none of the American armed forces had seen much glory. The Japanese had followed their surprise attack at Pearl Harbor with the successful conquest of the Philippines and Wake Island. They defeated Allied forces in Hong Kong, Malaya, Singapore, and Burma. They were even threatening Australia from New Guinea. Like the Germans in Europe, the Japanese appeared invincible in Asia. Every American military campaign against them was a disaster. But at least the navy was fighting back. A task force led by the USS *Lexington* was having some success with hit-and-run tactics in the Coral Sea. Her aircraft had even managed to bomb the Japanese at Rabaul.

The navy sailors and pilots were heroes. Meanwhile, the Army Air Forces pilots were sitting on their hands. They weren't even flying secret supply missions anymore.

As a result, Palm Beach was turning into a navy town. Girls were more interested in sailors than soldiers. The sailors, after all, were the ones about to see battle, shipping out first to Hawaii and then who knew where. They were the ones to receive the attention and the sympathies of the local women. Even someone as romantically accomplished as Jack found himself constantly competing with ship's officers or navy pilots. More than once he'd kissed the wrong girl, and the night ended with an army-navy brawl.

"The major? What about?" Bobby asked, forcing his mind back on course. Major Bovington had been preoccupied lately, constantly reviewing intelligence reports and consulting with the higher brass. He hadn't spent much time with the squadron outside of their training sessions, so it was a bit of a surprise that he'd asked to see Bobby.

"How should I know?"

Bobby folded up the love letters and put them away.

Five minutes later Bobby was sitting in squadron HQ, staring across a small metal desk from Major Bovington.

The desktop was a mess of papers. Tall filing cabinets flanked the major. He leaned back in his squeaky chair and folded his arms across his stomach. "What do you know about Russia?" he asked.

Bobby was slightly taken aback. This wasn't a question he'd expected from the major. "I don't know, same as everyone else, I guess. Communist dictatorship. At war with Germany. Enemy of my enemy's my friend, that whole bit."

"Isn't your girlfriend there?"

What did Major Bovington know about Karen? "Yes," Bobby replied cautiously.

"I heard she was in Leningrad."

"That's right. Studying music."

"And I heard you have letters from her. Dozens."

"That's true. They came all at once, a little over a week ago."

"What do those letters say?"

Bobby cleared his throat. "With all due respect, sir, they're private."

Major Bovington stood and threw up his hands, frustrated but amused. "For God's sake, son, I'm not asking you to tell me about your love life. I mean, what do they say about Russia?"

"I'm not sure I understand."

Major Bovington sighed. "I thought you were some sort of boy genius, graduated early from Columbia."

"I did graduate early; that's true."

"Seems you're a little slow on the uptake."

"Sir?"

"All right, I'll back up and start from the beginning." Bovington sat down and leaned across the desk. "In 1939 Germany conquered Poland. In 1940 Germany conquered France. Right now, they're trying to conquer Russia. They've conquered everyone they've attacked except one nation."

"England."

"Yes, England. You know why they haven't conquered England?"

"Because it's an island, sir?"

"Yes. It's an island with a very powerful navy. A navy more powerful than Germany's Kriegsmarine. Germany can't conquer England because England's navy won't let it get close enough to land troops."

"What does this have to do with Russia?" Bobby asked.

"You know who also had a powerful navy?"

"Who, sir?"

"France."

"England's strongest ally."

"Until they were conquered in 1940."

Bobby was starting to see the point of all this. "By Germany."

Major Bovington nodded. "And what do you think would have happened if the Germans had added the French navy to their own?"

"They could have invaded England?"

Major Bovington shrugged. "Perhaps."

"So why didn't they?"

"The English didn't let them."

"How so?"

"By destroying them. Operation Catapult, in French Algeria. England attacked the French navy in port and killed over twelve hundred French sailors. French sailors who had been, until only a few months earlier, among England's most trusted and powerful allies. French soldiers who claimed that they would never capitulate to Germany."

"But they had capitulated."

"Their government had. Their leaders had. And for that, they paid with their lives."

"Sounds like the English are as ruthless as the Germans."

"England survives because she was ruthless when she had to be."

Bobby thought of Karen's letter, of her distinction between the "real world" of war and the "dream world" of peace. "And now we're going to do the same thing to Russia."

Major Bovington leaned back in his chair and smiled. "I didn't say that."

"It's what you're implying, isn't it?"

"The Germans have conquered the Ukraine and Belarus. They've surrounded Leningrad. They're a summer campaign away from capturing Moscow. They've advanced over more ground and conquered more territory than any army in history. We've barely even fought. Our army is still a bunch of raw recruits. But we have something Germany doesn't have. Steel. Fuel. Factories."

"Industry."

"Germany can't keep up. But do you know what Russia has?"

"Steel. Fuel. Factories."

"Even more than us."

Major Bovington paused a moment, letting that reality sink in. "They've survived by moving their factories and their workers east. Most of their industry is now here"—the major pulled a map out from under the scattered papers on his desk and put his finger on a spot in the middle of Siberia—"at Chelyabinsk. But everyone's already calling it Tankograd. Because that's where the Russians now build their tanks."

"It's a long way from Moscow."

"It's a long way from anywhere. So far away the Germans can't bomb it. But they might not need to bomb it. If Russia capitulates, the way France did, the Germans would capture it. All those factories would start making German tanks."

"Unless we stop them."

"Like the English did to the French."

Bobby stared at the map, fascinated. He traced a line with his finger. "We could do it, too, flying B-17s in from the other side. Coming in from Alaska."

"I guess you're not so stupid, after all."

Alaska. That was the place Karen had mentioned in her letter. She was wrong, though—Alaska was far away, thousands of miles from Leningrad. But in a more important sense, she was right. Alaska was not so far from Siberia, from Russia itself. And thousands of miles through the Siberian wilderness seemed somehow less daunting than thousands of miles through German-occupied Europe.

If she was somehow making her way to Alaska, Bobby had to be there to find her.

"I'd like to be part of it," he blurted. "I'd like to transfer to Alaska."

"First, Russia has to lose."

"They will," Bobby said.

Judging from the way Major Bovington eyed him now, Bobby knew this must have been why he wanted to talk to him in the first place.

"You're sure?" the major asked.

"They're desperate," Bobby said. "They're starving. Every military campaign against the Germans has been a disaster for them. They can't possibly win."

"Is that what your girlfriend says in her letters?"

"In the parts that aren't redacted by Soviet State censors, yes."

Major Bovington stared down at the map of Alaska. Then he looked up at Bobby, deep in thought.

CHAPTER 28
THE TROUBLEMAKER

Krause marched with a sense of foreboding. He hated being this close to the front, and he knew that every crunching step through the snow took him closer to that dreadful location.

There was little chance he'd run into Red Army forces. The Soviet winter offensive on the Leningrad front had been an utter disaster for the Russians. The Second Shock Army had been obliterated. But a few Russian soldiers had survived, and they now formed isolated pockets of Red Army resistance—cut off, well armed, and desperate, hiding in the woods and slowly starving to death.

The Wehrmacht advised its soldiers never to travel alone lest they be jumped by the stray Red Army gangs, who could be as dangerous as cornered tigers. And yet here Krause was, completely alone, because *Unteroffizier* Oster had no runners left he could afford to send.

Krause's objective was to link up with the second squad, which was currently engaged in a forward combat patrol, probing the front line near Tikhvin. He was instructed to inform Corporal Greifer, the

Second Squad's leader, about the escaped prisoner and the death of the platoon's *Leutnant* and *Feldwebel*. Oster wanted the second squad to cancel its patrol and return at once to help defend the village's strategic bridge over the Neva.

Krause hated rivers, and he hated bridges. He hated them because he knew generals treasured them. Rivers halted an army's advance, and bridges bottlenecked supply lines, so generals always prioritized taking and holding bridges. They willingly threw lives away by the thousands to secure river crossings.

Krause was a professional soldier, but he wasn't a willing one. He hated soldiering. He would have preferred staying unemployed, like in the old days, before Hitler's rise. Despite being unemployed, Krause had never wanted for money. His various admirers always took care of him. Every morning Krause would wax his signature moustache and beard into a new, outlandish design. And every evening he would take a new admirer into Berlin's "Garden of the Beasts," the Tiergarten park. It was a wild, wonderful time, and for Krause, the happiest of his life.

Most of the men he knew back then were now dead. The Nazis were intolerant of homosexuals, whom they considered even more undesirable than Slavs and Jews. Krause had been smart enough to read the writing on the wall. He had shaved his head and beard and volunteered for military duty. For a time he flourished even there. He was provided for, given three meals a day, and expected to do little more than train and march in parades.

Krause wasn't the only homosexual soldier. There were thousands of them, many even high-ranking officers. So long as he kept his romantic interests discreet, he found almost as many admirers in the Wehrmacht barracks as he had in Berlin's cabarets.

But then Hitler decided to invade Germany's neighbors, and the real fighting began. Now Krause's friends and lovers were either dead or in convalescent hospitals. Krause was bounced from unit to unit until he landed here, in a platoon of straight men and under the command of a squad leader who evidently hated him. Krause wasn't just romantically frustrated, and he wasn't just scared—he was also bored. He fought that boredom by playing mental games of survival.

Unteroffizier Oster clearly judged Krause to be an unfit soldier. He would prefer Krause dead, because that would open a spot in the squad for a more competent replacement. But Krause wanted to survive. So he played a mental game with the *Unteroffizier*, a game of subterfuge. It was a delicate game, and one in which Krause couldn't be too obvious. The *Unteroffizier* would force Krause into a dangerous situation, and Krause would figure out some way of avoiding the duty.

Take his current mission, by way of example. The Second Squad and Corporal Greifer were probing troop strength near the front. It would stand to reason that wherever they were, Red Army refugees would be nearby. But such refugees were far more dangerous to a single runner like Krause than to a full rifle squad. It certainly didn't behoove Krause to expose himself to such a danger by getting anywhere near the Second Squad.

For that reason, Krause had no intention of actually finding the corporal. To do so would have been an unnecessary risk. Instead, Krause planned to stomp through the snow for a few hours, turn around, and report back to Oster that he was unable to locate the Second Squad. No one knew exactly where the squad was, after all. It didn't have a radio. All anyone knew was the path it was supposed to patrol.

Krause's plan wasn't without risk. When the Second Squad returned, and Greifer gave his report, Oster would know that the squad had followed its mission path and that Krause was lying. But he would never be able to prove it. Krause would claim he must have gotten disoriented in the mud, or perhaps it was Greifer and the Second Squad who'd gotten disoriented—perhaps they hadn't followed the route they thought they had.

These were the games Krause played and the thoughts occupying his mind as he sloshed forward. He was testing a dozen scenarios and coming up with a dozen excuses. It was how he passed the time. Then, suddenly, all those thoughts fled from his brain.

Curled up on the edge of the woods before him, not twenty-five yards away, lay a dog, staring at him. And not just any dog, but the very dog that had caused so much trouble.

Krause stopped moving, and his boots sank a few inches deeper into the snow. He didn't fully understand the significance of the dog. He didn't know whom it belonged to or why it behaved the way it did. But he did sense, deep down in his heart, that this dog had somehow been responsible for *Leutnant* Schaefer's death. Krause didn't like the *Leutnant* and was actually happy that Schaefer was dead. If only Oster, too, were killed, perhaps the platoon could be a safer and happier place. Enough of these Nazi true believers! What Krause wanted was a platoon leader who cared about only one thing—survival. He would happily follow that type of leader.

As Krause stared at the hound, he realized that Oster would want the dog dead. If Krause killed the creature, Oster might revise his opinion of him. Perhaps he'd judge Krause a fit soldier and stop giving him all the most dangerous tasks.

Krause unslung his Kar98k rifle, shouldered it, and aimed. He was more accurate lying down, but even standing he was quite sure he could hit the dog at twenty-five paces. He peered at the hound through the rifle's iron sights. Something was wrong with the animal. Its fur was matted and wet, and it was shivering. The canine stared at the rifle's barrel with sad eyes.

It seemed to recognize the weapon; it must really be a military dog, then, trained to understand the threat that a gun represented. But it wasn't doing anything about it. It just lay there, too weak to move, accepting its fate.

Krause hesitated. Even shivering and weak, the dog was a handsome creature. And suddenly he realized how it had injured itself and why it was wet. Krause had last seen the animal on the other side of the

Neva river. It hadn't crossed the river using the bridge because Krause's squad would have seen it. Instead, it must have tried to cross upriver and fallen through the ice.

That meant the weather must be warming at last. Even though it was late March, the snow was still deep, but now Krause noticed that the icicles in the trees were wet. Perhaps spring was finally coming. The dog must have broken through the ice into the cold water. That was why the animal was weak: it had hypothermia.

Krause reconsidered the scenario. Killing the dog would be no great achievement; it would soon die of hypothermia, anyway. But what if Krause were to capture it? Didn't the *Leutnant* want that all along? Here was Krause's chance. The animal could barely move; Krause could likely approach it easily.

He lowered the gun and cautiously approached. The dog whimpered. Krause held out his hand. The dog sniffed and then licked it. It appeared that the hound recognized Krause as the one who had cut it loose earlier. In fact, the rope Krause had cut still dangled from its neck.

Krause crouched next to the dog and took hold of the lanyard. Retrieving a length of line from his bag, he twined it to the rope with an eight knot and secured the dog to a tree. He then unfolded his *Zeltbahn*, an ingenious army camouflage blanket that could also be used as a poncho or strung up as a pup tent.

Krause draped his *Zeltbahn* over the shivering dog. He then proceeded to collect wood and start a fire.

By the time Krause had a good blaze going, he realized he'd lost track of time. The dim gray of twilight was already creeping across the sky. He should have been back to the village by now. Krause didn't care. Oster wouldn't send anyone looking for him. He'd just assume Krause was lost or dead. That's what Oster wanted anyway, wasn't it? Well, he'd be in for a surprise when Krause returned with the captive canine. Even Oster would be forced to recognize such a great achievement.

The dog was responding well to the heat of the fire. It had stopped shivering and had begun to drool. Krause remembered hearing somewhere this was how dogs sweated—through their tongues. If so, the dog's core temperature was back to normal. Krause was no doctor or veterinarian and had never even been a medic. But he'd already been around enough wounded men in his short military career to recognize the look of death. This dog didn't have it, not anymore. It would survive the night.

So Krause gave the dog a tablet of his *Erbswurst*, a sort of sausage made with dried peas that had been part of Germany's military rations since the Franco-Prussian War. Krause hated the stuff, but the dog loved it. It was still licking its chops as Krause lay down beside it, pulled over a length of his *Zeltbahn*, and slept beneath the stars. Between the warmth of the fire's embers and the dog's thick fur, he felt cozier than in their drafty cottage back in the village.

The next morning, Krause opened a ration can of *Fleischkonserv*, an unidentifiable minced, brownish-gray meat. Krause didn't bother spooning it into his mess tin but just set the open can onto the fire's ashes, hoping the embers were still warm enough to make the concoction somewhat more appetizing. Several minutes later he spooned it into his mouth, but the meat was still chilled throughout. He slopped it onto his *Hartkek*, a hard, crackerlike bread, to help camouflage its gooey coldness.

Krause threw the empty can on the ashes and was about to kick snow over it when the dog nosed its way in front of his foot and began licking at the can. Krause fed it another tablet of *Erbswurst* and bent over to pack up his few belongings. He secured his mess kit, *Zeltbahn*, gas mask, canteen, and bread bag to the rear of his combat webbing. Then, slinging his rifle, he untied the dog and started marching back toward the village.

Or, rather, he tried to start marching back. The dog sat down on its haunches and dug its front paws into the snow. Krause yanked at the cord and pulled, dragging the big dog a few feet. Then the hound lay down, trying to resist Krause with its full strength and weight.

Even as big as the dog was, Krause was still bigger, and he could drag it. But the cord dug uncomfortably into the palms of his hands, and he began to wonder whether he would be forced to drag the animal all the way back to the village. Krause gave up for a moment and crouched beside the dog. He scratched its head and encouraged it with kind words. He broke a stick off a tree and wove it in front of the dog's face.

Sure enough, the dog leaped to its feet and started bounding around, trying to bite the stick. "Come on, boy, that's it, come after the stick," Krause encouraged the animal, and then he ran forward with the cord still wound around his hand.

The dog fell for the trick and bounded after Krause, thinking he would throw the stick. But when Krause didn't, the dog stopped. Krause jerked on his end of the line. The animal once again dropped to its stomach.

Krause squatted down, catching his breath. Clearly the dog didn't want to go back. Something up ahead was luring the animal, had drawn it across the river, and was drawing it still. Krause wondered what that thing was and then realized it would be easy enough for him to find out. All he had to do was slacken the cord, let the dog go where it wished, and follow.

Oster would want him to do that, no doubt. Everyone, even Krause himself, wanted to discover the mystery behind the dog—where it had come from and to whom it belonged. But if it were trying to move forward, toward Tikhvin and the front line and away from the German rear, didn't that tell Krause what he already suspected—that, despite its German breeding, it was, in fact, Russian? Following the dog would likely lead Krause straight into a Russian unit, alone, armed only with a single rifle. The last place Krause wanted to be.

That left him with a new dilemma. Coaxing the dog all the way back to the village was more troublesome than it was worth. Following the dog to its handlers would prove too dangerous. And simply letting the dog go meant it would again be free to help kill more German officers like *Leutnant* Schaefer.

But, Krause suddenly thought, was that such a bad thing? He hated *Unteroffizier* Oster. He wanted Oster dead, too. Maybe this dog truly was some sort of magical devil creature capable of causing officers' deaths?

Krause smiled and let go of the cord. The dog just stayed where it was, lying on its stomach, watching Krause warily.

"Good-bye," Krause said. And then he added, "Good luck."

He turned his back and started marching back toward the village. A few minutes later, when he looked over his shoulder, the dog was gone.

CHAPTER 29

THE CELLIST AND THE

ORGAN-GRINDER

Their relationship had changed. Suddenly they trusted each other.

Petr could have left Karen to hang. He could have taken Duck, found another way across the Neva, and traveled on his own to the Russian lines and Tikhvin. But he hadn't. He'd come back for her. And Karen, too, could have left Petr to starve. But, instead, she'd given him the macaroni. And, perhaps more important, she'd left him a train ticket, her most valuable possession. She could have traded that ticket for anything. The two packets of pasta ensured that Petr didn't starve during the week that he hunted her down and planned her rescue. But he had little left, and the Germans had taken Karen's food. So now they had to share what remained and the old man's hard loaf of bread, rationing once again.

Petr didn't mind; he was growing confident that the Russian lines were near. Karen, too, had lost her map, but Petr remembered the important landmarks. The most daunting had been the Neva. Now that they were across that barrier, all they needed to do was follow the road and continue east.

They saw fewer German convoys but more barricades. Though snow still blanketed the ground, the weather had finally warmed enough to allow the Germans to dig. They'd learned that the T-34s handled Russia's snow and ice better than their panzers, so they crisscrossed the roads with antitank ditches.

Petr was slightly surprised by the fortifications; he'd assumed the Germans would use the spring to renew their relentless advance, not dig in. But clearly they were satisfied with their initial gains in stabilizing the front. Despite the absence of convoys moving down the roads, Karen and Petr still traveled inside the woods, just out of sight. The forest was much thicker here, birch trees growing in a latticework that Petr and Karen had to push through at times.

And then there was the razor wire. Tanks and vehicles could never drive through the thick vegetation, so the Germans didn't bother with antitank ditches anywhere but the roads. That didn't mean Russian infantry couldn't slip through, however. Knowing better than to risk getting surprised and outflanked, the Germans strung thick coils of razor wire from the road into the forest as far as the eye could see. This would slow down any Russian infantry offensive long enough for the Germans to organize a counterattack.

The barbed coils were pierced with wooden stakes tightly wound with more razor wire, an intimidating obstacle looking like a solid mass of spikes. Any attempt to climb over or through the dangerous morass would result in deep lacerations or, even worse, getting tangled in the barbs.

Karen and Petr found a deer that was caught in the wire and eventually died after bloodying itself trying to escape. Karen suggested eating the dead deer, but the crows were already feasting on it, and Petr worried the meat was spoiled. He didn't want to risk getting sick. So they ignored the deer, put their heads together, and tried to figure out a safe way through the barbed wire. But they didn't concentrate long. They were enjoying each other's company too much to solve even a problem like this.

For the first time in months, Karen was happy. The sun was out, high in the blue sky, and it warmed the crisp forest air. Bright light cut through the thick branches of birch and fir, dancing across the forest trunks and floor in dappled shadow patterns. The woods were coming alive all around them with the cawing of the nearby crows and the percussive drumming of a distant woodpecker.

Karen allowed herself, finally, to imagine a future. And so she told Petr about the past.

She told him about New York, about her father, about her concerts, what the city was like, and what it was like to grow up among artists and musicians.

Petr told her about his family. His youth was not so different from Karen's, it turned out. His father was a mathematics professor, deemed brilliant by his colleagues not just in Moscow but all over the world. But then on April 17, 1937, Petr's family history turned dark. Petr was out seeing a movie that night and returned to his apartment to find that the door had been kicked in, and his father was being escorted to an unmarked car by NKVD officers.

"Why?" asked Karen, horrified.

"Because of the purge," Petr responded grimly. "Anyone who was too rich or too smart or too powerful . . . anyone who could criticize or threaten Stalin or his government—they were arrested and made to disappear."

"And your father, he was critical of the government?"

"No," Petr replied, exasperated, "he was too tied up in mathematics. He barely even knew the government existed."

When Petr saw his father taken away, he tried to intervene, demanding that the NKVD officers release him. But his father told Petr to calm down, that it was all a misunderstanding.

Petr realized that his father was trying to save Petr's life. If Petr had persisted in his protest, he, too, would have been arrested. So, with a heavy heart, Petr said good-bye to his father, who assured his son he'd see him again soon. Petr knew it was a lie.

Karen sensed Petr's pain. "I'm sorry."

Petr smiled and wiped the back of his hand across his face. "It's OK, it turned out OK," he assured her. Because, it turned out, Petr's father had been right. The mathematics professor was so ignorant of politics that he befuddled his interrogators. Furthermore, NKVD investigators could never find evidence of a single incident when the math professor had criticized the government. As a result, Petr's father escaped execution. He even escaped the Gulags, the frozen concentration camps where many of his university colleagues died.

"They just let him go?"

"Not exactly," Petr admitted. "They agreed to let him go, but only if he proved his worth to society." He had to stop theorizing, Petr explained, and start working. The Soviet Union didn't need mathematicians, but it did need engineers. It needed railroads and bridges and factories and tractors. Surely a university professor, at the top of his field, could contribute to the greater good?

Unfortunately for Petr's father, his genius was in his head, not in the real world. He was a magician with numbers but not with measurements. When he had to account for the margins of error inherent in the manufacturing processes, he failed. His designs didn't fit together properly, and his bridges fell down.

Eventually he went into self-imposed exile, joining his brother-in-law, who ran a lumber mill in a small northern village. There, Petr's father found employment teaching arithmetic to children. And there he was left alone. The Politburo, the men appointed by Stalin to govern the vast Russian territories, concluded that there he could do no harm.

Karen realized that she and Petr were both children of very bright men whom some might even have considered geniuses. But despite their intelligence, both fathers were as irresponsible as children. They cared not for the world around them; they cared only about their very limited and individual passions. For Karen's father, that had been music. For Petr's father, it was mathematics.

Petr agreed. When his father worked at the university, his deficiencies had not been so obvious. The university took care of him and, by extension, took care of Petr. When, thanks to the purges, Petr's father lost his job and had to look after himself, he was helpless.

Petr sighed. "He often completely lost track of time. And when the first winter struck, he was completely unprepared. He worked on a math theorem for days, forgetting to feed or bring in the goat, who died. And he never bothered to cut new wood. I was forced to beg my uncle and neighbors to share their own provisions just so we could survive the winter."

"The same thing happened to me!" Karen replied, amazed. "Well, not the exact same thing, but . . ." She described the day she was forced to confront bill collectors at her apartment door who were threatening to turn off the gas and electricity. Her father hadn't failed to pay them because he was poor; he'd simply forgotten.

So Karen began to intercept the mail and pay the bills herself, taking the money from her father's wallet or the stash he left in a desk drawer. "He didn't even have a bank account. If we'd been robbed, we would have been destitute!"

"You *were* robbed though, weren't you?" Petr replied. "By the Germans."

"Yes, I suppose we were," Karen agreed, looking into Petr's eyes.

The girl and the boy soldier were sharing melancholy thoughts and disturbing memories, but these didn't make them sad. Strangely, sharing their memories made them happy.

Karen realized then that she'd spent her entire life alone, trapped in her own head and her own emotions. She'd assumed that no one lived the way she did and that her life experience was unique. She never talked about it because she was ashamed of it.

Now that she was sharing her past, she felt an immense sense of relief. She wasn't unique, after all. She wasn't so alone. Here was Petr, half a world away, living a similar life, struggling with similar challenges. If Petr had done it, how many others had done it, too?

Suddenly Karen felt part of a larger community—a community of human beings stretching back through history. She hadn't met any of them, but instantly she no longer felt alone.

As she sat cross-legged across from Petr, talking and listening, she recognized how grateful she was to have escaped that storage closet. If she'd been hung before learning to trust someone like Petr, she never would have had this conversation. She never would have realized that other human beings shared her experiences. She would have lived her entire life trapped inside her own soul, isolated and alone.

"Buried," replied Petr, with a knowing nod. His eyes were clear and shining with interest.

Suddenly Karen realized that they were holding hands. Somehow, during their conversation, their fingers had reached out and interlocked. It was an unconscious gesture, her hands and arms acting as if they had a mind of their own. But when she noticed that they were touching, she felt blood rush warm into her cheeks. She knew she was blushing. Her embarrassment only made things worse. And yet, she didn't want to let go. He was staring right at her. What would he think? She should let go of his hand, she should look away, but she didn't want to.

"Buried," Petr repeated, turning the word over in his mind. He glanced away from her for a moment, studying the barbed wire. "I think I know how to get through."

"How?" asked Karen, both glad and disappointed that his eyes had left her own.

"We could dig under it, through the snow."

It was so obvious. Petr still had his combat shovel. It wasn't difficult or particularly time-consuming to excavate a trench through the snow under the wire.

With the barbed wire behind them, they continued their journey. They also continued their conversation. But they no longer held hands. That spell had been broken. Still, they were having fun, talking about their favorite foods or most cherished childhood toys. But it was the same sort of idle chatter Karen might have had with Inna, no longer accompanied by the deep revelations she'd experienced next to the barbed wire.

They marched and chatted until nightfall, when they allowed themselves to lie back and look up through the branches. Stars had come out, forming a huge dome over the night sky. "I love nighttime," Karen whispered.

"Why?"

"Because in Leningrad, at night, with the electricity out and everyone indoors, all you can see are the stars. You can't see the rubble or the dead bodies. Just stars. Beautiful stars."

"That's not true," Petr responded. "I can see you."

Karen turned her head and saw that he was looking right at her. The movement caused her wool cap to pull sideways. Petr reached out to push it back on, but his fingers got distracted by her dark hair.

She enjoyed the feel of his touch. She wondered whether Duck felt like that when she petted him.

"What did you want?" she asked. "Before the war, before everything changed. What did you want to be?"

"Happy," Petr answered.

Karen thought he was teasing her. "Of course," she said, "everyone wants to be happy."

"No, they don't," Petr replied. "If everyone just wanted to be happy, there wouldn't be a war."

"The war must make somebody happy," Karen suggested.

"Who?"

"I don't know. The generals, maybe. Hitler. The men who work for the companies that make guns and planes and tanks."

"It makes them powerful, it makes them rich, it makes them famous," Petr admitted. "But that's not the same thing as happiness."

"Then what is it?"

"Ambition," Petr stated.

"Ambition leads to happiness."

"No, it doesn't," Petr replied as if the statement were self-evident.

"Then what does it lead to?"

"More ambition."

Karen conceded the point. "All right, then, what leads to happiness?"

"Right here, right now. This is happiness."

Karen blushed again. She pulled her hat back over her ears to stay warm, and Petr moved his hand away. And then she turned over, her back to him. "Good night."

"Good night."

Karen had trouble falling asleep. She wanted to turn over, take Petr in her arms, and cuddle him close. She couldn't be sure, but she suspected he wanted the same thing.

She tried to think of Bobby. She'd asked Bobby the same question when they'd first met, what he wanted. She asked a lot of people that question. She'd always thought of it as a trick to get to know someone, a way to move beyond small talk. But now she was realizing that wasn't her fascination with the question at all. She realized that she asked because she truly was curious. She wanted to know what others wanted because she wasn't sure herself.

Karen knew what she didn't want. She didn't want to be a musician. She didn't want to be a socialist. She didn't want to live in Russia. But there was a big difference between knowing what you *don't* want, and knowing what you *do* want.

She had loved Bobby's answer. It was flattering, hearing that he wanted her. So flattering that she decided she wanted that, too: love. And so she had fallen in love with Bobby.

But now Petr had given her a different answer, an answer both simpler and more complex. It was an answer she'd never heard before. Most people answered by describing their ambitions. Even Bobby's answer had been about ambition, in a way. He wanted her to marry him.

Disturbed, Karen turned back over. "Why? Why are you happy right now?" she asked, waking Petr up.

"Aren't you?" Petr asked.

"Yes," Karen admitted. "But why is that? I'm cold. I'm hungry. I'm scared. How is it possible that I'm happy?"

"Because it's not food or warmth or security that makes someone happy."

"Then what does?"

"People."

Karen thought for a moment. "That's not true."

"I think it is."

"If that were true, no one could ever be happy alone."

"Of course they could be."

"How?"

"By enjoying being with themselves."

"You make it sound so easy."

"No, it's not easy. Sometimes I don't even realize that I'm happy. That's why, when you feel it, it's so important to recognize it. And sometimes, some things make you happy that shouldn't."

"Like what?"

Petr didn't answer. He was thinking of the moment when he'd rushed inside the cottage, when he and Duck had killed the Germans. He'd been happy in that moment. He'd felt a strange ecstasy, a bloodlust, as he'd hammered the second blow of his spade.

He was ashamed of that feeling, so ashamed that he couldn't tell anyone, not even Karen. "I don't know," he lied. And suddenly he felt like changing the subject. "I think we should get some sleep."

Eventually they did fall asleep, but it was a troubled sleep, for both of them.

Karen woke feeling guilty and disloyal to Bobby.

Petr woke feeling ashamed of keeping a secret from Karen.

They ate their breakfast in silence. And then they set out for another day's march.

Gone was the joyful conversation that had characterized the previous day. But Petr didn't seem bothered by the quiet. Karen now realized that what she'd mistaken for gullibility or patriotism when she first met him was simple optimism. Petr had the ability to pick out the little joy details that surrounded them. He pointed out tiny animal tracks in the snow, stopped to appreciate melodious birdcalls, and even took off his cap and helmet to feel the warmth of the sun on his hair.

Karen was once again reminded of Bobby, of the letters he'd sent describing magical little details of New York. She loved those letters. Just as she loved being with Petr right now. As the sun warmed the forest, so did her mood. Soon she was chatting again, like a schoolgirl.

Petr was growing more confident that they'd finally passed through the German lines. They even risked coming out of the forest and returning to the road. There, they discovered that rough-hewn logs had been dropped lengthwise along the melting snow. It was an age-old Russian solution to muddy spring roads, and Petr said it confirmed that they'd crossed into Russian territory.

The logs provided a secure platform for their continued march and seemed to double their progress. Sure enough, no later than three o'clock in the afternoon, they approached a Red Army checkpoint. Sentries challenged them in Russian but let them pass. Petr and Karen were fed and given a basin of clean water to wash up. They were brought to the Red Army captain in charge of this forward position for a debriefing.

Petr took the lead in the conversation, claiming they had both been part of the ill-fated Second Shock Army. The Germans had surrounded their unit, and Karen had been captured. That explained her black eye and the loss of her military uniform. Karen lied that she escaped and found Russian clothes before meeting Petr and making their way through enemy territory back to the Russian lines.

The captain believed their story; he confirmed that the Second Shock Army had been cut off and surrounded, and even admitted that it was slowly being destroyed. Refugees from the fighting were occasionally finding their way back, as Petr and Karen had.

He asked them to describe what they'd seen of German military strength and to point out on a map the village with the bridge across the Neva. Then he gave Karen a new uniform and let them go, recommending they reach the retraining battalion as quickly as possible. Rumor had it that Stavka was preparing a new spring offensive, this time in the Ukraine near the city of Kharkov. They needed every soldier they could muster.

Petr and Karen thanked the captain and continued on their way. Karen had no intention of joining the retraining battalion, of course, or of fighting in Kharkov. She was still headed for Moscow by way of Tikhvin.

As they entered Tikhvin, they saw that the town had been bombed and shelled into a broken landscape of blackened timber and cracked concrete. Unlike Leningrad, its military value was too high to allow it to simply rot and die. The Wehrmacht and the Red Army had struggled against each other here in bitter street-to-street fighting—first Germany winning and then the Red Army taking it back in December. Red Army engineers wasted no time erecting hastily built shacks to shelter soldiers, and they jerry-rigged machines to keep the trains running, the supplies moving, and the reinforcements coming. The little city looked like an Old West boomtown built atop ancient Roman ruins.

To get on a train, Karen knew she and Petr had to change their story. Now they assumed the personas of the dead men who'd been issued the tickets. One of the men was named Dimah, which could be either a boy's or girl's name, so Karen pretended to be him.

A Soviet military policeman from the commandant's service confronted them. It was Karen's turn to take the lead.

"We were wounded at Nevsky Pyatachok," she claimed, referring to the bridgehead across the Neva that Leningrad's defense forces were stubbornly holding.

"What were you doing at Nevsky?" the commandant asked suspiciously.

"I was manning an antiaircraft gun. I don't know what he was doing . . ." She nodded toward Petr. "He was struck by shrapnel the moment he hit the riverbank. I barely got him onto an evacuation boat, and then I was hit, too."

"How did you get out of Leningrad?"

"Across the Road of Life."

"I didn't see you get off a truck."

"Because our truck got strafed by German planes. We barely escaped on foot." Karen showed the commandant her ticket. "Look, we have tickets to Moscow. We're to join a T-34 training battalion."

It wasn't a likely story, but there wasn't anything the commandant could flag as obviously untrue. So he stamped their ticket and directed them to the station.

Eventually, Karen and Petr procured a seat on the next train to Moscow. It wasn't a seat, really—it was just enough space to stand, in a crowded boxcar. "You ever been on a troop train before?" asked one of the grinning soldiers.

"No," Karen replied.

"You're gonna love it," the soldier assured her ironically. "You get a massage free with the ticket."

He was right. There was nothing to hold on to in the boxcar, so with every move of the train, the soldiers were falling all over one another. Karen and the other female passengers were constantly getting pinched and groped. Petr noticed and wanted to intervene, but Karen subtly gestured to him to swallow his anger and remain calm. The German beatings and NKVD torture were far worse than any pinching. She didn't mind the unwelcome attention so long as miles of Russia continued to pass beneath her feet.

Heading southeast, away from Leningrad and toward Moscow—*that* was what made Karen happy.

CHAPTER 30
THE CHOIRBOY

Bobby was starting to regret encouraging Major Bovington to move them all to Alaska. It had started promising enough, with a transfer back in April to the 57th Pursuit Squadron at Hamilton Field in California. Amazingly, Major Bovington's command now included some of the most experienced P-39 pilots in the Army Air Forces, so they were to help train the pilots of the 57th.

Bobby had embraced the duty because he knew that the 57th would soon be transferred from California to Alaska. Alaska was, he secretly hoped, one step closer to Karen.

No one else in his squadron shared his enthusiasm. And now that they were finally in Alaska, it was worse than any of them expected.

The facilities weren't bad—they were far better than the dump of an airfield in Eritrea. But it was colder than they'd feared. Even though it was now May, they had to plow snow off the airfield every morning. The roads were choked with more snow, and the shore was so clogged with ice it was hard to tell where the land ended and the water began. The icy wind gusted in from the sea, bringing large clouds of snow with it, and going outside was like getting caught in a blizzard. Everyone hated going outside, and nobody did unless they had to. The absolute temperature wasn't too bad: it hovered around thirty degrees. But the windchill brought that close to zero.

They huddled in their barracks, playing cards, and gambling with bottle caps they called "duty chips."

Jack had come up with the idea to deal in duty chips—you could win them to make someone else do your work for you. Scrubbing latrines was a duty chip. Peeling potatoes was a duty chip. But any task outside was several duty chips. Digging a defensive trench was ten duty chips. Plowing the airfield was five.

"Call," Bobby announced, and tossed a bottle cap onto the pile of tin heaped in the middle of the rickety card table.

Max grabbed the deck and tapped it a couple of times against the tabletop. Max was twenty-three and from San Diego. He'd joined their squadron at Hamilton Air Field, where he'd turned out to be a natural pilot. He looked to Jack expectantly.

"Two," Jack said. He slid two cards from his hand facedown toward Max; Max flicked Jack two new cards from the deck before glancing at Wally.

"Gimme a sec—I gotta think," Wally told him, eyeing his cards carefully.

Bobby used the opportunity to analyze his hand. It was garbage: a jack, a ten, a seven, an ace, and a three. It didn't add up to anything. He should have folded. Calling was a fool's bet.

"Just one, I think," Wally muttered.

"You think or you know?" Max grumbled.

"Yeah, just one." Wally slid one of his cards across, and Max flicked him a new one from the deck. His eyes shifted to Bobby.

"Three," Bobby said with a frown. He tossed the cards to Max, not really caring whether anyone saw what they were. Max flicked three new ones back.

"Call," Jack said after analyzing his new hand.

All attention passed to Wally, who hemmed and hawed and fidgeted, unwilling to commit.

Wally hated the cold more than anyone. But they all hated Alaska equally. Alaska was too far from the fighting they all craved. The only thing keeping the pilots from griping too much was the prospect of finally getting into a fight. It was why most of them had joined the Army Air Forces, and they'd begun to resent having spent their entire brief military careers in training and transport.

Combat was the official reason given for their being reassigned to the 57th, and it was why they'd been sent to this little airfield in Nome, Alaska. Army brass feared an imminent Japanese attack on American territory, and Alaska, so far off the beaten path, was deemed highly vulnerable. Wally, Jack, Max, and the rest only hoped the army brass were right.

Bobby had cards in his hand, but he barely looked at them. His mind was wandering. Alone among his squad mates, Bobby knew that the Japanese weren't about to attack Alaska. That was a mere cover story, intentional disinformation designed to obscure the truth.

Major Bovington had continued to confide in Bobby because of his special knowledge of Russian conditions, and Bobby was able to deduce the big picture.

Army Air Forces' real purpose in Alaska had very little to do with Japan and everything to do with Russia. In a technical sense, Alaska was as close to Russia as America could get. The Bering Strait, a tiny strip of ocean only fifty miles wide, was all that separated Russia from American territory. But there wasn't a lot of trust between the Russians and Americans. After all, only two years ago, Stalin had been Hitler's ally—Russia and Germany had invaded Poland together and divided the conquered country between them.

But that was then, and this was now. Hitler had betrayed his erstwhile ally, and now Russia was fighting for her survival. So Americans were forced to change their opinions of Russia and Stalin.

As Great Britain's leader, Winston Churchill was quoted as saying: "If Hitler invaded hell, I would make at least a favorable reference to the devil in the House of Commons." Even if Stalin was the devil incarnate, he was still the enemy of the enemy—enemy of Nazi Germany, a traditional enemy of Imperial Japan, and therefore a convenient friend of America.

The Soviet Union became an ally purely by virtue of mutual interest. But it wasn't a trusted friend. American military experts didn't believe that Russia could withstand another summer of German aggression. The Wehrmacht's war machine had been unstoppable everywhere it marched, including Russia. Mechanization—trucks, airplanes, and tanks—seemed to have broken those barriers that prevented Napoleon from conquering Russia 150 years earlier.

Germany's Army Group South had stalled, digging in over the winter and consolidating its gains. But there were already signs of it stirring. American generals believed it would soon be back on the move, driving south toward the rich oil fields of the Caucasus Mountains, in Baku, which appeared to be the key to the entire war. They provided an almost limitless supply of petrol. If Germany could secure that fuel, and by all appearances it seemed they would be able to, Russia was doomed.

And so, too, might America be. America's greatest advantage was her size and industry. Japan was an island nation with limited resources, and Germany was only slightly bigger than Texas. But Russia was vast. With access to Russian manpower and resources, German industry could dwarf that of the United States.

So the real reason Bobby's squadron had been transferred to Alaska was to help prepare a fallback strategy. If Germany's Army Group South were to succeed, if they were to capture the oil fields at Baku, America wanted to bomb those fields.

They couldn't stop there. They would have to bomb Chelyabinsk, so-called Tankograd, Russia's boomtown military-industrial complex, which had recently relocated to Siberia. America simply couldn't allow all that Russian industry to fall into Nazi hands.

The pretext was Lend-Lease. The United States would provide Russia with warplanes, flying them across the Bering Strait from Alaska. Russia considered the proposal, not suspecting that America's secret desire in flying the planes over themselves was to identify the Russian airfields they'd need to capture for a future bombing campaign. But things seldom work out according to plan. Contrary to everyone's expectations, the Russians ultimately refused.

They didn't refuse the planes; they wanted the planes. But it seemed they didn't trust the Americans any more than the Americans trusted them. They didn't want Americans flying through Russian airspace. They wanted to send their own pilots to Nome, where they would then take possession of the American planes and fly them to the Russian front themselves.

The whole plan was a bust, and as a result, the American pilots had nothing to do. They didn't know it was a bust. It was all top secret. But the truth was they were just wasting their time playing cards until the Russian pilots arrived, with no prospect of getting into a real fight.

"Raise," Wally finally announced, tossing another bottle cap on the pile.

"Call," Bobby said, matching Wally's bottle cap with one of his own.

"I'm out," Jack groaned, laying his cards facedown on the table.

"I guess that just leaves me," mused Max. "I guess I'll see your duty chip and raise you one more." He tossed two bottle caps into the center of the table.

Wally sighed. He tossed another cap on the pile. Bobby nodded and did the same.

Max eyed Wally before laying out his cards. "Two pair." He had two kings and two queens.

Wally beamed and put down his hand. "Straight." He had a three to a seven, all in order, a great hand. He leaned over to scoop up the duty chips.

"Hold on a second," Jack griped, hoping to save his friend Bobby at least. "Bobby? What you got?"

Bobby looked at his cards. His second draw had been extraordinarily lucky. All five of his cards were now spades, a flush to beat Wally's straight. But he just frowned.

"I got nothing," he said. He dropped the cards facedown. "Take your winnings, Wally. The duty's all mine. Guess I better start plowing the runway."

Grinning now, Wally scooped the duty chips into his pile as Bobby got up and started bundling himself into his parka, sweater, and hat.

CHAPTER 31

THE CELLIST AND THE
ORGAN-GRINDER

The train broke down fifty miles east of Tikhvin. No one seemed to mind. In fact, it was a relief to get out of the crowded boxcars. Soldiers stumbled down the railroad embankment and lay down in the grass.

It was a beautiful, warm day. April had come, and spring had finally sprung. White clouds surrounded the bright sun but never eclipsed it. Karen closed her eyes and relished the warmth of the sun on her cheeks. Somehow her fingers had found Petr's, and she enjoyed the feel of his grip.

There had been hundreds of soldiers on the train, perhaps even a thousand, but they hardly made a sound. All Karen could hear were the grinding chirps of the cicadas and the distant clang of an engineer trying to repair the locomotive. She hoped the engineer didn't succeed. She was so content lying in the grass, she could have stayed there for hours.

The other soldiers seemed to feel the same way. They were veterans—all of them—which meant they had fought the Germans, and they had lost. Most of them were all that remained of their platoons, companies, and even battalions, so they were being shipped back for reassignment. They'd all seen their fair share of death, and they knew they would be seeing it again. In their past was the war, in their future was the war, but right now was peace. They all just wanted the warmth of the sun and the smell of the grass to last as long as possible. But even in the most peaceful repose, some men grew restless. They began to mutter and to move. The sound of voices and laughter rose up in the sky, silencing the cicadas.

And then came the sound of music.

"Look," Petr said, gently tugging at Karen's hand.

Karen didn't want to look. She wanted to lie there forever, to forget about the war—and about the impossible journey before her. She began to wonder whether she could stay in Russia, after all. Maybe if she went far enough east, the Nazis would never reach her. Just keep going east, no real goal, just east. That would be so much easier than figuring out how to get back to America.

Karen giggled when she thought of America. She used to think it was so large. Her aunt was an opera singer who lived in San Francisco. Karen visited her every Thanksgiving, and it seemed so far away. It took three days by train. Now Karen realized that three days was nothing. It had taken far longer than that just to get from Leningrad to Tikhvin. How long would it take her to cross Siberia, to cross Alaska? Was there even a train in Siberia?

Of course there was. The Trans-Siberian Railway was famous. But even if she could get a ticket, that train went to China, not to Alaska. The Japanese had invaded China. It was as bad as it was in Russia. If Karen was going to escape, she needed to go northeast, not southeast. But that seemed impossible. Better to just keep running, keep hiding, outrun the Nazis.

The Russians couldn't win. Everyone knew that now. Maybe she could convince Petr to come with her. They could find a little cabin in the woods, like the hunting shack. They could hide there, Petr could hunt deer, and they could just wait in peace until the war was over.

"Look," Petr repeated, tugging Karen's hand again.

Karen propped her elbows behind her and lifted her head. The music was coming from an accordion. Soldiers had surrounded the accordion player, smiling and clapping along with the music. They were so happy. Karen remembered the water-bucket lines, when everyone in Leningrad started singing that silly song. Maybe her father was right. Maybe music was more important than bread or fire or security.

She recalled what Petr had claimed—things didn't make happiness; people did. And, Karen hoped, maybe music. Otherwise, her father had died in vain.

"We should dance," Petr suggested.

Karen was horrified. Petr couldn't be serious, could he? She looked at him, and although he was smiling, he *was* serious. And he was beautiful. His eyes were sparkling, and his joy and enthusiasm were infectious.

Karen attempted to inoculate herself from that infection. "But I don't know how to dance."

Petr, still smiling, looked her over with an appraising eye. "That's a lie," he playfully accused her. "You're a musician. You probably dance all the time."

Karen did dance and quite often, in New York. She loved to dance at her father's parties, after concerts. She loved jazz and Big Band music, and she especially loved dancing with Bobby.

But that was years ago, and this was different. "I don't know how to dance like *that*." She pointed.

Several soldiers were dancing, but they were thrusting their hands out before them and squatting and kicking out their heels in an impressive acrobatic display.

Petr laughed. "No one but the Cossacks know how to dance like that."

He grabbed Karen's hand and pulled her to her feet despite her resistance. He kept dragging her and didn't stop until they'd broken through the ring of clapping soldiers and joined the Cossacks. The soldiers cheered at the sight of Karen—she wasn't the only girl present, but she was the only one dancing. Her appearance reinvigorated the accordion player, and he increased the tempo.

Karen tried to mimic Petr as he placed her arm in his and led her back and forth. It felt more like skipping than dancing to Karen, and she was reminded of the square dances she'd seen in cowboy movies. But this was much faster than a square dance, and she had to admit it was thrilling to be the center of attention. Even the Cossacks turned toward her, jumping and yelling and clapping and smiling at her. The music got faster, and Petr swung her more quickly. She felt dizzy.

But she didn't stop. Her legs tired underneath her, but she didn't feel the sharp pain that usually accompanies exhaustion. Something about the music and the clapping and the cheering transformed the pain into euphoria. She didn't realize she couldn't keep going until her feet collapsed beneath her, and she tumbled, gasping, into the grass. But the crowd just cheered even louder. She looked over and saw that Petr had fallen beside her. They gazed at each other, smiling and trying to catch their breath.

And then the cheering changed. It became a chant. "Kiss her, kiss her, kiss her, kiss her!" yelled the crowd, clapping to accentuate each word, and the accordion player played along with the chant.

Karen saw that Petr had stopped smiling. He'd turned beet red with embarrassment. But that only made him look cuter. So she decided to rescue him from his predicament. She grabbed him by his hair and kissed him on the lips. She'd intended it as a simple gesture to help a friend out of a jam. But when their mouths touched, she had a sudden guilty urge to kiss him harder, like she'd once kissed Bobby. The thought of Bobby shamed Karen, and she reluctantly pulled her lips away. The crowd erupted into cheers of joy and finally parted to let Karen and Petr escape their impromptu dance circle.

"Thank you," Petr said to her when they'd settled back onto the grass of the railroad embankment. "They wouldn't have let us go otherwise."

"No, thank *you*," Karen insisted. "You were right. That was fun."

The train still wasn't repaired by dusk. The engineers didn't really know what they were doing, it seemed. They'd banged on the locomotive with a crowbar for about an hour before declaring that they needed to wait for specialized equipment.

They used the train tracks as a telegraph device, reporting their condition to the next station down the line. But even they couldn't predict when help would arrive. Like the soldiers, the engineers didn't really seem to be in any hurry at all.

That night Karen, Petr, and the rest of the soldiers ate gruel. The provisions were stored on the train, and military cooks lit fires to boil the oats seasoned with beef bouillon. It was really more soup than gruel, the oats thin and unfulfilling. Karen, remembering her meals of axle grease and wallpaper glue, found it delicious. But most of the soldiers complained, including Petr.

The moon rose, and still no help arrived. The soldiers lay back on the hill. Those lucky enough to have bedrolls used them, while others used the grass as their mattress and their bread bags as pillows.

Karen was tired, but she found it hard to sleep. Bugs were in the grass and in the air, buzzing near her ears and nostrils. They didn't bite—they were harmless—but they tickled when they landed on her nose or crawled over her legs.

Giving up on sleep, she turned on her side and looked at Petr. "How was the hunt?"

Petr opened his eyes and looked back at her. His expression made it clear he had no idea what she was talking about. "My what?"

"Your hunt. You know, when I left you, you'd gone hunting, look-ing for a deer."

"Oh yeah, that. It didn't go well."

Karen was disappointed. In her fantasy, Petr was such a good hunter he could keep them both well fed while hiding from the Nazis. "You couldn't find a deer?"

"No, I found one all right. I just couldn't get close enough to kill it. It kept smelling me or hearing me or something and running away."

"Didn't you have the pistol?"

"Yes, but you have to get close to use a pistol. They're not really accurate enough for hunting."

Karen's optimism returned. He could hunt—he just needed a bet-ter weapon. "What about this? Would it have helped?" She held up the MP40 she'd taken from the Germans.

Petr shook his head. "That's just like a pistol. It even uses the same type of ammunition. Throws out a lot of lead but not very accurately. What you really need for hunting is one of those." He pointed at a nearby Mosin-Nagant, the standard Red Army infantryman's rifle. They were everywhere.

"Maybe we could trade for one," Karen suggested.

"Why?" Petr said. "You planning to go hunting?" There was a twin-kle in his eye, as though he thought it was a joke.

"Anything to keep from starving."

The twinkle disappeared. He'd forgotten how close she'd been to dying in Leningrad. He hadn't meant to be insensitive. "You don't have to worry about that, not anymore. You'll be safe in Moscow."

"In a few months, Moscow could be just like Leningrad." Karen spoke the truth, even Petr had to admit—his face scrunched up think-ing about it. "Why Moscow, anyway?" Karen added.

"I don't know. I guess because it's the capital?" Petr responded, misinterpreting the question. "The Nazis probably figure if they can conquer Moscow, they'll have conquered Russia."

"No, I mean, why are you going to Moscow? You don't have to. You're a soldier. You could have rejoined the army in Tikhvin. You didn't need to get on the train."

"You're right."

"So why did you? Are you afraid of fighting?"

Petr thought hard about his response. It was a complicated question, with no clear answer. There was a part of him that wanted to get back into the fight, that wanted once again to experience that altered state of consciousness he'd felt in deadly combat. But he also knew he couldn't survive the war, and returning to it would eventually mean his own death. The problem was, meeting Karen had made his life matter again to him. "No, not afraid, not exactly," he told her. "I mean, everyone's afraid; even the Germans are afraid. You'd have to be insane not to be. But I'm no more afraid than anyone else."

"What will you do when we get to Moscow?"

"Probably join a retraining battalion. Let them decide where to assign me next."

"Couldn't you have done that in Tikhvin?"

"Maybe. But Duck was from Moscow. I was kind of hoping I could find his family first."

"His family? Why?"

"He was a soldier. When a soldier dies, the family gets a letter. I figure Duck's family should know what happened to him, know how well he fought, how brave he was."

"He was just a dog."

"A dog who saved my life. Saved your life, too. Twice."

Petr was right. Karen was ashamed of what she'd said. Of course Duck wasn't "just a dog."

"What about you?" Petr asked. "What will you do in Moscow?"

"Keep running east," Karen replied without hesitation. "East as far as I have to, all the way to America if I can."

Petr nodded. But his expression said that he didn't believe Karen could make it.

"How will you find Duck's family?"

"I have no idea," Petr admitted.

Karen reached out and took his hand. "I'll help if I can."

Petr smiled. "Thanks."

Dawn came, and still no help arrived. The cooks provided more gruel for breakfast, but it was even thinner than the night before. "How much food do you figure they have?" Karen asked.

"Only enough to get us to Moscow. A couple of days' worth. That's probably why it's so thin. They're already rationing it."

That afternoon, a supply train bound for Tikhvin neared. It was heading in the opposite direction of Karen and Petr's train, and when the engineers saw its smoke in the distance, they leaped up and ran toward it, waving their arms and yelling.

They'd let the broken-down locomotive's fire go out to conserve coal, and so had no steam to blow their whistle. The trouble was, they sat on the downward slope of a hill, only a few hundred yards from the crest. They were hidden from the approaching supply train coming up the other side, and the train was hidden from them. They wouldn't be able to see each other until the supply train crested the hill, and by then it might be too late. The supply train would be plunging downhill with only a few hundred yards to put on the brakes.

Karen and Petr didn't know this yet. They only saw the engineers jumping off the locomotive and running up the hill like madmen, yelling and waving their arms.

"What do you think they're doing?" Petr asked.

Karen pointed at the approaching plume of smoke. "You think that's a train coming?"

"I think so," Petr acknowledged, but he still didn't understand the danger. "But why are they yelling? Isn't that what we've been waiting for?"

They continued to watch the approaching smoke in contemplative silence. "I don't think it's slowing down," Karen commented.

"No, you're right," Petr agreed.

"I don't think that's the train we're waiting for."

"No wonder they're yelling," Petr blurted out, suddenly alarmed. He jumped up and started sprinting toward the boxcars. "Come on!"

Karen leaped up and raced after him. "What're you doing?"

"They're going to collide. We gotta warn that train!"

As they reached the tracks, Petr turned from the boxcars and jumped onto the antiaircraft flatcar, their protection against a Luftwaffe attack. It was directly behind the locomotive. Petr would surely be killed if the trains collided.

Karen jumped on right behind him.

"Break open one of those ammo crates," Petr commanded.

Karen leaned over and pried the lid off one of the metal boxes. It was filled with 37mm high-explosive shells. The flatcar was just a platform for the 37mm cannon mounted in the center. A stolen copy of the Swedish Bofors, the gun was basically a gigantic machine gun that could throw a stream of heavy shells into the air at eighty rounds per minute—enough to intercept the path of an approaching dive-bomber.

The trouble was, Petr didn't know how to operate it.

Karen dragged the open crate of shells next to the gun. "What now?"

"I have no idea." Petr ran his hands all over the gun in a panic. It looked nothing like a Katyusha rocket launcher. He couldn't even tell how to load it.

"What are you doing? Get away from there!" The gunnery sergeant of the 37mm cannon was running toward Karen and Petr, irate that someone was messing with his weapon.

"We've gotta get this loaded, we've gotta warn that train!" Petr shouted back, unintimidated.

The gunnery sergeant mounted the flatcar brandishing his pistol— and understood all at once. His eyes went wide with panic as he stared at the approaching smoke cloud. He dropped his pistol, letting it dangle on a tether attached to his holster. He elbowed Petr aside and cracked open the gun's breech. "Give me a shell!" he yelled.

Karen leaned down. The shell was heavier than she expected, almost four pounds. She picked it up with both hands and handed it to the gunnery sergeant, who slid it down the metal rack leading into the breech.

"More, more!" commanded the sergeant.

Petr helped Karen hand shell after shell to the sergeant. "Isn't that enough?" Petr asked, trying to judge the approach of the supply train out of the corner of his eye.

"Let's hope so." The gunnery sergeant yanked the charging handle, loading the gun. "Turn those cranks!"

Karen and Petr focused on their appointed tasks, spinning separate cranks that turned the cannon and elevating it to point up and over the approaching supply train.

"Fire in the hole!" the gunnery sergeant yelled, and pulled the trigger.

The gun roared and kicked as shells rocketed into the sky and arced over the approaching supply train like rapid-fired flares.

Karen then realized why they'd had to load so many shells. Every fifth one was a tracer round, filled with glowing phosphorous that marked their path through the air. They helped the gunner aim—the other rounds traveled too fast to be seen, so the tracers marked their direction and path. The gun was far louder than a train whistle, but they wanted the drivers of the supply train to see them as well as hear them.

The gunnery sergeant fired every last shell. Using a rag to open the red-hot breech, he yelled, "Reload!"

Karen and Petr had cracked open another ammunition crate and dragged it toward the gun. But the gunnery sergeant held up his hand. "Wait . . ."

They could hear the screech of metal on metal. It was the supply train's brakes. The engineers had seen and heard them.

But the supply train's locomotive was already cresting over the hill. "Run!" Karen yelled.

All three jumped from the flatcar and tried to run down the embankment.

The gunnery sergeant stumbled but didn't bother trying to find his feet. He just let himself tumble down, rolling painfully over the swinging pistol still tethered to his belt—fortunately, with the safety on.

Petr and Karen dove into the grass below and turned to watch the impending collision. The supply train's metal wheels sparked against the iron rails, but the engineers were letting go and then reapplying the brakes, forcing the wheels to regain their grip after each screeching skid. The supply train was slowing, but it came closer and closer to impact.

About twenty yards from contact, it halted.

Once everyone caught their breath, the engineers from both trains put their heads together to figure out what had happened. It seemed that no one had gotten the telegraph message, so no help was on its way. But now, with the broken-down troop train blocking the tracks, the supply line was cut.

The only solution was for the supply train to back up all the way to the previous station and report the problem. No one seemed surprised, or even frustrated. Everyone was used to Communist Russia's inefficiency. And a longer delay only meant a longer time before they were all redeployed for battle.

Meanwhile, Karen was getting used to the tickle of the insects. They didn't bother her as much that second night, and she fell fast asleep. She woke to the sound of wolves howling. All around her the encamped soldiers slept soundly, apparently not bothered by the haunting sound. Then, suddenly, the howling stopped. Karen stood up and listened. The night was perfectly quiet. Even the insects had stopped chirping.

She didn't know why, exactly, but she was worried. The howling had come from the northwest, back toward Tikhvin. Leaving Petr to sleep, she released the safety on her German submachine gun and began walking down the tracks in the direction from which they'd come.

After about ten minutes, Karen stopped. She suddenly felt frightened. She was alone, in the dark. She regretted not waking Petr and asking him to come with her. She hadn't heard the wolves this whole time, so they must have moved on. She took a deep breath and turned to head back to the train.

Then she heard something growl. It was behind her, farther down the tracks toward Tikhvin. She gripped the submachine gun in both hands and crept in the same direction she'd been marching. She saw figures in the starlight—wolves. They were stalking something on the tracks. What was it? It looked like another wolf, its form silhouetted. It was surrounded and outnumbered, but it stood its ground, snout curled back and growling. The wolves didn't growl. They approached cautiously and began to circle the victim. They didn't have to growl. They knew they would take it down.

But they hadn't counted on Karen. "Get away! Shoo!" she yelled.

They didn't. She jerked the trigger. The gunfire startled the wolves, and they bolted back into the woods. But the animal on the track seemed completely unafraid of the submachine gun. It straightened up and began loping toward her, its teeth flashing in the moonlight and its tongue lolling.

It was Duck.

Karen rushed toward the dog and embraced him in a tight hug. Duck pushed against her, and they tumbled together onto the railroad tracks. Duck pushed his wet snout into her face and began licking her. She nearly suffocated under Duck's tongue, but she didn't care; she just hugged him and savored the beat of his heart and the feel of his warm fur.

"Look who's here," Karen said.

Petr groaned and slapped at whatever it was that had woken him again. He opened his eyes to see a dog's snout—not just any snout; it was Duck's.

He grabbed the hound's head and drew him into a bear hug. Duck smiled and licked Petr.

"How'd you find him?" Petr asked in wonder.

"He was following us, straight down the railroad tracks."

Petr tugged at Duck's fur and rubbed him behind the ears. "I heard gunshots—was that you?"

Karen nodded. "A groggy sentry came my way, but he understood—once I told him about the wolves."

"Wolves?"

"They were after Duck.'

"Incredible," Petr marveled.

"Sure is," Karen said. "He's a survivor, that one."

Petr hesitated a moment. "I'm gonna take him back," he confessed.

"Back where?"

"To Moscow, to his family." Petr looked away, trying to gather his thoughts and express them coherently. "He's fought enough. He deserves to go home."

"We all do," Karen agreed.

"But for him it's different," Petr explained. "If the army gets ahold of him again, they'll just strap another bomb to him. He won't survive."

"Will you? Will anyone?" Karen gestured at the sleeping soldiers.

Petr shrugged. "I dunno. Maybe not. But at least we've got a chance. At least we're allowed to fight, not just forced to commit suicide like Duck."

But even as Petr said the words, he sensed they were untrue. He remembered their mass attack on the village, in waves. The soldiers in the front of that wave had no chance of surviving, not really. Weren't they being forced to kill themselves, too?

He pushed the thought out of his mind. "Anyway," he continued, "we should leave here now."

"Now?" Karen shot back, alarmed. "Why now?"

Petr grimaced. It was painful for him to say good-bye, obviously, but his mind was made up. "They won't let Duck on the train, and even if they did, it would only be as military property. How long do you think he'd last?"

Karen immediately realized Petr was right. She scrambled to gather her meager belongings. "I'm coming with you."

"Really?" Petr was smiling. Obviously it was what he wanted but had been afraid to ask. "Why?"

"I told you I'd help you find his family. Now let's go before someone stops us."

They began moving quietly toward the perimeter of the sleeping soldiers. Karen hesitated, leaned over, and picked up a Mosin-Nagant rifle. Its owner didn't stir in his sleep.

"What are you doing?" Petr whispered.

"It's a long walk. We've gotta eat," she replied, handing him the weapon. "Now hurry up, let's get out of here."

They headed off into the darkness, letting the railroad ties guide them, the first steps of a long march to Moscow.

CHAPTER 32
THE CHOIRBOY

It was already June, but you would never have known it by looking out the cockpit window. The rugged little Aleutian Islands far below were still capped with snow, and beyond them raged the cold and stormy Bering Sea.

Bobby wondered how long he'd last in those rolling waves. A matter of minutes, probably, before he numbed from hypothermia and slipped into the depths. Bailing out over water wasn't a good strategy for survival. But neither was burning up in a cockpit. To die either by fire or by ice, Bobby realized with dread, might be the final decision of his young life.

He closed his eyes and shook his head. That was just the fear talking.

Bobby had grown up Catholic. He was a believer, in his own way. But he was also educated enough to come to his own conclusions about human evolution. He believed men to be animals, subject to all the laws of biology that entailed. And he believed in Darwin's theory—that all animals, humans included, had evolved to embrace those characteristics that enhanced their chances of survival. Fear was one such characteristic. Fear had a purpose; fear helped the human race survive. Fear compelled men to run away from danger, and more often than not, those who gave in to that compulsion survived. That was why fear still existed, why it persisted after millions of years of evolution—a unifying characteristic of all humans.

But Bobby also believed that human intelligence had devised ways to surpass natural evolution. Men had never evolved wings, and yet here he was, flying into battle over the northernmost territories in the United States. His wings weren't provided by God or nature, but by engineering that human minds devised.

He wasn't running from danger, but flying toward it. He'd skipped evolution, and in return, his fear betrayed him. If fear was meant to improve Bobby's chance of survival, fear would have prevented him from getting into his plane. It would have prevented him from joining the Army Air Forces. It would have prevented him from falling in love with Karen Hamilton in the first place.

Fear hadn't done any of those things. Fear had come too late. And, like most things that come too late, fear had become less of a help than a hindrance. Bobby tried to change his thoughts and attitudes; he tried consciously to alter his mind-set and forget about the fear. But he found that exercise maddeningly challenging.

Despite the fear, Bobby was also feeling relief. All along, he hadn't been able to reveal to his squadron mates their real purpose for being in Alaska. This meant he didn't have to admit to his part in the fiasco. But the guilt had started eating him up inside. As a Catholic, he'd been taught to expel his guilt through confession. Yet in this case he couldn't confess because doing so would have revealed a military secret.

And then a miracle happened. Contrary to everyone's real expectations, the Japanese had attacked Alaska.

Naval intelligence had somehow intercepted Japanese communications and was able to warn Army Air Forces. When Japanese torpedo bombers attacked Dutch Harbor on Unalaska Island, P-40 Warhawks flown by the 11th Army Air Force quickly drove them off.

But the Japanese weren't about to go away, so Bobby's squadron of P-39s was hastily flown down from Nome to Fort Randall Army Airfield on the tip of the Alaskan peninsula. There they were refueled and fully armed.

The Airacobras intended as gifts for their Russian allies were suddenly desperately needed. They weren't Trojan horses anymore; they were warplanes defending America.

Every American airman knew an unfortunate truth, however: the planes weren't up to the task. The Airacobra was largely an example of failed aircraft development. Designed as a low-altitude fighter, it should have excelled against other low-flying aircraft like Germany's infamous Stuka dive-bombers. But the Japanese didn't stay low. Their aircraft operated at many different altitudes, and their Mitsubishi Zeros could outmaneuver any American plane yet built. The Japanese had become masters of the sky, outdueling the Americans in any but the most lopsided engagements. To win, they had to outnumber the Japanese. Every aircraft mattered. Bobby's Airacobras were desperately needed now.

On this spring day, Bobby and his squadron were coming in high, even though the Airacobras were low-altitude fighters. To compensate, American pilots had come up with a successful tactic called the Boom and Zoom. The American fighters were not as maneuverable as their Japanese equivalent, but they were faster. That advantage was multiplied when gravity helped accelerate them in a dive. Boom and Zoom tactics had them diving down from above and trying to knock out as many enemy aircraft as possible during that one good dive.

"Bandits, twelve o'clock low," Major Bovington announced over the flight channel.

It was good news. Twelve o'clock meant at the twelve on an imaginary clock—directly in front of the reporting pilot. Conversely, six o'clock was behind—"on my six"—meaning an enemy aircraft was on your tail, ready to kill you. "Low" meant the enemy bandits were below them. Bovington's report told Bobby that their strategy could work. They were above the enemy and would get one good pass, diving at high speed down toward their prey. With any luck, the Japanese planes would be "Kate" torpedo bombers, the same planes that had been driven off from Dutch Harbor the day before. The Kates, weighed down by their bombs, weren't as agile as Mitsubishi Zeros. If Bobby's squadron could damage enough of the torpedo bombers with their first dive, they might be able to break the enemy formation and blunt the Japanese attack before it began.

"Anyone got an ID?" Bobby asked, trying to hide the anxiety in his voice.

"Looks like Zekes," replied Max, Major Bovington's wingman, at the front of the American formation. "Zeke" was the Americans' nickname for the Mitsubishi Zero.

Each pilot was assigned a wingman. It was the most basic tenet of aerial combat. Since your guns faced forward, the worst thing that could happen to you was getting an enemy aircraft behind you on your six. You couldn't shoot behind you, so your only option was to try to shake him by performing a series of aerial acrobatics he eventually couldn't follow. But that took time, during which the enemy was relentlessly shooting at your tail with heavy-caliber machine guns or automatic cannons. You had to be both lucky and good to survive by yourself.

It was your wingman's job to protect you. If an enemy got on your tail, your wingman immediately tried to shoot him off. You did the same for your wingman. It was the buddy system. Despite his fear, it always gave Bobby confidence to know that his own wingman was also his best buddy, Jack.

"Yup," Max reported grimly, "definitely Zekes."

Bobby's chest tightened. The Japanese were covering their bombing attack with the more agile fighters. Bobby's squadron had a dangerous fight on its hands. He tried to swallow, but his mouth was dry.

"They're starting to climb," Max reported in. "They've seen us."

That the Zeros were climbing meant they were trying to negate the Americans' one advantage. Major Bovington commanded, "All right, boys, let's not give 'em all day. Attack formation. We're only gonna get one shot at this. Make it count. Whites of their eyes and all that. Ready . . . go! Go! Go!"

Bovington's voice was immediately drowned out by the scream of the aircraft, the engines' pitch rising to a deafening roar as they twisted and began to dive.

Bobby's stomach turned, and he felt like he was going to vomit. He'd dived at such high speeds before; they'd all trained in the tactic. But during training, the ground was the only point of reference, and it was so far away that it didn't provide a proper scale for measuring speed. Now came a new frame of reference—the Japanese plane before him—and he was shocked at how fast the Zero expanded in his view. What had first looked like a toy now grew to a threatening size.

Bobby momentarily panicked, fearing he was about to crash into the Zero. The Japanese pilot was craning his neck and looking up at Bobby in alarm. Then Bobby remembered his 37mm cannon. He triggered the weapon and felt the reassuring shudder of the gun's recoil vibrating through his fuselage. Then he was past the Japanese fighter. Had he even hit it? He couldn't be sure. It had all happened so fast.

But he did know he was losing the advantage of altitude. He was now below the Zeros, and he had to level out fast. His stomach sank into his bladder as he pulled back on the stick.

"Got him!" someone announced in triumph.

"I'm hit!" someone else shouted in terror.

"Bail out!" a wingman urged.

"They're coming around!" Max alerted them.

Bobby jerked his head back to look over his shoulder. A parachute bloomed behind him, but it wasn't Japanese. He'd missed. He realized too late that he should have used his higher-RPM machine guns instead of his heavy cannon. Somehow the Zero he'd attacked had passed right between his cannon's shells and was now circling around at an impossible angle. Already its nose was facing Bobby's flank.

Bobby jerked his stick forward and sent his plane back into a dive as the Zero's twin machine guns opened up. Tracer rounds zipped over Bobby's head, his sudden burst of speed saving him from the bullets. But he was flying right into the Japanese pilot's hands. He was still below the Zero, and it was child's play for the agile enemy fighter to lock on Bobby's tail.

"Zeke on my six!" Bobby yelled into his radio, not bothering to hide the panic in his voice.

"Hang in there, I'm coming!" Jack replied.

Again, Bobby heard the report of the twin machine guns, and he felt the Airacobra shudder as bullets punched through its frame. "I'm hit!"

"Almost there!"

Tracer bullets corkscrewed around Bobby. But Bobby recognized the illusion—the bullets weren't corkscrewing; he was. But his aerobatics gave no escape from the agile Zero. "I can't shake him!"

"Stop juking!" Jack responded.

"He'll hit me again!"

"But I can't get a bead on him!"

Bobby continued to dive, trying to maintain speed and outrun the Zero. "Stop diving!" Jack insisted. "You're gonna run out of real estate!"

His wingman was right. The ocean was coming up too fast. He pulled on the stick and started to climb, losing air speed. For a moment it looked like the Zero would shoot right past him. But the Japanese pilot cut his throttle just in time to stay on his tail. More bullets slammed into Bobby's plane. Smoke erupted from under the cockpit. "I'm on fire!"

"No, you're not; you're just smoking." Jack had a better view of the damage from outside Bobby's cockpit.

"You sure?"

"Sure I'm sure. Now level out and turn toward me."

"He'll tear me apart!"

"Believe me, it's your only chance."

Bobby closed his eyes, said a brief prayer, leveled off, and turned to his right. The Airacobra flew straight as an arrow, a sitting duck for the Zero behind him. The Zero leveled off and opened up with both barrels. Bobby opened his eyes to see bits and pieces of his fuselage and wings jumping up around him. But nothing penetrated the cockpit. This alone was the American airman's great advantage in 1942. Their planes were sturdy, their cockpits well armored. They couldn't outfly the Japanese, but they could often outlast them.

How much more punishment could the Airacobra take? The plane seemed to be disintegrating around Bobby. Then he saw a flash of light. He glanced over his shoulder to see the Zero in flames, plummeting like a comet toward the ocean.

Jack's tactic had proved perfect. He'd stopped trying to get a bead on the Zero and had pulled about sixty yards to Bobby's right. When Bobby turned, straight and level, he'd drawn the Zero into Jack's gun sights. The tactic would later be called "the Thach Weave," named after the pilot who codified it and taught it to all Army Air Forces flight cadets. But in June of 1942 it wasn't yet well known. Remarkably, Jack had instinctively figured it out for himself.

"Thanks," Bobby said to him with relief and awe. "Thanks."

But Jack remained all business. "You're losing fuel."

Bobby looked at his instrument panel and saw his fuel gauge dropping fast. The adrenaline was clearing from his bloodstream, letting him think more clearly—he confirmed the likely source of the smoke from the oil-pressure gauge. "I think I'm burning oil, too."

"Head back and try to land her."

Suddenly the sky flashed, followed by the sound of a deafening explosion. Bobby turned his plane for a better view of Dutch Harbor, on Unalaska Island. The entire airfield seemed to be on fire. While the Zeros kept the American Airacobras busy, Nakajima B5N2 torpedo bombers had snuck in and bombed the base.

"Shit." Bobby sighed.

"Don't think about it. Just get back and land that plane. Battle's over anyway."

Bobby knew Jack was right. Even though the dogfight still raged behind him, the Japanese had achieved their objectives.

He passed the enemy torpedo bombers going the opposite direction. But they didn't break formation to hunt him down. They'd already succeeded in their mission. Now they were heading back to their aircraft carrier. A few minutes later, Bobby was flying directly over Dutch Harbor. They'd hit the fuel-and-ammunition depots. The airfield was a cauldron of rising black smoke and flames, surrounded by snowy, jagged peaks on one side and an icy bay on the other.

Fire and ice, Bobby thought to himself, glancing nervously at his fuel gauge. It had settled. Apparently his fuel level had dropped below the leak in his shot-up gasoline tanks. All he had to do was keep it slow and steady, and he ought to get back to Fort Randall still in one piece.

CHAPTER 33

THE CELLIST AND THE
ORGAN-GRINDER

Karen never liked hoboes. She'd seen a lot of them in her young life, growing up as she had during the Great Depression and spending a lot of that young life on trains.

As a child prodigy, she'd traveled throughout the American Northeast, performing with her father at various venues, big and small, famous and unknown. Tanglewood, Jordan Hall, Alexander Hall, and Mortensen Hall were the more prominent stops during her so-called summer vacations, which were really just yearly concert tours organized by her father.

She enjoyed the travel, largely because she loved the New England countryside, and she enjoyed meeting artists of all genres and walks of life. She met Martha Graham in Boston, Sidney Bechet in New Jersey, and Rosa Ponselle in Connecticut.

But she dreaded the train stations because they were often haunted by destitute vagabonds riding the rails in search of work.

Her father, being a socialist, sympathized with the hoboes. It wasn't their fault they were poor, he tried to explain to her. In fact, they should be respected, if not applauded, for battling to rise above their unfortunate circumstances. And battle they did. Karen would never forget leaving Boston on a night train and looking out the window to see railroad workers hunting the switching yard for hoboes, dragging them out of boxcars, and beating them almost to death with baseball bats.

Karen realized then that she disliked the hoboes because she was afraid of them. She wasn't afraid they might attack her, mug her, or hurt her. She was afraid of becoming like them. And her father's lectures only made that fear worse. After all, if they weren't responsible for their own poverty, if they were simply victims of circumstance, couldn't that same circumstance happen to anyone? Couldn't it happen to Karen?

The answer was yes. Not only could it happen to Karen, it *had* happened to Karen. Now she was living like the hoboes she'd grown up to fear, walking long miles along the railroad tracks, hiding in the tall grass at the approach of a train, and jumping aboard for a free ride if an open boxcar passed by slowly enough. It was exactly what had always terrified her.

And yet she loved it. There was a strange peacefulness to the countryside, because the war was both behind and in front of her. Here, between the battle fronts, she had little to be afraid of. Karen never worried about violence. No one would attack her or mug her. Everyone was reserving their aggression for the enemy, it seemed, knowing they might have their fill of violence any moment if the Nazis came.

Even when Karen and Petr were discovered stowing away in boxcars, they weren't dragged out and beaten like the hoboes she'd seen in the United States. Instead, they were offered a cup of tea and asked whether their dog was friendly. They were still dressed in soldiers' uniforms, and everyone wanted to help a soldier, even if it meant help-ing a soldier desert.

The NKVD was nowhere to be found, either. Their agents were stretched too thin to bother with tiny villages and rural train stations. Even though those stations were on an important supply route, they were largely left to the management of locals. If trains started showing up in Tikhvin with half their cargo, or if there was any sign of theft or corruption between Moscow and Leningrad, no doubt the NKVD would have swooped in and found out what was going on. But that didn't happen because, unlike politicians or army officers, the civilian rail workers were mostly honest and simple folk.

Karen and Petr rode more often than they walked. The trains head-ing southeast were mostly empty because little in the way of supplies was being sent from Leningrad to Moscow. There was the troop train Karen and Petr had originally ridden in, which they then hid from as it passed two days after they went AWOL. And there was a train filled with Leningrad refugees that passed them a week later. But mostly the railway was traveled by supply trains on the return trip from Tikhvin—locomotives hauling lines of empty boxcars.

The engines rolled along at little more than a walking pace, which made it easy for Karen, Petr, and Duck to jump on and off. But it also made the journey a very long one, especially since the trains often had to wait hours at a time for more important traffic to pass in the other direction.

They ate well. During their fifth day of travel, they passed a herd of deer. The deer had obviously become accustomed to the trains, for they continued to graze unconcerned as the loud and smoky locomotive approached. Petr sat in the open door of a boxcar and waited patiently. Even when the car was only a hundred yards from the deer, the animals didn't flinch. It wasn't until he pulled the trigger and dropped one that the rest of the herd panicked and bounded away.

Petr jumped off, Karen and Duck close behind him. When they approached the deer, Petr was happy to see the shot had been a clean one, straight through the animal's heart. It hadn't suffered. But he was distressed to see that flies were already buzzing around the carcass. It would be only a matter of time before the meat was rotten with maggots.

Petr had to get to work fast, and he needed Karen's help. He taught her how to skin and quarter the animal, breaking it into smaller pieces for easier cooking and transport.

But even that wasn't enough. Until the meat was somehow preserved, it would continue to attract vermin. So he hung the large shanks of venison from the branches of a tree and built a large bonfire beneath them. It wasn't nearly as efficient as a smokehouse, but it would have to do.

The whole operation took the better part of two days, but they ended up with enough meat to last five more.

Karen was impressed. Here was proof positive that her fantasy of living in the woods might become a reality, after all. She hadn't eaten so well in almost a year, and it had cost them only a single bullet.

They began sleeping in each other's arms. It began by sharing the worn copy of *War and Peace* between them. They sat in a corner of a boxcar, backs propped against the walls, reading aloud. When Karen's voice grew hoarse, Petr would take over. And when Petr's voice grew hoarse, they would continue to read in silence, shoulder to shoulder, turning each page only after a nod indicated that they were ready.

Duck grew jealous of their closeness, so he wiggled and pushed his way between them. The three of them snuggled together, enjoying the feel of Duck's downy fur.

But eventually the dog got hot, that same fur trapping the excessive heat of three bodies. So he would get up and wander to a distant corner of the slowly rocking boxcar before flopping back down with a satisfied groan. That left Petr and Karen together. Neither one of them wanted to move. They just lay there quietly until they fell asleep.

Every night thereafter they did the same, without a word, without acknowledgment. Karen told herself it was innocent enough; they were still fully dressed, and they hadn't even kissed again since the day of the dance. It wasn't as if she was really being unfaithful to Bobby. She enjoyed lying in Petr's arms, and not because it was comforting. In fact, it was distracting. The feel of his body was electric, even maddening. But she didn't dare move, for fear of breaking the spell. Lying like that together, every night, prevented her from sleeping much, and it made the journey feel even longer.

Karen secretly looked forward to the sun going down so they could put down the book and once again lie together.

⸻◆⸻

When they finally arrived in Moscow, Karen marveled at how different it looked from Leningrad. Both cities had been fortified with a series of deep trenches bristling with log bunkers, machine guns, and antiaircraft cannons. And it was clear that, like Leningrad, Moscow had been militarized.

What little traffic traveled the streets and sidewalks consisted of civilians hurrying to accomplish specific daily tasks. There was no one just lounging around, and few people smiling. Yet the streets and buildings remained in good repair. Rubble had been cleared, and she saw no piles of garbage or corpses or junk.

As their train crawled through the city's back alleys, Karen could see into apartment-building windows. She observed well-fed civilians inside who, despite the threat from the German lines only miles away, seemed proud and confident. One young boy even looked up from a book he was reading and smiled and waved. Amazed, Karen waved back. There had been no friendly gestures in Leningrad. Even the smallest gesture required strength, and the starving population had to preserve that strength.

Petr was concerned about what might happen when they finally reached the end of the line. Undoubtedly there would be military officers at the train station who would recruit all three of them back into the Red Army.

Petr planned to rejoin the army. He wasn't a deserter, really, but he did want to save Duck first. Karen had agreed to help him find Duck's family, so they decided to jump off the train while it waited at a crossing.

They didn't know where they were. Petr had been born in Moscow and had grown up near Lomonosov University, where his father worked. But Petr was only thirteen when he and his father were forcibly exiled, more than seven years ago. And with his father focused entirely on mathematics, young Petr had never traveled far from the university. He didn't recognize where they were now and didn't know whether it was because he didn't remember or because he'd never been there. Nonetheless, he did remember that the campus was on Manege Square, and he assured Karen that if they could just find their way there, he'd be able to finally get his bearings.

It was surprisingly easy to find their way. Manege Square was famous, very near to Communist headquarters at Red Square, so asking directions was easy. It was a long walk, and they didn't have money for a tram, but by now they were used to long walks.

The campus itself was locked up tight. Petr recalled a secret way inside through a window with a broken latch; when he was a kid, he'd used that entrance to sneak in and out. He suspected that the window hadn't been repaired, and once again Communist inefficiency didn't let him down. When he pushed on the window, sure enough, it swung open.

Karen, Petr, and Duck spent an hour wandering the long halls of the university buildings. They quietly searched every floor, finding the campus deserted. The entire school—the staff, the professors, and the students—had been evacuated the previous winter and transferred to a temporary campus in Ashgabat, near Iran.

Karen found the huge, empty buildings eerie. The only sounds were the echoes of their footsteps and Duck's claws against the marble tiles. The electricity had been turned off, and the corridors were dim. Where it wasn't dark, along windowed chambers, dust swirled like ghosts in the shafts of sunlight.

As she got used to the emptiness of the buildings, Karen began to enjoy the solitude. She began to play with Duck, running in and out of offices and classrooms, having him chase her. She would hide and wait for him to sniff her out. Petr joined the game, and the three of them had more fun than they'd had in a long time.

Then they found the commissary. Someone had forgotten to clear out the cupboard, and there were leftover bags of flour and cans of soups and vegetables. Out of curiosity, Petr tried the stove and was thrilled to discover that the gas still worked. Karen immediately started grabbing random cans, declaring that they should celebrate their arrival in Moscow with a feast.

They didn't have a can opener, so they used Petr's military spade as an ax to chop them open. The first time Petr tried it, he was sprayed with stewed tomatoes. Most of it got on his face and in his hair. Karen laughed so hard that Petr made her open the next can. She, too, was sprayed, this time by creamed corn. Soon they didn't care. They just slammed open the cans, not worrying about the mess, pouring their growing concoction into a huge vat simmering over low heat.

The preparation of their feast had turned into a food fight. Duck was having a grand old time, licking up the mess they left behind. Neither one of them knew how to cook, and the strange vegetable stew they were creating looked thin, so Karen tried to make dumplings. Instead, she made unappetizing clumps of grainy raw flour. So Petr tried to make rice, which bubbled right out of the pot all over the floor. Duck happily jumped all over it and started lapping it up.

In the end, the soup was thin, the rice was hard, the dumplings were inedible, and the commissary was a complete mess. So were Petr and Karen. Their clothes were soaked and stained with all manner of food and sauce. Petr knew that what they ought to do is strip down to their underwear and boil their uniforms clean. It's what he would have done in the army. Living with soldiers had mostly cured him of modesty, though taking off his clothes in front of a fellow soldier, he now realized, was very different from stripping in front of Karen—a girl whom he undeniably found attractive. So the recommendation caught in his throat.

Karen also knew their clothes desperately needed washing. They'd worn them for weeks, and so the garments were filthy and stinking. But cleaning them required removing them, and she, too, was embarrassed to make the suggestion. They both mumbled and agreed that their clothes needed cleaning, but neither was willing to voice the obvious consequence: stripping. So instead they looked through closets and pantries for some miracle that would rescue them from their embarrassment.

Karen found that miracle in the form of janitors' aprons. They could wear them over their underwear, she reasoned, and after all, it really wouldn't be all that different from wearing a bathing suit, would it? That's how she justified it to herself, and how she justified it to Petr when she proposed that course of action.

They boiled a huge pot of soapy water and then slipped into separate rooms, where they stripped off their wet and sticky clothes and wrapped the aprons around their bodies. It wasn't quite like being in a bathing suit, after all, Karen realized with shame, since the apron didn't cover her backside. So when she returned to the kitchen to throw her clothes in the pot, she self-consciously made sure she was always facing Petr. Petr, she noticed, was doing the same. That realization made her giggle, and her giggle helped break the tension.

"When I was little and had stage fright," she said to Petr, "my father told me to imagine the audience in their underwear."

Petr laughed. "I guess if I'm in the audience now, you don't have to imagine."

"Exactly!" Karen said with delight.

When they finished boiling their clothes, they laid them out on commissary tables to dry. Then they slept on one of the few tables that had remained clean.

It was a hard and cold bed. They didn't sleep in each other's arms as they had on the trains. They were too self-conscious in their state of half dress. Their discomfort prompted them to wake up before dawn, at which time they were dismayed to discover their clothes hadn't yet dried. Teeth chattering, they opened the windows of a nearby classroom and hung their clothes out to dry.

As the sun rose, Petr tried his hand at making coffee, boiling water and dumping in grounds until it looked the right shade of black. Despite having a film with the same grainy consistency as Karen's dumplings, the coffee both warmed them up and energized them. But when they returned to fetch their clothes, they discovered that the wind had blown them into the bushes below. Someone had to go outside and rummage around to find them.

Petr reluctantly volunteered. He had to be cautious. They weren't supposed to be inside the university buildings and could technically be arrested. His state of undress only made him more timid. As bad as it would be to get arrested, it would be even worse to be arrested without any clothes on.

Karen served as the lookout in the window above. She was supposed to whistle if she saw anyone, warning Petr to duck down into the bushes. But she was having too much fun watching Petr's undignified tromp through the hedges, and couldn't help but giggle, which Petr heard. He hissed at her to be quiet, but then his apron got caught on a branch, and he found himself stripped to his underwear. Karen's giggle turned into a loud guffaw as Petr stood up and grabbed his apron, cursing. It was fortunate that no one was nearby, because the two of them couldn't have been making a louder racket.

An hour later they were finally dressed, wondering what to do next. Neither of them had any idea how to find Duck's family. Petr knew nothing about them; he only knew they lived in Moscow and had told the army that Duck enjoyed chasing birds in the park. Remembering this finally gave Karen an idea. They should find parks with lots of birds. If the family had spent time in such a park before the war, it would stand to reason that they'd still spend time there. And they might recognize their dog. Petr shrugged. It was worth a try, and he certainly didn't have any better ideas.

Petr and Karen spent three days visiting each of Moscow's parks. Duck lived up to his name, chasing everything with either wings or a tail, from ducks to geese to squirrels. In the rare instances he had no wildlife to chase, Petr and Karen threw a stick for him. It was fun at first, but the fun didn't last, especially since they didn't seem to be making much progress. Every park seemed much like any other. They would have to be extraordinarily lucky to be in the right park the very moment that Duck's family visited.

On the fourth day, frustrated and bored by the process, Karen and Petr decided to give up on the parks and do some sightseeing instead. Just up the street from the university was a memorial commemorating Russia's victory over Napoleon. Inna had often cited that glorious moment in Russian history as proof that they would also defeat the invading Nazis. And, of course, Karen and Petr had been reading *War and Peace*, so they wanted to see the monument for themselves.

As they approached Alexander Gardens, in which the monument was housed, Duck started to get excited. He ran ahead, turned around, and raced back, leaping up to Petr's chest and wagging his tail. When they reached the gate surrounding the gardens, Duck put his paws up on the wrought iron gate, beside himself with anticipation. And when

Petr opened the gate, the dog raced inside and immediately rocketed after a flock of ducks, sending the squawking birds into flight.

"I think he's been here before," Petr commented with a smile.

Karen nodded. "Maybe we've finally found the right park."

Nonetheless, no one came to Alexander Gardens whom Duck seemed to recognize. Petr and Karen had already been in Moscow for a week, and they seemed no closer to finding Duck's family than they had been in Tikhvin. They had no better ideas, however, so they simply continued to come to the Alexander Gardens day after day. It was a fifteen-minute walk from the university, which made things easy.

On Saturday they arrived to find a gathering crowd. Karen's heart filled with hope. Of course the family wouldn't have come to the park during the week. The boy would have been in school, and the father would have been at work. A weekend made much more sense. And from the size of the crowd, it appeared that Alexander Gardens was a popular destination for weekend leisure. It turned out that the crowd wasn't there for the gardens, but for a concert. An amateur youth orchestra was offering a free outdoor performance of *The Rite of Spring*. Karen knew the piece of music well. It had been a favorite of her father's and was the music she'd played the night she'd met Bobby.

She was not impressed with the youth orchestra's rendition, however. The conductor, a bespectacled woman with the severe appearance of a schoolmarm, proved strict and sincere in her approach to the piece. The amateur musicians simply couldn't keep up with the demands of her baton. The lead cellist, a scrawny boy about Karen's age with a gigantic Adam's apple and a peach-fuzz mustache, fell hopelessly behind and led his entire section into unintended cacophony.

The spectators didn't seem to notice. Indeed, they appeared to enjoy the piece more than the sophisticated New York audiences for whom Karen had often played. Russians, it seemed, really did love music, even bad music.

She noticed Petr smiling and unconsciously tapping his hand against his knee, trying to find the beat. "It's wonderful, isn't it?" he whispered when he noticed her watching him.

Karen was aghast. "Seriously?" she whispered back.

Petr looked at her, surprised. "What's wrong?"

"Everything. It's not supposed to sound like this."

Petr was mystified. "What is it supposed to sound like?"

At that point Karen realized she was ruining the experience for him. He was happy, and she was spoiling that happiness. So she consciously softened her expression and her tone. "Never mind," she reassured him. "You're right. It is wonderful."

She sat back in her metal folding chair, one of many set out to accommodate the audience, and tried to listen with new ears.

Petr was right. The music was wonderful. Not because it was melodic; it was not. And not because it was well performed; it was not. The music was wonderful because it was being performed at all, here in a beautiful park in the center of Moscow, in the middle of war, with the enemy only miles away.

If she'd been listening by herself, she would have hated it. She would have inwardly stewed and mentally criticized everything that was wrong. But thanks to Petr, she abandoned her cynicism and found a way to enjoy the experience. She was happy for that. She took Petr's hand and squeezed it in gratitude.

When the concert ended, Karen stood and applauded with the rest of the audience, genuine in her appreciation. The schoolmarm conductor stepped forward and smiled in acknowledgment of the standing ovation. She gave it time to quiet before making what she described as an important announcement. The youth orchestra was traveling to Chelyabinsk, a city she described as the "new heart of Russia." There, they would perform for Josef Stalin, who was hosting a summit with American officials. It was important to show the Americans the industrial might of Russia, as personified by the overnight growth of Chelyabinsk into the munitions factory for the entire nation. But it was also important to show the Americans that Russian culture still prospered, that the Russian spirit had not been crushed. It was for this second task that the youth orchestra had been chosen to perform.

But they needed help. The conductor assured the audience that any donations given her orchestra would be money well spent. Meanwhile, young members of her orchestra began handing out flyers advertising where to send donations.

Karen waited patiently for the woman to stop speaking and for the crowd to disperse. She then asked Petr to wait for her a moment. She was going to speak to the conductor personally. She had barely left her chair when Duck leaped to his feet, practically knocking her over, and scrambled through the assembled chairs, barking joyously.

"Duck!" she heard someone exclaim behind her.

It wasn't Petr. The voice belonged to a boy about eight years old. He rolled around with Duck on the grass, wrestling and petting him despite the fact that the dog weighed twice as much as he did. Duck licked him all over. A man and a woman, in their thirties and dressed in fine clothes, crouched beside dog and boy with broad smiles on their faces, petting Duck whenever he rolled within their reach.

Petr ran up to the family and caught his breath. "I take it this dog belongs to you?" he said with a smile.

The woman, presumably the boy's mother, nodded and laughed. "I didn't think we'd ever see him again!"

Then she noticed Petr's army uniform, and her smile faded. "Are you going to take him away?"

Petr shook his head. "No, no. I've been looking for you. I brought him back."

The woman smiled again, but this time in wonder. "Brought him back? But doesn't he belong to the army now?"

"He's been discharged," Petr lied, "for heroics."

"Heroics?" asked the son, looking up. "Duck's a hero?"

"Of course he is," Petr replied.

The man, presumably the father, was the only one not smiling. He looked at Petr and at Karen and then at Petr again. Then he looked around nervously. "Why don't we get Duck home, and you can tell us all about his heroics?" he suggested to Petr.

Petr nodded. "I think that would be wise."

CHAPTER 34
THE SUBVERSIVE

Danil Epinger had never believed he could fall in love with an animal. And yet a dog, a puppy he'd received as a gift, had stolen his heart. His son had named the dog "Duck," and the animal had become part of their family.

Danil was not an ambitious man. And yet he had prospered in a land where prosperity was eschewed, and he had grown wealthy in a country where wealth was essentially illegal. In part, he was wealthy and prosperous precisely because he was not ambitious. Danil was a patriot. He loved his country and was glad for the Communist government.

His father had been a factory worker, his grandfather a farmhand. In the old czarist economy of nobleman and peasant, he would never have been allowed to go to school, to become educated, and to pursue his passion for medicine. Communism, for all its flaws, had allowed Danil to become a doctor, and for that he would always be grateful.

Danil loved children. He loved children because he loved inno-cence. He himself was a simple and innocent man. But he was no simpleton. On the contrary, he had proven to be an intellectual giant. Danil had been drawn to medicine like a moth to a flame. It was both unambiguous and intellectually challenging. The puzzles were biologi-cal, not philosophical. And the goal was saving lives. No one—not even the most paranoid dictator—could find fault with that, especially when the lives Danil was saving were those of children, for he was a pediatrician.

But he knew what was happening around him. He recognized the excesses of Lenin and Stalin; he couldn't help but notice the bloody way they held on to power. He had personally witnessed political prisoners, the so-called Gulag labor, forced to reconstruct Moscow's Red Square, knocking down historic landmarks in order to clear a path for Josef Stalin's military parades. Danil had seen how thin the political prison-ers had been, how weak they were, and how they were forced to work despite that weakness and malnutrition. Danil knew that those prison-ers were being worked to death. His physician's eye was not fooled. These prisoners' assignments to Gulag labor were in itself a death sen-tence. And although Danil hadn't seen it for himself, he could guess at worse horrors occurring beyond the secret doors of NKVD interroga-tion rooms.

But he also knew that the masters of his country, the leaders of his government, and even the officers of State security weren't utter psycho-paths. The NKVD's victims weren't chosen at random. Neither were the Gulag political prisoners. There was a reason they were arrested. Their crimes of disobedience might not have been crimes in other countries, or in other times. But here and now, they were crimes.

Danil had no interest in crime. He was not a rebel, an agitator, or a resister. He didn't want to be a politician, nor did he want to overthrow the current regime. He had no ambition whatsoever, and therefore no interest in politics. And, he reasoned, he was not alone. Every govern-ment—no matter how corrupt, no matter how totalitarian, no matter how terrifying—ultimately ruled at the will of its citizens. Even the czar, most controlling of all of Europe's dictators, had ultimately been overthrown. If the czar could be overthrown, so could Stalin. Especially now, with the enemy at the gates, and defeat at the hands of the Nazis almost a certainty. But clearly, most Russians had no desire to overthrow Stalin. They did not rebel, despite the Gulags, despite the NKVD, despite everything. In fact, they had never been so united as now, in defending their homes, their land, and their country from the Nazis.

Adults were adults, Danil reasoned; they were free to make their own decisions, and they should live with the consequences of those decisions. Those who disobeyed should expect to be arrested. It was no secret that free thought and free expression were illegal. One chose to flout those laws at one's own risk. But children were different. Children were innocent. Children deserved to be protected.

Danil had grown wealthy tending to the children of Russia's politi-cal elite. He did not charge the leaders of his country more than he would have charged a Tankograd factory worker. In fact, he could not charge more, for he practiced medicine in an economy that was State run, where prices for everything, even a medical checkup, were fixed. But he could accept gifts. In fact, Danil had to accept gifts. It would have been an insult to his very powerful clientele if he refused to accept those gifts. The political elite claimed to be running a country of socio-economic equality. And yet somehow the rulers of the country had amassed far greater wealth than those over whom they ruled.

Danil never questioned the obvious corruption. But he did profit indirectly from it. His wealthy clientele made him wealthy through their gracious generosity. They were so grateful for his help in keeping their children healthy that they insisted he accept their extravagant rewards. Duck had been one such gift.

He was the puppy of a champion *Schutzhund* owned by Friedrich Werner von der Schulenberg, the German ambassador to Moscow until 1941. Von der Schulenberg's granddaughter contracted pneumonia while visiting the ambassador in the winter of 1938. Danil successfully treated the young girl, and von der Schulenberg gave him the puppy in gratitude.

It was the first gift Danil considered refusing. After all, it came from a German statesman, not a Russian politician. He felt confident there would be no repercussions for slighting von der Schulenberg. But hardly had the ambassador presented the puppy to Danil's three-year-old son, Maxim, before boy and dog were rolling around on the apartment floor, inseparable. Danil couldn't deny his child anything, least of all a new puppy.

Danil didn't know how to take care of a dog. He had lived with his father in a communal boardinghouse when he was a child. His only animal companions there were rats. But Duck wasn't difficult to manage. He was a smart dog and eager to please, so he caught on quickly that he wasn't supposed to urinate or defecate in the apartment, and he was remarkably vocal when he needed to be let out to relieve himself.

He was also a good watchdog, alerting them when anyone approached the apartment door, and barking when anyone knocked. He would growl if Danil's wife, Anya, stood at the door without letting the visitor in. But whenever she stepped aside to allow a guest within, Duck would sniff the stranger's hand and then let his guard down.

Danil believed that Duck was a mere animal, a nonsentient creature ruled by survival instinct, rather than reason or emotion. Despite that fundamental belief, he found it impossible not to project his own emotions onto the dog. Duck seemed so intelligent and seemed to love his family and Maxim, in particular, so much. Despite his best efforts, Danil had grown to love the dog, too. Duck seemed to him like a very strong and able child. And, like a child, he was innocent.

Then the Germans invaded. And Duck was drafted. Danil couldn't say no. To do so wouldn't just have been defying the army; it would have been defying the Communist Party. Danil knew better than that. Nonetheless, when he'd watched Duck being taken away, he'd felt like he was watching his own son marching off to war. He felt certain he would never see Duck again.

Maxim was less conflicted. He was proud of his dog and certain he'd become a war hero. Maxim still had the innocence of a child. He didn't know what would really happen to Duck. He had saluted the dog as Duck was loaded into an army truck.

And now, against all odds, Duck was back.

He came escorted by two young soldiers who were practically children themselves. Danil was grateful to the soldiers, and not just for bringing his pet home. He was grateful to them for preserving Maxim's innocence.

Maxim wanted to know all about Duck's adventures, of course; and the boy soldier, who introduced himself as Petr, obliged him. Petr described how Duck saved him from a German booby trap. He even demonstrated with sticks how the nefarious Nazis had rigged the booby trap with grenades.

He told the boy how Duck had helped destroy several tanks, running back and forth and confusing their commanders long enough for the antitank riflemen to fill the panzers with holes. But he didn't tell Maxim about the real horrors of battle. He didn't tell him about the death, the countless defeats, and the hopelessness of the resistance.

Danil didn't like to think about that, either, but he also didn't like to fool himself. His position as pediatrician to the politically powerful allowed him to overhear private conversations, which included discussions of defeat.

The Russians had engineered one great victory: the winter defense of Moscow. But overall, the German invasion had been a military disaster. Few believed the Soviet Union could survive another offensive, and the more practical individuals were beginning to plan for a future under Nazi rule. But Danil wondered if there ever could be a future under Nazi rule. The Germans weren't here to conquer; they were here to steal. And he could tell that the girl soldier agreed with him.

Her name was Inna, and there was something strange about her, something haunted. She hardly spoke, preferring to defer all questions to the more gregarious Petr. Danil had the strange feeling that this Inna girl had a better grasp of what was really happening out there than even his leaders in the Kremlin.

<hr/>

The time for stories had ended. It had gotten dark. Anya took Maxim to bed.

Duck hesitated, looking up at Petr for approval. Petr scratched the dog under his chin, encouraging the dog to go. "You're home, boy, you don't need me anymore."

Duck lowered his snout and licked Petr's hand, but Petr pulled it away. "Go on," he said encouragingly.

Duck didn't need to be told again. He trotted off, anxious to sleep at Maxim's feet. Petr then asked Danil whether they could speak in private. Danil led Petr and Inna to his office. They sat uncomfortably on a simple sofa while he took a position behind his desk. They stared at one another for a moment in silence, and Danil wondered whether he should offer them vodka. Were they old enough? They were soldiers; of course they were.

He reached into a desk drawer and held up a bottle. Petr nodded, so Danil silently poured three glasses. They clinked them together in a toast and took a sip. Danil noticed Inna grimace. She clearly wasn't used to strong liquor.

Petr looked down at his glass, then took another large gulp, as if for courage. He looked across at Danil, who'd retaken his seat. "I wasn't completely honest with your son," Petr said.

Danil nodded. He'd known that, and he was grateful for it. "I appreciate that. I'm sure you've seen things that I'd prefer he didn't know about."

"Yes, of course." Petr nodded. "But not just that. About Duck. About what he was trained for."

Danil hadn't expected this. "Why? Is there something wrong? Could he hurt us, hurt Maxim?"

"No, nothing like that."

Danil stared at the boy soldier and said, "The soldiers who took him, they warned me that he would be trained for war, trained to attack. They warned me that he wouldn't be safe around a family afterward. They warned me I would never see him again."

"They lied."

Danil was shocked. This he hadn't expected. "What do you mean?"

"He was trained for war, yes," Petr began, searching for a way to explain, "at least in a certain manner. But not to attack." He stumbled over the words. "I mean, he did attack, but it came naturally to him to defend me, to defend her . . ." He motioned toward the Inna girl. "I'm sure he'd do the same to defend your family, to defend Maxim. But that's not what he was trained for."

"What was he trained for?"

"He was trained to blow himself up."

Now Danil was confused. "I don't understand."

"We use dogs, so-called mine dogs. We use them to destroy German tanks. We strap explosives to them and train them to run underneath a tank, where the explosives go off."

Danil nodded. In a twisted, cruel way, it actually sounded quite brilliant. "Does it work?"

Petr shook his head. "Not that I've seen. The dogs get confused. They were trained on our tanks, you see. Ours run on a different type of fuel. So when they smell the German tanks, well, like I said, they get confused. Usually they just explode without really hurting anyone but themselves."

Danil was beginning to understand. "That's why they told me I'd never see him again. Because they expected him to explode."

"That's right. And that's why we brought him back. If he goes back into the army, they'll strap him to a bomb again. He's better than that. He deserves more than that."

So Duck had cast his spell over these soldiers, too. That made sense. They didn't want the dog to die any more than Danil did. They'd grown to love the animal. "I think I understand."

"I don't know if you can keep him hidden, but if you don't, you might lose him."

Hiding Duck would mean defying official policy. Technically, it would be a crime. It would be the first and only time Danil had resisted his government. It was a dangerous risk. Men had been arrested, had been tortured, and had been sent to Gulag labor camps for less.

Danil wanted to tell the boy soldier no. He wanted to send him away and make him take Duck away with him. But he couldn't. Much to his dismay, Danil realized he was still in love with the dog, too.

So instead, Danil just said, "Thank you."

"You're welcome. Duck's happy here. I'm glad we brought him home."

"If there's anything I can do for you?"

"No, nothing," Petr said. "We're fine—"

"You can give us clothes," the girl cut in.

Danil glanced over at her, surprised. She had been so quiet until now, so deferential. He had somehow assumed she was meek, despite whatever smarts she might have. Now her voice was direct and commanding. Petr's expression revealed that he hadn't expected it, either. But, unlike Danil, he didn't seem surprised.

"Nice clothes," Inna continued. "Formal clothes. A dress for me and a suit for him." She nodded toward Petr. "They don't have to be new. They don't have to be nice. They just have to be clean and presentable."

Danil nodded. He had an old suit he hardly wore anymore, and he was sure Anya could give up one dress. It was the least they could do, hardly a just reward for the return of their pet. "May I ask why?"

"I'd prefer if you didn't," Inna replied. And she left it at that.

CHAPTER 35

THE CHOIRBOY

Bobby was drunk. He stared at his whiskey glass instead of the card game.

He'd been drunk a lot lately. It helped him sleep. He'd had trouble sleeping. He kept having nightmares about his plane getting shot up, starting to disintegrate around him. In his nightmare, though, he had to eject. He drifted on his parachute through the cold breeze, the water below drawing closer and closer. As soon as his boots hit and he felt the icy chill of the ocean about to swallow him, he'd wake with a jolt.

In reality, he was one of the lucky ones.

Major Bovington had lost his life that day, as had seven other brave pilots in Bobby's squadron. To make matters worse, they'd lost their lives in vain. Dutch Harbor was destroyed and would be subject to Japanese assault no more. Dozens of American soldiers on the ground were killed. In the days that followed, the Japanese captured all of Unalaska Island. The top brass must have been shocked. The islands had little strategic value, but the defeat meant more American territory conquered by the Japanese.

If he was drunk enough, Bobby wouldn't have to think about it. If he was drunk enough, he'd just pass out and wouldn't have to dream in terror. So he spent more and more time sitting in the cold Alaskan barracks, playing cards as an excuse to drink whiskey.

"Bobby?"

He looked up from his whiskey glass. Jack was staring at him, expecting something from him. "Yeah?"

"What're you gonna do?" Jack asked patiently.

Bobby glanced down at the cards in his hand. "Oh yeah. Call."

Bobby was enjoying the liquor, but he wasn't much enjoying their latest game in the officer's mess. Gambling for duty chips had been bad enough. This was far worse. Unfortunately, it appeared he was the only one who thought so.

Wally was already down to his undershirt and boxer shorts, but he still had a wolfish grin on his face as he gazed across the table at the three Russian girls. They'd proven to be excellent card players. And they were hardly even tipsy, while the American boys were already beginning to slur their words. But everyone other than Bobby, it seemed, was certain his luck could change any minute. Hope springs eternal.

Strip poker had been Jack's idea, of course. Jack had never stopped trying to find a beautiful woman, not even here in the wilds of Alaska. He had braved the cold and the wind every weekend to travel into town on sightseeing tours, the "sights" in this case, pretty Inuit girls. One time he took Bobby with him, subtly pointing out which girls he'd already identified as the most promising. Bobby was amazed. He didn't know how Jack did it. The girls all looked the same to him, dressed as they were in thick sealskin parkas and big hoods—just big bundles of moving clothing.

Somehow, Jack had always maneuvered them into a situation where they took off their hoods and parkas so he could get a good look at them. Usually that meant following them into the general store, where they bartered local salmon and seal fat for imported flour or cornmeal. Other times he bought them coffee at the tavern. Although his intentions weren't innocent, his methods were. After all, he wasn't yet trying to seduce the girls. He was merely identifying the ones worth the effort.

The most promising of his potential prey was a girl in her early twenties with shiny, intricately braided hair and a geometric tattoo along her jawline. Jack found the tattoo both fascinating and erotic. He'd never seen anything like it. She had the opposite effect on Bobby. He agreed that the girl possessed rare natural beauty, but found the tattoo off-putting. His disinterest pleased Jack. It meant less competition.

But Jack's plan had one fatal flaw—none of the Inuit girls spoke English. He tried to tackle that problem by learning the native language himself. But he found it difficult. He fumbled even the simplest words, like "Hello," on his tongue.

After the squadron returned from its first action against the Japanese, Jack had become despondent—not because of losing the air battle, but because returning only reminded him that he was clearly losing the romantic battle with the local girls. That had changed with the arrival of the Russian pilots. They were female pilots, just like the ones they'd met in Iran. In fact, most were the same pilots they'd met back then. The Soviet military had decided to keep trusting the transport flights to women, reserving the men for combat duty against the Germans. The main difference between then and now was that the Russian girls had begun to learn English. That meant Jack could finally talk to the girl he'd danced with four months ago. Her English was still basic, but it was a lot better than Jack's nonexistent Russian.

Jack invited the girls into the officer's mess while the mechanics prepped their Lend-Lease Airacobras for the transport flight across the Bering Strait to Russia.

The girls clearly expected more dancing and were disappointed to discover there was no jukebox in Nome. Jack flashed a smile and promised he'd order one for delivery—maybe next time they came it'd be there for them. In the meantime, he suggested a round of drinks and a game of cards.

The round of drinks turned into four and then five rounds of neat whiskey—for the men, anyway; the women would soon have to fly back, after all. And the game of cards turned into strip poker. At first the girls didn't want to risk having to disrobe, so Jack upped the ante to make things more interesting. The losers didn't just have to strip; they had to run out to the airfield and back in their underwear. The Russian girls thought it would be funny to watch the Americans shiver in the cold, so they agreed to the terms.

Wally was quickly reduced to his undershirt and boxer shorts—and that wolfish grin. Jack had already lost his jacket, his necktie, his shoes, and his socks. Next to go would be his shirt and trousers. Bobby was only a little better off than Jack, having retained his socks and necktie. The girls had lost their boots and their hats and their jackets, and Jack's favorite girl, a plump twenty-three-year-old named Bel, had also lost her belt.

To make matters worse, Jack had raised the current bet to two articles of clothing, and it was time to lay down the cards. One more loss would see Wally running to the airfield in bare feet through the cold.

Bel eyed Jack. "You nice legs? I hope," she teased, then laid down two pairs: fives and kings.

"And I hope you're wearing a clean bra," Jack retorted with a grin, laying down a set: three tens.

That left Bobby out in the cold. He had only a pair of aces. He folded with a groan and drained his whiskey. The two other girls, Katia and Lenka, folded.

But Wally stood in triumph. "Read 'em and weep!" he announced, dropping a full house. Delirious with joy that he'd finally won a hand, he gestured at the entire room, chanting, "Take! It! Off!"

Jack hammed it up, pushing back his chair and raising his leg like a choir girl, his bare foot resting on the table. "Tra ra ra boom de-yay," he sang, mimicking a well-known cancan while he pulled off his pants as if rolling down a pair of silk stockings.

The girls laughed at the show and joined his song. "Tra ra ra boom de-yay!"

Jack stood on the chair and swung his pants around his head, letting go so that they flew across the table and landed on Bel's shoulder. He then swiveled his hips as he unbuttoned his shirt. But before he finished, he pointed at the girl. "You, too!"

Bel laughed and stood on her chair. While everyone sang, she and Jack unbuttoned together. When they were finished, they wiggled out of their shirts and threw them at each other, wearing only undershirt and bra, respectively.

Suddenly a cold draft hit them as the officer's mess door swung open, bringing sunlight with it. "What the hell is going on in here?"

Everyone spun toward the door, where Colonel Harris stood, fully dressed, aghast at the scene before him. Colonel Harris was Major Bovington's replacement, and the men hadn't yet gotten to know or to trust him.

"Just a little recreation, sir," Jack answered, managing not to slur his words.

"Looks like a damned whorehouse," the colonel growled in outrage.

"I wouldn't know, sir," Jack replied, slyly turning the accusation back on the colonel.

The colonel flushed red. "Just get your damned clothes on and report to HQ." He turned on his heels and marched back out into the cold.

Jack frowned at Bel and shrugged. "Sorry, beautiful. Duty calls."

Bel frowned back at him.

Colonel Harris's office was ice-cold. He even had a fan on. But Bobby was hot anyway, from the liquor. When he, Wally, and Jack entered, Colonel Harris made them stand at attention before him.

"Do you know why we're here?" he asked, pacing back and forth in front of his desk, a scowl etched on his face.

"Lend-Lease," Wally replied. "Helping to give the Russians airplanes."

"Funny, and here I thought we were supposed to be fighting the Japs and the Krauts," the colonel growled.

"With all due respect, sir, so did I," Jack agreed.

With his talk of fighting, the colonel was fast gaining their respect.

"So I bet you're wondering why we're cooling our heels here, out in the middle of nowhere instead of down south helping 11th Air Force kick the Japs out of the Aleutian Islands?"

"I'll admit I had that thought," Jack said.

"We all did," Wally added.

The colonel turned his appraising eye on Bobby.

"What about you?"

"I know why we're here," Bobby admitted. "It's not to give the Russians airplanes, and it never was."

The colonel nodded, keeping his eyes on Bobby. "So why don't you tell your friends?"

Wally and Jack both gawked at Bobby. They had no idea of the true, secret mission they were supposed to be on. Bobby took a deep breath and laid it out for them: how the army was afraid Russia would lose the war, how they didn't want Russian oil and industry to fall into German hands, and how they were using Lend-Lease as a pretext to scout out potential bombing routes.

The fact that he was drunk made it easier. He was ashamed to have kept it from them this long, and he was relieved, finally, to be letting the cat out of the bag.

The colonel nodded with satisfaction. "They warned me you were smart." He turned to Jack and Wally. "So you see, our mission in Nome is a helluva lot more important than kicking the Japanese out of some islands nobody really wants anyway."

He let that settle in for a moment, holding the silence.

"But sir," Bobby began, then stopped.

"Yes, Lieutenant?"

Bobby wanted to continue. The trouble was, the room was spinning. He took another deep breath and steadied himself. "I thought that mission was scrubbed, on account of the Russians insisting on flying the planes themselves."

"It wasn't scrubbed," the colonel said, "just put on ice." He looked over the assembled pilots. "Believe it or not, you three are among the most experienced pilots we have. Navy's been in a few scraps, but we've mostly been sitting on the sidelines. Didn't it ever occur to you how strange it is to ground three experienced army pilots in northern Alaska?"

"Of course it did, sir," Jack offered.

"We were waiting. Hoping that our time would come. And guess what? It's come."

"How so, sir?"

"Russians want a summit. A face-to-face with General Marshall. Of course the Russians can't leave the USSR, seeing as they're fighting for their lives. Which means they want the general to come to them." The colonel smiled and leaned back in his chair. "We agreed."

Like Jack, Bobby was even beginning to like the colonel. Because he immediately caught on to what the colonel was implying. He might be drunk, but he wasn't stupid. "Under the condition that we fly the general there?"

"Of course. We can't entrust the safety of one of our most important generals to Soviet pilots, can we?"

"I shouldn't think so," Jack said.

There was still one piece that Bobby couldn't wrap his head around. "But we're fighter pilots."

"So?" the colonel said.

"The general will be in a transport, won't he?"

The colonel's smile got bigger. "We're in a war, son. Who knows where the front will be by the time the summit takes place? Gotta protect General Marshall from a potential German air attack. It would be stupid to let him fly naked, without fighter support." The colonel winked.

Then he leaned forward. "The summit's taking place in Chelyabinsk. I want you three to remember." He pointed at Bobby. "This one here has a photographic memory, or so I'm told. But that doesn't mean we're not counting on the rest of you, too. We need to know everything you see. No detail is too small."

Jack nodded. "We'll take good notes."

"No, no notes," the colonel scolded. "This is the Soviet Union. Their NKVD is no joke. They catch wind of why we're really there, you three won't make it out of the country alive. Understand?"

Bobby replied for all. "Yes, sir, we understand. When do we leave?"

"Summit's in two weeks. You leave in five days."

Bobby nodded at that. Five days was plenty of time to sober up.

By the time the three American aviators were dismissed, the Russians' planes were already prepped.

Bel, Katia, and Lenka were now covered up in full-body flight suits. They were just climbing into their Airacobra cockpits when Jack, Bobby, and Wally walked up to wave good-bye. Katia and Lenka smiled and waved back, but Bel jumped back off the ladder and trotted over to Jack. "Come, I need to show you," she said, taking his hand, mischief in her eye.

She and Jack ran through the snow and disappeared into one of the hangars. Some moments later, they reappeared and then separated, Bel to her plane and Jack to the company of his two friends.

"What was that all about?" Wally asked.

"She wanted to show me something."

"Oh yeah? What?"

"Her panties."

Wally gaped at him.

"She said a deal's a deal," Jack continued. "And she wanted me to know that she, too, has nice legs."

"Did she?" Bobby asked.

"Bobby, boy, I think I'm in love."

"Yeah? Well, join the club."

The engines roared above, and the three pilots looked back toward the runway. The Airacobras were lifting up just in time, speeding toward the ocean, their metal finish gleaming as they rose up into the cold sunlight.

Bobby couldn't wait to follow them, across the sea and deep into Russia.

CHAPTER 36
THE CONDUCTOR

Madame Nadia put down her baton and looked out at her orchestra. They timidly avoided her eye, expecting her to berate them at any moment.

That was her instinct. Their concert in Alexander Gardens had sounded awful, and today's rehearsal was no better. The young musicians were sufficiently skilled at their craft to impress a group of uncultured proletariat, but they would need to do far better if they hoped to impress an American general, or Josef Stalin himself.

Madame Nadia had berated the children dozens of times already, to no avail. She couldn't rap their knuckles, either; that might detrimentally affect their playing abilities. She considered paddling them, but that would require making them get up and leave their instruments, and the lesson would be lost. So what was left? What could she do? She had to reassess.

"That's enough for now," she told them. "Let's take a break for lunch."

The children looked relieved. And then began the scrape and shuffle of putting down instruments and folding up music.

Madame Nadia turned her back on the orchestra and walked out of the auditorium. Her office was only a hundred feet from here, but her mind was a thousand miles away, in Chelyabinsk. How would Josef Stalin react to their performance? He wouldn't be pleased, she was sure. On the other hand, perhaps his expectations would be as low as that of the proletariat they'd just performed for in the park. After all, they wouldn't be presenting a full concert in Chelyabinsk; they'd be performing only a sort of background music during the summit's opening dinner.

No, Madame Nadia decided, hoping for an uncultured audience was a fool's game. She had to find a way to impress them, regardless of their level of sophistication. Perhaps the piece was the problem. *The Rite of Spring* was difficult to perform, and it wasn't exactly easy on the ears. It was clear that many of her young musicians didn't like it. Who was to say Stalin or the American general might not feel the same way?

Madame Nadia had chosen the composition because it showcased a living, famous Russian composer. But perhaps that, too, was a mistake. She thought she was being patriotic, but in truth she had no idea how Stalin felt about Stravinsky. After all, Stravinsky had never returned to Russia after the Revolution. Perhaps he was a czarist. Perhaps, in her desire to seem patriotic, Madame Nadia was unwittingly celebrating an enemy of the State. That wouldn't just lead to a cold reception at the summit; it would also lead to a one-way trip to the Gulag. By the time they arrived in Chelyabinsk, it would be July—the summit was set for July 4 in order to honor their American guests. That gave them just enough time to rehearse a new piece of music.

Madame Nadia reached her office and sat down behind her desk with a sigh. She'd made an enormous mistake. But it wasn't too late to fix it. She began rummaging through her desk drawers for sheet music. *Peter and the Wolf?* Prokofiev was still living in Moscow, and the kids loved his little musical drama. But she was performing for adults. She tossed it aside. She considered *The Nutcracker* next, another child's favorite and another ballet like *The Rite of Spring*. She tossed that, too, in the discard pile. Tchaikovsky, though, was a good choice. Everyone loved Tchaikovsky, and he died before the Revolution, so he couldn't be criticized as being anti-Bolshevik. But which piece?

The echo of a door knocker interrupted Madame Nadia's thoughts. It was the auditorium's stage door, and the sound made her drop everything. That door was the address she'd given for donations. She stood up and brushed her hands down the front of her dress. Then she checked her hair in a hand mirror. Her bun had come undone. She hurried to reknot it as the knocker echoed once more. She put down the mirror and hurried to the stage door.

She didn't need donations, not really. But potential benefactors didn't have to know that. The trip to Chelyabinsk had already been paid for by the Soviet government. A patriotic fervor was gripping Moscow, especially since the Siberian divisions had miraculously delivered them from the Nazis' clutches this last winter. Everyone was eager to do their part by working hard and donating to the war effort.

Madame Nadia had been sly in associating her orchestra with war morale, and she wasn't about to deny anyone the satisfaction of pledging a donation. Even though her orchestra didn't need the money, she sure could use it. It was her way of making a few extra rubles on the side. There was nothing wrong with it. So long as it remained a secret, no one would be hurt, and everyone would win.

She arrived at the stage door, hesitated a moment, put on her most serene smile, and swung it open. Greeting her were two teenagers, a boy and a girl, dressed smartly if not in the latest fashion. They were not quite what Madame Nadia had expected, but she had to be careful. You never knew, after all, who had money these days. Perhaps they were the children of important Party officials, bearing a gift from their parents.

"Welcome," she announced. "I am Madame Nadia. How may I help you?"

"Good morning, Madame Nadia," the girl replied with the slight dip of a curtsy. "My name is Inna Kerensky, and this is my brother, Petr."

The boy glanced at the girl with momentary surprise, but he quickly gathered himself. "I am pleased to make your acquaintance," the boy declared with a bow.

Madame Nadia stared at the two teens. There was an awkward silence. Why were they here? Had they brought a donation, or hadn't they? Madame Nadia didn't want to ask outright. That would be uncouth. Then she noticed one of her flyers dangling from the girl's hand. "Ah, I see you have one of my flyers. Were you at the concert in the park?"

"I was, Madame," the girl replied eagerly.

"I very much hope you enjoyed it," Madame Nadia continued.

The girl hesitated, so the boy added, "We enjoyed it immensely. Thank you, Madame."

Madame Nadia smiled. But the girl frowned. She opened her mouth, hesitated again, and gathered her courage. "Actually, I felt it sounded a bit amateurish."

Madame Nadia reddened with anger. She knew it was the truth. She'd told the orchestra the exact same thing herself. But she wasn't about to be lectured by a teenage nobody. "And I suppose you could have done better?" she shot back.

"Yes, I could have," the brazen girl replied. "I am quite familiar with *The Rite of Spring*. Your lead cello, in particular, was poor. If I had been playing, I think I could have made a significant difference."

Madame Nadia was getting angrier by the moment. This wasn't a donation, after all. It was an audition. The girl wanted to play lead cello in the orchestra, in *her* orchestra. "I'm sorry, but this is a youth orchestra. You must be under eighteen."

"I am seventeen," the girl told her.

"Auditions are on the first of every year," Madame Nadia continued, unyielding. "That was six months ago."

"I could not attend the auditions on account of being trapped in Leningrad."

Madame Nadia was left speechless. The nerve of this girl, claiming to have been in the martyred city of Leningrad! Everyone in Russia knew about the city. The Soviet propaganda ministers had recently decided to publicize its fate. Rather than keeping it secret, they now celebrated its starving citizens as martyrs to Nazi villainy.

This girl was obviously hoping to play on Nadia's patriotic emotions. Well, it wouldn't work, because it was clearly a lie. No one escaped from Leningrad, no one. "I am sorry for your misfortune," she said curtly. "But you are welcome to audition on January first of 1943."

Madame Nadia stepped back and began to swing the door shut. But it stopped before latching. The girl had stuck her foot in it. "Please, Madame, I need to get to Chelyabinsk."

"Then you will have to find your own way there," Madame Nadia snapped. "The orchestra, and the train, are full." She kicked the girl's foot away, then quickly bolted the door.

CHAPTER 37

THE CELLIST AND THE ORGAN-GRINDER

Karen glared at the stage door, wanting to kick herself. She'd overplayed her hand, acting like a prima donna know-it-all. She hated prima donnas but had assumed the persona intentionally. She'd been around musicians long enough to notice that prima donnas usually got their way. But only because they were talented, Karen now realized. That had been her mistake. Karen had talent, but this Madame Nadia didn't know it.

Madame Nadia had never heard of Karen Hamilton. And, even if by some miracle, Madame Nadia *had* heard of Karen, had somehow known Karen was studying on a performance scholarship at the Leningrad Music Conservatory, she still could not know for sure that this girl knocking on her door had talent. Besides, the girl knocking on her door wasn't even claiming to be Karen Hamilton but someone completely different—a girl named Inna Kerensky.

Karen may have bungled it, she might be down, but she wasn't yet out. All she had to do was demonstrate to Madame Nadia that she had talent. To do that, she needed to audition.

The fact that formal auditions were closed was meaningless. Karen's father had always reminded her that an audition could take place anywhere, anytime.

"Can you get me inside?" Karen asked Petr, her eyes glued to the door.

Petr ignored the question. He was dwelling on something else. "Why did you tell her I'm your brother?"

"Oh, that," Karen replied, breaking her concentration on the door. "I don't know. It just came to me."

"Came to you? Why?"

"You're a war hero. They wrote about you in Pravda. I didn't want her to recognize your name."

Petr thought about that. He'd been lucky. Not even Duck's family had recognized him. If they had, they might have asked why he wasn't at the front.

"I had to say something, didn't I?" Karen added. "We couldn't use your real name, could we?"

"But why claim I'm your brother?"

Karen suddenly realized that she'd been acting as much on emotion as on logic. Pretending that Petr was her brother had seemed like a flash of brilliance that would serve both her personal and emotional goals. But she had never admitted those emotions, not even to herself. And she now hesitated admitting them to Petr. The silence between them grew.

"Is that how you think of me?" Petr asked, almost timidly. "Like a brother?"

"No," Karen said, wondering at the source of Petr's sadness. Had he begun to think of her as more than a traveling companion—more, even, than a friend? She hoped so, because she'd begun to feel the same way.

"Then why did you say it?" Petr persisted.

Karen looked him in the eye. "Because you're not a musician. Unless we're related, you'll never be allowed on the train."

"Of course not. Why should I be allowed on the train?"

"Because I want you to come with me."

There, the truth was out. Karen was afraid of saying it, afraid of how Petr might react. But now it was out, and there was no taking it back. Petr stared at her in silence, his mind turning, trying to process Karen's bold statement. Their conversation had just moved across a slippery slope, their emotions vulnerable. It was difficult enough being honest with themselves about how they felt. Being honest with each other could lead to rejection.

He thought he knew what she meant, but was that just wishful thinking? He needed clarification. "You want me to come with you to Chelyabinsk? Is that it?"

Karen shook her head. "I want you to come with me to America." In America, Karen knew, Petr would be safe. But that's not really why she'd asked; it wasn't for a selfless reason but for a selfish one. She loved Petr's company. She treasured being with him. She wanted him to come with her because she didn't want to be apart from him. Absence didn't make the heart grow fonder, she now knew. It made the heart grow absent, too. She'd been apart from Bobby for so long now that he didn't even seem real anymore. She didn't want the same thing to happen with Petr.

Nothing physical changed in Petr's facial expression. But something behind his face did. His eyes flickered, and Karen recognized that in that moment his emotions had transformed from sadness to joy. He wanted to come with her. He likely had just wanted her to ask. It all gave Karen a profound sense of relief. She hadn't been rejected. Still, he hadn't yet accepted her proposal. She took both his hands in hers. "Will you?"

Petr was struggling with conflicting desires. Clearly, he wanted to be with Karen, wherever she was. But America was not just a foreign country; it was a foreign concept. What would he even do there? How would he fit in? And Russians were not free the way Americans were. He couldn't just travel to New York City and see how he liked it. If he were to desert from the army and emigrate to America, he might be declared a traitor. He might never be allowed to return to Russia. He would never see his father or his uncle again.

Then again, would he ever see his family again, anyway? He still didn't expect to survive the war.

"I don't know," he admitted. "I'd like to, I think, but I don't know. Let's go to Chelyabinsk first, and then we'll see."

Karen smiled and hugged him tightly. He returned her embrace, powerfully, practically crushing her rib cage.

He suddenly let go. "But I guess first we have to find you a way inside."

They circled the auditorium, which was difficult, as it was flanked on either side by attached apartment buildings—it meant going around a vast city block.

The buildings were of varying heights, forming a chaotic series of stepped rooftops, many with glass skylights, others transformed by tenants into summer patios.

Finding no unlatched windows or unlocked doors on the first floor of the complex, Petr climbed a tree and reached a low garden patio. From there he stood on the patio railing and was able to lift himself onto a second-story roof. Thank goodness for warm weather! One of the windows flanking the roof was open, and Petr crawled inside.

Karen waited at the stage door for five minutes, but it seemed like hours. She worried less about whether Petr would be caught, and more about what would happen to him if he were. But that was silly: he was a soldier and had faced far more dangerous foes than Madame Nadia and her youth orchestra. But still, she worried.

Then the stage door opened. Petr's smiling face popped out, and relief washed over Karen. "Come on, I don't think we have much time," he warned her.

Karen hurried inside.

"They're all eating lunch," Petr whispered as he led her into the auditorium. "I don't know when they'll start rehearsing again."

Karen nodded and halted at the edge of the stage. The instruments and music stands were already set up, awaiting the musicians. She took a deep breath, crossed to the position of the lead cello, and sat down.

Petr followed. "What are you going to play?" he whispered, sounding like a fan now.

Karen reached into her coat and pulled out a folded sheet of music. It was the music she'd taken from her father the day she'd found him dead, the same piece he'd been working on with Dmitri Shostakovich, even after the composer had fled to safety. It was the music Karen's father had died for, and she treated it with the gentle care of a valuable artifact as she unfolded it and then smoothed it on her music stand. Then she picked up the cello and put bow to string.

The cello was in tune, thank goodness. The lead cellist might have been an unimpressive musician, but at least he knew how to tune his instrument. Karen couldn't risk taking the time to tune it herself. If she did, the sound would only draw Madame Nadia, who Karen was certain would forbid her from performing her audition.

Her father's music flowed from the cello, rich and deep. It wasn't just his music, of course, it was also Shostakovich's, but Karen so hated the famous Russian composer that she couldn't admit to anything beautiful and moving coming from his mind. And the music did sound very beautiful and very moving.

As Karen played, she lost herself in the composition. The sound of the cello spoke to her like the voice of her father's spirit, speaking to her from beyond the grave. It told her he was sorry for having taken her to the doomed city of Leningrad, for having trapped her against her will. It told her he was proud of her for finding the strength to survive. And he thanked her for not giving up.

As Karen continued to play, her father's voice began to change, subtly. It became less personal. He wasn't just sorry for Karen, he was sorry for all the unfortunate men and women who were trapped and starving. He was proud of all the survivors, and he wished he, too, could have found the same strength. He couldn't, but he could leave them this one gift, this gift of music, one he knew was inadequate compared to the lifesaving food and comfort the brave Leningraders really needed. That was what the strong, defiant, starving citizens of Leningrad deserved, not just some symphony. But Karen's father couldn't give them that. Neither could Dmitri Shostakovich. They could only give music.

The music brought back vibrant, horrible, sad memories. Karen remembered the dead body of the old woman in the fountain. She remembered the hungry faces of the cannibals. She remembered Sasha's face, brutally beaten and bloody. She remembered Inna's face, as beautiful in death as Sasha's had been gruesome. She remembered the city lit up by dozens of separate fires. She remembered smelling food while being interrogated by Sasha's father.

But most of all, she remembered the singing: all those men, women, and children, starving almost to death, standing in line and passing buckets in a desperate attempt to keep the bakeries open—barely having enough strength to pass the buckets, and yet, somehow, finding the inner reserves of energy to sing.

Karen agreed with the voice she was hearing in her inner ear, saying that music was not the most important gift Leningraders could have received. But it had worth. It was a beautiful gift. Karen no longer hated her father. And, more miraculously, she no longer hated Dmitri Shostakovich.

She finished the movement and put down her bow. She couldn't see because her vision was blurry with tears. She wiped her eyes with the cuff of her coat and looked across the stage.

Madame Nadia and the entire youth orchestra were standing there, gazing at her with rapt attention. It surprised her for a moment. She had lost herself so completely in the music that she'd forgotten where she was. She'd even forgotten she was auditioning. She didn't know what to do.

Madame Nadia had her conductor's baton in one hand. She placed it under her armpit to free both hands and started to applaud. The rest of the Youth Orchestra joined in the ovation.

Karen put down the instrument, stood awkwardly, and bowed. She had never been so reluctant to accept an audience's praise. She felt that the power of the music had not come *from* her; it had merely come *through* her.

"*That* is how you play with emotion," Madame Nadia lectured her students. Then she turned her attention to Karen. "Where did you learn that piece?"

"I studied under Mr. Shostakovich at the Leningrad Conservatory."

"And he gave you a copy of his work?"

Karen wanted to tell her no, that the copy was from her father, a talented composer collaborating with Shostakovich. But she couldn't. That would reveal that she was Karen Hamilton, not Inna Kerensky. That would reveal that she was American, not Russian. No matter what the circumstances, Madame Nadia would never allow an American in her Russian orchestra.

So instead, Karen just said, "Yes."

"A copy of the whole symphony, or just that one movement?"

"The whole symphony."

Madame Nadia nodded with satisfaction. "I will need to make more copies if we hope to learn the symphony in time for the concert in Chelyabinsk. I will need to begin immediately."

She held out her palm, expecting Karen to hand over her father's score.

But Karen didn't hand over the score. Instead, she grabbed her father's composition, folded it back up, and stuffed it in her coat pocket.

"Yes, you will need to," she agreed warily, "assuming, of course, that I am in the orchestra."

The old Karen was back, the practical Karen, the survivor.

Madame Nadia frowned. "I think that can be arranged. Do you have an instrument?"

"I was forced to destroy my cello in Leningrad."

Madame Nadia wrinkled her nose in contempt. "Whatever for?"

"I needed the firewood."

Madame Nadia sighed. "Very well. Then we will have to find you an instrument. You are our new lead cello."

CHAPTER 38

THE CHOIRBOY

Bobby hadn't believed anything could be bigger than Alaska, but Siberia was just that. They flew over vast stretches of taiga wilderness. Up ahead, the Russian girl pilots were leading his formation of P-39 fighters as they escorted General Marshall's C-47 Skytrain. They'd stopped briefly to refuel at no fewer than seventeen different airfields, mostly for the P-39s.

The C-47 would have needed to refuel only once before reaching Chelyabinsk, as a B-17 bomber would have. But General Marshall wanted to land at as many fields as possible to gain a complete picture of the proposed route. Most of the airfields were tiny and remote, little more than gravel runways ground into the permafrost. But, as Bobby observed, all were adequate way stations for a potential B-17 bombing run.

At one such airfield, Seymchan, the American pilots had spent their first night. Their barracks were a log cabin with a sod roof. It was cold enough in June; Bobby couldn't imagine what it must be like in the middle of winter. It took him ages to fall asleep, and it felt like only moments later when Jack woke him.

1

"I need your help," he said.

"Help doing what?"

"Help with Bel."

"Why? What's wrong with her?"

"Nothing's wrong, everything's right. That's the problem." He looked around, making sure no one else was waking up. "Lenka knows this hot spring. She's willing to show us, but only if you come along."

"Why me?"

"Why do you think? Lenka's sweet on you."

Bobby groaned. "All right, but you owe me."

It was an hour hike through the darkness. Pine and fir trees climbed all around them, the bushy needles of their branches blocking the sky.

Bobby heard a strange sound as they hiked—a sort of grunt or a growl. "What's that?" he asked.

"Bear," Bel responded with a smile. "How you say . . . white, big?" she gestured with her arms to indicate a bear's enormous size

"A polar bear?" Bobby blurted in alarm. "What if it attacks?"

Bel shrugged. "Then it eat. Us."

Lenka leaned close, draping her arm around Bobby's shoulder so she could whisper in his ear. "Do not worry, she tease," Lenka reassured him. "Most likely just wild pig."

The forest parted to reveal a wide circle of barren ground. Bobby gasped at the horizon. Bright-green streaks rose like reverse lightning into the sky: the aurora borealis. It was so bright, it illuminated everything, including the girls' glowing faces.

Lenka led them across the icy dirt interspersed with granite boulders. In the center of the clearing was a small, perfectly circular pond. Thanks to the light of the aurora borealis, Bobby could see steam rising off the pond's surface.

"Turn around," Lenka told the boys.

"How come?" Bobby asked.

"Just do it!" whispered Jack, turning around. Bobby frowned and followed suit.

"No look!" Lenka called out.

Then came a long pause, broken by one splash and then another.

"OK, you can look now!"

Bobby discovered both girls up to their necks in the warm water. Though the black, murky depths obscured their bodies, Bobby knew they were both naked because their clothes were draped neatly over nearby boulders.

"Now your turn," teased Lenka.

"What? You want us to strip right here?"

Lenka shrugged, revealing her bare shoulders as they briefly rose above the surface of the black water. "You must not walk back cold in wet clothes."

"Aren't you gonna turn around?" Bobby asked incredulously.

"No," Lenka stated. Bel giggled beside her.

Bobby looked around. The clearing was at least fifty yards in circumference. There was not a single bush or tree to hide behind.

"What're you waiting for?" Jack urged, practically tearing off his shirt and trousers.

Bobby sighed and followed suit, disrobing and jumping into the water as quickly as possible so the girls wouldn't see his naked body too long. His clothes lay in a tangled pile on the cold ground. The warm water of the hot spring immediately relaxed him. It smelled bad, like rotten eggs, but he couldn't deny it felt wonderful.

The foursome began to chat, with Jack telling the story of how he'd learned to fly. That prompted the girl pilots to tell their own stories.

Bel had grown up worshipping Maria Raskova, a sort of Russian equivalent, Bobby decided, of Amelia Earhart. Bel always dreamed of flying, and when she was twelve, she jumped off her apartment balcony with homemade wings. The experiment ended with her breaking both her legs. But it didn't end her desire to fly. When she turned eighteen, she applied to the Zhukovsky Air Force Engineering Academy, where her hero, Marina Raskova, was now working as an instructor. When Germany invaded, all the student pilots were conscripted into the military.

Lenka admitted that her reasons for becoming a pilot were much more practical than Bel's. She, too, learned to fly at the Zhukovsky Academy, but Lenka had never heard of Marina Raskova. Lenka's mother believed that pilots would make good husbands, since their jobs were both respected and in demand. She'd sent Lenka to the academy not to succeed, but to fail, trusting that her daughter would hitch a man before flunking out.

"But she not flunk," Bel declared, proud of her friend. "Lenka was best in class."

Lenka blushed.

"Your mother must be proud," Bobby observed.

"She still want I marry rich pilot," Lenka replied with another shrug of her cute bare shoulders.

"But if you're a pilot now," Bobby reasoned, "you can be rich yourself. You don't need a husband."

"Nobody rich in Soviet Union," Lenka informed him. She leaned forward so that the steam parted around her smiling face. "So maybe I marry rich American pilot instead."

Bobby suddenly realized how hot it was getting. "Hey, I'm starting to sweat. What do you say we head back?"

Lenka smiled, as if proud of herself for making Bobby uncomfortable. "OK, you first."

Bobby knew there was no arguing. He just had to swallow his embarrassment, get out of the water, and get dressed as quickly as possible. "You coming?" he asked Jack.

Jack looked over at Bel, who shook her head with a grin. "No, I'm just fine. Why don't you two go ahead?"

Bobby pulled on his clothes in seconds, and turned around to let Lenka dress in private. As they walked away, Bobby glanced over his shoulder and noticed that Jack and Bel were no longer across from each other. Jack had slid up beside her.

Obviously, something happened that night between them. For the rest of the trip, on through Yakutsk and Kirensk and Krasnoyarsk, Bobby caught Jack and Bel kissing. And for every time he caught them, he was sure there were at least a dozen more times that he didn't. Bobby was glad for his friend. But he also had to admit he was a little jealous, because it reminded him of all those good times in New York with Karen. He could only hope he was getting closer to bringing them back.

CHAPTER 39

THE CELLIST AND THE
ORGAN-GRINDER

Karen had never been on a train that was so luxurious. It was more like a rolling resort hotel than a means of transportation. After all she'd been through, she tried not to smile the whole time.

The youth orchestra was sharing the train with the Soviet delegation, which was the reason for its elegance. Despite Josef Stalin's rhetoric about serving the proletariat, about hating the bourgeoisie, about eliminating social class and unifying Russia's economy, he and his cronies lived exactly the way the czars had before them.

For once Karen was glad of their hypocrisy. She never met Stalin, of course, nor did she meet his top general, Chuikov, nor any of the lesser members of the Politburo. Karen's and the rest of the young musicians' movements were carefully orchestrated to avoid chance meetings with the leaders of Russia's totalitarian regime. It would be a disaster, Madame Nadia knew, if one of her music students inadvertently disturbed the important men heading to the summit. So she admonished the children to remain hidden in their berths until they could be sure of no inadvertent encounters, threatening them with dismissal from the orchestra and, more important, immediate expulsion from the train.

Neither Karen nor Petr minded. The members of the youth orchestra did not have sleeping cabins. Those were reserved for the important politicians and generals. But they did have beds or, more accurately, bunk berths. Those bunks were stacked on top of each other against one wall of a sleeping car, with a narrow aisle providing access along the other wall.

Since Karen and Petr were believed to be brother and sister, they were forced to share a single bunk. It was the only way to allow Petr on the train, since he wasn't part of the orchestra. The bunks were stacked so tightly that Karen could barely sit up in theirs without smacking her head, and Petr, much taller than she, had to remain prone or just slightly propped up on his elbows. At least the thin curtain gave them a small amount of privacy from the aisle and the other berths.

They left Moscow at midnight, in secret. The summit was no secret, but their departure had to be, for the safety of the delegation. The young musicians were sent immediately to bed. But, of course, they were all too excited to sleep. They peeked out of the curtains dividing their bunks, gossiping and giggling with one another all night long.

The constant chatter gave Karen and Petr the audio camouflage they craved. They could whisper to each other without fear of eavesdroppers.

"What are you going to do when you get there?" Petr asked.

"I'm going to play the concert," Karen replied after giving this careful thought, "and see who is in the audience. If I can identify the Americans, I should be able to find a way to approach them."

"Won't it be difficult to see past the stage lights?"

"There won't be any stage lights," Karen explained. "It's a dinner concert; we'll just be background music." She hesitated, thinking. "But if you could get inside, you could help. We need to identify all the Americans, not just the ones I can see from the stage."

"I'll try."

"Then, once we know what they look like, I need to find a way to approach them in private so that I can reveal who I am and tell them my circumstances."

"And just like that," Petr replied skeptically, "they'll take you home?"

"They'll have to."

Petr shook his head in disbelief. "No, they won't. Why should they care? They could just leave you. Worse, they could report you to the NKVD."

"They'd never do that."

"How can you be sure?"

"America isn't like Russia. Our government cares about us. It protects us."

"I hope you're right."

"Of course I'm right. It's why you should come with me."

"The only reason?"

"Of course not," she whispered, taking his hand in hers. "Have you decided?"

"Not yet," Petr admitted.

"Don't you want to come with me?"

"Convince me," Petr teased.

Karen smiled coquettishly and leaned forward. She kissed Petr on the lips.

It wasn't their first kiss, but it was their first romantic one, and it was something they'd both desired for a long time. They closed their eyes and enjoyed its erotic pleasure. She'd kissed and been kissed like this before, by Bobby in New York. But she hadn't been back to New York in almost two years, and hadn't heard from Bobby in more than six months. He had most likely forgotten her. Now, lost in the thrill of this kiss, Karen forgot him, too.

It was as if their souls lived not in their bodies or in their hearts, but in their mouths. Touching their lips together was like touching their inner selves. That kiss lasted as long as either of them could hold their breath.

It was their first real kiss, but it wasn't their last. It stripped away all their emotional defenses and laid bare their feelings for each other. No longer did they have to worry about rejection. They knew how they felt about each other; they knew they were both in love. The kiss proved it. It meant they could kiss again, without fear, all night long.

They didn't just kiss each other's lips. They kissed necks, shoulders, chests, and stomachs. They sought out bare flesh, slipping their hands under pajama and nightgown, seeking to feel bodies that were as naked as their emotions. But they still had to be careful. They were pretending to be brother and sister, after all. Their movements were restricted. They couldn't make a sound for fear of revealing what they were doing. Oddly, that made the experience even more exquisite.

Neither knew exactly when they fell asleep. But they couldn't have slept more than a couple of hours before Madame Nadia appeared, rousing all the student musicians from bed and admonishing them to get breakfast quickly.

Breakfast was another indication of how luxurious this trip would turn out. Madame Nadia and her orchestra were allowed in the dining car only after the last Russian dignitary had left, but even then the banquet of food was amazing. They chose from scrambled eggs, smoked salmon, kippers, sausage, pâté, an assortment of hard and soft cheeses, black bread, butter, and jam—all served from silver trays from which the young musicians could take as much as they pleased. Matching silver pitchers provided coffee, hot water for tea, and cream.

Lunch saw a return of the black-bread-and-cheese platter, along with an assortment of sliced vegetables, including onions, tomatoes, cucumbers, and radishes. Black caviar was added to the menu, complete with crackers to eat it on.

Karen had tried caviar once before, with her father, when they'd celebrated their arrival in Leningrad. She didn't much like it then and didn't like it now, either, until Petr found an open, half-empty bottle of champagne that the dignitaries had left behind. Somehow the bubbly, sweet, sparkling wine perfectly complemented the salty fish eggs, and Karen learned to savor the slight crunch of the caviar bursting between her teeth.

Dinner brought kidney soup, pork pies, dressed herring, potato dumplings, and traditional goulash, in addition to foods with which Karen was more familiar, like beef stroganoff. Crepes and lemon pie were served for dessert. While the other students picked at only those items they particularly liked—the lemon pie was especially popular—Karen made it a point not only to try but also to finish an ample helping of everything that was served. She devoured as much as she could, until she felt as though she would burst. It was an orgy of food, and she was determined to make up for those months of deprivation she'd experienced in Leningrad.

Between meals the young musicians were allowed to explore, so long as they restricted their movements to the back of the train.

Petr and Karen were more interested in exploring each other's bodies. They looked for hiding places where they might indulge in each other's kisses. They were like drugs, those kisses, that first real one igniting their addiction, and now they couldn't stop.

But they had to be even more careful than the night before. They couldn't be certain someone might not come around a corner and catch them. It made their romantic encounters both more frustrating and more exciting. They would duck around a corner and embrace and kiss each other for mere moments before hearing approaching footsteps and quickly separating, catching their breath so they could act as if nothing had happened. This went on for days. Karen indulged all her senses, devouring both the dining car's exotic food and Petr's erotic passion, barely hesitating long enough to look out a window and notice the passing countryside.

Nights were excruciating. It was an enormous test of will to stay apart in their single bunk. But they couldn't risk making any noise. After that first night, the musicians had settled down, and they slept sound and silent. Karen and Petr remained silent for fear of blowing their cover. But they always made up for those nights of yearning with days of romantic indulgence.

On the third day, they were almost caught. They'd found what seemed like a private corner of the baggage car. No one ever came into the baggage car, and even if they did, the young paramours' spot was behind several stacked trunks, well hidden from view.

Confident in their privacy, perhaps too confident, they overindulged in romantic flirtation. Karen unbuttoned Petr's shirt and stripped off his undershirt so she could feel his chest hair on her cheek and taste his nipples with her tongue. Aroused and unwilling to be outdone, Petr lifted Karen atop a stack of suitcases and lifted her skirt up over her waist so he could kiss her inner thigh. Karen closed her eyes, savoring the touch of Petr's lips and running her fingers roughly through his hair.

Then they heard the baggage-car door slamming shut. Someone had come inside. Karen scooted off the stacked suitcases, pulling down her skirt in a panic. Petr crouched behind the barrier of trunks, holding his breath and trying to pull on his undershirt silently. They froze at the sound of high heels clicking across the metal floor. That meant the intruder could only be one person: Madame Nadia.

The clicking stopped, and Petr grabbed his shirt, fumbling with the buttons and trying to smooth down his tousled hair. By attempting to do both at once, he was accomplishing neither but was so desperate, he wasn't thinking clearly. Karen licked her palms and brushed down his hair, letting him concentrate on finally tucking in his shirt.

With their appearances finally assembled properly, they peered out from behind the stacked trunks. They weren't surprised to discover

Madame Nadia, but they were surprised to discover a man with her. He was a portly man, with a bald patch on the top of his head, and he and Madame Nadia were acting exactly as Karen and Petr had been only moments before. The man had already pulled loose Madame Nadia's bun so he could run his fingers through her hair, and she yanked off her steaming glasses before twisting him around and pushing him against the baggage car's bulkhead.

"Oh, Boris," she moaned between kisses.

"Oh, Nadia," he moaned back.

Karen grabbed Petr's hand and led him to the door in a crouch. With Madame Nadia so distracted, they snuck out easily. Once they were safe, they leaned against a window of the rocking train and gazed at each other.

"Oh, Boris," Karen moaned.

"Oh, Nadia," Petr replied.

And they both convulsed in laughter.

When they finally recovered, Karen asked, "Do you think she's using him for his money?"

"What makes you think that?"

"He's fat and bald. What else could she see in him?"

"She's not exactly easy on the eyes, either," Petr joked.

The mystery was solved that night at dinner when one of the cooks appeared to clear the leftovers. Petr recognized the cook as Boris, then noticed Boris and Madame Nadia sharing more than a few sly glances. He pointed out the spectacle to Karen, who couldn't help but giggle.

Karen felt bad about accusing Madame Nadia of seducing Boris for his money. She'd assumed that Boris was part of the Russian delegation, a privileged politico with access to public money and expensive perks. Instead, he was a mere cook, no more privileged than Nadia herself. If it wasn't for the money, the two must really be in love. Karen thought the whole thing was cute, and she began to think differently about her stern conductor.

Madame Nadia changed, too. Now that she was in love, she became less strict. She began to wear her hair differently, experimenting with wavy curls that draped over her shoulders. She wore her collar open, revealing the tiniest line of cleavage for the first time. She even tried not to wear her glasses, using them only when she had to identify a sign or a person far away.

But more important than her change in appearance was her change in demeanor. Once they arrived in Chelyabinsk, her youth orchestra had only a few days to rehearse. But in those few days, they improved more than they had in months. Some credit went to Karen, their new lead cellist, but it was mostly thanks to the change in Madame Nadia. That emotion she'd demanded of her students but could never force them to express now began to flow out of her while conducting, and in turn it flowed from them. Her orchestra was more a reflection of herself than she ever cared to admit. The music lacked emotion for the simple reason that Madame Nadia lacked emotion. But now that she had embraced romance and passion, those things were reflected in the music.

Their final rehearsal came on the morning before the concert. They, and Karen, sounded brilliant. They were ready.

CHAPTER 40

THE CHOIRBOY

Bobby loved Chelyabinsk's speakeasies. Most started as tiny buds and sprouted into enormous vines, a series of adjoining apartments with their walls knocked out to provide enough space for bars, musicians, and crowds.

They were owned by collectives of factory workers supplementing their incomes with bootleg vodka. A group of ten or so workers would form the collective, giving up half their apartments to form the speakeasy, and doubling up in the remainder, sleeping on the floor. They mixed beer in the bathtubs and distilled vodka in their bedrooms.

The speakeasies were as illegal as American ones during prohibition, but not for the same reason. In Russia it was not the alcohol that was illegal, but free enterprise. The NKVD could have arrested everyone involved for participating in this black market. But the proprietors of the speakeasies didn't care. They felt secure in their anonymity. So long as they maintained at least the facade of secrecy, they knew the NKVD didn't really mind and wouldn't interfere. But that facade of secrecy was important. If they were too public, it would appear that they were flaunting their illegal activities. Then they wouldn't just be black marketers, they'd also be subversives.

Because they were secret, Bobby couldn't have found any of the speakeasies by himself. Chelyabinsk was a boomtown, though unlike most American ones, it was planned. Wide avenues and bridges had been built to accommodate the heavy machinery required for the huge factories that gave the city the nickname Tankograd. Uniform apartment buildings, the housing units for the factory workers, lined the streets like concrete monoliths.

Yet Chelyabinsk was still a maze. So it was all the more fortunate that Bobby had Lenka and Katia as guides. The girl pilots, it turned out, were celebrities. They were welcome everywhere and treated like American movie stars. To the average Russian, an airplane was an absolute miracle, and a pilot an angel. Girl pilots, therefore, were objects of both fascination and erotic fantasy.

Bobby loved the Russian factory workers. They labored through twelve-hour shifts but didn't go home and go to bed. Instead, they spent the next six hours in speakeasies, drinking and singing until they passed out. But there was always someone in charge of waking them up again, usually a kid about eleven or twelve years old. Armed with buckets of cold water, the kid would douse every unconscious worker, waking him or her early enough to get to work on time.

The source of the Russians' limitless energy, Bobby eventually discovered, was their fatalism. Each one believed they would eventually be drafted and killed by the Nazis.

Bobby wasn't surprised that this fatalism led to drinking. He'd done the same thing after his battle with the Japanese over the Aleutian Islands. But he was surprised that it led to a lively social atmosphere rather than a maudlin one. The Russian response to the inevitability of death was to live life to the fullest. They wanted to drink, sing, and make love today, because they didn't believe there would even be a tomorrow.

Bobby so enjoyed his nights out at the speakeasies that a part him was secretly dreading the summit itself.

The Russians didn't even want the American pilots to attend. They weren't dignitaries, after all. They were mere soldiers, which from the Soviet perspective meant sacrificial pawns in the great games of power. The Americans couldn't disagree more. America celebrated the Everyman, and these pilots, college-educated young officers from all walks of life, epitomized the American dream.

So a compromise was struck. The pilots could attend, but only in pseudosecret. After all, the Russians didn't want to be forced to invite their own pilots. So the Americans wouldn't wear their uniforms. They could hear the concert, but would have to eat dinner in the kitchen, with the staff. Bobby wished General Marshall and the rest of the American delegation hadn't bothered. He fully expected the summit to be uncomfortable and gloomy.

When the summit came, they put Bobby and the pilots in the kitchen, as proposed. As he ate his meal, he couldn't help but wish he was spending another evening at one of the speakeasies. But the music was interesting, at least—much better than the accordions and fiddles he'd sung to every night. It seemed like ages since he'd last heard a proper symphony.

He started to listen more attentively. He tried to identify the piece and eventually had to admit he'd never heard it before. But it was good; it was emotional. The cellist was particularly good. Bobby had become something of an expert on cellists after he started dating Karen. He knew she resented his father's demands of her talent and, as a result, even resented her talent itself. But Bobby couldn't help but be proud of his girlfriend. She was just so darned good at it. And this cellist was as talented—clearly better than the rest of the orchestra.

Curiosity overcame Bobby. He'd never known a cellist as good as Karen. He snuck to the kitchen door and peaked out, careful not to reveal himself. And he saw her. The cellist was as good as Karen because the cellist *was* Karen. Bobby's heart leaped. He felt dizzy with joy. It was fate; there was no other explanation. Never before had Bobby so completely believed in the power of faith. Yet he had kept his faith, doing everything he could to be near her again, despite having no communication with her or even knowing whether she was still alive.

Karen, too, had clearly kept her faith, somehow escaping Leningrad and finding her way east, to head closer to Bobby. Fate had rewarded their faith by bringing them together for this chance encounter. God, it turned out, was a romantic.

Bobby stared at Karen, feasting on her beauty. She was even more striking than when he'd first met her. She looked too thin, practically emaciated. But what Bobby noticed most was that she was no longer a girl. She was a woman.

Bobby looked away from the spectacle and rushed out of the kitchen through the back door. It was difficult, like tearing off a bandage, but he had to. He had so much to do. He returned to his hotel, where Jack had ditched the summit to spend another night alone with Bel. Bobby knocked loudly on Jack's door to give them fair warning, and burst inside.

Jack and Bel were in bed. "What are you doing?" Jack yelled, pulling the covers over Bel.

Bobby ignored Jack. He told Bel, "I need a gift quick, something romantic."

Bel smiled. "Romantic? For Lenka?"

Bobby shook his head. "No, I'm sorry. It's for someone else."

Jack stared at Bobby. "You're not talking about . . ."

Bobby grinned, nodded. "I am. I found her. I found Karen."

Bel did her best. There was no florist in Chelyabinsk, and few gardens. But there were wildflowers. She helped Bobby gather a bouquet of exotic steppe colors.

Finally prepared, he returned to the summit and waited outside the stage door. It was like the first time they'd met, two and a half years ago, except this time Bobby was sweating in the humid July heat. The door swung open and the musicians spilled out. Bobby searched their faces. He didn't see Karen. In broken, halting Russian, he asked where the lead cellist was. One of the young musicians pointed back inside the building.

He pushed past them. The hallways were quiet, dark, and abandoned. Where could Karen be? He began to panic, thinking he'd somehow lost her. Then he heard something—a girl—giggling. He followed the voice. It sounded like Karen, but why was she hiding in the dark? He saw shadows but couldn't fully make them out. He brushed the wall with his hand, found a light switch, and flipped it on. He immediately wished he hadn't. He'd found Karen, all right. But she wasn't alone. She was with a boy. And she was kissing him.

CHAPTER 41

THE CELLIST, THE ORGAN-GRINDER, AND THE CHOIRBOY

Bobby grabbed Petr's shoulder, spun him around, and hit him in the jaw.

The blow took Petr completely by surprise. One moment he was kissing the woman he loved, the next his brain flashed with pain and confusion. But he didn't pass out. He'd had time to flinch, which made Bobby miss the nerves leading from the jawline directly to the brain. He fell back against the wall, gathered his legs under him, and steadied himself.

Bobby had his hands up, his elbows tight, ready to protect face and stomach from a rain of fists. He'd learned to box in high school.

Petr had never learned to box. The Red Army hadn't trained him to brawl, only to kill in combat. And he had no idea who Bobby was; all he knew was that some strange man had attacked him for no apparent reason. In Petr's world of Nazis and NKVD assassins, Bobby could have been any number of deadly foes.

Petr launched himself at Bobby and tackled him, knocking him down. He was going to kill him. He instinctively reached for the sharpened spade that hung from his belt. It wasn't there. Of course it wasn't—this wasn't his infantry uniform.

Bobby took advantage of the opening to roll out from under Petr and climb back to his feet. He returned to his boxing stance. He was ready for Petr now; he wouldn't make the same mistake twice. When Petr lunged to tackle him again, Bobby would shuffle out of reach and hammer Petr's downturned skull with crosses and jabs.

But instead, Petr grabbed a chair and flung it at Bobby, who ducked and deflected the flying furniture with his left forearm. The chair spun past him and cracked against the wall.

His forearm hurt like hell, but Petr charged again, trying to knock him down. Bobby stepped back, reducing Petr's tackle to a mere clinch around him. He hammered Petr's sides with hooks, aiming at his solar plexus. Petr didn't let go. He twisted and pulled, nearly dragging Bobby to the ground again.

"Stop it! Stop it!"

Karen had been screaming from the start, but neither Petr nor Bobby had heard her. Adrenaline and instinct had pushed her pleas to the back of their minds so they could focus entirely on what both now realized was a life-or-death struggle.

But Karen grabbed at them, pushing herself between them.

If they kept fighting, they'd hurt her. But she was the whole reason they were fighting in the first place. So they let her separate them, warily, glaring at each other as they caught their breath.

"Who the hell is he?" both demanded simultaneously.

"Bobby, this is Petr," Karen explained in English. "He helped me escape from Leningrad." Then she switched to Russian: "Petr, this is Bobby, my ex-boyfriend."

Bobby sneered. He straightened up, chest out, and snarled, "Stay away from her. She's my fiancée." He turned to Karen. "Tell him."

Karen was confused. She'd told herself that she would never see Bobby again, that he'd likely forgotten about her. That's how she'd justified loving Petr. Now she realized the justification was a lie, and she didn't know what to do; she didn't know what to say.

"Tell him," Bobby insisted.

Karen obeyed, reluctantly. "He's not just an ex-boyfriend, he's my ex-fiancé," she admitted in Russian.

"Your ex?" Petr said. "Does he know that?"

Petr was demanding confirmation, but Karen couldn't give it to him.

"I'm sorry," she muttered meekly, to both and yet to neither of them.

They moved to the kitchen, where Karen found ice to numb their wounds and reduce the swelling of their bruises. They leaned against a counter as Karen admitted to Bobby that she'd been unfaithful.

"But, please," she told him, "you have to forgive me. You have to help me escape Russia." She needed to hitch a ride with the American delegation. She pleaded with him. "If you don't, you'll be leaving me to die."

Bobby knew that. But he could only shake his head. His heart ached for her. He wanted to forgive her. He hadn't suddenly stopped loving her because he'd caught her kissing another boy.

"I can't let you die," he muttered.

Finding her had been the sole focus of his life for the past six months. To abandon her now would be to admit that all his ambitions had been foolish.

"I can take you in my own plane, sneak you into the cockpit," he told her, analyzing the plan in his mind. "You could sit in my lap. Then, when we reach Krasnoyarsk, I can introduce you to General Marshall. He'd be forced to take you then."

"Would that work?"

"It'll work. There's nothing at Krasnoyarsk. They couldn't possibly leave you behind."

"No, I mean hiding in your cockpit, sitting on your lap."

"I've done it before," Bobby admitted with a nod.

Petr was watching, slumped and helpless, unable to understand.

"What about Petr?" Karen asked Bobby.

"What about him?"

"Can you sneak him out, too?"

Bobby glared at Petr. "Not a chance."

"You have to."

"He's Russian. The Soviets will never let him leave."

"That's why you have to hide him."

"General Marshall will never risk it."

"If you don't, he'll die."

"That's probably true," Bobby admitted.

And then he told Karen that the Russians couldn't win this war, that even America's top generals were expecting Russia's defeat. He didn't have to tell her the rest—about how the Nazis treated so-called undesirables. He didn't have to tell her that the Germans would either place the Russians in work camps or let them starve. She'd experienced it all firsthand.

"And if Russia does lose," Karen asked, "what happens to the United States?"

"We have a plan for that."

"What sort of plan?"

"That's classified."

"Russia's huge," Karen said. "If it loses, so will we."

"That's not true. We can beat the Germans."

"No one has yet."

Bobby didn't reply right away; it was a tacit admission that Karen was right.

"Either way," she continued, "Petr has to come. You'd be killing him, otherwise. And I owe him my life."

Bobby glanced at Petr. "Nobody's gonna want him riding in their lap." Bobby sure didn't.

"Couldn't you sneak him on the general's transport plane?"

"Maybe," Bobby admitted. "Maybe he could stow away with the luggage. You'd better dress warm, though." Bobby was addressing Petr directly now. "Because it's gonna be damned cold."

Petr didn't respond. He just stared back at Bobby, his face an emotionless mask.

Karen answered for him. "He doesn't speak English. But don't worry; Russians are used to the cold."

Bobby turned back to Karen and gazed at her.

She was so beautiful. He wanted to grab her, to hug her and kiss her, like he had in Central Park and at her father's parties, like this boy Petr had been doing moments before.

Petr was the whole problem. He had spoiled their reunion. Bobby said, "Why do you want him to come along, anyway? He's not American."

"He saved my life."

"But he belongs here."

"If he stays, he'll die."

Petr still didn't say a word. He felt numb and emotionless. Moments ago, his life had been certain. He'd found a girl that he loved. They were going to spend their lives together. And he had decided: he'd come with her to America—not because he hated Russia, or that he was afraid of the Germans. He'd come to America to be with her because he loved her. She'd proven that she loved him.

But this new boy, this ex-boyfriend, threw all his certainty into confusion. No, Bobby was more than an ex-boyfriend, he was an ex-fiancé. That was even more serious. Petr had no idea what to think, what to feel. He just stared at the two of them.

Bobby reached out and took both of Karen's hands. "I'll do it under one condition."

"Anything," Karen replied, desperate.

"Tell me that what I saw was a mistake. Tell me you're bringing him to America to help him—only to save him, not to be with him. Tell me you still love me."

Karen stared into Bobby's eyes. She did still love him. There was no denying that. But she also loved Petr.

"I still love you," she admitted. The truth of that statement made her next lie easier. She added, "I'm not doing it to be with him. I'm doing it to save him."

Bobby nodded. He let go of her hands. "Meet me at the airfield an hour before dawn. We'll need it to be dark if we want to sneak you on board."

"Thank you, Bobby. Thank you for never giving up."

Bobby wished that he, too, could thank Karen for never giving up, but she had. She'd given up on him.

He hoped that someday he could forgive her for that. So he only said, "Thanks for staying alive."

Later that night, Bobby kissed Lenka. He'd always been attracted to her, in part because he knew she was attracted to him. She wasn't beautiful, not like Karen. But she was pretty, with a round face that matched her round figure.

Lenka flirted with Bobby; she flirted with everyone. Lenka loved to flirt. Until now Bobby had resisted her advances because he wanted to remain faithful to Karen. But why should he? Karen hadn't remained faithful to him. His spiteful thoughts made him angry. And a few glasses of moonshine vodka only fueled that anger. So later in the evening, in a speakeasy, when Lenka played her usual games and started to flirt with Bobby, he kissed her.

It caught Lenka off guard. She had played this game so many times with Bobby that she felt safe. No matter what she said, no matter how she teased him, he would just maintain a chaste distance with a respect-ful demeanor.

But this time he practically jumped on her. Lenka didn't know what had caused Bobby's sudden change in attitude, but she wasn't going to look a gift horse in the mouth. She grabbed the handsome American aviator and kissed him back with gusto.

And then it was Bobby's turn to be surprised. Lenka wasn't letting go. And a part of him didn't want her to let go. He'd never been kissed like this before. Lenka wasn't just older, it turned out; she was far more experienced. She used her lips and tongue in inventive ways that Bobby would never have imagined.

Lenka would have made out with Bobby for hours. That was the Russian style, kissing in full public display. When Bobby had first seen a couple making out like that right in the middle of a speakeasy, he'd been shocked. But Lenka made fun of his prudish ways, and eventually Bobby got used to it, though he never thought he'd ever engage in such public displays of affection.

And yet here he was, kissing this girl at a packed party, with no regard for the spectacle he was causing. She didn't even notice the spec-tators around him. But he did. They made him uncomfortable, and he immediately regretted the kiss. Before things could get out of hand, he peeled the giggling Lenka off his lips, and he said good-bye.

He headed to the airfield.

Karen had to spend one more night alone with the youth orchestra. After their arrival in Chelyabinsk, she and Petr had been separated. The male and female musicians bunked in different dormitories, separated from one another by a thin wall.

Petr had been allowed to stay with the male musicians until he could find the apartment of his fictional father. In the chaos created by

Chelyabinsk's rapid expansion, finding anyone was difficult. So, while Karen rehearsed in the days before the summit, Petr did his best to find Inna's father. The perfect cover, he'd decided, was actually to perform the task he was pretending to do. Fortunately for him, he failed at that task.

It meant he could continue to spend his nights close to Karen. They'd both chosen bunks pushed against the wall that divided their rooms. They couldn't kiss anymore, let alone talk, but that didn't mean they couldn't communicate. Late at night, until this one, when Karen could tell that everyone else was asleep by their breathing, she would tap three times on the wall to represent three words: "I love you." A moment later she would hear a response from Petr: four taps.

After the first time this happened, when they found a moment alone together, Karen asked Petr what his four taps had meant. "I love you more," he answered.

Karen was astonished. She had never told him what her three taps had meant, but Petr had instinctively known and responded with the same code. They used that code every night thereafter, whenever they felt lonely, whenever they couldn't bear to be so close to each other, yet separated by that thin wall. Karen would tap "I love you," and Petr would respond, "I love you more," and it gave them both the comfort to sleep.

But on the night after the concert, after their chance encounter with Bobby, Karen tapped "I love you," like she always had. Petr never tapped back.

Karen had never felt so alone in her entire life.

<hr/>

She'd arranged to meet Petr early the next morning when it was still dark. They were to sneak out of their respective dorms separately and meet on a street corner three blocks away.

Despite the early hour, the city wasn't dark.

Here in Siberia the July summer sun hadn't let the city slumber in full darkness for long. In the early light, the street lamps still blazed, and electric light spilled from factory and apartment windows as if dawn had not yet come. After Karen's long months without power, in the deepest darkness of Leningrad nights, the streets of Chelyabinsk seemed brighter to her now than anything she'd ever experienced.

It didn't brighten her dark mood. Petr was late, and she was worried. Had he changed his mind? Is that why he hadn't tapped his usual response back to her? Had he stopped loving her? Had he decided not to come with her to America, after all?

She had once felt so confident. She had always trusted herself. It was other people, like her father and Sasha and even Inna, whom she didn't trust.

Leningrad had done terrible things to her, but it had never broken her confidence. Even in her most trying moments, when she was burying her father, when she was being led back to NKVD headquarters at the Smolny, when she was watching her friends die—she'd felt let down by others, never by herself.

Now, for the first time, that confidence was gone. If Petr had changed his mind, only one person was responsible: Karen. She hated herself. She had somehow won the love of two remarkable men. But she had squandered that love. She couldn't help but fall in love with Petr. Like Bobby, he was one of the few people she knew she could count on. She trusted him as she used to trust herself. But she should have been satisfied to keep that love unrequited. She should never have allowed Petr to fall in love with her; she should never have led him on.

It had been a betrayal of Bobby, and now it was a betrayal of Petr. It served her right that Petr had stopped loving her. She didn't deserve to be loved by anyone. He probably even hated her now, with good reason. He hated her and couldn't bear to be near her. So he'd miss this one opportunity to escape. He'd be forced back into the Red Army, and he'd be killed. This was the truest source of her anxious worry. She worried now that her own failures would lead to Petr's death. Karen had made him hate her, and that hatred would cost Petr his life.

Then she saw movement in the distance. A man was walking toward her. He was too far away for her to see his face. But she recognized Petr instantly from the way he moved, the way he walked. There was no doubt in her mind. So she ran to him. And she didn't stop running until she'd wrapped her arms around him and buried her face in his chest.

"Thank God," she said. "Thank God."

Petr held her stiffly, as if being forced by etiquette to hug a stranger. Then he unwrapped his arms and stepped back.

"We're going to miss our flight," he warned, his voice icy.

Karen nodded and wiped her eyes with her sleeve. She'd been right all along. He'd stopped loving her. That was proper; that was what she deserved. But was he such a good man that maybe he didn't hate her? Even if he did, by coming with her now, he wasn't letting that hatred destroy his life. He was still the Petr she'd fallen in love with, the Petr she could rely on. He was still a survivor.

They turned and walked together in silence. It was a long walk, all the way past vast blocks of apartment buildings and huge factories and endless motor pools of lifeless tanks. The city was still asleep, its factory-worker residents catching the last few hours of slumber before their shifts began.

It was a sorrowful walk. Karen desperately wanted to take Petr's hand, as they'd done so many times before. It seemed they'd marched across half of Russia holding hands. But she knew that this time she couldn't. She kept stealing glances at his hands, lamenting inside that she'd never hold them again.

CHAPTER 42

THE CELLIST AND THE
ORGAN-GRINDER

Twenty years before, Shagol Airport had been rolling pasture for heavy oxen and shaggy steppe ponies. Then, with the construction of Chelyabinsk, those rolling pastures were bulldozed into runways to service the new industrial center of Siberia. Still, air transport was expensive and rare, so the new airport sat mostly idle.

Then the Germans invaded. Once the industrial cities like Leningrad with munitions factories vital for the war effort were threatened, Stalin made the decision to evacuate Russia's industrial might east.

But the trains were too slow, the advancing Wehrmacht too fast. The evacuation had to be by air. So, in the summer of 1941, sleepy Shagol became the busiest airport in Russia.

But now that two of the three fronts had been stabilized, the little airport languished again. Apart from two ribbons of runway and a double row of humped aluminum hangars, it was beginning to look more like the rolling pasture on which it was built, dusty and weedy.

The landing strips were lined with the hastily constructed hangars, and a single control tower jutted above their rooftops like a camel's head over its humps.

The entire facility was surrounded by a chain-link perimeter fence patrolled twenty-four hours a day by Red Army military police driving GAZ-64 jeeps. By agreement, the American delegation wasn't allowed to post its own sentries inside. Despite the Soviet security, someone had cut a hole in the wire fence right below a **No Trespassing** sign.

"The runways are built next to a pond," Bobby explained, "And the fishing's too good to keep the locals out."

"When do they have time to fish?" Karen wondered.

"They never sleep," Bobby replied. "Get down."

Bobby, Karen, and Petr flattened themselves on the cool ground as a GAZ jeep rumbled by. First its headlights, then a top-mounted spotlight, swept over their heads as its brake lights showed, and it then continued on its patrol.

Bobby checked his watch. "If you go now, you'll have three and a half minutes before they make another round."

Karen didn't hesitate. She was already crawling through the hole in the fence as she translated Bobby's instructions to Petr.

Petr nodded and crawled through behind her.

"Remember," Bobby continued, "hangar eighteen."

"Aren't you coming with us?" Karen whispered in alarm.

Bobby shook his head. "I've gotta go through the main gate. Otherwise they'll be suspicious."

"OK," Karen replied reluctantly. "Hangar eighteen."

She lowered her head and sprinted into the alley between two hangars. Petr sprinted next to her, and they caught their breath in the shadows. The GAZ jeep made another pass.

"What number is this?" Karen asked, looking at the curved slope of the hangar rising up beside her.

"Seven," Petr reported.

"How do you know?"

"I looked at the number when we ran past."

Karen realized she should have done the same. One number didn't help much since they didn't know how the hangars were organized. "We'll wait until the jeep comes around again and run down the line," she advised.

"Of course," replied Petr, as if he'd come up with the same plan ages ago.

The jeep drove by, and Petr took off running. Karen sprinted after him.

She read the number of the next hangar—nine—before turning into the next alley, following Petr.

As she turned the corner, she ran right into Petr's open arms. He'd hidden, and he was waiting for her. He pulled Karen close and kissed her.

She closed her eyes and relished the feel of his mouth on her own. Tears welled up and ran down her cheeks—not tears of anguish, but tears of relief. And she kissed him back.

The jeep drove past once again. She dimly heard the rumble of its engine and sensed the brightness of its headlights, and still she kissed him. Her nose ran, and she couldn't breathe, but still she kissed him. Whatever happened, she didn't want to be the one to pull away; she didn't want to be the one to end the kiss. She wasn't. Petr withdrew his lips and caught his breath. "I'm sorry," he whispered.

"For what?" Karen wondered.

"For kissing you like that."

She shook her head vehemently, sniffling as she spoke. "Don't be sorry; be the opposite of sorry."

"But you're crying."

"I'm crying because I didn't think we'd ever kiss again."

"I know," Petr admitted. "I wasn't sure, either. I needed to see how you'd respond."

"Like this," Karen whispered, and she kissed him again.

That kiss might have lasted a moment, or it might have lasted an hour. They lost all sense of time, and they nearly forgot where they were. They felt and remembered only one thing: each other.

Too much of that passion finally drew them apart. They wanted more from each other, more from their bodies, and it reminded them both that this was neither the time nor the place to give in to their desire.

So they parted once more, this time letting go of each other entirely. They leaned back against the hangar's cool aluminum siding and closed their eyes, each relishing this moment of relief.

They'd both thought they'd lost the other. But they hadn't. Petr gently tapped the aluminum three times: "I love you."

Her eyes still closed, Karen smiled and tapped four times back: "I love you more."

She stole a glance at Petr and saw that he, too, was smiling.

"Listen," he whispered.

Karen heard frogs croaking in the distance. "It must be the fishing pond," she said.

"They weren't croaking a minute ago." Concern had crept into Petr's voice.

Karen's eyes popped open in panic. "I don't hear the jeep."

"Shh," Petr warned.

And Karen heard the soft tread of boots on gravel.

It was the military police. Something had aroused the guards' suspicions, and they were sneaking up on their position.

Petr took Karen's hand and pulled. He couldn't risk speaking, but he needed her to follow him. Karen instantly obeyed. She trusted Petr, she'd discovered. She trusted Petr more than she even trusted herself. He led her back around the opposite side of the hangar, keeping off the gravel runway so that the wild grass muffled their footsteps. Then

Petr crouched down and removed his shoes. Karen did the same. Petr held both his shoes in one hand and let go of Karen with his other. He counted with his fingers: one, two, three . . .

They sprinted across to the neighboring line of hangars.

The gravel runway hurt Karen's stockinged feet. Her heel came down hard on a large pebble, and pain jarred up her leg. She grimaced but refused to cry out or even slacken her pace. Soon they again landed in the safe embrace of the hangars. Petr didn't pause to catch his breath. He took Karen's hand again and led her to the opposite side of the hangars at a brisk jog.

Karen read their numbers as they rushed past . . . twelve, fourteen . . . and realized how the buildings were organized—the other row was odd numbers, and this one was even.

They passed sixteen, reached eighteen. Petr, with trepidation, tried the door. It opened. They slipped inside and locked the door behind them. They'd made it. Karen let out a breath of relief. And once more, Petr kissed her.

This time Karen pushed him away. "We can't. Not here. I don't know when Bobby's coming, and if he sees us . . ." She hesitated; she didn't want to tell him the reason.

But Petr wanted to know. "If he sees us, what?"

"He'll never take us back to America."

Petr nodded. It was obvious to him that Bobby still loved Karen. He'd worried that she still loved Bobby, too. But he'd been wrong to worry. Karen loved Petr. She'd proven that with her kiss. So Petr trusted her again, and he felt slightly ashamed that he'd ever stopped trusting her.

If she needed to pretend, if it was crucial that they spend the entire flight back to America without touching again, Petr could handle that. He brushed his lips against hers.

"One last one for the road," he said before pulling away and walking to the opposite side of the hangar.

CHAPTER 43

THE ORGAN-GRINDER
AND THE CELLIST

The front landing gear of the C-47 Skytrain was so tall that Petr barely had to duck to fit under it.

Petr was surprised by how big airplanes were on the ground. He'd never flown before; he'd traveled across Russia with the army mostly on foot, sometimes by truck, and most recently by train. He'd seen plenty of planes up in the air during his time in combat. German airplanes were what his Katyusha battery feared the most. The Luftwaffe was always hunting for the Russian rocket batteries, and the Red Army pilots didn't fare any better in their aerial duels against the Luftwaffe than the rest of the army did on the ground. As German aviators began to establish air superiority, Petr and his comrades always had to make sure they had cover nearby, whether a ditch or a trench or a tree line— anything to get away from the Katyushas' truck and stay hidden. Petr's unit had lost three trucks to air attacks. One time he'd watched from only a few dozen yards away as the German warplane dove low and strafed the Katyusha truck into oblivion. But even then the plane had been deceptively high in the sky, its small size an optical illusion.

Parked here before him in a hanger, the C-47 stood even bigger than most. It had been designed as a civilian aircraft, built to ferry wealthy Westerners between New York and London, stopping in Greenland to refuel. Each of its giant propeller engines was the size of a truck. Petr knew it was the plane Bobby intended him to stow away in. But Petr wondered where he would hide in that behemoth, and hoped its engines wouldn't deafen him.

As he stared at the plane, Petr once again began to have doubts. He knew he wasn't doing the right thing, the patriotic thing. Not just the Soviet Union, but Russia herself, was fighting for her life. He didn't care about Stalin and the Communist Party, but he did care about his father and his uncle and his cousins. He even cared about all the regular Russians he hadn't ever met. He wasn't sure why he cared about people he didn't know, but he did. He cared about them more than the nameless, faceless people he'd soon be meeting in America.

Despite all that, Petr didn't regret his decision to travel with Karen to Chelyabinsk. The brief time they'd spent together on the Trans-Siberian Railway was the happiest time of his life. He wouldn't have given up that experience for anything. It still drove him now—the promise of future bliss with Karen in America. That was all. Some Russians might assume he was motivated by cowardice. They might say he was betraying his country. So be it.

He wasn't afraid to fight. The bitter truth was that a part of him was anxious to experience once more both the terror and the thrill of combat. They came together, Petr had discovered—terror and thrill. As a rocketeer, he'd only felt terror, since he'd never had the sensation of fighting back, apart from his one-man stand against the panzers. But when he was made a tank killer, he discovered a latent aggression inside himself. He liked to fight. And worse, he liked to kill. So, no, it wasn't cowardice that motivated him to betray his country.

It still wasn't too late to change his mind.

Chelyabinsk, too, had an army recruitment center. Petr had just been there last night. He never went back to sleep in the dorm with the musicians. Instead, he'd wrestled with himself and with his decision to escape Russia. He'd approached the army recruiters, pretending to be his own nonexistent cousin. He wasn't there to enlist, he explained, but there at the behest of his grandmother, who was desperate to find out what had happened to her grandson hero, Petr.

The recruiters obviously tried to do their job, admonishing the boy to join up by assuring him that it would be better than getting drafted. But they also both had grandmothers of their own, and they couldn't resist helping her. So they looked up the grandson's record. The hero, Petr, they sadly reported, was missing in action and presumed either dead or a prisoner of war, which, they seemed to think, was even worse than being dead.

The report had given Petr some comfort. He knew that no one would be hunting him now. He could escape with Karen and make a clean start. But he still hadn't been sure what he *should* do. He'd spent the remainder of the evening walking aimlessly through Chelyabinsk's streets, trying to decide.

When the time came to meet Karen, he still wasn't sure. So he resolved to let a kiss decide. At his first opportunity, he would kiss her, and he'd know by how she responded whether she still loved him. If she did, he'd go with her to America. If she didn't, he'd rejoin the army and help defend his homeland.

Petr looked away from the Skytrain and across the hangar at Karen. She was so beautiful. She'd long since recovered from the Nazi beating she'd received, and she was no longer the filthy, scrawny girl he'd first met outside Leningrad. She'd put on weight during their train trip so that her stomach even slightly swelled, pushing up against her tight, borrowed dress.

Petr stared at Karen's tummy, finding it maddeningly erotic. He desperately wanted to rub his hands and lips over it. He had to look away, lest he cross the hangar once more and give in to those compulsions. He knew he'd made the right decision. After all, what difference could he, one person, make to the Russian war effort?

Despite the assurance of a Hollywood reporter, he was no John Wayne. He was a simple man, a simple kid, really, a Russian boy with simple desires and modest ambitions. Better to live than to die, better to love than to fight, and most of all, better to spend a long life with that gorgeous woman.

He gazed at Karen then, and she gazed back at him. "You would be blushing," he told her.

"Why?" she asked, with a coy smile.

"If you knew what I wanted to do right now."

And Karen did blush, because she was thinking something similar.

Right then the door unlocked, and Bobby entered. "You made it," he said with relief.

"We made it," Karen confirmed.

"Well, then, let's do this. We don't have much time."

CHAPTER 44

THE CELLIST AND
THE CHOIRBOY

It had been awkward at first, climbing into Bobby's lap—not because it put Karen in an uncomfortable physical position, but because it put her in an emotionally difficult one.

She had once yearned for Bobby's touch. That yearning had helped her survive the dark days of Leningrad. But, she was ashamed to admit, since meeting Petr, that yearning had left her.

Now, as she leaned back against Bobby's chest, it was as though her body was becoming reacquainted with a long-lost comfortable chair. Despite the growl and rumble of the Airacobra's powerful engine, Karen felt Bobby's heartbeat thump against her back. The pressure of his arm across her stomach was strong and reassuring.

She moved her fingers gently up his forearm and bicep, feeling the curve of his muscles under his shirt. He wasn't wearing his flight jacket; he'd given it to her, and she'd pulled it over her simple, straight dress.

She felt strangely proud to be wearing it, the way she'd seen those silly cheerleaders wearing their boyfriend's letterman jackets. At the time she'd found the ritual vaguely demeaning, as if the boys were laying claim to the cheerleaders and confining them in a straitjacket. But now she understood the comfort it provided. It made her feel wanted. More than that, it made her feel protected.

Only a few months ago, Karen had felt neither. No one wanted her in Leningrad, and certainly no one had protected her. Even her own father seemed to care more about the symphony than about her. She now knew she was wrong in that perception; her father had loved her, but he was simply incapable of protecting her. She'd learned to forgive him for that.

Karen had been left on her own. And now she had two men protecting her. Two men, she knew, however, was one too many. She indulged herself, comparing the feel of Bobby to that of Petr. They were both long and lean, but Bobby's skin was softer. She remembered that his chest had been smooth when she'd left New York, but that was a long time ago, and she wondered whether he'd grown the same coarse hair that bristled across Petr's chest.

If Bobby had brown hair on his chest, Karen imagined it would be soft. She was tempted to push her hand between the buttons of his shirt and satisfy her curiosity. But she resisted that urge, not out of fear that he'd reject the gesture, but out of fear that he'd welcome it.

She began to wonder whether that would be such a bad thing. Somehow, unconsciously, she'd found a way to turn in his lap so that she could twist her neck and look at his face. It was long, angular, even slightly patrician. Yet it was simultaneously trustworthy and trusting. Bobby's lips were full, and they were perpetually curled at the corners into a dimpled smile.

It was an inviting face, and a familiar one, but there was something new there, too. Karen could detect a darker quality behind Bobby's eyes that she'd never sensed before. They were not as dark and brooding as Petr's eyes, but they'd lost the playful twinkle she remembered.

"What are you staring at?" Bobby asked, glancing away from the sky and up at her face.

"You," Karen answered. "You've changed."

"So have you," Bobby acknowledged.

Karen nodded and turned back forward, breaking eye contact with her fiancé and staring once more through the cockpit window. She didn't want to think about how she'd changed. She knew she wasn't the same person who'd left New York, and she wasn't sure she liked the person she'd become. She felt selfish for what she'd put Bobby through, and what she was currently putting Petr through. She tried to tell herself that it was all for Petr's own good, that her actions were a necessary evil to rescue him from certain death.

But was that just an excuse to keep him close? And if she loved Petr, wasn't she just using Bobby? Who else had she simply used to survive? Inna? Sasha? Could it be that she felt compelled to save Petr not because she loved him, but because she felt guilty about her dead father and dead friends, and she needed to somehow redeem herself?

She honestly didn't know. Her brain and emotions both seemed to be betraying her.

"So what do you think?" Bobby asked her.

"About what?"

"About this . . ."

Bobby twisted the aircraft into a roll and a dive. Karen smiled as her stomach climbed up into her chest and Siberia's treetops revolved over her head. "It's incredible!" she yelled, exhilarated.

"Lieutenant Campbell, are we under attack?" It was the voice of Captain Hart coming over the radio. As General Marshall's personal pilot, the captain was their squadron's tactical commander. He knew they weren't under attack, and his sarcastic tone was his way of reprimanding Bobby for breaking formation.

"No, Commander," Bobby responded. "I thought I saw an antiaircraft emplacement and wanted to take a closer look."

All the pilots had been briefed on the secret objective of their mission, so Bobby knew he could get away with insubordination by claiming it was to scout Russian air defenses. He'd volunteered to fly in the rear of the formation so that no one would see Karen in his cockpit. Only Jack knew the truth, and Bobby intended to keep it a secret until they all landed in Krasnoyarsk and it was too late for them to forbid bringing Karen home.

"Machine gun or flak?" Captain Hart asked, all sarcasm suddenly absent from his tone.

"Neither. Just an abandoned tractor," Bobby reassured him, twisting and climbing back into formation.

"Do you ever get used to it?" Karen asked after Bobby quieted his radio.

"Get used to what?"

"That feeling in your stomach. It's like the roller coaster at Coney Island, but a hundred times more intense."

Bobby laughed. "Yeah, they call it g-force. You gotta get used to it, some, but not too much. Get used to it too much, and it could be dangerous."

"Dangerous? Why?"

"That sensation you feel, it's your equilibrium warning you to cool it. You press the g-forces too hard, you can black out."

"That's possible?"

"Not flying like this, but in combat, with a Zeke on your tail, yeah, you could start to lose your vision and then fall unconscious before he even shoots you down."

Karen suddenly felt cold. She hadn't ever considered Bobby fighting in combat. But he was an Army Air Forces pilot; that's what they did, what they were trained for—to fight, to kill. Just like Petr. The whole reason she was doing this was to save Petr, and now she realized Bobby was in just as much danger. Why wasn't she trying to save him? "Have you . . . have you fought yet?"

"Yeah, I've fought," Bobby replied, without a trace of bravado.

"Have you killed?" Karen asked with trepidation.

"No, not yet," Bobby admitted. "But not from lack of trying."

"But you survived, anyway," Karen said, as if to reassure herself.

"You don't have to worry about me."

But Karen *was* worried, suddenly. She'd been so stupid, so short-sighted, and she now understood why his eyes looked haunted. She wrapped both her hands around his arm and squeezed. "Don't try too hard," she said.

"To do what?"

"To kill. Just try to survive."

"One doesn't go without the other," Bobby confessed.

"You're right," Karen sadly admitted.

And they spent the rest of the flight in silence.

Krasnoyarsk was a surprisingly beautiful city built up along either bank of the wide, flat Yenisei River. The formation of Russian and American warplanes circled the entire area before lining up, one by one, for landing.

Bobby's aircraft was last, giving Karen the opportunity to admire the city in silence. She was surprised by the historic architecture; she'd imagined Siberia to be a wild land only recently and forcefully populated, as Chelyabinsk had been. But Krasnoyarsk's skyline was spotted with the tall spires of Russian Orthodox cathedrals that were hundreds of years old, and its docks were lined with beautiful old mansions that in czarist times belonged to adventurous nineteenth-century merchants made rich by their exploitation of Siberia's vast resources.

Emerald hills and forests surrounded the city, which in turn sur-rounded beautiful green islands serving as parks in the middle of the river. A ribbon of railroad track twisted through the forest and over the short mountains before passing through the city across a magnificent bridge. Karen realized that the tracks belonged to the Trans-Siberian Railway, and her eyes followed them southeast until they disappeared over the distant horizon.

They finally landed. There was no hiding Karen now. Before Bobby slid back the P-39's cockpit canopy, the Russian ground crew spotted an extra passenger in his lap. They watched in openmouthed wonder as Karen climbed out and hopped down, still wearing Bobby's leather flight jacket.

"Hello," she greeted them in Russian, with a smile. The Red Army soldiers didn't say anything; they just avoided her gaze and went about their business checking the airplanes. The same could not be said of Lenka, one of the Red Army pilots escorting the Americans out of Siberia.

"You'll be reported," she threatened as soon as she caught Karen alone outside one of the airplane hangars.

"Reported for what?" Karen kindly asked.

"Treason."

"But I'm not even Russian. I'm American," Karen replied in English.

That surprised Lenka, who stared daggers at Karen. "Who are you?" she asked.

"My name is Karen."

Lenka didn't offer her own name. Karen only discovered it later when she asked Bobby. Instead, Lenka just stormed off in anger. Now that it was an open secret Bobby had brought a stowaway, it was only a matter of time before General Marshall himself found out. When he did, he invited both Karen and Bobby to dine with him.

Karen was nervous. She expected the dinner to be much like the ones she'd had to avoid on the train to Chelyabinsk. She was worried she'd somehow spoil the formal occasion, saying or doing the wrong thing in front of this important American dignitary.

She was surprised to find dinner presented on a folding card table in the general's ad hoc office. And it wasn't caviar on silver platters; it was salted pork and mashed potatoes—the same food the pilots ate.

"I know it doesn't look like much," the general said, tucking his napkin into his collar, "and I'm afraid to admit it doesn't taste like much, either."

The general was a distinguished gentleman with graying, slicked-back hair. His soft face and warm eyes immediately made Karen want to trust him. He would have looked perfect in a priest's collar or a judge's robes. His military uniform wasn't starched and covered in medals like those of the Russian generals she'd seen on the train. Instead, it was well worn and looked comfortable.

"Isn't that right, Lieutenant Campbell?" Marshall continued. He was smiling at Bobby, who nodded. The general winked back. "I think they call it slop."

"Call it worse than that sometimes, General," Bobby confessed.

The general laughed. "I'm sure they do. But whatever it tastes like, it'll fill you up, and that's the whole purpose of food, isn't it?"

"It looks delicious," Karen politely replied.

"Maybe it does, maybe it does at that," the general murmured thoughtfully. "Well, dig in."

He mixed the pork and potatoes and scooped a helping into his mouth, his eyes never leaving Karen's.

"I can understand wanting to sit in your boyfriend's lap," he continued, "but that isn't exactly the safest way to fly, is it, Lieutenant Campbell?"

Bobby paused midbite. "It's safer than it looks," he replied defensively.

"But what if we come under attack? What if you were shot down? You don't have two parachutes."

"General, you and I both know we won't come under attack," Bobby said.

Karen was shocked by Bobby's boldness. No one would dare speak to a Russian general like that.

But if Marshall was offended, he didn't show it. "All right, then," he conceded, "but what if we run into bad weather? What if we have to climb? You got two oxygen masks?"

Bobby knew the general was right. Flying double in a single-seat aircraft was dangerous. But it would have been far more dangerous to leave Karen behind. Somehow, he had to convince Marshall of that fact.

"I know you're right, General, but you've got to understand. She's not Russian, she's American. She's a refugee. It's our duty to bring her home safely."

The general chuckled as he raised his hand to make Bobby stop talking. "Don't worry, son, we're not going to leave her behind. I just meant it would be safer for her to ride in the C-47." He looked at Karen. "What do you think? There's plenty of room."

"I'd be honored. Thank you, sir."

"No, thank *you*," the general replied, shoveling another spoonful into his mouth.

Karen was intrigued. There was something in the general's tone that suggested he wasn't just being polite. He seemed genuinely thankful. But what had she done? She was mystified.

"Thank me for what?" she said.

"Excuse me?"

"I'm sorry, sir, I was just wondering . . . what have I done? What are you thankful for?"

The general peered over at Bobby. "You didn't tell her?"

"No, General," Bobby replied, blushing.

"Tell me what?"

"Well, Miss Hamilton," the general began to explain, "the whole country owes you a debt of gratitude. For the intelligence you provided."

"Intelligence?" Karen still didn't know what he was talking about.

"Your letters," Bobby told her.

"My letters?"

"From Leningrad," the general continued. He quickly added, "Don't worry, we didn't read them. A gentleman never reads private mail."

"I told them the important stuff," Bobby explained. "About what was really happening in the city, about how Russia was losing."

The important stuff was what she'd written to Bobby about how she felt about him, how she was surviving for him. Until this moment she'd almost forgotten about those letters, and now, thinking about them, all the emotion she'd felt writing them came crashing back over her.

"That wasn't the important stuff," she muttered.

"I know," Bobby reassured her. He took her hand and squeezed it.

"I can understand how you feel," the general told her, his words heartfelt. "I wouldn't want anyone reading my wife's letters, either, but I can assure you, whatever you wrote that was private—that stayed private. At least to us."

"'At least to us'—what does that mean?" Karen asked, suddenly worried.

"The Soviet State censors read them," Bobby replied, never letting go of her hand.

Karen closed her eyes. She was so embarrassed. Those letters had been intimate. She never expected anyone but Bobby to read them.

"I'm sorry," the general continued quietly, "but we have no control over the Soviet postal service."

Karen's voice caught in her throat now. So she just nodded. At least the general hadn't read them. She didn't have to be ashamed in front of him.

That gave her the courage to open her eyes again. And once again she wondered what was happening to her. Against all odds, she'd survived Leningrad. Somehow she'd managed to hold it together through that entire trying time. But now that she was safe, she was an emotional wreck.

"I can assure you," the general said, "that what you communicated in those letters was important." His tone was fatherly now, but not like her own father, who'd always seemed so distracted. General Marshall seemed like the ideal father, both proud and protective. Karen took comfort in that, even if she was finding it difficult to find comfort in his words. He added, "So important, in fact, that this entire mission was based on them."

"Mission? You mean the summit?"

"The summit was just cover," Bobby said gently.

"Cover for what?"

"We can't afford to let Russian industry and resources fall into German hands." Once again the general's voice had changed. Now he was strong, commanding. How had he learned to be so many things at once? No wonder he was one of America's top military leaders.

"Our objective," Bobby explained, "was to scout Russian air defenses, so we might come up with a way to bomb them."

Karen was horrified. America was going to bomb Russia? They were allies. "You're supposed to help Russia, not attack them!"

"And we are helping them," the general insisted, "and we will continue to do so, right up until they capitulate. But when they do, when they've lost this war, America has to protect herself."

Karen looked at the general's earnest face, then at Bobby's loving one. A silence stretched across the room. "Russia can't lose," she whispered.

"But they will," the general insisted.

"They won't," Karen protested. "I was wrong in those letters. Things have changed."

"What's changed?" Marshall asked, acutely curious now.

"They're committed."

"France was committed. Poland was committed," Bobby said. "It takes more than commitment to win a war. It takes industry; it takes resources."

"They have both," Karen argued. "There are hundreds of tanks in Chelyabinsk, fresh off the factory floors."

Bobby nodded. "Hundreds of tanks and no one trained to drive them."

"And even with industry and resources," the general conceded, "even with commitment, it takes something else to win a war."

Karen looked at him with despair. "What?"

"Leadership."

Karen knew instinctively that he was right. He was a leader, a great leader. That was obvious from only a ten-minute conversation. Russia didn't have leaders. It had dictators.

The general leaned back in his chair. "Sometimes you have to be practical. And practicality demands that you make sacrifices, however distasteful, to survive."

This was not what Karen wanted to hear. She'd been practical, and she'd already made so many sacrifices to survive. It was what she hated about herself. But her sacrifices until now had been insignificant compared to the sacrifice she had unwittingly engineered. She was about to sacrifice a whole country. Chelyabinsk would be bombed. Russia would be conquered, its entire population enslaved or starved to death.

"I'm sorry," she said. "I'm not really hungry."

"I guess you're not a fan of army slop, after all," the general replied, trying to lighten her mood.

"That's not it," Karen said. "It's the flight," she lied. "My stomach hasn't recovered."

General Marshall nodded with a smile. "Teach your boyfriend to show off, won't it?"

"Can I take it with me? In case I get hungry later?"

"Of course," the general replied. "I'll see you tomorrow."

"Tomorrow?"

"On the C-47. I'll save you a seat."

"Yes, thank you." Karen grabbed her plate and retreated from the room.

Bobby hurried after her. He caught up to her on the airfield. She'd stopped to stare at the aspen-ringed mountains rising above Krasnoyarsk's shingle rooftops. "Are you OK?" he asked.

"Of course not," Karen replied.

Bobby sighed and put his arm around her shoulder. "It's going to be OK."

"For you, maybe. For me. But what about them?" Karen lifted her chin toward the city.

"We can't save the whole world."

"I want to see Petr."

"It would be safer if you didn't."

"I don't care. He's been cooped up in that thing for almost twelve hours!"

Bobby took a deep breath and placed his hands on Karen's shoulders. "I know you're upset, but you've got to understand . . . the world's different now."

Karen stared at him with disbelief. "You don't think I know that?"

"Of course. It's just, you've been trapped here. You haven't been able to see beyond Russia's borders. In order to understand, you've got to see the big picture."

Karen stepped back and angrily pushed Bobby's hands off her shoulders. "I want to see Petr."

Bobby stared at her. "OK, I'll take you to him. But you can't say anything."

"Why not?"

"Why do you think? He's Russian."

"Don't be such an idiot."

Bobby sighed. Karen could tell he'd be rolling his eyes if she hadn't been looking right at him. "He's over here," he said simply.

Bobby led Karen to the airplane hangar sheltering the enormous C-47 Skytrain. Before he unlocked the door, he paused. "I already promised to take him home," he cautioned. "It may not be comfortable, but you can trust me. He'll make it to America."

"I know."

"If you tell him about the mission, I won't be able to protect him."

Karen was surprised, but she shouldn't have been. Bobby was smart. Of course he would have anticipated what she was considering. If she told Petr everything, it might force General Marshall to help Petr emigrate or even seek asylum. The general couldn't afford to leave behind a Russian who knew what the US War Department had in mind. But that wasn't the general's only option.

"If General Marshall finds out," Bobby continued, echoing Karen's thoughts, "he'll have Petr killed."

For a moment Karen had a hard time believing Bobby. The general didn't look like a killer. But, of course, neither did she or Petr or even Duck. They were all killers. And you didn't get to be a top general by being kind and gentle. "You made your point," she said. "Now let me see him."

Bobby nodded, and unlocked the hangar door.

CHAPTER 45

THE CELLIST AND THE ORGAN-GRINDER

The C-47 Skytrain was quickly becoming the workhorse of the US Army Air Forces. The large side-facing cargo doors provided access to a spacious main compartment once designed for civilian passengers, but now stripped of its comfortable seating. Barely padded benches lined the cylindrical walls, with seat belts and harnesses riveted into the bulkhead so soldiers wouldn't be injured during evasive maneuvers. The middle aisle was empty so that cargo—including anything up to the size of a three-quarter-ton truck—could be strapped down for fast air transport.

To the rear of the main compartment was a toilet cabin that did double duty as a storage closet. Farther back, between the toilet and the tail cone, was a small maintenance duct. Mechanics used the duct to service the rudder controls and tail air flaps. The tight space was used as a hiding place.

Petr was folded up there, knees against his chest.

Finally, Bobby came to release him from the boxlike prison. The first thing Petr did was stretch his legs and crack his spine. The next thing he did was eye Bobby warily. Bobby eyed him right back. They exited the plane and faced each other with their feet planted far apart on the hangar floor. It seemed for a moment that the two of them might launch into another fistfight.

But Karen was there. "Can you leave us alone for a minute?" she asked Bobby.

"I don't know, can I?" Bobby replied.

"If I wanted to tell him anything in secret, I'd just say it in Russian."

Bobby nodded at that. "All right. Just remember what I told you," he warned.

And he left Karen and Petr alone in the hangar.

"I brought you some food." Karen held out the plate of army slop for Peter.

"Thanks." Petr took it, leaned against the C-47's tail cone, and began to eat. "What was that all about?" he asked between bites.

"If I tell you, they'll kill you," Karen confessed.

Petr laughed. "Just like the NKVD."

"No. Not exactly."

"But close enough."

"Close enough," Karen conceded.

"So why don't you tell me?"

"Because the whole reason I'm doing this is to protect you!" Karen blurted out in frustration.

Petr paused and looked at her. "I had hoped you were doing this because you love me."

Karen didn't know what to say. She thought she loved him. What she felt seemed like love. What else could it be?

But it couldn't be love, because she felt the same way about Bobby. It wasn't possible to love two people at once, was it? Not true, real love.

There had to be something wrong with her, something wrong with her emotions. She'd told Petr she loved him. And she'd told Bobby the same. Had she lied about that? Had she lied to them both *and* lied to herself? She couldn't be sure anymore. And if it was a lie, Petr at least deserved some form of truth, even if it was a different truth. "They don't think you can win the war," she said finally.

"They're not the only ones," Petr replied bitterly.

"What do you think?"

Petr considered the question. He'd seen precious little during his time with the Red Army to put much faith in victory. But he'd also seen chinks in the Germans' armor. He'd seen despair in the faces of the Wehrmacht soldiers. He'd seen them living in squalor; he'd seen them cold and hungry. He'd seen them building barbed-wire fences and digging antitank ditches instead of capitalizing on their victories with new attacks. The Wehrmacht had hesitated; for the first time the Germans seemed uncertain. But most of all, Petr had seen how he and Karen were treated during their travels to Moscow, how they were seen as heroes just because they wore military uniforms.

He remembered the old man by the village bridge. He still had the man's copy of *War and Peace* and had even been reading it in the cramped confines of the C-47's maintenance duct.

"I think the Germans have made a mistake," he reasoned. "I think that if they were here to conquer us, topple the government, and take over, like they did in France, I think maybe they'd have already succeeded."

"They almost have."

Petr nodded. That was true. But there was something else, something he wasn't eloquent enough to put into words. But the concept he was trying to express deserved eloquence, so Petr just described how it had formed in his mind. "That music you've been playing, the music your father and Mr. Shostakovich wrote—"

"The symphony."

"I've heard that a lot, during your audition, during our rehearsals, the summit. That symphony's more than just music. It tells a story."

"About a dying city."

"No, not about a dying city. It tells a story about a city that refuses to die."

Karen gazed at Petr. He wasn't particularly clever, and he'd never claimed to be. He didn't think of the world as a chess game, didn't think three or even two moves ahead, not like Bobby did, not like General Marshall did. But that didn't mean he wasn't smart. He'd surprised her before with his astute observations. And he was surprising her again.

Maybe he was the one who could finally solve the riddle that had perplexed her for so long. "There was an old woman," she told him, "who died, frozen to death in Leningrad."

She paused, half expecting Petr to interrupt her. That was what Bobby would have done. He would have asked for clarification or an explanation as to why she was changing the subject. But Petr just stared at her, patient and attentive.

Karen continued. "She could have died anywhere. But she chose a fountain. You know, one of those symbolic fountains with a statue of workers building the new Russia." She painted a picture with her words, of a scene she'd seen every day walking to the State bakery. "I never understood why she did it," she concluded. "Why she chose to die there, on public display like that."

"Maybe she just didn't want to be a burden. Maybe she did it so someone else could eat her bread ration," Petr postulated.

"I thought of that," Karen replied. She described the story she half remembered of an old Eskimo walking into the forest to die. "But if the old woman were doing the same thing," she continued, "she would have died someplace hidden, someplace private."

Petr nodded thoughtfully. "You're right."

"The only thing I can figure is that she did it on purpose. She *wanted* to be seen. She wanted her death to mean something. But what?"

Petr thought about it in silence for a long time. Karen waited for him. Finally, he said, "Maybe it's not just one thing or the other."

"What do you mean?"

"Maybe it's both. Maybe she was dying like the Eskimo in that story. So that other people could live. Maybe she figured that since she was going to die anyway, better to die now so someone else could eat her bread. But she also wanted people to see the sacrifice she was making. She wanted people to witness her death."

"Why?" Karen asked, though she feared she already knew the answer.

"To serve as an example. As an inspiration. Like that symphony."

"Die so that other people can live," Karen repeated. She felt ashamed. She'd worked so hard to live. It had been her entire focus. And it had been so difficult. But to what purpose? What had she achieved that Inna and Sasha hadn't?

Petr nodded. "You know what I saw more than anything during the first months of the invasion?"

"What?"

"Russian soldiers running away, trying to save themselves. We all ran away. I ran away, my unit ran away. And those who couldn't run, they surrendered. We didn't know, then—we didn't understand what the Germans were doing to the villages they occupied. We thought they were just conquering. We didn't know they were killing and enslaving. How many people in those villages died because we ran away?"

"More would have died if you hadn't."

"I'm not sure that's true," Petr confessed. This notion had been bothering him, especially now that he'd chosen to run all the way to America. "Eventually, I don't think there will be anywhere left to run."

"America thinks that when that happens, you'll surrender."

"We would, if we could. But Germany's not offering us that choice." There was no bluster in Petr's expression, no blind patriotism—just thoughtful, honest contemplation. "Everyone realizes that now. We're not France. The Germans don't want anything to do with us. Leningrad showed that. Your father's symphony showed that. We fight or we die. It's a simple choice, really. Makes things easier in a way. Either fight or die."

"It's not quite that simple." Karen used the same argument Bobby had made only moments before. "You need guns to fight—planes, tanks."

"We'll have those," Petr assured her. "Even if Stalin was assassinated tomorrow, the factories would keep running. Even if the workers were under attack, they'd keep building and rolling tanks off the production lines so that drivers could get inside and go straight to battle. Because that's the way the workers can fight. And everyone realizes now that we have to fight. We fight or we die."

Petr took the last bite and handed the plate back to Karen. "Everyone but me."

Karen sensed what was coming next. She wanted to stop him, but she knew that she couldn't. Because she believed that Petr was right. So she held her breath, dreading the words.

"I'm sorry," he said. "I wanted to do this for you. But I can't."

"I know," Karen replied, the words almost catching in her throat.

They stared at each other for a long time. Karen's eyes were welling with tears, but she didn't dare blink. She felt that as long as she could hold that stare, as long as they looked at each other, the spell that united them would force Petr to stay.

"Bobby's a lucky man," Petr said with regret. "Don't ever let him forget that."

Then he stood up and walked toward the hangar door.

"Wait!" Karen grabbed Petr and spun him around. If she couldn't stop him with words, if she couldn't stop him with a look, maybe she could stop him with a kiss.

Maybe it would have worked, too, if Bobby hadn't interrupted them. He came in through the hangar's side door, the sound of it clicking open prompting Petr to pull away.

Bobby eyed how close Petr and Karen stood together, and how both seemed out of breath. "What's going on?"

Then Bobby saw the tears on Karen's cheeks, and he softened. He went to her, putting his hands on her shoulders, looking at her downturned face with concern. "What's wrong? What happened?"

Karen couldn't answer; she didn't want to say the words.

"Tell him I'm leaving," Petr urged her in Russian.

"Petr's leaving," Karen echoed in English. She didn't know why, but it made it easier that Petr was telling her what to say.

"Leaving? Leaving where?"

Petr said, "You can tell him I'm going back to the Red Army."

"He's going back to fight," Karen translated.

Bobby stepped back. For a moment he didn't believe what he was hearing. He looked at Petr and then back at Karen. Their expressions confirmed that it was the truth. "Do you need anything?" he asked Petr, knowing he couldn't understand English but trusting that Karen would translate. "Food? Money?"

Hearing Karen's translation, Petr shook his head. "The Red Army will provide."

Bobby approached Petr and took his hand firmly in both of his own. "Good luck," he said, and he meant it.

Petr nodded. He knew the English expression even if he didn't know the rest of the language. "Thank you," he replied in heavily accented English. And then he added something in Russian before turning and exiting the door through which Bobby had come in.

Bobby turned back to Karen. "What did he say?"

"He said, do not die. For my sake, do not die." And then she couldn't say anything more because she was crying again.

Bobby wrapped her in his arms and held her tight. "I won't," he assured her. "I won't."

Karen didn't stop crying, and for as long as she sobbed, Bobby held her. "It's OK," he assured her. "You did what you could." But still she cried. "It's better this way," he continued. "He's Russian. He belongs here."

Finally, Karen stopped crying. She unwrapped herself from Bobby's embrace, wiped her eyes with the palms of her hands, and nodded. "You're right," she conceded. "It's better this way. But I need to talk to him. I never even said good-bye."

"All right," Bobby said, stepping back.

Karen left then, out the hangar and through the fence, running into the streets of Krasnoyarsk.

346

CHAPTER 46
THE CHOIRBOY

Bobby watched Karen go. She looked like a ghost for a moment, her coat flapping behind her, gray in northern Siberia's late twilight.

And when, at last, she disappeared completely, Bobby examined his heart. He didn't resent Petr, not anymore. The boy was doing the right thing, the courageous thing—the right thing for his country and, more important, for Karen.

Bobby wondered whether he would have had the courage to do the same, to go back into a fight he knew he would probably lose. Bobby knew he would have to fight again; he had no choice. He'd given up that choice when he joined the Army Air Forces. But Petr did have a choice. He could have flown to America. He could have emigrated. He could have sat out the rest of the war.

What would Bobby have done if he'd been in Petr's place?

He went back to the barracks to find them empty. He knew where everyone was, and he knew he could use their company, and he could use a drink. So he headed to the mess hall.

Sure enough, Bobby found Jack, Max, Wally, Bel, Lenka, and Katia there. Even Captain Hart was with them. As usual, they were passing the time drinking and playing cards. They hadn't noticed Bobby yet. They were too busy drinking and laughing. Bobby paused just inside the doorway and watched them. As he did, he knew the answer to his question.

Yes, he'd have the courage to get back into the fight, he realized, even a fight he knew he'd probably lose. He'd do it for Jack, he'd do it for Max and Wally. Hell, he'd even do it for Bel, Lenka, and Katia. They were his friends. More than that, they'd become his brothers and sisters. So long as they fought, Bobby knew, he'd fight beside them.

But that was different from what Petr was doing, he realized. Petr wasn't only fighting for his friends, wasn't only fighting for his brothers and sisters. He was stubbornly fighting for people he didn't even know.

"Next round's on me!" Bobby declared as he stepped forward and took a seat next to Jack.

Lenka eyed him from across the table. "What are we celebrating?"

"Russian courage," Bobby replied. He raised his glass in a toast.

Lenka smiled and raised her glass. "To Russian courage."

"To Russian courage!" everyone toasted, including Captain Hart.

As soon as Bobby emptied his glass, someone else entered the mess hall. To his shock, it was General Marshall.

"Attention!" Bobby announced, standing and saluting. The other American flyers did the same.

"At ease. At ease, boys," the general told them. He took a seat at the table. "What's the drink, and what's the game?"

"Vodka and five-card stud," Jack said with a wry smile as he filled a glass for the general. "But first you've got to join our toast."

"Oh yeah? And what are we toasting?"

"Russian courage," Katia responded with pride.

"I think that's a worthy toast," the general acknowledged. Marshall looked at the clear liquor, swirled it, and took a draw, evaluating. "Not bad," he said with surprise.

"My brother makes it himself," Katia revealed.

"Moonshine vodka?" the general replied, even more surprised. "Where does he distill it? In the woods?"

"In his bathtub."

"Isn't that illegal?"

Katia shrugged. "I won't tell if you don't."

The general laughed and pushed his glass back to Jack. "Fill me up another and your secret's safe with me."

Jack did as requested and then dealt the cards.

At first the general's presence made the boys ill at ease. But Marshall had the grace not to criticize, and the good sense not to win. Pretty soon the pilots let their guard down and talked as if the general were just another junior officer. Bobby was impressed. He wondered how much the general learned this way, just making conversation, pretending to be one of the boys.

"I'm looking forward to spending the flight with your girlfriend tomorrow," the general said to Bobby.

"Thank you. I'm sure Karen is looking forward to it as well."

Lenka glanced up at the sound of Karen's name. "Who is this Karen, anyway?" Her words dripped with venom.

"She's a winner," the general replied, oblivious to Lenka's tone. "Smart, practical, a survivor. And I've got to admit, she's a looker. Who'da thought a scrawny kid like Bobby could reel in a catch like that?"

Everyone laughed, and Bobby blushed. "Thank you, sir."

Lenka stood up from the table. "I turn in," she announced with frustration.

Katia and Bel stood in support of their friend. "Us, too."

"Good night," said the general, oblivious to their angry tone, "and thank you for the vodka."

The other officers stood respectfully as the female pilots headed back to the barracks. Then the general turned his attention back to Bobby. "Could I have a minute, son?"

"Of course, General."

The general led Bobby back to his office, where he produced a whiskey bottle out of a desk drawer. He poured it into two paper cups and leaned back in his chair. "I'm beginning to wonder if we shouldn't keep Karen for ourselves," he mused. "What do you think?"

"'Keep her for ourselves'—what do you mean?" Bobby asked.

"OSS wants her, of course."

OSS was short for the Office of Strategic Studies, a brand-new agency specially created for the war. In previous wars, each arm of the military relied on its own spies to gather intelligence on the enemy. But recently someone had had the foresight to create a central agency that could coordinate espionage activities across all military branches.

"Speaks fluent Russian," General Marshall continued, "knows the lay of the land. Pretty valuable asset. Anyway, I happened to meet another lady—though I don't know if you can call a proven spy a proper lady. Now, this other lady, she's pretending to be a foreign correspondent for the *Los Angeles Times*, but really she reports to the OSS. She was very interested in your girlfriend. Very interested, indeed. Sent her bosses a coded message via shortwave radio promising I'd let them debrief her when we get home."

"You mean, recruit her?" Bobby asked with suspicion.

"Well, they're going to try. They need analysts, she has the language skills, and her experience will give her an edge."

Bobby took a deep breath. "I don't think after all she's been through that she'll want that."

"In a way, I hope you're right. You said she's a musician, right?"

"A cellist."

"Pretty girl like that, talented. With her story, I have a sneaking suspicion she'd do more good working for us selling war bonds."

Bobby tried to imagine Karen dolled up in a fancy dress, barnstorming from town to town, playing cheesy musical numbers and appealing to humble Americans to support the war effort. He couldn't.

"I think she'd rather work for the OSS," he confided.

The general laughed. "Well, then, let's see if you and I can't convince her."

CHAPTER 47
THE HARD GOOD-BYE

Karen spent the entire night searching for Petr. She finally found him coming out of a Red Army recruitment center.

He had a bundle of clothing—a new uniform—and a rifle. Obviously, he'd joined up again.

The recruiter had been suspicious—even though Petr was a war hero—that Petr had somehow deserted. But Petr claimed he was captured by the Germans and kept as a prisoner of war during their summer campaign. He'd managed to escape and wandered back until ending up here.

It was an unlikely story, but since the Second Shock Army had been completely destroyed, there was no way to verify it. They couldn't have proven that Petr was lying even if they'd wanted to. And the truth was, they didn't want to. The Red Army needed every soldier it could muster, especially veteran heroes like Petr.

Petr and Karen faced each other on the sidewalk. He halted when he saw her, then composed himself. "What do you think?" He held up the new uniform against his chest. It was tan instead of green, and it wasn't quilted like the winter uniforms.

Karen had to admit that the earthy color complemented Petr's blond hair, and she could imagine its straight cut would also complement his broad shoulders and angular physique. "It looks smart," she said.

Petr shrugged as he bundled it back up under his arm. "Doubt I'll be able to keep it that way."

"When do you leave?" Karen asked.

"First thing in the morning. Another boxcar," Petr added with a smile.

"I'll see you off," Karen promised.

Petr gazed at her sympathetically, then shook his head. "No you won't—you have a plane to catch."

"Aren't you . . ." Karen hesitated. Then she gathered her courage and said what was on her mind. "Aren't you going to ask me to come with you?"

Petr stared at her in silence, for a long time. "No," he said finally. "I'd never do that to you, not where I'm going."

"I would," Karen replied.

Petr shook his head. "No, you wouldn't, not if you loved me."

Karen knew he was right.

"It was a beautiful dream," Petr continued, "our dream of living the rest of our lives together. But that's all it was: a dream. The war's reality. We should have known that someday we'd have to wake up."

Karen was surprised. She'd written those same words months ago, in her letters to Bobby—the same letters now being used by army intelligence against the Russians.

How was it that she and Petr could be so alike, having grown up so far apart, so differently? She hugged him, uniform bundle and rifle and all, and again she cried. This time, so did Petr.

But eventually they parted because, as usual, Petr was right. Someday they had to wake up from their dream. And today was that day.

Or was it?

Karen began to wonder during her walk back to the airfield. Not everything dies. Her father died, but his symphony didn't. Why should dreams have to die?

The airfield was dark when Karen returned. But the moon and the stars were out, providing just enough light for her to see Bobby, already there. When she walked up, he turned to her, smiling, apparently relieved. "I was worried you'd be late. The general wants to depart at dawn."

"I'm sorry," Karen said, "but I've come to say good-bye."

She turned and walked away. She didn't look back; she couldn't bear to face Bobby. She couldn't bear to talk to him.

"You are coward," said a voice from the darkness.

Karen turned toward the voice. It sounded familiar. There was a flash and a flame. The flame rose to a cigarette, and Karen saw a girl's pretty face.

It was the Russian pilot who'd accosted her earlier. What was her name? Lenka?

"No, I'm not," Karen shot back.

"Look at him," Lenka insisted as she inhaled the cigarette's smoke.

Karen glanced over her shoulder. She could barely see Bobby's dark outline. His shoulders slumped as he stared up at the moon. He looked defeated.

"He deserves explanation." Lenka held the cigarette out to Karen. "Take this. It will help."

Karen did as she was told. She inhaled and immediately coughed. But the nicotine's narcotic effect soothed her brain. It gave her strength.

"Now tell him," Lenka advised.

Karen nodded, handed back the cigarette, and returned to Bobby. He didn't seem to hear her approach. He didn't turn around.

"I love him," she said, to Bobby's back.

Now Bobby turned. There were tears on his cheeks, glistening in the moonlight. "You said you loved me."

Karen nodded. "And I still do, I think. But could you love me back?"

"Of course," Bobby stated. "I've always loved you."

Karen shook her head. "You don't deserve me. You know that now. You'd never forget what I did to you."

"I'd try."

"You'd try. I know you'd try. But still, you'd never forgive me."

It was true. Karen knew it was, even if Bobby didn't. "Good-bye," she continued. "I wish I was more like you."

Once again Karen walked away. And once again she was interrupted by that voice from the darkness. "I was wrong. You not coward."

This time, Karen just kept walking. She went to the train station. The sun was rising by the time she arrived. Soldiers were everywhere. She pushed through the crowds, searching for Petr. She began to call out to him. Eventually she heard him call back in surprise: "Karen?"

He was standing in the open door of a boxcar, wearing his new summer uniform.

Karen was right. He did look dashing with the flared breeches and knee-high brown leather boots. It wouldn't look dashing for long, she knew. Soon it would be filthy and probably even bloody. But right now it was beautiful.

She pushed through the crowd until she stood next to the boxcar.

"What are you doing here?" Petr asked, looking down at her in wonder. "Aren't you supposed to leave?"

Karen wasn't, generally, a stupid girl. She'd proven that with her remarkable escape from Leningrad and her subsequent survival. Both those accomplishments had required no small degree of common sense. So her decisions this morning were not the result of dim-wittedness. She wasn't being a fool. She was certain that her actions this day would eventually result in her death. A sensible voice in her head told her to turn around and run back to Bobby, to beg his forgiveness and ask him to fly her back to America.

Russia was horrible. She'd grown to hate Russia. And her terrible experiences had made her love America even more than she ever had before. But it wasn't a very loud voice, because although Karen hated Russia, she loved a Russian. And she no longer really cared if she lived or died. Her life no longer mattered to her. All that mattered was that she spend the rest of it with the man she loved—with Petr.

Suddenly a formation of warplanes roared overhead—Russian and American P-39s escorting General Marshall's C-47 Skytrain back to Alaska.

"I think I missed my flight," Karen said with a smile.

Petr beamed at her and reached out his hand. Karen grasped it, and he pulled her up into the boxcar. A whistle blew, and the boxcar lurched, knocking Petr and Karen into each other's arms. They kissed as the train pulled out of the station, destined for a city Karen had never heard of.

Its name was Stalingrad.

HISTORICAL NOTE

"Stalingrad is no longer a town," wrote one German officer involved in the fighting there. "By day it is an enormous cloud of burning, blinding smoke; it is a vast furnace lit by the reflection of the flames. And when night arrives, one of those scorching, howling, bleeding nights, the dogs plunge into the Volga and swim desperately to gain the other bank. The nights of Stalingrad are a terror for them. Animals flee this hell; the hardest stones cannot bear it for long; only men endure."

The Battle of Stalingrad is believed by many historians to have been the largest and bloodiest battle in the history of warfare. That means it was more horrible than Gettysburg, than Gallipoli, even than D-Day. It is into this nightmare that Petr and Karen will be thrust, with slim chance of survival. Karen's dim awareness that her commitment to Petr will lead to her death is, most likely, an accurate prognostication.

Meanwhile, the Siege of Leningrad would last for two more years. By the time the siege was lifted in 1944, more than 1.5 million residents had died. The human losses in Leningrad exceeded those of the atomic bombings of both Hiroshima and Nagasaki.

Most of the events I've described in Leningrad actually occurred. The corruption of city government officials, their dishonesty, and their profiteering from the misery of the people they were supposed to govern is documented, as is the appearance of antigovernment pamphlets calling for revolution.

But it took until the fall of the Soviet Union and the declassification of those documents in the mid-1990s for anyone to discover the truth about what had really gone on in that city. The plight of Leningrad wasn't just a result of reprehensible Nazi policies; it was also a result of shameful Soviet ones.

Although Petr is fictional, the battle he fought in the second chapter is not. There is some disagreement among historians about the importance of the Siberian divisions to Soviet military successes in the winter of 1941–1942. According to legend, Stalin received information from a Japanese spy that Japan would not attack Russia's Siberian border. That information allowed the Red Army to transfer all its Siberian military assets from Asia to Moscow.

Those Siberian soldiers, veterans of recent battles against the Japanese defending the border with Manchuria, are usually credited with the defeat of the Germans at the very gates of Moscow. Not all the Siberian divisions defended Moscow, however. Three of them were sent to the Northern Front, where they successfully drove the Germans back far enough to secure the railroad lines from Moscow to Lake Ladoga. Had that military adventure also failed, even more innocents would have died in Leningrad.

The ill-fated attack by the Second Shock Army also occurred, and it failed spectacularly. Most of the Russian soldiers who took part in the attack were either killed or taken prisoner. The Russian commander of the Second Shock Army, General Vlasov, later betrayed his country by fighting alongside the Germans. Petr would have been one of the lucky few who escaped this disastrous defeat.

The description of Bobby's mission from Eritrea to Iran is entirely fictional. But the transfer of trucks and planes from America to Russia using that route is not.

The Lend-Lease route from Alaska to Siberia was also real, as were the female Russian pilots who flew the planes to the front lines. Although the Airacobra was a failed aircraft design for the US Army Air Forces, it proved quite successful for the Soviet air force, owing to the different combat conditions on the Russian front. In fact, Russian fighter ace Grigoriy Rechkalov scored more victories in his Lend-Lease P-39 Airacobra than any American airman did in any other plane during the war.

Although a number of real summits took place between American and Soviet officials in Siberia during the war, the specific summit described between General George Marshall and Josef Stalin is fictional. So, too, is the proposed strategy of bombing the Soviet Union if it surrendered. It is not hard to imagine, however, that such a strategy might have been debated, especially considering what Winston Churchill had already done to the French navy.

The Leningrad symphony is generally considered to have been Shostakovich's crowning achievement. It is certainly his most famous work. His collaboration with an American—Karen's father—is fictional. The microfilm of the score was flown to Tehran and smuggled to the West in April of 1942, however.

ABOUT THE AUTHOR

Photo © 2016 Kate Thumann

Chad Thumann, a Los Angeles native, has written for the stage, theater, and television. While earning a master's degree in colonial Latin American history, he wrote plays that premiered at the Substation Theater and New Playwrights' Arena. In film and television, he has had a long and fruitful writing partnership with Laurence Malkin; together they have developed screenplays for US studios and independent production companies, including Sony Pictures Studios, Paramount Pictures, Universal Studios, Lionsgate, Bold Films, and Pathé. In television, they have created shows for NBC, FX, Syfy, and AMC. *The Undesirables* is Thumann's first novel.